STAR WARS
THE HIGH REPUBLIC

PATH OF VENGEANCE

CAVAN SCOTT

Disney
LUCASFILM
PRESS
LOS ANGELES·NEW YORK

Printed in the United States of America

First Edition, May 2023

10 9 8 7 6 5 4 3 2 1

FAC-004510-23076

ISBN 978-1-368-08288-4

Library of Congress Control Number on file

Design by Soyoung Kim, Scott Piehl, and Leigh Zieske

Visit the official *Star Wars* website at: www.starwars.com.

STAR WARS
THE HIGH REPUBLIC
QUEST OF THE JEDI

There is conflict in the galaxy. Chaos on the Pilgrim Moon of Jedha has resulted in a devastating battle. In its aftermath, the Jedi have learned of the involvement of the seemingly benevolent group THE PATH OF THE OPEN HAND in violent interplanetary conspiracies.

With communications down, the leader of the Path, THE MOTHER, races back to the planet Dalna to make her ultimate escape.

Little do the Jedi know that the Mother is about to unleash mysterious, nameless creatures with the power to destroy the Order once and for all. . . .

STAR WARS TIMELINE

THE HIGH REPUBLIC

FALL OF THE JEDI

REIGN OF THE EMPIRE

AGE OF REBELLION

REBELS

ANDOR

ROGUE ONE: A STAR WARS STORY

A NEW HOPE

THE EMPIRE STRIKES BACK

RETURN OF THE JEDI

THE NEW REPUBLIC

THE BOOK OF BOBA FETT

THE MANDALORIAN

RISE OF THE FIRST ORDER

RESISTANCE

THE FORCE AWAKENS

THE LAST JEDI

THE RISE OF SKYWALKER

PROLOGUE

Marda spoke and the Path of the Open Hand listened.

The deck plates vibrated beneath her with the gentle thrum of the ship's engines. It still amazed her how powerful and yet serene the *Gaze Electric* was, the gigantic craft finally launched after years of construction on the dusty plains of Dalna. Marda had spent most of her life dreaming about this moment, and there she was—there they *all* were—speeding toward Jedha, the fabled Pilgrim Moon, to spread the Path's message. Most unbelievable of all, she was leading the way: Marda, who had always been left behind as her cousin Yana struck out with the Children, the Mother's elite group of disciples that traversed the galaxy liberating Force artifacts from those who would misuse them. Marda had petitioned to join the Children time and time again, only for her requests to be denied. While Yana was out among the stars, Marda was destined to remain on Dalna, looking after the Path's Littles, wondering why she wasn't worthy of the Mother's blessings.

Kevmo Zink had changed that; beautiful, exhilarating Kevmo had made Marda doubt everything she'd ever believed before proving that she'd always been right. The young Padawan had turned her head—that was sure enough—coming to Dalna with his Jedi tricks and reckless manipulation of the Force, with little or no thought for the consequences of his actions. Marda had begged him to think of what he was doing, sharing the truth that the Path knew all too well. Misusing the Force, even in the most trivial ways—such as levitating flower petals to delight the Littles, the way he had on their first meeting—could trigger a chain of events with unforeseen and potentially catastrophic consequences elsewhere in the galaxy. What started as a ripple on Dalna could become a tidal wave far, far away, laying waste to everything in its path. Kevmo and those like him had no way of knowing what pain and suffering they were inflicting on others. Marda had tried to persuade Kevmo of the transgressions he unwittingly committed, but he wouldn't listen. She couldn't blame him entirely, of course. He'd only been an apprentice, beholden to his Jedi Master, a pale Soikan called

Zallah Macri. Zallah had insisted that the Force didn't conform to the Path's teaching, and Kevmo, indoctrinated as he was, swallowed the lie hungrily.

Marda's heart ached when she thought of the young Pantoran, the only boy she'd ever loved. She'd never again see his brilliant smile or witness those smooth blue cheeks flushing beneath intricate tattoos when they kissed. His foolishness taunted even her memories of the Padawan. When she closed her eyes, all she could see was Kevmo's cold body lying in the caverns beneath the Path's compound on Dalna, his soft skin calcified at the touch of the strange creature the Path called the Leveler—the same beast that now watched from the shadows of the gathering hall, an avatar of the Force itself.

Kevmo and Zallah had abused its power and the Force had punished them, extinguishing their light in the most terrifying way. The Jedi had been reduced to lifeless husks, their robes collapsing as their bodies crumbled to dust.

Marda wore Kevmo's lightsaber beneath her robes as a reminder of what she had both lost and gained in that one dreadful moment. Kevmo's death had broken her heart, and even as the Mother announced that the Path would leave Dalna to travel to Jedha, Marda had pledged that she would never let anyone else suffer the pain and emptiness she felt. She would warn everyone of the inherent dangers of misusing the Force so no one would experience the same sorrow. Kevmo was dead because he had refused to listen. She wouldn't let others share his fate. The Mother had recognized Marda's potential, installing her as the Path's spiritual guide, inviting her to lead devotions and offer teaching in the Mother's stead. Finally, she could protect the Force. Finally, she could save those who would follow in Kevmo's footsteps.

Marda smiled as she spoke, her dark eyes glistening with tears, and the Path listened, weeping with her.

Yana didn't weep. She wanted to. She probably needed to, but she couldn't, not there. Everything had changed so fast. Just a few weeks earlier, she had been planning to leave the Path, to begin anew with the love of her life, far from the Mother's influence, far from Dalna.

She *was* leaving Dalna, but not how she'd expected. First of all, Kor wasn't with her. Instead, her girlfriend's body was deep beneath the ice on a frozen world light-years from anywhere, where Yana had been forced to abandon Kor to escape the same fate. In her darkest moments, Yana found herself imagining Kor Plouth as she was now—not the vibrant Nautolan she'd known since she was thirteen, but a corpse stripped of its flesh by Thelj's deep-sea scavengers. The image, grotesque and horrific, made Yana's claws ache for justice. The Mother had betrayed Kor, selling out the four Children on their last doomed mission. Yana had survived only by the skin of her sharp Evereni teeth. Across the galaxy, Yana's people were feared by those who didn't know them but judged them on their reputation and appearance—their slate-gray skin, razor-sharp teeth and nails, and coal-black eyes. They were seen as little more than vicious predators, and by the Great Storm, Yana wished she could prove them right. How many times had she daydreamed about knocking the Mother to the ground and tearing out the false prophet's throat in front of her adoring congregation? Instead, she did nothing, standing at the back of the *Gaze Electric*'s gathering hall, listening to Marda deliver yet another naive address on the intricacies of Path doctrine.

Marda had changed most of all. Yana had protected her cousin from the moment they'd arrived on Dalna as refugees, wishing that she would stand up for herself, that she'd grow a spine. Yana had thought . . . had hoped . . . that Kevmo Zink would be Marda's catalyst, that the feelings that had blossomed between her cousin and the young Jedi would help Marda realize who she was, who she could be. Marda had realized, all right, but not in the way Yana had hoped, instead reinventing herself as a fanatic Yana barely recognized. The most outward sign was the change Marda had made to the three blue lines that all Path members daubed on their faces using crushed brikal shells. Symbolizing freedom, harmony, and clarity, the lines had always been drawn as gentle waves, like the rise and fall of an ocean, but since Kevmo's death, Marda had adopted three vertical lines that slashed straight down from her forehead to her chin. She had told Yana the new pattern represented her belief that the Path needed to become more assiduous in their work, actively seeking out abuse of the Force and removing it like the corruption it was. Others had followed her lead, applying their own face paint in the same way as Marda's popularity grew. Yana's own markings, applied in the traditional manner above her eyes, were definitely in the minority.

"Look at them all," came a faint voice beside her. Yana didn't respond, keeping her dark eyes locked on Marda. "They adore her. The Path's new Guide."

Yana's people had many curses to endure; that was certain. The Evereni had no real home, no real identity other than slurs applied by others, no real purpose. Then there were the more outlandish rumors about them, stories Yana never had entirely believed, not until now.

She had first heard the most macabre of them in a bar on Rekardia while trying to ignore the mutterings of a group of smugglers who had glared at her the moment she stalked through the doors.

"They talk to the dead, you know, the Evereni," she'd overheard one of the spacers tell his companions, fueled by ignorance and cheap ale. "They see the ghosts of those they've slaughtered, lost souls doomed to follow those damned sharks wherever they go."

It was superstitious nonsense, of course, as she'd reminded the green-skinned Argazdan after she'd smashed his nose against the bar. She'd even recounted the story to Kor when they were reunited at the spaceport, Kor's head-tresses shaking as she'd laughed. And yet the fact that the stories were undoubtedly nonsense hadn't stopped Yana from spotting an achingly familiar figure standing at the back of the crowd as they'd boarded the *Gaze Electric* for the first time. The head-tresses had been the same, and her lime-green skin was fortunately still on her bones, but Kor's once-dark eyes were cloudy as she looked at Yana from across the crowd, ice water spilling over cracked lips when she smiled.

Kor had been there ever since, always a few steps behind, invisible to everyone but Yana, her voice as clear as if they were lying in their bunk back on Dalna.

"You left me, but I'm still with you. I will always be with you, as long as you need me."

It wasn't her, of course, not really; Yana knew that. Kor was dead. This apparition was Yana's guilt and anger given shape. It was the fury that burned deep within her, the same fury that had led her to throw in her lot with Kor's grieving father, Werth Plouth, the Herald of the Open Hand, who in turn was biding his time to unseat the Mother when the moment was right.

"When *he* decides, you mean?" Kor whispered.

Yana clenched her fists and focused on the pain of her nails cutting into her dry palms. And yet she still couldn't cry, even as the members of the Path echoed Marda's closing words: "The Force will be free."

"The Force will be free," Kor said coldly in Yana's ear.

"Yes, but will we?" Yana asked, not taking her eyes from her cousin.

Marda stayed after the congregation had filed from the hall, the Elders thanking her for the comfort her words had brought. The Mother hadn't attended the gathering, of course. Elecia spent most of her time in her private chambers, communing with the Force. Marda had been surprised that the Herald was absent, though. She had gotten used to the Nautolan standing at the back of the crowd, his eyes almost as dark as hers and the stubs of his shorn tentacles stark against his green head. Perhaps he had business elsewhere in the massive ship? That was probably it, but Marda doubted he would tell her if so. Their relationship had been tenuous before her elevation to Guide but now was positively frosty. Werth's resentment toward her came off him in waves, but she had no idea why. She wasn't a threat, especially to him. They both shared the same goal: to spread the Path's message far and wide. Was it her newfound closeness to the Mother, the bond they shared? Was the Herald jealous?

His nose had undoubtedly been put out of joint when the Mother sent Sunshine Dobbs ahead of the *Gaze Electric* to announce the Path's coming on Jedha. That was, in part, understandable. As his title suggested, the Herald was supposed to be the Path's messenger, and Sunshine Dobbs, well . . . Sunshine was little more than a con man. At least, he had been before he'd dedicated his life to the Path. The former prospector positively beamed whenever he was in the Mother's presence, so much so that Marda wondered if he had developed feelings for Elecia since his conversion, not that the Mother would take advantage of such an obvious crush.

But Sunshine's exuberance only made the Herald's demeanor all the more upsetting. Werth's grief for his daughter had sucked the joy from his life and calling. He barely spoke to anyone these days, not even his wife, Opari, who, already gravely ill, had retreated into herself since Kor's death, hiding away in the quarters she shared with the Herald on board the *Gaze*. His only confidant seemed to be Yana, which was surprising considering their past differences, but Marda couldn't begrudge him whatever comfort he found in her cousin's company. No doubt it was their combined grief that had drawn them together, their shared link to Kor, the daughter and girlfriend they loved.

Whatever the reason, Marda just wished Yana would speak to her.

"Marda?"

The sound of her cousin's voice made her gasp in surprise. She had been so lost in her thoughts as she gazed out the viewport that she hadn't heard Yana approach. Or maybe it had been Yana's training. If she didn't want to be heard, Yana could be as stealthy as a slink-cat, but she was there now,

Force be praised, a literal answer to prayer. Marda whirled around to greet her cousin, her grin faltering only when she saw the long fighting sticks in Yana's hands.

"Cousin?"

"Cousin," Yana acknowledged, her voice devoid of emotion as she thrust one of the staffs toward Marda.

"What is this?" Marda asked.

"What it looks like—training."

Marda laughed, not quite believing what she was hearing. "This is the gathering hall. A sacred place!"

Yana gave the barest of shrugs. "Faith is a battlefield."

Marda took a step toward her cousin. "Yana. Let's talk. Let's . . . eat."

Yana snorted. "Eat?"

"The stores are packed with provisions from Dalna. Elder Sarevelin even brought candied nuts. If you fancy something more substantial, there are liters of curried chowder in the galley. Your favorite."

Yana continued to hold out the staff. "We can eat later."

Marda's shoulders slumped. "After training?"

She was rewarded with a curt nod that wasn't a promise. "After training."

Marda considered the weapon. Perhaps this was her cousin's way of breaking the ice that had formed between them, the first step in rebuilding their relationship. It was certainly the most they'd talked since boarding the *Gaze*. She should grab the opportunity before Yana changed her mind.

Marda took the proffered staff and dropped into a defensive position, and Yana immediately launched into an attack.

"Not good enough," Yana snarled as Marda somehow managed to evade the blow, swinging her staff around to attack on the other side. This time Marda didn't even have a chance to respond.

"Aah!" she cried out as the tip of Yana's weapon found her ribs.

"You're not trying."

"I shouldn't have to!" Marda countered, attempting her own strike only for Yana to sidestep it, the end of Marda's staff hitting the deck plates at her cousin's feet.

This time Yana's stick jabbed into Marda's breastbone, knocking her back.

"And that could've killed you."

The staff whipped around again, catching Marda in the back.

"That could've broken your spine."

Marda roared in frustration, bringing her staff up in an arc that Yana was forced to bat away before it connected with her jaw.

"Better."

Marda continued to bellow, spinning around, the momentum of the staff leading the way. Again Yana blocked; again she complimented Marda in the same way Marda used to praise the Littles in the crèche for completing their finger paintings.

Clack.

"Better."

Clack.

"Again."

Clack.

"Concentrate."

For a moment, Marda lost herself in the dance, thrusting, blocking, striking, and parrying. Images danced in her head as they sparred in the cool air of the ship, memories rushing through her mind unbidden, little more than flashes. Coming to Dalna as children, lost and scared. Seeing the Mother for the first time. Seeing Kevmo, feeling her heart jolt, feeling his mouth against hers.

"Enough!"

Yana's staff swept low, taking Marda's legs from beneath her. Her weapon clattered to the deck, her body following suit, the air shocked from her lungs as she hit the floor. Yana stood above her, and for a second Marda thought her cousin was about to bring the end of her staff down to finish the job. Instead, Yana relaxed, her fighting stance shifting to one of annoyance as she rapped the wood against the deck plates.

"You're not ready for Jedha."

Marda struggled to catch her breath. "We're going in peace."

Yana laughed sharply. "In peace? To tell everyone who has gathered in the holiest of places that their beliefs are wrong? To tell this 'Convocation of the Force' that they need to change their ways or face the end times?"

"The Jedi are corrupting the Force," Marda spat, pushing herself up on shaking arms.

Yana held out a hand. "I didn't say Jedi."

Marda took it and allowed Yana to haul her back to her feet. "I know. But the Jedi are a corrupting influence in the Convocation. . . ."

Yana let go of Marda's hand. "A corrupting influence? Now you sound like the Mother."

"Thank you," Marda said softly, claiming the jibe as a compliment. She looked her cousin in the eye as she fought to catch her breath. "The Convocation has representatives of every major belief system in its number. If we can persuade them that they are endangering the Force . . ."

"They won't believe you."

"But we have to try."

The two Evereni stood in silence, Yana's jaw clenched, Marda finally able to breathe. Marda could see the pain in Yana's expression, the anger she knew her cousin felt. If only Yana could channel that rage to help spread the word, to find peace in the simplicity of the one true Path. Marda wanted to wrap her arms around her, to tell her that she understood, that everything would be all right, but it was Yana who made the first move, bending to retrieve Marda's staff from the floor.

"One hour," she said, thrusting the weapon back into Marda's hands. "We'll meet in the secondary hold. You need to prepare for every environment. Nights are dark on Jedha."

"It's the Moon of Light!"

"It's a moon filled with pilgrims who won't take kindly to what you have to say."

Not *we*. *You*.

"What about the chowder?"

Yana turned and stalked from the chapel without looking back. "Maybe later."

Marda knew she didn't mean it, even as the door swished shut and she was left alone.

No. Not alone. Not anymore.

"She'll see," Marda said aloud. "She'll see how wrong she is. Jedha will listen. They will all see the truth."

"They will see the truth," Kevmo repeated, standing behind her. His once-vibrant skin was now chalky and white, his voice like gravel crunched underfoot. "The Force will be free."

"The Force will be free," Marda agreed, smiling.

PART ONE
THE BATTLE OF JEDHA

ONE

Jedha didn't listen. *No one* listened. And now Marda was alone.

The calm Marda had felt standing in the *Gaze Electric*'s gathering hall—bruises from the beating Yana had administered already forming on her arms and side—had lasted all the way to the Pilgrim Moon. If anything, it had only increased, becoming something akin to rapture as she had strolled down the ramp of the *Gaze*'s landing shuttle.

At first, Marda had been proven correct. The people had been more than ready to receive the Path's message, to welcome it, even. Sunshine Dobbs had been better than his word, his ancient cruiser—appropriately named the

Scupper—landing a few days ahead of the *Gaze*. Sunshine had worked his dubious magic, greasing the palms of anyone who could stand in their way, reducing if not completely removing obstacles, even investing some of the Path's surprisingly healthy coffers to purchase an almshouse that was in danger of closing its doors, as a show of the Path's benevolence. The Convocation of the Force had agreed to meet with the Herald, and the Mother proved to be a valuable help in the peace talks between Eiram and E'ronoh, worlds that had been in conflict for generations.

Everything had been working exactly as planned, and then the fighting started.

The dusty streets of Jedha were now running with blood. What had started as a quarrel between the Herald and the Convocation had become a riot, the Herald taking to the steps of the Convocation building and whipping up passersby into a mob, preying on their own distrust of both the Convocation and each other. Insults were thrown first, and then punches, the violence spreading like wildfire. Such an event would have been calamitous enough on its own, but the fighting escalated as the peace talks between Eiram and E'ronoh broke down, and armed guards and enforcer droids from the two warring planets took to the streets. The already frightened people of Jedha responded in fear, rioters clashing with enforcer droids and guards, the various skirmishes rolling together until the city was at war with itself, centuries of religious grievances boiling over.

Marda had tried to do the Force's work, to calm the mob and tend to the injured, but then the Jedi had taken over, as they always did, lightsabers blazing. They'd only made it worse, the violence escalating until no one remembered why the fighting had started. . . .

The Jedi *always* made it worse.

Marda ducked as fighters screamed through the sky above her, engines like thunder. In the next street, an explosion bloomed, followed by a jagged scream. So many explosions. So many screams.

Marda pulled a comlink from her belt and thumbed the control.

"Yana? Yana, can you hear me? I've lost the Mother, haven't seen her since the almshouse was destroyed."

Now Marda's failure was complete. Now Yana would gloat. Everything her cousin had said would happen *had* happened. The people of Jedha had responded to their message with violence. All was lost.

"Yana? Please come in. *Yana!*"

There was no response at all, not even a mocking laugh or a smug "told you so."

One of the fighters erupted into flames overhead, its twisted fuselage dropping from the sky to plow into the temple of some half-forgotten faith.

"What do I do?" Marda asked, but no one answered. Not Yana and not even Kevmo, who hadn't appeared to her since Jedha had started to turn itself upside down. Maybe he'd never been there in the first place. Marda couldn't be sure of anything anymore.

Another scream sounded, nearer this time. For a moment, an irrational fear flooded Marda's mind: Was that the Mother? Was she in danger? Irrational or not, Marda was already running in the direction of the cry. Yana would say it was her imagination, but Marda had to believe it was the Force, spurring her on.

Her heart leaped to her mouth as she tore around the jagged ruin of a once-mighty shrine and spotted the unmistakable sight of a tattered blue tunic lying in the dust, its folds blackened with dirt and blood. The figure was curled in a ball, arms over their head as a gang of rioters kicked and punched, hurling abuse at the victim they pummeled. Was it the Mother, after all? There was no way to tell for sure, not with the mob doing their level best to beat the person to death. Marda needed to do something, needed to save *whoever* it was. If Yana had been there, she would've dived headfirst into the fray without hesitation or fear, but if there was one thing Jedha had proved once and for all, it was that Marda wasn't Yana. She didn't even have a weapon.

"Yes, you do," said a dry voice in her head.

Marda glanced down at her razor-sharp nails, wondering if they would be enough but knowing in her heart of hearts they wouldn't.

"No, not them," Kevmo told her, finally reappearing to whisper in her ear. "Beneath your robes. My lightsaber."

Before she could think what she was doing, Marda fumbled with her belt, slipping her hand beneath dust-caked robes to find the cool hilt waiting for her. She yanked it free, turning the metal shaft over and over to find the activator, panic stopping her from seeing what was in front of her eyes.

"It's there. Under your thumb. Use it."

Marda pressed down and the hilt thrummed with power as the yellow blade of burning plasma burst to life, taking her breath away. The last time she'd seen the weapon, it had been in Kevmo's hands. She had toyed with the idea of lighting the blade ever since he'd died, but it felt disrespectful somehow, an affront to both his memory and the Force itself. Now she had no choice.

"Stop what you're doing," she called out, her voice containing an edge she didn't feel and hadn't known she possessed. "Step away from them."

The gang whirled around, two humans and a gold-eyed Kyuzo.

"Crukking Jedi!" the Kyuzo snarled, glaring at the humming blade. "This has nothing to do with you. Walk away. Walk away now."

"I can't do that," she replied, her voice wavering almost as much as the weapon in her hands.

"Why, pretty-pretty?" sneered one of the humans, a broad-chested male with a mane of red hair and a mouthful of uneven teeth. "Because the Force told you to?"

That confirmed everything she needed to know. The

red-haired brute was no believer, misguided or otherwise. He was just there for the sport, and the Path member still curled at his feet had been in the wrong place at the wrong time.

Marda took a cautious step forward. "I told you to leave them alone."

The body on the ground wasn't moving. Stars, why weren't they moving? At least the thugs were stepping away from them, if only because all three were stalking toward Marda instead.

It took everything she had not to run.

"You're no Jedi," the Kyuzo realized, grinning beneath the translator strapped over his mouth. "You're like him. One of those cultists."

"We're not a cult," Marda said, seizing on the *him*. So it wasn't the Mother, thank the Force. Guilt almost overwhelmed her a second later. It didn't matter who they had been beating, only that they didn't start again.

"Stay back," she warned, shifting the hilt in shaking hands.

"Or what?" the redheaded brute sniggered. "You'll strike us down with your laser sword?"

"Crukking planet killer. She doesn't know what she's doing!" the Kyuzo said, actually stepping *toward* the blade. "Probably found it on the street." He held out a gauntleted hand. "Hand it over, girlie, before you hurt someone. Probably yourself."

Marda didn't know if it was the use of the slur that had

dogged her people since their exodus from Everon or the casual dismissal of the threat she posed, but fire erupted in her belly. She moved with more grace than she had ever shown in her training sessions on the *Gaze*, sweeping up the lightsaber so it took the Kyuzo's hand. He sank to his knees in pain, clutching the cauterized stump with his remaining hand. He didn't look up as Marda lunged forward without thinking, driving the glowing blade deep into his chest. His yellow eyes went wide and a curious gurgle escaped through his translator as he slid to the side to land with a heavy thump on the ground.

Marda let go of the lightsaber as if it were on fire, the blade immediately spluttering back into the hilt. What had she done? She didn't even notice the other members of the gang calling their fallen comrade's name or reaching for their blasters. She could only stare as the Kyuzo she'd killed stared lifelessly back.

That was when the blasters started firing.

TWO

Marda closed her eyes and waited for blaster bolts to cut her down. She had failed them all. The Mother. Yana. Even Kevmo. *Especially* Kevmo. He had been wrong, so wrong about everything, but she knew he would never have used his weapon to kill. Perhaps she could apologize when she met him in the Force, because that was where he was; she was sure of it—as sure as she was that she would see him again, not how he'd appeared to her since death but how he'd looked when they first kissed in the marketplace on Dalna. Perhaps if she opened her eyes now she would see him grinning back, skin the color of the Strukian Ocean.

But the bolts never found her. Instead, when she opened her eyes, she saw only a kaleidoscope of colors, the red of the blaster bolts bursting into starlight against a sweeping blue arc. There were shouts and cries and the unmistakable hum of a lightsaber. Marda glanced down, but Kevmo's hilt was nowhere to be seen, nor was it in the hands of the Jedi who now stood between her and the gang, a glinting shield strapped to one of her wrapped arms, a gleaming lightsaber in the other hand. She moved like water, graceful and yet deadly if she wanted to be. With a bellow of anger, the red-haired brute charged at her, but the tall, lithe woman didn't even break her stride. Instead, the shield jumped from her arm as if punched forward by an invisible power and slammed into the man's broad chest, knocking him onto his back before returning to its home on her wrist. Marda felt a familiar curl of disgust in her gut as she realized that once again she'd witnessed a Jedi using the Force as their plaything, even if it meant that they'd saved her life. The remaining member of the gang grabbed the stunned human and dragged him back, deciding this was a battle they didn't need, especially with one of their own in a heap on the floor. The Jedi didn't move, standing guard, a human wall between Marda and the retreating gang. It was only when they had gone that the Jedi turned and looked at Marda with deep brown eyes.

"Are you hurt?"

Her voice had a strange lilt to it, calming even amid such terror, but it did nothing to quell the storm that burned within Marda—shame, anger, and condemnation churning at once.

"Marda?"

A familiar voice spoke before she could answer, her head snapping around so fast that her neck was cricked, but Marda didn't care.

"Mother," she stammered, not quite believing her eyes. "Mother, you're alive. You're alive."

She moved with instinct, throwing her arms around the prophet who had brought them to Jedha, holding her close. The woman stiffened, and Marda broke away.

"Are you hurt?"

The Mother smiled, her face looking strangely older than when she'd arrived on the Pilgrim Moon, the lines somehow deeper, the gray streaks in her hair more pronounced.

"I am safe, Marda, thanks to Silandra Sho." She nodded at the Jedi who was now crouched in front of the fallen human, her saber back in its holster and her shield attached to the harness she wore on her back. "A true servant of the Force," the Mother concluded, her voice as tired as her eyes. Marda looked from the Mother to the Jedi and back again, confusion replacing her joy that Elecia had survived the battle. Why was the Mother lavishing such praise on a Jedi, of all people? How could *anyone* think they were servants of the Force? They were its captors. Its torturers.

"What happened here?" Sho said, cutting through

Marda's thoughts, the Jedi's graceful hand resting beside the scorched hole in the man's chest.

"I . . ." Marda's throat constricted, her guilt gagging her. She could only stammer the same short word again before another, deeper voice rang out.

"We found that poor brute lying on his back."

All eyes turned to the Ovissian who was pushing himself up from the ground. Marda marveled that she had ever mistaken him for the Mother, with her slight and slender form. The wide-mouthed Ovissian, barely older than Marda herself, was easily two meters tall, his shoulders as broad as the wide horns that swept out from his flat head. The dried blood she had seen on his robes had obviously not belonged to him, his own copper-green blood pouring liberally from a gash on his forehead and crusted around the root of the missing tusk that should have jutted from the left of his chin. Had he lost it in the beating?

"My friend here tried to revive him," he continued, glancing over at Marda, "but to no avail."

"A lightsaber through the heart will do that," the Jedi commented flatly.

"Then those . . . monsters jumped us," the Ovissian wheezed before sinking to one knee, his voice little more than a croak. "Blaming us for what has . . . has . . ."

He was gasping for breath. Sho went to catch him, but Marda got there first, flashing a look that stopped the Jedi in her tracks. If only she could have done the same to the attackers.

"Thank you," she whispered to the emerald-skinned giant, grateful for the lies that had saved her from the Jedi's wrath. He looked at her with his one good eye and grunted deep in his throat.

"The saber rolled beneath the rubble to your right," he said, his voice suddenly stronger now he was whispering directly to her. "After you dropped it."

Marda didn't dare look, in case her glance betrayed her in front of the Jedi. It wasn't that she didn't want to face the consequences of her actions . . . not really . . . but she wasn't ready to surrender what had been Kevmo's just yet.

"Your poor injuries," the Mother said, crossing to take the Ovissian's huge hand in hers, careful not to scrape torn knuckles that showed he had given as good as he got before being overpowered.

"I will recover," he said, bowing his head in reverence. "By the will of the Force."

"The Force will deliver us all," the Mother replied. "That I can promise you."

Marda, however, was only half concentrating on the conversation between disciple and prophet. Instead, she was looking back to where the Jedi was still examining the wound at the center of the Kyuzo's chest. Beside her, beneath a chunk of masonry, Marda could see the telltale glint of Kevmo's saber. If Sho looked to her side . . .

"We should go," Marda said, turning decisively toward the woman. "Master Jedi, I thank you for delivering the Mother to us, but now we must get her to our ship."

Sho stood, leaving the body where it was. "I will accompany you."

Marda took a step forward. "No."

The word came out more forcefully than she'd intended, and the Jedi's eyes narrowed slightly. Marda raised a hand in apology, softening her voice as she continued. "I mean, it is our responsibility. I am the Guide of the Path of the Open Hand."

"*You* are?" Sho asked, and Marda tried not to bristle at the disbelief in the Jedi's tone.

"I will get my people to safety."

Still the woman didn't move. Were all Jedi this stubborn? Somewhere behind her, Marda thought she heard a dry voice whisper, "Yes."

You're not helping, she told Kevmo silently, her mind racing. If the Jedi let them go, she could double back and retrieve the lightsaber. But what if Sho called more of the Order to their location? What if she could somehow sense Marda's guilt?

The barrage of concerns was halted by the sudden bleep of the Jedi's comlink. Sho raised her wrist to her mouth, turning slightly to answer the call.

"Sho here."

"Where are you, Silandra?" a gruff male voice asked, the line thick with static. "We're expecting you back at the transport ship."

"I was escorting the Mother of the Path to her craft," Sho replied.

"A task she performed admirably, Master Sun," the Mother interjected, raising her voice so she would be heard over the comlink. "But now I am safe in the hands of my people. Master Sho should return to her duties, with our gratitude."

"Are you sure?" Sho asked, casting a curious look at Marda, who felt her gray cheeks heat under the Jedi's scrutiny.

The Mother smiled benevolently, pressing her palms together in the universal symbol of peace. "Please. While we may never agree over your use of the Force, I can never . . . *will* never . . . deny the importance of your work. Jedha needs you, Silandra. Go with my blessing."

Marda had to force herself not to sigh in relief when the Jedi offered a short bow of deference. "May the Force be with you."

"It always is," the Mother replied as the Jedi finally took her leave, sprinting off with her comlink close to her lips.

Marda wanted to sink to the ground and weep but didn't want to show such weakness in front of the Mother and this unfamiliar Ovissian disciple. The tears could come later. Instead, as soon as she was sure that the Jedi wasn't about to double back, she rushed to the pile of rubble and retrieved the lightsaber from where it had fallen.

"You did well," the Mother told her when Marda turned around, the hilt safely back in her hands.

"Did I?" Marda said, trying desperately not to look at the body at her feet.

"You saved my life," the Ovissian said.

"And you saved mine," Marda told him. "I was sure that Jedi would know . . . at least suspect . . ."

"What she suspects isn't important," the Mother said, "only that they leave us alone."

"You said they were servants of the Force," Marda pointed out, still mystified. "Gave them your blessing."

"I gave them what they wanted to hear," the Mother responded sharply. "Flattered their egos, nothing more."

"But—"

"But nothing. We were in danger. I needed to—" The Mother broke off, sucking in air as her hand shot to her side. Marda darted forward, the Ovissian already moving to support their leader as her legs gave way.

"You *are* hurt," Marda said, the blood between the Mother's fingers clear to see.

"It is nothing," the Mother insisted, although the strain of her voice told them otherwise. "I will apply a rejuv pack once we are on board Sunshine's ship."

"Sunshine's?" Marda asked. "But the shuttle—"

"The shuttle was destroyed," the Mother said, her face deathly pale as the Ovissian managed to pry her hand from the wound.

Marda gasped as she saw the metal buried in the Mother's side.

"Shrapnel," the Ovissian grunted, examining the wound. "And in deep."

"Are you a doctor?" Marda asked, but the Ovissian shook his head.

"Let's just say I've seen a lot of combat injuries." His attention turned back to the Mother, admiration written all over his broad face. "To continue in such a condition and inquire about my injuries while the severity of your own . . ."

The Mother brushed a hand over the Ovissian's cheek. "The Force provides . . ."

"Bokana," the Ovissian said, supplying his name with pride. "Bokana Koss. A recent convert to your cause."

"To *our* cause, Bokana," the Mother said gently. "To our cause."

"Which will lose its figurehead if we don't get you to the *Scupper*," Marda cut in, suddenly feeling more than a little sidelined by the conversation. "Do you know where it is?"

The Mother nodded, licking her dry lips. "At a private landing field, near the Roalj Temple . . . property of one of our donors."

Unfortunately, the temple proved to be a long trek across the city, a journey that would be treacherous even if the Mother weren't fading with every step. Much of the city was burning, battles between the Guardians of the Whills and Eiram's enforcer droids still raging as opportunists looted places of worship in plain sight. Marda kept trying to get through to Yana, switching from one comm channel to the next in search of one that wasn't disrupted by the chaos. The Jedi had managed to talk to each other, so why couldn't they?

"This way," Bokana grunted as they found their path blocked by even more fighting. He darted toward an alleyway sandwiched between a pair of sandblasted buildings that were miraculously still standing.

"Are you sure?" Marda asked.

"Don't argue with him, Marda," the Mother snapped, her reproach stinging, although hurt turned to concern as the prophet stumbled and fell.

"Mother!"

"I can't go on," Elecia breathed. "Too tired."

"I'll carry you," Bokana said, moving to pick the woman up.

"You're injured yourself," Marda told him.

"I can manage," he insisted, bundling the Mother into his powerful arms, although there was no mistaking the slight whimper that escaped his split lips as they hurried into the alley.

"Are you *sure* this is the right way?" Marda asked as the explosions seemed to get nearer by the second. Bokana's only reply was to thunder on, his steps becoming noticeably more unsteady.

Something caught Marda's eye at the periphery of her vision as they ran, a flash of red on the top of the wall to their right. Was that an animal running alongside them? Marda drew Kevmo's saber without thinking but stopped short of igniting the blade. There was every chance she'd accidentally slice into one of Bokana's legs as they ran, but its presence in her hand made her feel better, even if the memories it evoked were more complicated than ever.

"Almost there!" Bokana grunted, turning a sharp corner. Marda followed him instinctively, having to stop herself from barreling into the giant as he came up short, nearly dropping the Mother in the process.

"Careful!" Marda snapped before realizing why they'd suddenly stopped. "It's a dead end!"

The Ovissian swayed slightly on his feet, his words slurring as he replied: "I'm sorry, I . . . I thought I knew where I was going. I was so sure . . ."

His voice trailed off, and he swayed, breathing heavily. One thing was certain: they couldn't stay there. It was down to Marda to get all three of them to safety.

"Good luck with that," said the dead voice in her head, the impossible words instantly drowned out by a deep guttural snarl behind them.

Marda spun around to see rabid eyes glaring hungrily at them.

Kevmo was right; she was going to need all the luck she could get.

Swallowing hard, Marda lit the saber.

THREE

Jedha had been as bad as Yana expected. No, actually, it had been worse. Far worse.

She should've predicted how things would go the moment she'd walked off the *Gaze Electric*'s shuttle into the throng of pilgrims. The air was thick with cloying spices and simmering tension, religious groups and Force factions arguing in the street. All the time, the so-called Convocation of the Force was trying to promote peace and harmony among the various belief systems, pushing ahead with a festival that was supposed to unite the Holy City but in reality only deepened years of division.

In many ways, it all played into the Mother's hands. The

plan she had concocted with the Herald was simple enough. Werth Plouth was to petition the Convocation to prohibit all use of the Force within the city's walls, a request they would naturally dismiss without discussion. Once spurned, the Herald would appeal to the crowds gathered outside the Convocation building, convincing them that the council wouldn't listen to reason, that they sought to serve only themselves, not the Force. Everything proceeded exactly as the Mother said it would, the mob so incensed by the Herald's words that they turned on the Convocation as soon as the Force users had rushed out of their chambers to see what was happening.

That was when Yana played her part, releasing the Leveler into the crowd. The walking nightmare hadn't attacked, hadn't fed, but its mere presence was enough to drive the Force users insane. Unable to distinguish what was real or hallucination, the members of the Convocation lashed out, unleashing their powers on the crowd, who in turn responded in fear, a riot breaking out in the Square of the Supplicants. The violence spread like wildfire, and having lit the fuse, the Herald and Yana made their retreat, ready for the second phase of their plan.

It turned out that the Mother had operatives all across Jedha. She'd been working the city for months—no doubt the reason she'd been so opposed to the Path setting out for the Pilgrim Moon when Marda first suggested it. Her agents had been looting shrines and temples for weeks, stealing religious artifacts that could be sold on the black market to fund the Path's work. But Elecia's network was small, made up of petty thieves and ne'er-do-wells who would have been out of their depth locating the real reason the Path had come to Jedha. The Rod of Daybreak was a legendary relic that, when combined with the Rod of Seasons—already liberated by Yana from the Hynestian royal family—could control the Leveler fully and without question. But the Rod of Daybreak was lost, and to recover it, the Mother needed her Children—a problem as Yana was the only survivor, the Mother having sacrificed the others on the altar of her ambition.

So a new team was assembled from those who had shown promise in the past, the Herald handpicking several new members, such as Shea Ganandra, a talented engineer with a surprising gift for armed combat, and Barkov, a hulking Lasat who Yana suspected had been selected more for his size than his skill. As the authorities tried to calm the rabble, the Mother's new Children raided Jedha's more significant archives, following leads provided by one of Elecia's most trusted contacts in the Holy City. Soon they were rampaging through the Temple of the Whills and the Dragigan Annals, but there was no sign of the damned rod.

With time running out, Yana had been ready to abandon the mission when a new lead came to light, rumors of a secret Jedi vault out in the desert, specifically an area known as the Dunes of Contemplation. For centuries a gigantic statue of a lone Jedi had stood guard on the spot where the vault was said to be. However, when they'd reached the dunes, the mighty effigy had already been pulled to the ground by anti-Jedi protestors. For once, the Force had smiled on them when they learned that the statue hadn't been guarding the vault; it *was* the vault, with thousands of artifacts hidden within its structure, including the fabled Rod of Daybreak.

The Herald had been ecstatic, especially when the Mother's contact warned that Jedi reinforcements were on the way. He'd been waiting for the chance to test the power of the combined rods, and he grabbed the opportunity with both hands.

The legends were correct. With the rods slotted together, the Leveler could do nothing but obey. Yana saw for herself the full horror of the creature feeding on a Selonian Jedi, the Force user's gray pelt turned to stone before their eyes.

Then everything fell apart. Another Jedi arrived, accompanied by a purple-skinned Sephi, who turned one of the vault's many treasures against them.

The Leveler had been the first to fall to the relic's power, eldritch energies flowing from the ancient gauntlet the Sephi had slipped over his hand. Maybe the Mother's avatar of the Force wasn't as invulnerable as they'd first believed, and neither, it appeared, was the Herald, who had been foolish enough to grab a lightsaber and attack the Jedi, a bruiser of a Kiffar who fought through the Leveler's influence to defend himself.

They were still fighting, and the Herald, skilled though he was, was unable to overcome years of training on the Jedi's part. At any other time, Yana would have helped him, but she had bigger concerns, namely the Leveler that was laid out on its side, whimpering like a wounded kath hound.

"Get up," she barked at the savaged creature, the combined rods held tight in her hands. The Leveler tried to obey but was unable to haul itself from the ground near the petrified corpse of its latest victim.

"Yana!"

A cry went out, not from the Herald, who was still locked in a lightsaber duel, but from Shea Ganandra. She was fighting the Sephi, now stripped of his gauntlet but proving to be more than a match for the engineer.

Yana looked from the creature—knowing how furious the Mother would be if they returned without it—to the engineer, who was pitifully outmatched.

"For storms' sake," Yana hissed, leaving the Leveler where it lay and running to Shea's side.

The Sephi's eyes went wide as he saw Yana pelting toward him, but he reacted before she could run him through with the rods' curved blade. He grabbed the staff, twisted its length around his body, and snapped the artifact in two. Yana barreled forward, still gripping the Rod of Seasons, while the Sephi held on to the Rod of Daybreak. Shea tried to grab him as Yana regained her balance, only to be rewarded with a well-placed boot to her chest. The Sephi barely hesitated, whirling around to face Yana and jabbing with the rod. She met the lunge, the Rod of Seasons' blade glancing off the razor-sharp edge of its counterpart. Still she couldn't get the upper hand, the Sephi swiveling around to connect the flat edge of the staff with Yana's head.

Stars slammed across her vision and she went down, smacking the floor hard. Before she could recover, the Sephi was standing over her, the Rod of Daybreak's blade aimed firmly at her heart.

"Just stay down," the Sephi commanded, breathing heavily. "It'll be better for you. Better for both of us."

And for a moment, Yana wondered if that was true. It would be so easy to jump up at her victor, force him to thrust down with the curved blade. That would end it all, one way or another. No more anger. No more grief. She could even hear Kor calling for her. *Yana. Yana!* Storms, how Yana wanted to be with her. . . .

But the universe had a different idea. The Sephi turned as a growl sounded behind him. The Leveler was back on its feet and charging at them, its injuries not as severe as any of them had thought. Maybe it was a thirst for revenge driving it forward, or the call of the Rod of Seasons still in Yana's grasp. Either way, the Sephi didn't stand a chance as the monster launched itself into the air and landed on the humanoid's chest, knocking him back. The Rod of Daybreak skittered from the Sephi's hand, sliding across the floor as the Leveler pinned him down, saliva from the creature's fronds splashing onto the Sephi's straining face as he tried to push the monster's jaws away.

And still Kor called from the beyond. *Yana. Yana.*

"Yana, can you hear me?"

But that wasn't Kor's voice. It was Marda!

Yana twisted to her right, spying her comlink on the floor beside her, its tiny speaker broadcasting Marda's terrified voice.

She flipped over, snatching up the device to answer the call.

"Marda? Marda, I hear you. And we need help."

But Marda either couldn't hear or was in no position to offer assistance, the latter explanation becoming more and more likely as her pleas continued through the static.

"Near the spaceport . . . they're . . . they're going to kill us, Yana . . . the Mother . . . hurt . . . I need you, Cousin . . . need the Leveler . . ."

Yana looked up, seeing the Herald fall to the Jedi, who, true to his vows, stopped short of killing his foe. As for the Rod of Daybreak, it was nowhere to be seen, lost in the wreckage of the vault. Shea, meanwhile, was already on her feet, pulling at Yana as the Sephi fought with the Leveler, the situation only worsening as a second Jedi, a brown-skinned woman clutching her midriff, burst into the chamber.

"Yana, we need to get out of here," Shea said, yanking her up. "There are speeders outside. We can take them back to the city."

"But the Herald—"

"The Herald has lost. We can still live."

As could Marda, Yana thought, making a decision.

They ran, Yana still holding the Rod of Seasons, leaving the Herald to his fate and finding the speeder bikes waiting outside. Yana jumped onto the nearest seat, gunned the engine, and roared away, realizing she and Shea were being followed only a moment later. It wasn't the Jedi but the Leveler, running at full pelt, compelled to follow the rod.

The mission had been a disaster, but at least Marda might still make it through the night alive . . . if they weren't already too late. . . .

FOUR

The creatures were called wargaran, and Marda had already encountered them in extremely close quarters.

Incredibly rare and even more dangerous, the predators had been brought to Jedha by an unscrupulous showman. He had hoped to make his fortune displaying or even selling the beasts as part of the Festival of Balance, an interdenominational gala organized by the Convocation to bring the people of Jedha together. Unfortunately for everyone, including the showman himself, the animals had been released from their cages by one of Marda's Littles, who was desperate to do the right thing and completely unprepared for what happened to her. Marda had been with Naddie when they first saw the wargaran looking both beautiful and tragic within their cages. Their bodies were large but sleek, more reptilian than mammal, covered in feathers the color of a blazing sunset. They lay behind the bars of their cages, gazing mournfully out onto a world they could never explore. Naddie's heart had gone out to them, especially when the trader had leaned into the story, keen to spin a yarn for prospective customers.

"Wargaran are hunters," he'd said with a grin, showing a mouthful of golden teeth. "Predators. And clever with it, too. They can sense the Force, you see, hunting in packs—never less than three—feeling out their prey through murmurations in the Force."

Naddie had been so appalled by their plight that she had slipped back when Marda wasn't looking and thrown open the animals' cages, telling them to get away while they could.

They'd repaid her kindness by ravaging her the moment they were free. Naddie survived only thanks to Marda's quick thinking, although the poor girl would carry the scars of the ordeal for the rest of her life. The same couldn't be said for those who had perished as the creatures tore through Jedha's primary marketplace, slaughtering anyone who couldn't run fast enough. It wasn't the wargaran's fault. They were merely following their instincts, but many more would have died if the Mother hadn't marshaled the Path to corral the creatures, returning them to their enclosures. The survivors had hailed them as heroes, and the Mother was even invited to take part in the ultimately doomed peace talks between Eiram and E'ronoh.

The fact that two large, hungry wargaran were now staring at them proved that either the Path's efforts to recapture the animals hadn't been as successful as previously thought or the wargaran had escaped once again in the subsequent battle. The animals weren't as majestic as they had once been, both missing clumps of plumage, while deep slashes across their flanks only added to their savage appearance. The only thing stopping them from leaping forward was Kevmo's lightsaber. Marda held the blade out like a brazier, swinging it back and forth, the wargaran watching the yellow plasma as if hypnotized. It was evident from the way both were coiled, ready to spring, that the spell wouldn't last long.

"Put me down," breathed Elecia, still supported by Bokana, who looked as though he was about to collapse any moment himself.

"No way," Marda insisted, gripping the hilt even tighter. "Absolutely not. You're too weak."

"And you're not a fighter. Not like your cousin."

The Mother's words stung because Marda knew they were true. Just as the words Yana had spoken on the *Gaze Electric* had proved true after all. But Yana wasn't there. Marda had called for her over the comlink, but there was no way of knowing if the message had gotten through, and Bokana, for all his bulk, could barely stand. Even Kevmo had deserted her, his brittle voice gone when she needed it most.

The larger of the two wargaran braved a step forward, and Marda swung the lightsaber to block its path. Immediately, its partner lunged forward, and Marda swung the other way. The tip of the blade nicked its feathered cheek and it wailed, jumping back, the larger taking up the attack a second time. Now she wasn't just swaying the lightsaber back and forth; she was slashing the blade wildly through the air, not caring if the plasma met feather and bone, anything to force the creatures back.

The larger of the wargaran lunged forward, and she gave ground, the other following suit. Soon it was Marda who was backing up, Bokana retreating with her, Marda's head full of taunts that suddenly seemed so crushing.

You're not a fighter.

You need to prepare yourself, Marda.

Not a fighter like your cousin.

Behind her, the Ovissian lowered Elecia to the ground.

"What are you doing?" Marda shrieked, the largest wargaran howling as Kevmo's blade declawed it, more by accident than design.

"I need to fight," Bokana replied thickly.

"You need to protect her!"

"He is," the Mother insisted.

That's when Marda heard the growl, not from the furious wargaran in front of her but from the third standing on the wall behind them, teeth bared and hackles raised high.

Never less than three.

The wargaran pounced, but Marda couldn't turn to defend herself from the claws she imagined would soon rake her back, not without dropping her defense against the creatures that had trapped them in the alley.

Everything happened at once. Her back remained unmauled, Bokana putting himself between Marda and the leaping wargaran and raising his muscled arms as if to welcome the creature into a hug. The force of the animal dropping onto him sent the Ovissian stumbling back into Marda, who lost her balance, the tip of the lightsaber sizzling into the ground. The smaller of the two advancing wargaran was on her in an instant, slamming her onto her back. Only the fact that she had previously taken its claws stopped her shoulder from being shredded as the giant paw pinned her down.

But the thing's teeth were still as sharp as ever and currently the only thing she could see, the wargaran's maw wide as it lunged for her throat. Marda acted on instinct, bringing Kevmo's lightsaber up to protect herself. The wargaran's teeth sank into the hilt, puncturing the weapon that Kevmo had carefully crafted so many years before. The creature snarled in frustration, thrashing its head back and forth, the sudden powerful movement snatching the lightsaber from Marda's grasp. It flew across the alley, out of reach, not that Marda could have gone after it even if she wanted to. Instead, she used the only weapons she had left to her. The wargaran wasn't the only one with claws, after all. The predator howled in pain as Marda slashed her nails across its face with enough force to knock its long head back. A moment of defiance, but a fleeting one. She had drawn blood, but the wound was only superficial. The wargaran's jaws snapped back, and this time there would be nothing to stop them. She grabbed its throat, pushing with all her might, but the animal was too strong for her. Marda retched as the beast's foul breath washed over her, the last thing she would ever smell.

Or so she thought.

The wargaran howled as a shining blade burst through its side, the blue beam brighter than a sun. It was already dead as it slumped to the side, the lightsaber slipping from its body to strike the other beast. For a moment, Marda thought that Silandra Sho had returned to save her from death a second time, but the whirling robes were not those of a Jedi but the Mother of the Open Hand. Elecia had a lightsaber of her own gripped tightly in her hands, one that had belonged to Kevmo's master, the Soikan who had died with him on Dalna. The Mother must have hidden it beneath her robes, the same way Marda had kept Kevmo's hilt since his death—another example of how the Mother and Marda, the prophet and her guide, were becoming increasingly alike. Unfortunately, the prophet was almost dead on her feet, despite her enthusiastic if clumsy performance with the blade. Bokana, meanwhile, was still wrestling with the wargaran that had attacked them from above, the pack down by one but still stronger than three pacifists already wearied by fear and injury.

"A pacifist order that kills rioters in the street," a voice said deep within her, "stabbing them through the heart."

No, Marda told him, looking around for Kevmo's saber. That had been an act of defense, never to be repeated. If they made it out of this alley alive, she would never light the damned thing again; on that he could have her word. And there it was, lying a meter or so away, where it had been thrown from her hand. Marda scuttled for the weapon on all fours, snatching it up and spinning around, her thumb finding the activator as if it had been designed for her.

Now the wargaran would pay.

But nothing happened. Almost nothing.

There was no majestic yellow blade, but there was a brilliant, burning spark of unfocused energy that scorched Marda's hand, forcing her to drop the weapon. The wargaran's teeth had done more damage than she'd thought. In fact, they seemed to have turned the tide of the fight. On the ground, Bokana lost his wrestling match with the other wargaran, the creature's jaws finding his thick green shoulder. At the same moment, Elecia stumbled as she overswung, Zallah Macri's lightsaber still clutched in her hands as her knees went out beneath her.

The larger of the original two wargaran howled in victory and leaped for the Mother, and Marda reacted out of sheer instinct. There was no pain in her burned hand, no ache in her impossibly tired limbs. In that instant, Marda Ro was pure Evereni, as feral as her species' unwarranted reputation. She fell upon the pouncing wargaran, slamming it to the ground. They rolled, the creature scrabbling to gain purchase as Marda sank her sharp teeth into the wargaran's neck, holding tight. The animal roared in pain, flipping Marda over onto her back and crashing down on top of her. Her jaws released and she gasped for air, winded by the creature's weight. It floundered for a moment and then . . . was gone. There was a whimper and a wail and the sizzling zap of a blaster bolt, and the next thing Marda knew, she was staring up into a face that could've been her own if it wasn't for the sharp cut of the hair and the three lines of brikal shell brushed horizontally across the furrowed brow.

"Marda," Yana said, her dark eyes full of concern. "Marda, are you all right?"

"Yana . . ." The name was like a breath escaping from Marda's lungs as, dazed and most probably in shock, she reached up with nails caked in blood and gently brushed her cousin's cheek.

Then reality came crashing back and Marda remembered. "The Mother! Yana, she was attacked."

Yana pulled back as Marda leaped to her feet, expecting to be greeted by the sight of both Elecia's and Bokana's dead bodies. Instead, the Ovissian was lying on his back, blood pumping from a messy wound on his shoulder, while the wargaran he'd been fighting lay dead from the blaster bolt Yana had expertly delivered to its head.

As for the Mother, Elecia was leaning heavily against the alley wall, transfixed, as if she was watching the most beautiful thing she'd ever experienced.

"Look at it," she breathed, eyes gleaming despite her injuries. "Just look at it, Marda."

Marda did as she was told and immediately regretted it.

The third and final wargaran, the one that had been plucked from her, was lying on its side, limbs twitching, as an even larger creature fed noisily on its rapidly calcifying corpse.

Marda felt her gorge rising as the Leveler finished its meal and looked directly at her, its hideous, twisted body three times the size it had been when they'd left Dalna.

But that wasn't the worst of it. What disturbed Marda most was that those huge baleful eyes—the very same eyes that had hunted Kevmo and Zallah to their deaths—still weren't sated, even after a fresh kill.

They wanted more. So much more.

FIVE

Yana didn't know which was more horrifying, the Leveler or the sight of her cousin, robes torn, long hair tangled, and chin slick with blood.

Not that Marda seemed to care. She was too busy fussing over the Mother, who was watching in ghoulish delight as the Leveler turned its attention to the wargaran Yana had shot.

The Ovissian she'd rescued scrambled away as the monster continued its feast, dropping on the carcass like the carrion feeder it was.

"Whoa, there," Yana said, ignoring the horror show beside her as fresh blood pumped from the wound on the

Ovissian's broad shoulder. She dropped onto one knee beside him, putting herself in between him and the Leveler's meal.

"Let me see."

The Ovissian did as Yana told him, his eyes wide as he continued staring at the sight behind her.

"You were lucky," she told him, examining the bite.

"Yeah," he said, distracted. "I feel like it."

Yana pulled a rejuv pack from a pocket of her belt and ripped it open with her teeth.

"It could've caught an artery," she said, unfolding the pad and slapping it hard on the wound with no warning.

The Ovissian cried out, the pain snapping him back to what Yana was doing.

"Thanks, I guess," he eventually said as Yana ran a finger across the edge of the pad to seal the dressing. "Never realized signing up with the Path would be so dangerous." He glanced at Yana's tight-fitting combat suit. "You *are* Path, aren't you?"

"Unfortunately, yeah." The words were out of her mouth before she could stop them, but neither Marda nor the Mother seemed to hear. The Ovissian, for his part, merely frowned, his deep brown eyes wandering back to the Leveler.

"Can you stand?" she asked him, and he nodded, seeming grateful as she helped him up. "Looks like you've been through a lot."

"Bokana is a hero," came the Mother's voice from beside them. "As are you."

Yana turned to see Elecia leaning heavily on Marda, who looked ready to collapse herself.

"That thing did most of the work," she said, nodding at the Leveler, which had moved on to the third wargaran before deciding that there was nothing for it there. "It moves fast when it wants to. I struggled to keep up."

For a moment, Yana thought Marda was going to stop her from examining the wound on the Mother's side, but she shifted so Yana could guide Elecia's hand away. Rough metal glinted in the afternoon sun.

"Do you have any more rejuv packs?" Marda asked.

Yana shook her head, trying to see how deep the shrapnel had cut. "I'm afraid not."

Behind her, Bokana went to rip his from his shoulder. "She can have mine."

"Don't you dare, hero," Yana warned him. "I've only just patched you up. Besides, we don't want to introduce any infection from that animal's bite to her wound."

"Infection?" The big lug sounded worried. She couldn't blame him.

"You will be treated when we are back on the *Gaze Electric*," the Mother said, her voice shaking along with the rest of her.

"She's going into shock," Marda said.

"You're *all* in shock," Yana said, pulling the comlink from her belt, her eyes taking in the extinguished lightsaber gripped tight in the Mother's left hand. "Have the Jedi seen you with that?"

The Mother shook her head.

"Thank the Force for small mercies." Yana flicked the head of the comlink to open a channel. "Herald? Are you there?"

"Communications have been down," Marda commented. "I didn't even know if my message had gotten through."

"It barely did," Yana told her, trying to raise Werth a second time, but there was only static.

"Is there a problem?" the Mother asked.

Yana snorted. "Where do I start?" she asked, snapping the link back to her belt.

"With the Rod of Daybreak," the Mother replied, her eyes suddenly alert. "Do you have it?"

Yana shook her head. "We know where it is, or rather where it was, but the Jedi . . . they found us . . . captured the Herald and—"

"You must go back," the Mother interrupted, her voice as hard as slate.

"Back?"

"Find the rod. Finish the job."

"The job? The job is a bust," Yana insisted. "The Jedi found us. I barely escaped with my life."

"Then take the Leveler," Marda told her. "They won't be able to stop it."

"No," the Mother said. "The Leveler comes with us."

Yana couldn't believe what she was hearing. "And where exactly are you heading while I risk life and limb?"

"To Sunshine Dobbs and his ship."

"That ship is a disaster at the best of times, and I don't know if you've noticed, but this is very much *not* the best of times."

The Mother held out her hand, the palm streaked with blood.

"The Rod of Seasons. Give it to me."

Yana took a step back, subconsciously putting space between the Mother and the rod that was attached safely to her back.

"You gave it to me. You said I was the Leveler's champion."

"And the Leveler is my protector. I need it near me at all times, especially now."

"You can't send me against Jedi without that thing. I wouldn't last five minutes."

"You will do what you are told."

Yana knew full well who the Mother was, having seen through Elecia's act the day Kor had died, but the authoritarianism in the woman's voice took even her by surprise. She was so stunned she didn't react as the rod was unceremoniously slipped from the harness between her shoulder blades. She spun around, her hand going to her blaster, to find Bokana gripping the rod in both hands.

"She said she wanted it," he said, at least having the decency to look embarrassed, an expression that gave way to worry as the Leveler's head swung around to face him, fronds writhing beneath its gaping jaws.

"Maybe next time I won't be so quick to patch you up, *hero*," she told the Ovissian as he gingerly handed the rod to the Mother, looking as if he half expected the Leveler to jump up and attach itself to his arm.

"Don't worry," she told him bitterly. "I don't think you're its type."

"Recover the Rod of Daybreak and bring it back to Dalna," the Mother said, holding the Rod of Seasons tight as the Leveler padded obediently to her side.

"To Dalna?" Yana repeated incredulously. The surprises just kept coming. Even Marda seemed uncertain at the sudden decree.

"Mother, are you sure?" Marda asked, moving closer to the woman. "Dalna is behind us now. We need to press on with the mission."

"We *need* to regroup," Elecia insisted.

"We have the *Gaze*."

"And Dalna has the caves. They will protect us."

"Protect us from what?" Bokana asked, no doubt wondering precisely what he'd signed up for when he'd slipped on his now-tattered robes.

The Mother looked out across the Holy City, thick plumes of smoke rising from the fires that raged in the streets.

"From those who will seek to blame us for this carnage. From those who will want revenge. Help me, please. We must hurry."

Yana could only watch as Marda let the Mother place

an arm around her, the pair of them walking away, with the Leveler slinking behind. Bokana kept his distance, shooting worried glances at the strange creature, pausing only to recover something from the ground.

"Running won't work," Yana called out to them. "They'll know exactly where to find you. Where to hunt you down."

"Which is why you need to recover the Rod of Daybreak," the Mother answered, not looking back. "Come to Dalna as soon as it's in your hands, Yana. Not a moment before."

And then they were gone, disappeared around a corner, leaving Yana alone and more confused than ever.

"You could just leave," a voice said behind her. "Marda has made her decision. You could, too."

"Not now, Kor."

"But—"

"Not now."

When she turned, Kor had gone, not that she was ever really there. Yana was alone in the alley with a trio of slaughtered wargaran, one still flesh and blood, the others . . . the others something else.

SIX

The flight deck of the *Gaze Electric* was a hive of activity. Path members were at every station, some having come from space-faring backgrounds, while others had gotten a crash course over the previous few weeks. All, however, had a strange, distracted look in their eyes if you examined them carefully enough. They, like Marda, had expected great things from Jedha. It was supposed to have been the beginning of the Path's big push into the galaxy. Even Elder Delwin, the Weequay who had been so antagonistic toward Marda in the past, had allowed himself to be swept up in the frenzy of excitement, going so far as to propose a new community on his home planet, Sriluur. Now Delwin was dead, caught in the crossfire between Eiram and E'ronoh, and many of the Elders were missing, including Aris Ade and Sarevelin. Only Old Waiden was present on the flight deck, blue face paint temporarily removed so a nasty gash on his forehead could knit together under thickly applied kolto paste. The elderly human sat hunched over in a chair, looking out at the stars, his already craggy features seeming to have aged all the more since the troubles on Jedha. Marda wanted to go to him, to rest a hand on his frail shoulder, even offer him a cup of warming muru tea, but she worried he'd throw it back in her face. Many of the faithful blamed *her* for what had befallen them. Was it not Marda who had suggested going to Jedha? Was it not Marda who had influenced the Mother to leave Dalna in the first place? Was she not supposed to be their Guide? A guide into what, exactly? Disaster. Infamy.

On top of everything was the Mother's concern that the galaxy would blame the Path for what had happened in the Holy City. Rumors were already circulating that a member of the Path had been working with the Grafs to sabotage the peace talks, the tittle-tattle compounded with reports that the Herald's speech had sparked the initial riot. If only Werth hadn't taken to the streets to decry the Convocation. If only he had stuck to the plan. So much blood. So much violence. It could all have been avoided if *Marda* had been allowed to petition the Convocation, as she'd suggested.

"If only they had trusted you."

"No."

Marda hadn't meant to respond to Kevmo out loud, certainly hadn't meant for others to hear it, several of the Path turning quickly to glance at her. With the Herald still on Jedha and the Elders . . . crumbling, she was the Mother's proxy on the flight deck in Elecia's absence. She was the Guide, and whether she agreed with Yana or not about the logic of returning to Dalna, that was what they were doing, albeit still in realspace for the moment, as the Mother had instructed Shea Ganandra to monitor communications to and from Jedha.

"You could order them to stop, Marda. You could take control. The Mother is in the infirmary having her shrapnel removed. If she trusted you, she would let you act."

This time she didn't reply to Kevmo. She didn't need to. The Mother was right. It was prudent to gather as much data as possible. As she'd told Yana, they needed to prepare for every eventuality.

"Yana thinks you're a child. She never listens to you. I wish *I'd* listened to you."

Yes, Marda thought wistfully, *I wish you had, too.*

"Oh, varp," Shea said from her station on the other side of the flight deck, the engineer still in the combat fatigues she'd been wearing when she returned to the *Gaze*.

"What is it?" Marda said, marching over to her, hoping Shea was being typically overdramatic.

The red-haired woman pointed at a report scrolling over her screen. "I intercepted a report on the Hutt communications network."

"The Hutts'?"

Shea shrugged. "What can I say? It's farther reaching than the Republic's and more stable, too."

"But you got into it."

"I got into it when I was eight, Marda. The important thing is *that*." She tapped the screen with a grimy finger.

"I don't speak Huttese," Marda admitted.

"It doesn't matter. This is Rigariam, the dead language of an even deader species. Many Hutt transmissions still use it."

Was there anything this woman didn't know? Marda tried not to let her irritation show. "And?"

"And it says that the Path is being investigated for attempting to derail the peace conference."

"We know. The Mother has promised to make her own inquiry into—"

"The traitor in our midst," Shea interrupted, pouring melodrama into her voice. "The problem is that the Hutts seem to think that it was *several* traitors."

"And they care, why?"

Shea rolled her eyes. "Stars, you're naive. The Hutts obviously had a fathier in the race. They've profited royally from the war, but could profit even more in peace. All those planets needing help to rebuild? You can be sure the benevolent Hutt Cartel will be there to wheedle their grubby little hands into local governments, preferably before the Republic sweeps in with its glittering reforms. Who knows how many strings those overgrown slugs pulled to get the peace talks to the point they were, and now things are worse than ever? One thing is certain: our name is mud as far as Nal Hutta is concerned."

"And what of the Mother?" Marda asked, increasingly infuriated by Shea's tone. "Has she been named?"

"Named for what?"

Every head turned at the voice that rang out from the back of the flight deck. The Mother was leaning on a stick near the main doors, the Leveler at her feet. She had changed into fresh robes, her hair covered with a wrap. She was pale, yes, but her voice was more robust than it had been on Jedha, her gaze clear, even from this distance. Behind her loomed two figures, the Wookiee Jukkyuk, who had made it off Jedha after being separated from the Mother in a street scuffle, and Bokana Koss, his injuries dressed, wearing the livery of the Mother's honor guard.

"He wormed his way in nice and quick," said the voice in her head, and Marda felt her lips thin in annoyance. The Mother always repaid those loyal to her, and the Ovissian had protected her when she needed him most.

"He pulled you out of the fire, too," Kevmo reminded her, "before you destroyed my lightsaber, before you left it lying in the dust."

Yes, she had left it lying where it had been tossed by

the wargaran. She'd told herself that she had forgotten the weapon in the rush to leave Jedha, but the truth of the matter was that she'd never wanted to pick it up again, the memory of what she had done with the damned thing too painful.

She'd extinguished a life. The thought of lighting the blade again made her feel sick, but Bokana had come to her aid once more, thinking the saber was special to her. He'd picked it up as they ran for Sunshine Dobbs's ship, handing it over as soon as they were on board. Now the hilt was in her quarters, hidden beneath a neatly stacked pile of robes, its once pristine lines punctured by the wargaran's teeth. She should throw it away, toss the thing out of an airlock, but something stopped her.

"It's because you love me," Kevmo wheezed. "You just can't bear to let me go."

On Jedha, Marda had longed to hear Kevmo's voice, but it had changed, becoming harsh and bitter. Worst of all, it was another distraction, which was the last thing she needed right now.

"Mother," she said, crossing the deck. "Word has started to spread about Jedha, as you said it would."

"All lies," Elecia said, raising her head to make the comment public.

"Exaggerations," Marda said hurriedly. "Everyone knows about the incident with the Grafs."

A look of annoyance flashed over the Mother's face. "You told them?"

"The word was already out, and we have nothing to hide, not from each other."

The Mother's nostrils flared, but she decided not to push the point.

"But she will when you're in private," Kevmo murmured. "Or maybe she'll just talk about you behind your back to her new friend, the Ovissian."

"People *will* talk, but ultimately the truth will prevail," the Mother continued. "They will know that we had no part in the troubles on Jedha, that the real villains here are those who misuse the Force for their own ends. If it weren't for Force users like the Jedi, the violence would never have broken out in the first place. We would have been able to spread our message in peace, as you intended, Marda. The Path would still be whole, rather than grieving those who are no longer with us."

She broke off to look back at Bokana, a gesture everyone understood. Before Jedha, the human known as Qwerb would have stood in his place, but Qwerb was dead, killed defending Elecia.

The Mother began walking across the flight deck, leaning heavily on her cane.

"Here," Marda said, offering her arm. "Let me help."

"I am not one of your Littles," Elecia snapped with a

ferocity that surprised Marda. Even the Leveler looked up, whimpering slightly in the back of its long throat.

The Mother closed her eyes and took a breath. "I apologize, Marda. I apologize to you all. My temper is short, a result of the pain, but my injuries are already healing. The shrapnel is removed, and Elder Jichora says that the Force has spared me from any lasting damage. I need to meditate, to reconnect with the Force." She looked down at the creature at her feet. "The Leveler will help, our avatar for the Force itself, a living miracle, and when the triple rod is complete . . ."

"I don't want to be the bearer of bad news," Shea piped up from her screens. "But you might have to start praying for another miracle."

"What is it?" Marda asked, a feeling of unease settling into her stomach.

Shea's only reply was to flick a switch, a stuttering hologram projecting against the wall. A defiant face glared out at them, dark eyes robbed of their luster by static, but there was no mistaking the stubs where Nautolan tresses should fall.

"The Herald," Elecia breathed.

"You're looking at a mug shot, courtesy of the Convocation of the Force," Shea told them, jabbing a finger at the holo. "The Herald is under arrest."

"For what?" Marda asked.

Shea tapped some keys, summoning a datafeed. "It's patchy, but according to this he's being charged . . ." She paused when she found the answers she was looking for, closing her eyes and sighing.

"Well?" Marda prompted.

Shea swiveled her chair toward them, her eyes defiant. "I was with them, Yana and the Herald."

"You were a member of Yana's team?"

"Of the *Herald's* team. Continuing the work of the Children, looking for artifacts that we could . . . that we could liberate. There was an . . . incident in the Jedi vault. That's where we were when you called Yana back. . . ." Her eyes flicked down to the Leveler. "Us and that creature."

"Yana told us that the Jedi found you," the Mother said, her voice even.

"Did they ever. Yana and I ran, but the Herald was left behind. I honestly thought he would get away."

"But he didn't," Marda pointed out. "Werth was captured and his accomplices . . ." Her mouth went dry as she read the rest of the report. "His accomplices were killed."

Marda turned to the Mother, icy fingers gripping her heart. "We sent Yana back there. Is she—?"

But the Mother ignored the question, raising one of her own: "What are the charges leveled at the Herald?"

"Looting of various archives, including the Temple of the Whills," Shea said, reading ahead before sighing again. "And murder."

"Murder?" Marda parroted, her head still reeling. "Of whom?"

Another flick of a switch brought up a picture of a proud-snouted Selonian. "The representative serving on the Convocation. Jedi Master Leebon."

"A Jedi," the Mother commented, almost to herself, before directing a question at the engineer. "And how did they die?"

Shea's eyes dropped down to the Leveler.

"I see," the Mother said, a bandaged arm dropping to touch the creature's head. She looked like she was about to collapse, despite her cane. Jukkyuk and Bokana obviously thought the same, stepping forward from where they had been waiting beside the flight deck doors.

The Mother merely raised a hand, warding them off. "Do not fuss." Her eyes were flicking left and right as her mind raced to process the information Shea had provided. Marda felt the same way. She found herself glaring into the impassive eyes of the Herald on the screen.

"This is all his fault, you know," Kevmo whispered in her ear. "If he had allowed you to go to the Convocation . . . if he had followed the plan, Yana would still be alive. They would have retrieved the rod and escaped. She'd be here, by your side. But perhaps . . . just perhaps . . . he did you a favor. . . ."

His words hung in the silence, Marda suddenly realizing their significance. Kevmo was right. Maybe the Herald would prove to be the instrument of their salvation after all.

"Mother," she said, drawing close to the frail-looking

woman. "This is the opportunity we need . . . to protect the Path."

Elecia studied Marda's face curiously. "In what way?"

"We find a way to distance you from the Herald. To distance our entire organization. We say that the Herald was working alone."

"Or as part of a conspiracy," Kevmo suggested.

"Yes," Marda said, ignoring the puzzled look on the Mother's face. "That's better. He was part of a splinter group—"

"Radicalized by the death of his daughter."

"—who wanted to sabotage the peace conference and force the Convocation to listen to our message."

"A message he misunderstood."

"We say he argued with you. That his actions provoking a riot were his alone—"

"His and Yana's."

"—that he believed in direct violent action, while we—"

"The true Path."

"—while we believe in peace and dialogue. That we believe in the Force."

"That's good. This will impress her. This will prove your value. This will prove that you're worthy of being the Guide."

The Mother was silent. She just stood there, examining Marda's face. Why didn't she answer? Could she hear Kevmo's voice? No, that was ridiculous. He was dead. Like Yana. Like they'd *all* be if the Jedi decided to retaliate.

"Good," Elecia finally said. "Yes, that is very good."

Marda's shoulders relaxed. She hadn't even realized that she'd been holding her breath as she waited for the Mother to answer.

"You think it will work?" Marda asked, immediately kicking herself. Why did she always have to second-guess her own ideas?

"Because you know they don't trust you yet. They don't believe in you."

No. The Mother had said it was good. It was a good plan.

"Shea," the Mother said, turning to the engineer, "can we send a message to Jedha?"

"To anyone in particular?" Shea asked.

"To the Jedi," the Mother replied. "To the Convocation . . . the Guardians of the Whills . . . to everyone and anyone."

Shea was already flicking switches. "Shouldn't be a problem. We're not too far. At the very least, we could send a courier droid."

"No," the Mother said sharply. "It needs to be an open signal that all can hear."

Shea looked at the prophet as if she was losing her mind. "You know the relay network around here is as patchy as a moth-eaten bantha skin, don't you?"

"Can you do it?" Elecia pressed, rapping her cane against the floor for emphasis.

Shea swung back, as nonchalant as ever. “Of course I can. This isn’t my first podrace.”

“But what are you going to say?” Marda asked.

The Mother smiled.

SEVEN

Padawan Matthea Cathley—Matty to her friends—tried to keep calm as she walked through the chilled corridors of the Temple of the Kyber in Jedha City. Her head was high, her lekku straight, and her hands steady around the tray she carried, laden with a small but surprisingly nutritious meal. Say what you wanted about the Guardians of the Whills—and plenty on Jedha did—but they treated their prisoners well, as was right and proper. That said, Oklane Viss, the captain of the guard, had been surprised when Matty offered to take the food down to the holding cells.

"You know me," she had said with her typical breeziness. "I want to help, and you're all busy enough."

That much was true. The Guardians, protectors of the temple's many treasures, had stepped up to help rebuild Jedha. An uneasy peace had fallen on the Holy City, although tensions were still running high. It didn't hurt for the Guardians to be seen in the streets, a steadying hand. Anywhere else, that would be the Jedi's role, but Jedha was different in so many ways. Long before, the Jedi had governed there, withdrawing when resentment started to grow within the other Force religions on the Pilgrim Moon who claimed that the Jedi were overreaching, putting themselves forward as the one true faith. Nonsense, of course, but the events of the past few days had shown that the old grievances were still there, simmering under the surface, ready to boil over. And boy, had they boiled over.

None of this was a surprise to Matty. She'd been here for years, ever since Master Leebon had taken her as a Padawan and brought her to Jedha. There was no Jedi Temple on the moon, although the existence of the towering statue of a Jedi in the desert still caused consternation. At least, it had. That problem had been solved spectacularly by the protestors who had brought it crashing to the ground. Instead, Matty's home for just over a decade had been the Temple of the Kyber itself. The bond between the Jedi and the Disciples was still strong, although the recent bloodshed had put a strain on the relationship. The sight of Jedi marching through the streets like a small army would do that!

But they had come through it, all the plots and the violence and the . . .

Matty paused for a moment, her grip around the tray tightening as she finished the thought. And the death.

Blowing her breath out to center herself, Matty continued walking, her head-tails bouncing against her back. A Jedi didn't fear death, nor did they grieve when one of their own fell. Of course, the not grieving thing was more challenging when she heard the lesson in the voice of her late master. Leebon was gone—the respected Selonian who had taught her so much, who had granted her independence unheard of among other Padawans, allowing her to follow her studies wherever the Force led. And yet Master Leebon had always been there when Matty came back from the Sabracci collection or the Reflection caverns or wherever she had wandered, the old Selonian brewing a mug of nubussian cocoa, ready to listen to what her inquisitive apprentice had discovered. Matty knew she talked a lot—and she knew how often that habit annoyed people, as it had annoyed her new master Jedi Vildar Mac when he first arrived on Jedha—but not Leebon. She would listen come what may. But now Leebon was gone, her body reduced to ash by an unknown weapon, Vildar unable to explain what had happened in the lost Jedi vault. Matty couldn't blame him. His mind had been clouded by the same dreadful malady that had swept over them all on the Convocation steps. The confusion and terror she'd felt was still all too raw at the back of her mind, the sensation that she had been suddenly cut off from reality, from the Force itself.

Matty halted again, not because her emotions were in danger of running out of control (which they were) but because she had come to the door that led to the holding cells, a pair of burly Guardians standing, well, guard.

"Hello!" Matty said, lifting the tray slightly so they could see its contents. "Grub's up. Not for you, sorry. For the prisoner. Although if you're hungry, I could pop back up to the kitchens and bring you down something to eat. A bhillen wrap, maybe, or a nice crisp salad?"

She was rambling. This in itself was nothing new, her motormouth being her preferred method for covering up her nerves.

"Sorry," she said, feeling her already red cheeks darken several shades. "I'm sure you're more than capable of fetching your own food." The Guardians continued to stare at her. "But the offer still stands, if you get peckish," she added, unable to help herself.

"Do you want to go in?" the brown-skinned human asked.

"Yes," she confirmed, although she wanted to say: *Nope. Not at all. Not on your nelly.* She didn't really know what a nelly was and considered asking the guards before thinking better of it. "Yes. Thank you."

Ignoring the look of relief from the other guard, a towering buzzard-faced Hiitian, Matty waited for the human to fish a key-laden ring of metal from his robes and unlock the door. It swung open without a sound.

"Ooh, I expected it to creak," Matty said, unable to help herself. "In fact, this entire place is *very* well maintained, all things considered. Most dungeons are gloomy . . . you know, dank. . . . This is . . ." She searched for the word, fully aware that it would probably be better if she shut the heck up. "Roomy."

"Yes, it is," the human said, holding the open door. "Don't let us keep you."

"Of course," Matty said, taking the hint and stepping over the threshold. "Thank you. And have a think about that food. I'd be happy to pop back down."

"He's at the end," the Hiitian said. "Just knock when you want out."

The door slammed shut, although Matty couldn't help noticing that the hinges did creak this time.

Perhaps she'd bring down some grease with the guards' food. Yes, that was what she'd do. In fact, she could just head up to the supply closet now.

She was spiraling, another of her habits, one she'd worked on time and time again with Master Leebon.

"You need to learn to anchor yourself," the Selonian used to say. "Close your eyes and quiet that glorious mind of yours." She did so now, hoping that the guards weren't watching through the viewing hole in the door, wondering what the foolish Jedi was doing. "Now, when you're ready, open them again and focus on the first thing you see. That is your anchor, as effective as any thrown overboard during a storm. Focus on that object, whatever it is, and describe it to yourself. Its color. How you imagine it would feel beneath your hand. Does it smell of anything? What is its purpose? If your mind starts to wander, acknowledge the thought and return your full attention to the object. Make it the center of your world at that moment."

Matty reopened her eyes and did as she had been instructed, focusing on the cell at the other end of the brightly lit corridor, the wooden door dark in the light from the glow-orbs set into the walls. Matty took a breath and marched the entire length of the passage, ignoring the other doors, all of which led to empty cells. All the time, she kept her eyes locked on her anchor, getting nearer, seeing blemishes in the wood. She stopped in front of it. Balancing the tray on one hand to slide open the small window at the top, she looked inside.

The prisoner was kneeling in the middle of the cell, his palms raised to the low ceiling. He looked like he was praying, his eyes closed, head slightly forward.

Werth Plouth. Herald of the Open Hand.

Thief. Murderer.

Finally, Plouth opened his eyes and looked up to meet

her gaze. His face was impassive, the stubs where his tresses should have been as stark as when she'd first seen him being brought in by Master Vildar and Tey Sirrek, the impish Sephi who had become an unlikely friend.

"Well?" he asked, his expression not changing, his low voice reverberating around the small room, empty except for a bed and a squat evac tube. "What do you want of me, Jedi?"

For once, Matty didn't speak. She wanted to. By the Force, she wanted to; she wanted to tell him *exactly* who he'd killed—the wonderful, generous, at-times-a-little-scary life he'd snuffed out for a few trinkets stashed in an archive no one even knew existed. She wanted to tell him of the pain he'd caused, of the damage. Most important, she wanted to tell him that it had all been for nothing, that whatever he'd been planning, whatever his motivation, the people of Jedha had rallied, that they had stood together in the main square and sung songs of unity, even though Matty's heart had been breaking because Master Leebon's voice hadn't been among them. But even in that, he hadn't succeeded, because Matty Cathley would go on. She would remain a Jedi, be the best Jedi she could be, in honor of the teacher he'd slaughtered. She wanted to tell him all that and more but instead slid the window shut and opened the hatch to slip the tray into the cell. The hatch closed again, and she walked purposefully to the door at the other end of the corridor and rapped twice on the wood, waiting patiently for the Guardians to turn the lock.

"Are you all right?" the human asked as she swept past them. She nodded and carried on, promising herself that she'd come back later to check if the Guardians really did want something to eat. She couldn't ask now, because if she opened her mouth, she worried she'd never stop screaming.

EIGHT

Matty hadn't expected to find a summons from Vildar Mac waiting for her when she walked up the stairs from the cells, counting every marbled step to quiet her thoughts.

Actually, *summons* was too strong a word. It was a request delivered by SK-0T, Tey Sirrek's spherical scout droid. Skoot, as Tey called him, had burbled the message excitedly, asking her to head straight for the Convocation chamber to meet with Vildar and Oliviah Zeveron, the Jedi Knight who had served as Master Leebon's aide—and a woman Matty felt had never warmed to her, as frosty today as when they'd first met five or six years earlier. Oliviah had been expected to succeed

Leebon as the Jedi's representative on the Convocation but had been badly injured at the hands of the Herald and advised to return to Coruscant to recuperate, Vildar taking her place on the advisory council instead. Matty was surprised Oliviah was still on Jedha, to be honest. Skoot didn't know why she hadn't left, and for once, Matty wasn't in the mood to speculate. Instead, she followed the droid from the Temple of the Kyber in uncharacteristic silence, taking in the sights and sounds of the streets. What she had wanted to say to the Herald was correct; the people of Jedha *were* rallying, the streets crowded with folks working together to clear up the damage from the fighting. Members of different factions stood side by side, sweeping and gathering rubble, while a Republic cleanup crew did its best to shore up a scorched wall that looked like it was on the point of collapse. One thing was certain: Jedha would need more than brooms and scaffolding. The cooperation required was more than the Convocation had achieved in all its years of service. The scars would run deep for many years to come.

Amazingly, the Convocation building itself was still standing, having weathered the angry mob whipped up into a frenzy by Werth Plouth. The smooth walls, relatively new compared with those of the buildings that surrounded it, were pocked and blackened but still holding, its grand doors already rehung.

Vildar and Oliviah were waiting for Matty in the Jedi representative's chambers, a room that still smelled of the meditation candles Leebon used to burn. Tey Sirrek was there, too, the pointy-eared Sephi sitting cross-legged on the desk rather than on one of the ornamental chairs, a habit that would've once raised Vildar's blood pressure by several digits.

Both Master Vildar and Tey had only recently come into Matty's life; Vildar had been posted to Jedha, while Tey had been there since he was a child. Once, the pointy-eared Sephi had been a Guardian of the Whills, until a tragedy forced him to question his calling. Tey had abandoned his post at the Temple of the Kyber, adopting the life of a thief while helping those worse off than him. He'd originally clashed with Vildar when their paths had crossed while investigating a series of robberies, but a fierce friendship had developed over the course of the adventure they'd subsequently shared, a bond strengthened by the trials and tribulations of the conflict that had engulfed the Holy City. Both men had been there when Master Leebon was killed by Werth Plouth, although neither could explain exactly what had happened. Master Vildar had been overcome by the same strange sensation that had swept over all the Jedi on the Convocation steps, while Tey was suffering memory loss from his use of a forbidden artifact in the Jedi vault. The ancient Sith gauntlet had saved Vildar's life but scrambled Tey's short-term memory, leaving only a vague recollection of Master Leebon's final, tortured moments.

The danger had passed, the relic the Herald had been searching for given into the safe hands of archivist Oranalli of the Disciples of the Whills, and Tey had been rewarded with a place at the Convocation table, representing those who didn't belong to any of the major Force factions. Matty had a suspicion that the bond between Tey and Vildar would last a lifetime, although that didn't stop the Sephi from relentlessly testing her new master's patience. Vildar tolerated the constant ribbing with a wry smile that was nothing compared to the wide grin that Tey gave Matty as she entered the chamber.

"Matty," the Sephi exclaimed, leaping down from the table to throw his arms around her. Tey hugged everyone. In the past, that had probably been so he could lift their wallets, but now that he was once again a respectable citizen, the former Guardian had promised that he'd changed his ways. That said, Matty *had* caught Vildar checking that his saber was still on his belt the last time Tey had locked him in an embrace. Once bitten, twice shy . . .

"Perhaps if you could let my Padawan breathe?" Vildar eventually said, and Tey released her with a wink.

"Oh, he's so *masterful* these days," the Sephi said, plonking himself back on the table, his legs swinging. "Have you noticed that, Matty? You don't think power has gone to his head, do you?"

" 'A Jedi does not act for personal power or wealth . . .' " Oliviah Zeveron intoned from the side of the room, the brown-skinned woman's hands resting on her belt.

" 'But only seeks knowledge and enlightenment,' " Vildar

Mac added, concluding the older version of the Jedi's mantra, one Matty knew only from history crystals. "But I didn't call Matty here for a lesson in the Code." He turned to his Padawan and smiled almost bashfully, their new relationship as strange to him as it was to her. "Thank you for coming so promptly."

"Of course," Matty replied before glancing at Oliviah. "Although I thought you'd be halfway to the Core by now, Jedi Zeveron?"

"That's still the plan," the Jedi replied.

"At least, officially," Tey slipped in.

"Officially?" Matty replied, leaning forward. "Okay, now I'm interested. What's going on?"

Vildar stepped around the desk, unable to stop himself from straightening the tray Tey had knocked when he'd returned to the table. Matty felt a twinge of sorrow to see someone other than Leebon on that side of the desk but swallowed it. There was business to discuss.

Vildar flipped a switch, and the image of a woman flickered into existence above the holoprojector set into the marblewood desk. She was tall, with an almost noble face decorated with three wavy lines. Her simple robes marked her as a member of the Path of the Open Hand, but Matty already knew who she was.

"The Mother," she said, remembering the woman's appearances in images from the peace conference. "Their leader."

"Their *prophet*," Vildar corrected her. "Or shaman. We're not sure which. Either way, she's already left Jedha but sent a message for the Convocation."

Another flick of the switch and the holo sprang to life, the Mother's lilting voice edged with static.

"My friends in the Force," she said, smiling benignly, "I am sorry not to be with you in person. I speak from the flight deck of our ship, the *Gaze Electric*, where I was regretfully forced to flee from the violence on Jedha's streets. To see such devastation in such a holy place saddened my heart, but nothing could prepare me for the terrible news that a member of the Path, my very own Herald, would be discovered to be the instigator of the tragedy that has befallen your great city, not only fanning the flames of discontent but lighting the fire to watch it burn.

"Please believe me when I say that we knew nothing of his plan or that of his fellow conspirators. Our mission to Jedha was always one of peace. We sought to spread our message, a message of truth and love. A gift freely given to all who would listen.

"Werth Plouth betrayed us by acting upon his own selfish desires. While the Path of the Open Hand seeks only to illuminate, Plouth sought to spread hatred and chaos, to tear down while we sought to build and unite. Through his actions, he has shown his true nature. He is not a man of the Force. He is a man consumed with greed and a lust for power. He is a viper whom we brought into your community, and for that, we ask your forgiveness. Know that we irrefutably renounce his actions and his agenda. Know that we are sickened that someone we trusted so wholeheartedly, someone we loved, could betray that trust, betray that affection, striking at the heart of everything we hold dear. Trust me, my friends, that we will contemplate what has happened and ensure that such a malign presence will never again be allowed to fester in our community. Even as we speak, the Elders and I are taking our people to a safe place where we can learn from our mistakes and teach those Plouth might have influenced that his way was never . . . will never . . . be the path we tread.

"I ask you to respect our privacy as we deal with the ramifications of this great betrayal. However, as a sign of our good faith, as a sign that we take responsibility for our part in this tragedy, the Path of the Open Hand will be sending a donation of one million zukkels to aid in rebuilding the Holy City."

Matty glanced at Tey. Jedi had no need for money, but even she could understand that was an astronomical amount.

"And to Plouth himself, if he is listening . . ."

At this, the Mother faltered, her voice cracking with emotion. She paused, raising a quaking hand to her lips before continuing.

"To Plouth himself, I say this: Werth, you know what you have done. For all our sakes . . . for the Force itself . . . I beg you to take responsibility for your actions, to accept whatever punishment the people of Jedha deem appropriate. You have brought this upon yourself, and only *you* can be held answerable for your crimes. Show the faithful of Jedha . . . show the *galaxy* . . . that in your heart of hearts you are still a good man, a good *father*, that you know you have done wrong and, by the will of the Force, you are sorry."

Matty suspected that he wasn't, not if his expression in the cell had been anything to go by.

"I hope that one day Jedha will forgive us," the Mother continued, "and that we will be welcomed back to your streets to continue our vital work. Until then, I wish you peace, and I wish you harmony. The Force shall be free."

With that, the woman smiled and the hologram blinked off, leaving only silence in the small room, a silence that Matty immediately shattered with a whistle.

"One million zukkels? That's a lot of money in anyone's currency. Is she serious?"

"Apparently so," Vildar confirmed. "The sum has already been transferred."

"Transferred where?"

"To the Convocation," Oliviah told her. "With the promise that more will be available if needed."

Matty smoothed her lekku, a sign to anyone who knew her that her mind was racing. "But . . . how does an organization like the Path of the Open Hand have access to those kinds of funds? Most *Hutts* would kill for such riches."

"And many have," Vildar agreed. "The Republic has—"

"Snooped," Tey cut in.

"Has made discreet *inquiries*," Vildar said, more diplomatically, "and discovered that the Path has benefited from some wealthy patrons over the last few years. This Mother of theirs is remarkably . . . persuasive."

"She seemed sincere," Matty admitted. "And truly appalled that this has happened on her watch. This can't have been the impact she wanted to make when they arrived from . . ." Matty paused, realizing that she knew nothing of the Path's origins.

"They appear to come from Dalna," Oliviah informed her, leaning across Vildar to reactivate the projector. This time a peaceful-looking planet appeared above the table. "A small world on the very edge of the frontier," Oliviah continued, "orbiting twin suns."

"I can't say I've heard of it," Matty admitted.

"Very few have," Vildar said, deactivating the holo. "And even less seem to visit, although I hear the waterfalls are magnificent. Maybe you could let me know when you get back."

"Me?" Matty looked from one Jedi to the other in confusion. Just what was happening?

"As you know," the Kiffar continued, stroking his beard, "Jedi Zeveron is due to return to Coruscant to convalesce after her trauma in the desert. . . ."

Beside him, Oliviah placed a hand over the spot where the Herald had run her through with her own saber, the wound now covered in kolto-infused synthflesh beneath her tunic. "A plan that is one hundred percent my intention," she agreed, "eventually."

"Eventually?" Matty asked, almost burning with questions.

"Oliviah has planned a slight detour on the way to the Core," Vildar said.

"Taking the scenic route," Tey added, flashing his most infectious smile.

"To Dalna?"

Oliviah nodded. "And Vildar has asked for you to come with me."

"Me?" Matty's mind boggled. "Why?"

"Because she trusts you," Tey said happily.

"Because we *all* trust you," Vildar added.

Matty's cheeks burned, but this didn't answer the question of why Oliviah wanted to go to Dalna in the first place, an answer that Tey, in his own inimitable way, decided to provide.

"She has a bad feeling about this Mum character and the cult in general."

"They are not necessarily a cult," Master Vildar cut in, drawing a snort from the Sephi.

"They are *obviously* a cult." Tey started to count on his long fingers. "There's the clothes, the rhetoric, the wiggly lines on their faces."

"*I* have lines on my face," the Kiffar pointed out.

"And you, my uptight little friend, are part of the biggest cult in the galaxy. All three of you, for that matter. No offense meant."

"Quite a lot taken," Vildar replied, crossing his powerful arms, although Matty suspected that his outrage was all part of the banter. It was hard to tell with these two.

"Yeah, yeah," Tey continued, the smirk never leaving his lips. "Go cry into your robes, Saber Boy."

This, at least, caused Vildar to smile. "You wish, you no-good Lepi."

Tey slapped a hand over his heart, feigning an injury.

"Oooh, *Lepi* . . . because of the ears . . . I see what you did there, although try not to crack that one on Coachelle Prime. They'll shove a space carrot right where the suns don't shine."

Oliviah had mirrored Vildar's pose, her arms neatly folded in either annoyance or despair; Matty couldn't tell which.

"Are you two finished?"

Tey winked at Matty, shrugging off the rebuke. "Not in the slightest, but I take your point. Time is money and the fate of the galaxy may hang in the balance."

"We don't know that," Vildar cut in. "At the moment, it is only a feeling . . . a hunch. . . ."

"A nudge from the Force," Tey added. "To go stick your pretty noses where they don't belong, for the greater good."

"Say my nose is pretty one more time, and I'll break

yours," Oliviah said flatly, which only seemed to amuse Tey all the more.

"Ha! Not very Jedi of you. I must be rubbing off on you all, and about time, too. But yeah, that's the gig. Hotfoot it to Dalna and investigate the Path to see if they're on the level."

"And if they aren't?" Matty asked.

"Then you return here," Master Vildar told her, "and we come up with a plan."

"Which will probably feature laser swords and throwing people around with the Force." Tey grinned.

"As a last resort," Vildar added.

"Says the man who delights in throwing people around with the Force at the very first opportunity."

"Don't tempt me."

"Okay," Matty said, raising her hands before they could continue. "Okay."

"You'll come?" Oliviah asked. "Even though this mission is distinctly off-the-record."

"If it's all right with my master, who am I to refuse?" Matty said, glancing at Vildar.

"I'd be happier if you were there," he said, smiling.

"Then you'll need a ship," Tey said, clapping his hands together and launching himself from the chair. "I know just the Hoopaloo."

"We're not taking Master Leebon's shuttle?" Matty asked, instantly correcting herself. "Sorry, I mean *your* shuttle, Master."

"As Oliviah said, this can't be an official visit," Vildar said. "Not until we know more about these people."

"Then the Hoop it is," Tey said, sweeping from the chambers. "You'll like him. Beautiful plumage. Just let me do the talking. Old Strat can haggle in his sleep."

Oliviah followed, telling the Sephi that she had no intention of letting Tey do *any* of the talking, which only made the former Guardian all the more determined. Oliviah allowed him to continue into the corridor before pausing to look back from the doorway. "Are you coming, Matty?"

Matty was about to spring forward before Vildar stopped her. "Perhaps I could just have a moment with my Padawan?"

Oliviah bowed and took her leave. "Of course. Someone needs to stop Tey from getting carried away."

"Good luck with that," Vildar said with genuine affection as Oliviah closed the door behind her.

"Master?" Matty asked, sensing the Kiffar's desire to speak once they were alone.

He looked at her thoughtfully, perching on the edge of his desk.

"You've known Jedi Zeveron a long time. Longer than me, at least."

"Oliviah? Sure. She's great."

"I know, and I agree. . . ."

You didn't have to be a Jedi to sense the *but*.

"You're worried about her."

Vildar nodded. "I'm sure it's nothing, but while I believe that Oliviah *has* sensed something about this Path—"

"You think she's not telling you everything."

The older man smiled. "You are a very perceptive Padawan."

"I learned from the best," Matty said, returning the grin, which soon fell away, replaced by an expression of concern. "Do you think Oliviah is . . ." She paused, not wanting to complete the sentence.

"Doing something wrong? No, I honestly don't. At least, I hope I don't. But she *is* holding something back, maybe even from herself, and I know how damaging that can be. What with everything that has happened and the way Leebon died . . ." He let the sentence fall away, for both their sakes. "Just be there for her, Matty. I'm not asking you to spy on her or keep her in line. . . ."

"As if I could. She's a strong-willed woman. One of the strongest I know."

"As she's proven by walking around with a saber wound through her gut," Vildar agreed. "But if there is one thing I've learned on Jedha . . . one thing you and Tey have taught me . . . keeping secrets, especially from ourselves, never ends well. We are Jedi. We're always better when we work together."

"And with the Force," Matty added, drawing another smile from her master.

"Yes. With the Force."

NINE

There had been many perks to being one of the Mother's Children. The biggest was the freedom, being able to leave Dalna to search for Force artifacts just begging to be "liberated" from religious houses and private collections alike. Then there was the ability to keep your distance from the rest of the Path when the rituals got too much. Which they had for Yana. A lot.

The most significant benefit had been spending time with Kor on missions. Time alone, just the two of them, breathing in each other's scents, exploring each other's bodies. It wasn't just the sex, although the sex had been incredible; it was the companionship, fitting together with someone who couldn't have been more different in so many ways. Kor, with her family and her easy smile; Yana, with a past that was best forgotten and her habit of making things hard.

They had liked each other from the moment they met. Yes, that sounded like a cliché, but it was true. Yana could still remember the first time she'd laid eyes on Kor, the first time her breath had been taken away. Things had been so different then. Yana and Marda were still new to Dalna, the bloodshed and the trauma of their escape from Genetia still raw, still painful. Marda coped by immediately trying to fit in, learning everything she could about the Path and its teachings. She was so eager, like an excited pup charging from one new experience to the next. Yana, on the other hand, kept everyone at arm's length. It wasn't that she found it hard to trust; she just couldn't. Getting near people only made it easier for them to stab you in the back. Yes, she allowed them to drape the robes of an initiate over her scarred body, but only because she didn't want to draw attention to herself. It wasn't so much trying to blend in but making it easier to slip away in a crowd. Don't let them notice you. Don't let them target you. It had been that way for years, first when she was a youngster and then later as an adolescent, until the day everything changed.

"Hi."

One tiny word. That was all it had taken. One tiny word

as Yana had sat at the edge of the group, with the moon hanging low over Dalna's purple mountains. It was harvest festival, just one of the many celebrations the Path enjoyed.

There had been feasting and singing and dancing and joy, and a huge bonfire blazed at the heart of the compound, the flames rising and crackling to a clear, star-filled sky. Marda was in the thick of it as usual, playing with the Littles, who squealed as she allowed them to ride her like a dewback. The good people of Ferdan probably heard the music, too, played on batanga and concertinium, but to Yana it was all noise. She'd been sitting there, planning her escape, wondering if she could stow away on a ship leaving Ferdan, wondering if she could persuade Marda to come with her.

That was when someone had flopped down beside her, a slim but deceptively strong green hand holding out a bottle of gnostra berry wine.

"Hi," Kor had said.

"Hi," Yana had replied, wondering what to do.

"Thought you might be thirsty."

Thirsty? Yana's mouth had definitely gone dry. She'd seen Kor Plouth around the compound. It was hard not to when her father was the Herald, an imposing figure in every sense of the word. But even if he'd been a nobody, Yana would have noticed Kor. She was beautiful, the most beautiful person Yana had ever seen, with her long, sensual tresses and perfect green skin. Even as Yana had planned her escape, a new fantasy had formed uninvited in her imagination: Yana slipping away in the middle of the night, heading for Ferdan, a hand grabbing her, pulling her back. She'd spin around and find herself face to face with the young Nautolan, their lips dangerously close, Yana's breath catching as Kor told her she couldn't leave.

Now, after all those imagined moments, Kor was sitting beside her, the bottle still outstretched.

Yana shook her head, looking back at the fire.

"No. I'm good. Thanks."

"Whatever you say." It had been so hard to keep focused on the flames as she listened to the Nautolan swigging wine from the bottle. She could imagine Kor's head tipped back, her tresses tumbling down her back. . . .

"I should go," Yana had muttered, standing up.

"Where?"

"What?"

"Where will you go? Do you want company?"

Yana had looked down, seeing Kor looking up at her with those gorgeous, rich eyes, lips parted and moist from the wine.

"I-I don't know," Yana stammered. "I'm just . . . I'm just not very good around people."

A smile had spread across Kor's lips. "Then I know the perfect place."

She had taken Yana to the old torinda tree on the other

side of the compound, the very same tree Yana had discovered on her first day on Dalna, the same tree she had climbed a thousand times to be alone.

"It's my favorite place," Kor told her.

"Mine too," Yana replied.

They had climbed it together that night, finishing off the bottle and laughing, firm friends from that point on. Yana's tree. *Their* tree. Where they first kissed, a year to the day from that first fateful meeting, where Yana told herself there would never be another.

Yana set the glass down on the bar's table. "Another?" the insectoid barkeep asked, two of his seven arms cleaning a flagon.

Thought you might be thirsty.

Kor stared over the Villarandi's shoulder, from the mirror on the other side of the bar, her once black eyes milky and distant.

"No," Yana said, shaking her head.

No. I'm good.

"Not a problem," the curious barkeep said, sliding the now-clean flagon along the bar. "You sit there. Relax. Think. Do whatever you do. Then, when you are ready, you call Kradon, yes? Kradon will fix you up."

Satisfied that he had done his duty, the Villarandi barkeep turned to a large Sullustan sitting three stools away, offering him another glass of retsa. The Sullustan, obviously a regular, asked for two.

NINE

Yana looked around, anything to avoid looking up at that mirror. The place—apparently called Enlightenment—was two steps away from being a disaster zone. Something bad had gone down there, like in most of the city. There were fresh blaster marks on the already pitted walls, and the once-glorious tapestries that hung from the low ceiling were tattered and scorched. Even the doors were temporary fix-ups, the originals blown to pieces if the splinters and debris swept into a corner were anything to go by. Yana had a sense that there should have been at least twice as many tables, and it was clear the music droid that lay on its side by the smashed novacrown board would never play again. Still, Enlightenment was open for business and a haven from trouble if the hulking Gloovans at the door were anything to go by. Yana had certainly gotten the impression that they would enjoy pummeling her into the ground if she took a step out of line, even if one of them rocked a painful-looking magna-cast on her left arm.

Kradon had been welcoming enough, but Yana hadn't wanted a drink. She just needed to get off the streets, to find a place to think, and the one thing Jedha didn't have was a torinda tree.

Yana looked up, finally braving the mirror, but Kor wasn't there. Good. She needed to work out her next move. Everything was in turmoil. Not only had the Mother abandoned them in the middle of a war zone, but then she had twisted the knife. The broadcast from the *Gaze Electric* had soon been playing on every holonet channel—well, the ones that could get a signal as far as Jedha, anyway. Yana had stared in disbelief as Elecia had casually thrown the Herald under the landcrawler. The people of this Void-forsaken moon had swallowed the lies as Yana knew they would, the various factions—both secular and religious—desperate for a scapegoat to absolve themselves from blame.

It wasn't us. It was the agitator with the shorn-off tresses. It was the traitor to his cause. It was that radical.

However, the Path of the Open Hand wasn't off the hook completely, no matter what the Mother had planned. There were plenty of folks who lumped them all together. Even now, Yana tried not to wince as two dockers seated at a back table discussed what they would do if they came upon one of those galaxy-hugging cultists. The Force may well be free, but no Path member would be free from danger on Jedha, even if Elecia emptied the entirety of the Path's coffers into the Convocation's lap. In times like this it was the ordinary people who mattered, and the ordinary people wanted the Path's blood. Yana was grateful she wasn't wearing her usual robes. She could probably take the dockers, but she'd be in trouble if news got out that a member of the Path of the Open Hand was nursing an empty glass in a backstreet bar. The Evereni were used to angry mobs, but that didn't mean she went looking for trouble.

But what *was* she looking for? The Mother had basically washed her hands of Yana the moment she betrayed the Herald, and Marda was becoming more radicalized by the day.

"This is your opportunity to run," Kor's voice said. "To start again. Find a new torinda."

"But what about your dad?" Yana whispered under her breath.

Across the bar, Kradon's antennae twitched, and he scuttled back over to her.

"If Kradon can't get you another drink, what else can Kradon fetch?"

She sighed, pushing away the glass and starting to dismount the stool. "Nothing, thanks. I was just going."

"Kradon could rustle you up something to eat. Our chef is unfortunately deceased, but Camille makes a mean pancake. Her zoochberry cream is delicious."

Yana frowned. "Camille?"

The Villarandi nodded at the Gloovans by the door. "One of the Twinkle sisters. The attractive one."

"There's an *attractive* one?"

"Careful," Kradon said, a gleam in his bulbous eyes. "Their ears are almost as keen as their fists."

"And I thought Villarandi were the ones with the excellent hearing."

The barkeep clucked. "You have heard of us. Kradon will have to watch himself around you."

Yana tapped the bar as she stood up to go. "I'm willing to bet it's the other way around. Bye, Kradon."

"Wait," the insectoid said. "If not a pancake, then maybe entertainment? A game of flikflak?" He leaned closer. "Information."

Yana paused, looking over to the improbably named Twinkle sisters and wondering which was Camille. When she looked back to the bar, Kradon was waiting patiently.

"Just go," Kor urged, far away. "You don't need to do this."

Yana slipped back onto the stool.

"What kind of information could you get me, hmm? The kind I can trust? The kind that won't see me end up dumped near the Old Shadow, a knife in my back?"

"Ah, information never gets you killed. It's what you *do* with it that gets you killed. Kradon is just a humble barkeep. Kradon gets what people need."

"For the right price?"

"Or maybe a favor. Kradon collects favors."

"Cashing them in when the time is right, I suppose."

The insectoid shrugged. "What else would you do with them? Keep them in an album with the Twinkle sisters' holiday snaps?"

Yana leaned in. "I don't like being in debt."

Another shrug. "Then flikflak it is, although Kradon is not sure we have all the pieces anymore."

"Then I'll get you a new set," Yana said. "How's that for a deal?"

The barkeep clicked his tongue against the roof of his

mouth. “Kradon likes it, although you may need a great many sets, depending on the size of the favor.”

Yana studied the Villarandi, wondering if she could trust this strange little being or whether she was about to make the biggest mistake of her life.

“Yes,” said the voice in her head. “Yes, you are,” but Yana plowed on anyway.

“Tell me, Kradon,” she said, leaning in closer still, “is Enlightenment the kind of establishment where a girl can find out where a certain prisoner is being held?”

TEN

"Can you help me?"

Bokana spun around, the Ovissian's twin blades glinting in the lights of the room the Mother had given him for his morning calisthenics.

"I didn't see you there," he said, sweat glistening on his olive green skin.

"I'm sorry," Marda said, regretting not knocking before entering, or clearing her throat. "I didn't mean to make you jump."

"You didn't," he said before correcting himself. "Well, you did. I was . . ."

"Concentrating, I know."

Now she just sounded creepy, like she had been standing there watching him for hours rather than the minutes she'd actually spent in the doorway as he sliced the daggers through the air in a series of curated moves.

If he *was* unnerved, he didn't show it, walking over to a nearby bench to place the daggers back into their felt-lined box and pick up a towel.

"I couldn't believe it when I saw those in the armory," he said, drying the sweat from his broad bare chest. "I don't know what was more surprising, that the *Gaze Electric* even *had* an armory or that it would contain a pair of katachi blades." He glanced up, his skin still glistening. "Looks like you've visited the weapons rack yourself."

Marda licked her lips, her mouth having suddenly gone dry. "My cousin found them on the way to Jedha," she said, self-consciously rapping the ends of the wooden fighting staffs against the metal floor.

"Yana," he said, sympathy filling his dark eyes. "I heard that they, er, they think . . ."

"They think she's dead," Marda said for him, trying not to let her voice quiver.

"I'm sorry. Truly I am. If I had known, when I helped take the rod from her—"

Again, Marda stepped in. "She knew the risks," she said sharply, the words almost catching in her throat.

"And she was brave," Bokana said. "At least, that's what they say."

Marda tried not to feel a sting of jealousy. "You've talked about her."

"About her . . . about *you*." A bashful smile pulled at Bokana's broad lips, and Marda was suddenly aware of just how close the room had become.

"I've never met an Evereni before," Bokana continued, kneading the towel in his hands. "I've heard stories. . . ."

"I'm sure you have."

"But you're not what I expected," the Ovissian added quickly. "The Elders said you came to the Path as a child."

"It was a long time ago. We had nowhere else to go."

"I know that feeling," Bokana said, throwing down the towel and holding out a hand for a staff. "May I?"

She handed it over and watched him twirl it in his strong hands, nodding in appreciation. "Shyrran wood from Kashyyyk. Rarer than wroshyr, but just as strong."

"It certainly hurts," Marda admitted, mock grimacing at the memory.

"Why me?" the Ovissian asked, clasping the staff tight in his fists and looking at her pointedly. "When you first met me, I was being beaten to a pulp. . . ."

"You were outnumbered," she reminded him.

Bokana returned his attention to the wood, rubbing it with his thumb.

"It wouldn't have been a problem in the past."

She moved in closer, the tang of his sweat surprisingly pleasant. "You were a warrior?"

He snorted, looking back up. "Of a sort." A pained look tugged at his expression, as if he was worried she'd think less of him. "A soldier of fortune."

"A mercenary."

He nodded. "I went where the money was, but after a while . . ." His voice trailed off, and he swallowed hard, flicking an invisible flaw in the wood with his thumbnail.

"Bokana?" she prompted, moving closer still and fighting the urge to reach up and place a hand on his chest. A comforting hand, she told herself. Nothing more.

"It started to eat away at me," he said, his voice thickening. "Every battle, every kill. I even signed up for the war on the side of the E'roni—a side I thought I could believe in—but it just felt worse. Piece by piece, I was being whittled away, emptied of everything I thought I was."

"You don't have to tell me," she said softly, regretting pushing him, even if it was with the best of intentions. "Not if you don't want to."

"No," he said, sniffing. "It's good. I want to." He rapped the end of his shyrran staff on the floor, anything to avoid looking at her. "There was a battle, on Eiram. I was sent in as part of a contingent assisting the crown forces. We were to storm a munitions plant, or that's what we were briefed. The first wave blew the walls and we went in." His voice caught. "They were everywhere."

His eyes glistened with the horror she was forcing him to confront. She waited as he chewed his lips, summoning the courage to continue.

"They were families, Marda. Civilians. The plant was a shelter for refugees who had lost their homes. They didn't stand a chance, and those still alive were screaming. So, so scared. I mean, why wouldn't you be? The rest of the squad, they kept firing, salvo after salvo. I couldn't take it anymore. I turned and ran, straight into one of the E'ronoh commanders. He called me a deserter and ordered me back, even after I told him what we'd found. What we'd done."

"Oh, Bokana," Marda breathed, no longer stopping herself from reaching out. She pressed her palm to his muscular chest, the skin beneath her fingers tattooed with scars. "I'm so sorry."

The Ovissian took a shuddering breath. "The commander pulled his blaster on me, but I shot first. I didn't even wait for him to hit the ground. I ran and didn't stop running until I found myself on a shuttle heading for Jedha. I don't even remember buying the ticket, but it suited me, you know? If there was anywhere I could find answers . . ."

That, Marda *could* understand, and she only wished she'd found answers herself.

"That's where you found the Path," she said, and he nodded, wiping his eyes with the back of a hand.

"They were speaking outside the almshouse on the

Invocation Way, talking about gifts from the Force, for each other. Next thing I know, I'm on my hands and knees bawling my eyes out." He laughed, embarrassed. "I must have looked such a sight."

Her hand slipped up to his face, cupping his cheek. "No one will have judged you. Not among the Path, at least."

"Yeah," he agreed, not pulling away. "They were so kind. I felt . . ." Bokana swallowed. "I felt like I'd come home."

Marda smiled sadly. She couldn't help herself. The way he'd talked about the refugees, and the warmth when he described his experience at the almshouse. Her chest tightened when she thought about the brutes who had beaten him in that backstreet. It made her so angry that someone could be so cruel to someone who was already broken, someone who was struggling to find his way back. She looked deep into his eyes, seeing the pain and the hurt . . . and Bokana leaned closer to her, his lips parting. . . .

No. Marda had no idea if she'd said the word out loud, but she stepped back all the same, her hand snapping away.

"I'm sorry," Bokana said quickly, but she had already turned away from him, her face burning.

"This was a mistake," she said, her voice thick. "I had no idea what you had gone through. I should never have asked. . . ."

She made for the door, forgetting that he still held the other fighting staff.

"We've all been through things," he said, calling out to her. "And we all have scars. What matters is how we help each other heal. A gift freely given."

Marda stopped, turning back. Bokana was already in a defensive position, his shyrran staff raised, a playful smile on his lips. "Why don't you show me what your cousin taught you."

That first lesson had been hard, and not because of any awkwardness over what had almost happened between them. Bokana hadn't held back, pushing Marda, encouraging her when she fell and praising her on the rare occasions she slipped a hit past his defenses.

The second and third sessions had been just as bad, but by the fourth Marda was actually looking forward to their time together. Her body was a mass of bruises, but Bokana said she was making progress, which only made her smile all the easier. She liked it when he was pleased with her, her pride and her confidence growing with each compliment.

And that was the problem. Now, sitting in the *Gaze Electric*'s dining hall at one of the long tables beautifully carved by the Path's finest artisans, Marda could feel eyes boring into her skull, eyes that had no business looking at the living.

She liked Bokana, not quite in the same way she'd liked Kevmo, but there was something there, something that made her feel both excited and guilty in equal measures.

“Not *that* guilty,” said the dead voice behind her.

Marda tried to block it out, focusing on what she wanted above all.

“We both know what you want. What *he* wants.”

Freedom, balance, and clarity. That’s all she needed. Freedom, balance, and—

“Marda?”

Marda jumped at the voice, not that of the dead but the living, if very, very tired.

“I’m sorry,” Elder Jichora said, the Twi’lek’s eyes rheumy and concerned. “I didn’t mean to startle you.”

“Elder?” Marda said, swinging her legs off the bench as she turned. “Is everything all right?”

“It’s the Mother,” Jichora said, dropping her voice to a whisper. “You need to come with me.”

Elecia was laid out on a bed in her quarters, her face dangerously pale. When she’d first entered the chamber, Marda had feared the worst, that while she was absorbed in her own drama, the Mother had passed away. But Elecia opened her eyes, smiling sluggishly as Jichora led Marda toward the bed. Not that they could get very far, of course, with the Leveler blocking their path, a growl escaping its fronds.

“No, my sweet,” the Mother said, dropping a shaking hand over the side of the mattress to soothe her monstrous protector. “Let them come. It will do me good to see my Guide.”

The Leveler didn't move.

"Mother," Marda said, circling the creature. "Are you well?"

"Of course she's not well," Jichora said, joining Marda at the Mother's side. "She won't rest. She won't sleep."

"There is so much to do," Elecia said, lifting a hand, which Marda took gratefully in her own. It was like holding a skeleton. "We must prepare for our arrival on Dalna. There will be questions. The people of Ferdan . . ."

"Need not concern you," Marda told her. "We can deal with any questions they might have."

Somewhere in the back of her head, Kevmo laughed.

The Mother squeezed her hand weakly. "The Force will uphold me." She pulled on Marda, struggling to get up. "But the Path should see their Mother."

On the other side of the bed, the Leveler rose like a sand whale breaching the dunes.

"There is no need," Jichora said. "The Path is doing just fine."

"It almost sounds like you don't need me," Elecia joked, swinging her feet off the bed.

"She collapsed," Jichora told Marda. "On the way to the dining hall."

"I was hungry," Elecia claimed.

"You were exhausted!"

"Perhaps I can bring you something?" Marda suggested, knowing this was an argument Jichora was unlikely to win with words alone.

"Give me your arm," the Mother said, ignoring the question. Marda did as she was asked, Elecia leaning on Marda as she got to her feet, not that there was much weight to support. It was as if the Mother was wasting away in front of their eyes.

"See?" Elecia said, her voice regaining a little of its usual defiance as she let Marda slowly lead her forward. "She lives. But maybe you're right, Jichora. I have been pushing myself, but only because the Force . . ." Elecia suddenly faltered, gripping Marda's arm tight. "The Force . . ."

"Mother?"

Elecia went rigid, her muscles knotting. She fell back, toppling like a tree, and Marda cried out in alarm as the Mother began to convulse.

"What's happening?"

"And they call you the Guide," Jichora said, joints cracking as she knelt by the Mother. "Elecia? Elecia, can you hear me?"

The Leveler leaped onto the bed, and Marda thought for a second that it was about to pounce on them.

"Don't just stand there gawping," Jichora snapped as foam bubbled across the Mother's pale lips. "Call for help. Send for Dinube."

"Of course," Marda said, fumbling for the pouch on her belt. The comlink slipped through her fingers as the Mother continued to thrash, the communication unit breaking in two as it hit the floor.

"For Aakaash's sake," Jichora hissed, fishing out her own communicator and calling for help.

Marda just stared at the Mother, Elecia's bloodless lips drawn back, clenched teeth red where she had bitten through the tip of her tongue. *Just stop it,* she wanted to yell. *Just stop.* This wasn't how it was supposed to be. None of it. This wasn't what the Mother had promised.

On the bed, the Leveler's fronds writhed beneath its jaws as Dinube burst through the door, the rest of the Elders following close behind.

Marda could only step back as they fussed around Elecia's convulsing body like a brood of scratch-hens.

"She's going to die," Kevmo whispered in Marda's ear. "She's going to die and it's all your fault."

"No!" Marda screamed, and the Mother snapped her eyes open, gasping for breath.

"Oh, thank the Force," Jichora breathed as the woman tried to sit up, the Leveler pacing back and forth behind them.

"You had a seizure," Elder Dinube said, speaking slowly and deliberately as if she believed the Mother was no longer capable of understanding her words. "We must get you back to bed."

Still, the stricken prophet tried to rise. "No," she croaked, her throat parched. "The Path needs me. . . ."

"*We* can lead the Path," Jichora insisted, grabbing the Mother's hand. "You are unwell. You need to recover."

Elecia snatched her arm back. "No. You don't understand. It wasn't a seizure. I don't have seizures."

Marda's mouth dropped open as she realized the truth. "It was the Force." She dropped down in front of Elecia, looking her straight in the eyes. "Did it speak to you, Mother?"

The ashen-faced woman licked her dry lips and nodded. "Yes, my Guide. The Force has shown me what we must do. It has shown me the true way of the Path."

ELEVEN

Even before the troubles, the streets of Jedha had been dangerous. It was often the way in cities deemed sacred. The reasons were obvious. Just like Kalimahr and Daclavian 3, Jedha attracted pilgrims from all over the galaxy, their hearts brimming with hope and their pockets full of credits. The more guileless would be targeted almost immediately, "helpful" locals hitting them with promises of ancient relics and even the opportunity to witness a miracle in a forgotten shrine far from the beaten track. The only miracle would be if they made it out of the labyrinth of dingy back alleys with their vital organs still in one piece. The blood of gullible believers had washed the cobbled lanes of Jedha for generations and showed no sign of slowing. Yana hoped that at least some of the poor unfortunates had ended up in their afterlives of choice. Just because she didn't believe in a better place after death didn't mean it didn't exist. She'd been wrong about matters far more trivial.

But the one thing she'd never been wrong about was that Feric Oranalli was a stinking piece of crap. Oranalli, a pale-skinned Dressellian with shifty eyes and a mouth that spouted only untruths, had recently been elevated to chief archivist at the Temple of the Kyber. He'd been a lowly assistant when they'd met, second to the late lamented archivist Zumeg, but Yana had made a point of noticing the Dressellian's habits just in case things went wrong, which they subsequently had.

Despite his relatively high office, Oranalli regularly used the same back alleys that had proved the undoing of so many pilgrims over the years. The reason was that the Dressellian had an almost pathological fear of crowds and was liable to panic if caught in a throng. The alleyways were dangerous, but Oranalli had been walking them for years.

All Yana had to do was wait, crouched high on the roof of a particular tavern at a particular time, and the archivist would come bumbling along, the red robes that marked him as a Disciple of the Whills hidden beneath a heavy cloak the color of his sunken blue eyes. At least that was the plan.

As NaJedha started to set in the cold winter sky, Yana wondered more than once if her information was incorrect and it would be better just to brazen it out at the Temple of the Kyber. So far, the only thing that had scurried down the alleyway was a family of creepmice chased by a mangy felnox. Her legs cramping, she was about to give up when the sound of footsteps found her ears. There he was, hurrying through the night, heading home after a long day doing whatever chief archivists did. Yana waited until he was almost directly below her before silently vaulting over the side of the roof and landing perfectly in front of him. The shrill scream that issued from his lips was a little too satisfying.

"Hello, Feric."

"Yana Ro!" he gasped. "I thought . . ."

"You thought I was long gone, along with the rest of the Path."

Oranalli looked around, a vein pulsing on his elongated skull.

"It's fine," she said, raising a hand to show it was empty. "I'm alone."

"Yes," Kor said in her ear, "and that's why you should get as far away as possible."

"What do you want?" Oranalli stammered, holding his cloak tight to his thin chest.

"I hear you have a guest in your holding cells. A mutual acquaintance of ours."

The Dressellian ground his already blunt teeth. "Do we have to do this here? If we're seen . . ."

"Someone might put the pieces of the puzzle together," Yana said. "Work out that it was *you* helping the Path steal religious artifacts all across the city and you who let us know that the Jedi were onto us."

"Shhhh!" he said, stepping in close and then, questioning putting himself in slashing distance of a known killer, taking an instant step back.

"Oh, relax," she told him. "No one's here. That's why you use this route every day."

"How do you know the way I walk home?"

"I make it my business to know everything about those we deal with." That was a lie—or at least an exaggeration—but it didn't hurt to pile on the pressure. "Like the fact that you have the Herald rotting in your kyber-lined dungeon."

"Not me," he insisted. "I had no part in that. You were the ones who got caught. You were the ones who lost the Rod of Daybreak after I delivered it to you on a platter."

"Hardly. We had to turn over a dozen shrines before we hit the jackpot. I should kill you where you stand."

"Well, that would be stupendously foolhardy," Oranalli scoffed, "even for an Evereni."

Now it was Yana's turn to take a step forward.

"What did you say?" she said, baring her teeth.

"I have it," he said quickly, cowardice winning out over his bigotry. "I have the Rod of Daybreak. The Jedi gave it to me for safekeeping."

Yana couldn't believe her luck. The Force was shining on her, whether she believed in it or not. It was about time.

"Where is it now?"

He shook his head. "I've already said too much."

"Is that so?"

"You can't intimidate me."

"Yes, I can, but I don't need to. You see, *I* haven't said enough, not by a long shot. All it would take is a few words to the wrong people . . ."

"You said you weren't going to intimidate me!"

"I said I don't need to, not that I won't."

All at once, he moved, and with a flurry of his cloak, Yana found herself staring down the muzzle of a gently shaking disruptor. Oranalli stared down the barrel at her, trying desperately to smirk despite his obvious fear.

"Did you really think I wouldn't walk this way without protection?"

Yana moved without hesitation, grabbing the blaster and twisting it, ignoring the cry of pain as she snapped at least one of Oranalli's fingers disarming him.

"And did you think I couldn't do that?" she said, pointing his weapon back at him. "I need the rod, and I need to see the Herald, in that order."

"It's impossible," the Dressellian burbled, cradling his injured hand. "The temple is shut down. No one is allowed within the Old Shadow, except for the Jedi or the Whills themselves."

Yana smiled, reminding Oranalli just how sharp her teeth actually were. "Then I think it's about time I convert."

TWELVE

Marda didn't know what reception would be waiting for them when they returned to Dalna, but perhaps it shouldn't have been a surprise to find Ferdan's formidable sheriff standing there, arms crossed and jaw set, as the shuttle's ramp squelched into the mud.

"Well, well, well," Jinx Pickwick said, fixing Marda with a glare that could have frozen a supernova. "Look who's crawled back. I thought you were gone for good."

So did I, Marda thought, but turned on her most diplomatic smile. "Sheriff Pickwick, we were hoping to speak to the port master."

"Well, you can talk to me," Jinx said, brushing a lock of her golden hair over her ear. "Because, trust me, you're not exactly flavor of the month around here."

"Were you ever?" Kevmo asked, his reflection clear in the sheriff's mirrored visor.

"Our ship has returned into orbit," Marda told the law enforcer.

"So I hear."

"And we were hoping that we could obtain permission to send shuttles straight to our camp rather than via the port."

"No."

The short, sharp response took Marda by surprise.

"I'm sorry?"

"So you should be." The sheriff's aggression wasn't improving. In fact, it was getting worse, making Marda wonder whether she should return to the relative safety of the shuttle as Jinx placed her hands firmly on her hips, dangerously close to the twin blasters that hung from her belt. Had Pickwick always worn two blasters?

In the visor, Kevmo shook his head. "She does now."

"I honestly don't know where you get off, Marda," Jinx continued. "Waltzing back here as if nothing has happened."

"I don't know what you mean."

Jinx jabbed a finger at her. "Don't play the innocent with me, missy. The communication network may be shot to hell at the moment, but ships come and ships go and people talk.

Do you know what they're talking about, Marda? What is the topic of every conversation from here to the Mid Rim?"

Marda had a horrible feeling she was about to find out.

"They're talking about Jedha," Jinx said, not waiting for her to respond. "Now, I'd never heard of the place before last week, and not knowing suited me just fine, but then folks started to gossip about battles and riots and *droids* fighting—actually fighting—in the streets. And then I hear that a member of your little group, someone I've known for a very long time, was the ringleader, that he incited the riot, that he was looting and killing and responsible for all kinds of terrible things—the same guy who has lived down the road for most of my life."

Marda stepped off the ramp, hoping to stop Jinx's rant. "Sheriff, I—"

It didn't work.

"And do you know what I thought, Marda?" Jinx tapped the side of her head. "Do you know what went through my mind?"

"You were glad that we were gone," a voice rang out behind them. Marda turned to see the Mother walking down the ramp, the Leveler slinking beside her, with Jukkyuk and Bokana close behind. "You thought you'd had a lucky escape."

Marda couldn't help feeling relieved that the Mother had decided to join her, even though Sheriff Pickwick was staring open-mouthed at the Leveler as Elecia's party disembarked.

"What in the name of all things luminous is *that*?"

"A pet," the Mother said, not looking down. "Nothing more."

"Ugliest-looking pet I've ever seen."

On that, Marda had to agree. The Leveler, whatever it was, had continued to grow on the journey home, its body somehow even more twisted than before, its expression more pained. Even now, it wheezed horribly as it swung its misshapen head around, every person in the spaceport staring back in disgust, not just at the monster but at the people with it.

"Mother," Marda began, wanting to be out of the hateful gaze of people she had once called neighbors, "Sheriff Pickwick has refused our request and says the shuttles must land here in Ferdan. . . ."

"Rather than going straight to the compound," the Mother said, still not taking her eyes off Jinx.

"That's right," Pickwick said, although some of the steel had gone from the sheriff's voice. She looked uncertain, licking her lips as if they'd suddenly gone dry. "I don't know what you've all been doing, but I want to see what you're bringing to Dalna with my own eyes."

The Mother stepped closer, her voice purring. "And why is that, Sheriff?"

Jinx cleared her throat, a deep flush rising from her chest. "Because we don't want any trouble like they had on Jeddy."

"Jedha," the Mother corrected.

This time the sheriff rubbed her mouth with the back of her hand.

"That's what I said."

"We don't want trouble here, Jinx," the Mother continued, smiling coyly. "Not on Dalna. Dalna is our home."

"Yeah, I guess it is." Jinx coughed, trying to reassert her authority and almost immediately failing. "We've missed you folks."

"You have?"

"S-sure," Jinx stammered, her frown showing she was just as confused as Marda. What was happening? The Mother had always had a calming influence on people, but Marda had never seen someone crumble like the sheriff. The fact it was *her*, of all people, made it all the more bewildering. If ever there was a woman who knew her mind, it was Jinx Pickwick. Everyone said so, and yet there she was, almost simpering in the Mother's presence.

"Surely you understand that we want to get our people home as quickly as possible," the Mother said, keeping her tone steady. "It's been such a trying time."

"I'm sorry to hear that," the sheriff said, her eyes becoming wet.

"You want to help us, don't you, Jinx?"

A single tear rolled down the sheriff's cheek, and the Leveler snapped its head up, nudging the Mother's leg. The Mother gasped, nearly bending double.

"Mother," Marda said, grabbing the woman as she

staggered back, a deep growl coming from the Leveler's throat. Bokana and the Wookiee had also taken a step forward, neither seeming to know what to do.

"Is that thing safe?" the Ovissian asked, and Jukkyuk said something in Shyriiwook that didn't sound encouraging.

"It's just tired," the Mother rasped. "We all are."

"Okay, you can land on your damned compound, but only this once," Jinx said, pulling her brimmed hat down to cover her eyes. "You're not the only one who's tired. I'm tired, tired of the questions folks are asking about you. Of the way they're looking at us, as if *we're* part of whatever circus you have going on at that camp of yours. First the spacers and then that damned investigator."

The Mother stiffened in Marda's arms, pushing herself up.

"Investigator?"

"They said they'd come here on vacation, if you can believe that," Jinx said, not quite meeting the Mother's gaze. "I didn't. Who comes to Ferdan for their holidays? So I asked her outright, and she admitted she was here to find out about you."

"About the Mother?" Marda asked.

"No, about all of you. About your cult."

"We're not a cult."

"Well, that's the problem, isn't it? No one *really* knows who or what you are, especially now."

"You said you'd missed us," Marda reminded her, and a fresh look of doubt flashed across Jinx's face, just for a second.

"We're a welcoming town, but we don't like trouble. I don't like trouble."

"Then we truly are neighbors," the Mother said, pushing herself from Marda's arm and raising a hand to hold off both Bokana and Jukkyuk when they moved to offer support. "Yes, there were . . . difficulties on Jedha, but we have no desire to bring them with us. We only wish to reflect, to mourn our dead, and to start again. Is that so very much to ask?"

The sheriff sniffed, her jaw set. "I guess not."

"As for this investigator," the Mother continued. "Marda will speak with them."

Another surprise. "I will? What do you want me to say?" Marda asked.

"Do I have to think of everything?" the Mother snapped, her temper flaring. "You are supposed to be our Guide, Marda. You choose the way." She staggered, this time allowing Bokana to catch her. "I must rest."

"Of course," Marda said, trying to appear calm even though she was churning inside. "Help the Mother back inside the shuttle."

Bokana shot Marda a sympathetic look as he and Jukk helped Elecia back up the ramp, the Leveler loping behind.

The ramp began to lift, and Marda raised a hand to

protect her eyes from the dust and dirt the shuttle's thrusters kicked up as it rose into the air before speeding off in the direction of the camp.

"Bet you wish you were going with them," Kevmo pointed out.

Marda ignored him, turning back to the sheriff, who was watching them go, her head cocked to the side as if she was trying to work out what had just happened. Marda was wondering that herself.

"The investigator," she asked, smoothing her robes in an attempt to quiet her mood. "Where will I find them, Sheriff?"

"Where do you think?" Jinx replied, her foul mood having returned with a vengeance. "Where do *any* off-worlders stay when they come to Dalna?"

THIRTEEN

Yana always found things more manageable when she had a role to play.

Yana, the Child of the Open Hand.

Yana, the professional.

Yana, the badass.

Only one person had ever seen beyond the performance, the same person who was now watching from the polished surfaces of the sculptures that lined the Temple of the Kyber's walls.

Yana had hoped that Kor would smile when she saw what Yana was wearing, but the Nautolan's dead eyes only looked sorrowful in the cut crystal.

No, more than that. They looked worried.

Not that Yana could blame her. Oranalli had also been concerned, telling her that her plan would never work. Why couldn't he simply bring the Herald and the rod to her? She could wait outside, hiding in the very shadows that gave the temple's walls their name. There was no need for her to even step through its doors.

"'Why can't I?'" she'd repeated, chuckling at the suggestion. "Well, let me think. Perhaps it's because you're a slippery wormsucker who only thinks of himself?"

"Can you blame me? Your own leader threw the Herald to the wolves. If she'd do that to one of her own, what do you think she'll do to me?"

"The Path works in mysterious ways," she replied, reiterating that if she wasn't inside the temple within the hour, the Convocation would be *very* interested to hear what she had to say.

And now there she was, playing yet another role, her most outrageous one yet. The Jedi robes were slightly out of date, Oranalli had said, as if the protectors of light and justice were always one step ahead of the trends, but they did the trick nonetheless, covering her fatigues.

She had asked him if he had a lightsaber to complete the look, but he had just glared at her, offering her a stylus that she could hang from her belt.

Yana had declined the offer.

Sarcasm or not, it turned out that, for once, the Dressellian had been telling the truth. The temple *was* swarming with Guardians, but Yana had no way of knowing if this was more than usual. Luckily, no one had reason to suspect a Jedi taking a stroll through the treasure-lined corridors with the chief archivist, even when they descended the steep stairs that led to the detention block.

Only the guards on the door leading to where Werth was being held seemed suspicious, eyeing Yana as they approached.

"What's this?" asked the shorter of the pair, a brown-skinned human who was still a good head taller than both Yana and Oranalli.

The archivist pulled the Rod of Daybreak from beneath his robes, having previously fetched the artifact that was behind all this trouble, its crescent-shaped blade glinting in the light of the glow-orbs.

"We need to question the prisoner about why he was searching for this object."

The other guard—a surly-beaked Hiitian—narrowed their eyes as they peered at Yana's borrowed robes.

"Never seen you around here before. Are you with that Twi'lek, the one who never stops squawking?"

Not knowing whom the avian was speaking about, Yana was about to say yes when Oranalli cut in.

"No. Jedi Ro has only recently arrived on Jedha, direct from Coruscant."

It was all Yana could do not to grind her teeth. She

appreciated the save, but why on Everon had he given her real name?

"I'm an expert in esoteric relics from the pre-Republic period, a particular hobby of mine," she said, noting the Hiitian's apparent dislike of chatterboxes. "Do you have any interest in such items? I find them *endlessly* fascinating. The shaft the archivist is holding, for example—"

The hulking avian simply turned and unlocked the door, Yana's gamble having paid off.

"You know where he is, Archivist," the Hiitian said, ushering them through, all while desperately trying not to make eye contact with Yana in case she continued her monologue. "Knock when you want to come back through."

"Thank you, Marr," Oranalli said, sharing a look with the guard that screamed, *Bloody Jedi.*

They passed through, and as the door shut firmly behind them, the archivist shook his ridged head.

"You're too good at this," he said, mopping his lips with a handkerchief produced from his robes.

"Years of practice," Yana acknowledged. "And you're not too bad yourself."

"Perhaps I should take to the stage?" the Dressellian grumbled as they reached the door at the end of the corridor. "Anything would be better than this."

Oranalli checked the observation window before unlocking the door with a datacard he produced with a flourish.

"Anything else in those robes?"

"Do you honestly think I wouldn't have made myself a copy of the master key?"

"I'm beginning to like you, Feric."

"Such a shame the feeling isn't mutual."

Unlocked or not, Oranalli struggled to pull the door open, that vein in his forehead pulsing more than ever.

"Allow me," Yana said, leaning over and opening the cell with little effort. Controlling her emotions as she laid eyes on the Herald proved more problematic. Seeing him brought back the pain that she'd never see his daughter again—not alive, in any case. The thing that haunted her every waking hour wasn't Kor. Yana knew that. It was a figment of her imagination, the part of her that didn't want to let her girlfriend go, the part that had led her down into the depths of the Whills' temple to save a man she'd never truly liked but Kor loved. Werth Plouth was all that she had left of her girlfriend, alongside Opari, Kor's mother, back with the Path. Kor wouldn't have left Jedha without springing him from this cell, and neither would Yana.

The Herald sat cross-legged on the floor, leaning against a remarkably clean wall. At least the Whills didn't make their prisoners live in squalor. At first he didn't look up, staring instead at a point somewhere beyond his bare feet, refusing to give his captors even the satisfaction of acknowledgment that they were there. Instead, he rumbled a familiar mantra into the relative silence of the room: "The Force shall be free. The Force shall be free."

"Still as stubborn as ever," Kor said. "Some things never change."

Fighting the urge to clear her throat, Yana spoke up, attempting to keep her voice as calm as possible.

"Hello, Werth."

The Herald finally looked up at her words, a smile spreading across his features, the same smile Kor used to have when she knew she'd won an argument, because, yes, there had been arguments, as that was the way of relationships—and Yana wished she'd savored them as much as the good times. Every moment spent with Kor had been precious. She just hadn't realized how much.

"You came. You came for me."

No, Yana wanted to say to him, *I came for her,* but Oranalli spoke first.

"Okay, I brought you to your Herald. I brought you the rod. Now what?"

Werth was on his feet within seconds. "You have the Rod of Daybreak? Here?"

"Show him," Yana urged.

Oranalli held out the rod, and Werth went to grab it, only for the archivist to pull it away.

"Oh, no. No, no, no, no. You can't just take it. It's too valuable."

"You were paid," the Herald rumbled. "You were paid *handsomely*."

"And you kriffed it up. I told you the Jedi were coming, and you allowed yourself to be captured. This," Oranalli said, brandishing the rod, "belongs to the Temple of the Kyber now. It was handed to *me*, for me to keep it safe."

"And *now* you decide to take your responsibilities seriously?" Yana asked, not believing the gall of the man.

"My only responsibility is to myself. I had the rod valued, tried to discover why it was so important to you . . ."

"And?" asked the Herald.

"And no one could tell me. I mean, it's worth a fortune, that much is obvious, but money doesn't seem to be a problem for you people, what with the riches the Mother has lavished on Jedha since your arrest."

Yana's stomach tightened. She'd wanted to be the one to break the Mother's treachery to Werth. The Nautolan's attention switched to her, his dark eyes searching her face for answers. "What is he talking about?"

Yana breathed out, not knowing how he would react. "The Mother fled."

"On board the *Gaze Electric*?"

"Yes. But just after she left . . ." She hesitated, realizing she knew *exactly* how the Herald would react to the news. What he would say.

"Yes?" he prompted, his face already darkening.

It was now or never.

"The Mother announced to the galaxy that you were the ringleader on Jedha, a traitor to the Path's cause, and that the rest of the Open Hand had nothing to do with it. She offered a vast fortune to help rebuild the city and appealed to you to accept the punishment for your crimes."

The Herald didn't respond to her but turned to the archivist, fixing Oranalli with a steely gaze.

"And you knew this? You knew this, and you never came down here to tell me?"

"*Everyone* knows it," Yana told him. "Your face is everywhere, on every news broadcast and holo."

Werth closed his eyes, barely moving.

"They will all hate me. They will hate me and love her, because I destroy and she rebuilds. She's clever. Far more than we gave her credit."

"Can you *see* why I didn't know what to do?" Oranalli bleated. "What if she was right? What if you *were* some kind of lunatic? After everything I did for you, after everything I *risked* . . . I only ever wanted what was due to me, what I deserved, and everybody is watching. Everybody! The Convocation . . . the Jedi . . . my own people! You and the Mother have made things very difficult for me. And then what happens?" Oranalli turned toward Yana, looking her up and down. "Your pitdog jumps me in an alleyway and demands I bring her here, threatening me in the street, risking what little security I have left. I should lock her in here with you. Let you fight it out between yourselves, or maybe screw each other's brains out. Whatever this is."

"It is not that!" Yana said, her claws suddenly itching for the kill. "Never that. We are . . ."

What? What could she say? Friends? Family? Neither was true.

"Yana, please." Werth's quiet voice cut through her rage. The Nautolan had reopened his eyes and was looking straight at her, his palm raised to stop her from making a mistake. His face calm, he turned to the archivist, his hand dropping back to his side.

"You're right, my friend. You did as you were asked, and we let the situation . . ." He smiled wryly. "Well, we let the situation spiral out of control. You owe us nothing, and yet we ask, over and over, for your help. Thank you. Thank you from the bottom of our hearts."

Oranalli shifted on his feet, jutting out his chin, surprised but pleased that the Herald saw things his way. Yana had to admit that she was a little shocked, too.

"Is my friend safe?" Werth asked.

"Friend?" Oranalli parroted dumbly.

"Yana," the Herald responded, nodding toward her. "Is she safe on the streets? Is she safe on Jedha?"

Oranalli nodded. "If she keeps her head down." He looked pointedly at her. "If she stays out of trouble."

"And the people . . . they still trust the Path?"

At this, the Dressellian scoffed. "I don't think they *ever* trusted the Path. All I know is they despise *you.* She'll be safe as long as no one knows that she has anything to do with you . . . that *neither* of us does."

The Herald clasped his hands together, fingers interlocked. "I understand, and have one more favor to ask."

Oranalli didn't look convinced.

"Which is?"

"Go to the Convocation, to the Jedi. Tell them I am ready to make a full confession. Tell them I am ready to expose a network of saboteurs who want to start a war between the various Force religions of the galaxy, that the violence on Jedha's streets was only the beginning. Tell them that I will give them the truth and the truth shall free the Force of bloodshed and tragedy."

Of all the things Yana expected, this wasn't one of them. The Herald was so contrite, so sincere. She liked the idea of blowing the Mother's plans out into the open, but never believed for one minute that the Herald would cooperate with his enemies to bring Elecia down.

"Will you do that for me, Oranalli?" he said, looking the traitorous Disciple straight in the eye. "Will you help me put things right?"

Yana could almost see the Dressellian's mind whirling, imagining the opportunities the Herald's confession would bring. His position in the temple would be protected, his standing beyond reproach, and as the crisis passed, the eyes of the galaxy would once again turn away from Jedha. Oranalli's scams could continue right under the Convocation's noses, just the way he liked it.

"Yes, I will," he finally said, "as long as you promise that I will be kept out of it. I cannot be implicated in any way."

"You won't be," the Herald told him. "You have my word."

Oranalli nodded, satisfied. "Very well." He waggled the Rod of Daybreak at Werth as if the Nautolan were a naughty child. "Stay here and keep quiet. Eat your slop and don't cause a fuss."

"I won't," Werth said, looking at the rod. "I'll even tell you why we wanted that. The *power* it possesses."

"Yes?" Oranalli said, his curiosity piqued.

The Herald looked at Yana. "Do you have the other half of the rod?"

She shook her head, frustrated. "No."

"The Mother?"

She nodded, and the Herald sighed.

"Perhaps I can still show our friend what it can do, even from this distance." He held out a brikal-stained hand to Oranalli. "May I?"

The archivist paused, considering his options, before holding out the relic.

"I suppose so, but you better be quick about it."

"Oh, I will," the Herald said, taking the Rod of Daybreak and, without pause, thrusting its sickle blade into the archivist's chest. Oranalli slammed back into the cell wall, pinned like a flutterbug against a board.

"You say you only ever wanted what was due to you," the Herald spat into the Dressellian's startled face, "what you deserve. Well, I have news for you, my friend. Good news. *Marvelous* news." The archivist tried to scream, but no sound would come, only a thin dribble of blood that ran down his bobbing chin. "Today," the Herald continued as Yana heard a gurgle at the back of Oranalli's throat, "your wishes are granted."

The light went out of the archivist's eyes, his arms suddenly limp. Yana looked away as the Herald released his body, the corpse slapping to the floor.

"You told him you would cooperate," Yana said, her voice thick.

"And spend the rest of my life locked up in this place?" the Herald asked, examining the blade for damage. "Do you think the Path would survive if we revealed the truth about the Mother? I am fully aware that you don't care about our group, but I do, as did Kor."

Forget the archivist, Kor's name was like a blade to *Yana's* heart.

"The Path looks after its own," the Herald concluded. "I assume they are heading back to Dalna? To the complex?"

Yana nodded.

"And they have the Leveler?"

"The *Mother* has the Leveler."

"Then we need a ship."

Yana's mind went back to Enlightenment. It looked like she was about to notch up another debt.

"The bigger issue is getting you out of here. It's not like we can squeeze you into Oranalli's robes."

"How many guards are there?"

"Two, on this level—a Hiitian and a human—but the entire temple is lousy with them, unless . . ."

Remembering something, she crouched down and rifled through the dead archivist's pockets.

"What are you doing?" the Herald asked.

When she stood, Yana had Oranalli's master key in her hand.

"Looking for a way out."

FOURTEEN

The investigator wasn't in Lady Jara's lodging house in the thick of town, nor were they in Ferdan's marketplace, talking to people Marda had known for years but who now avoided her eyes or hurried away before she could approach them. Had the Path become so infamous since Jedha? Marda had thought that the Mother's generosity would have helped regain their trust.

"They *never* trusted you," Kevmo pointed out to her, and Marda found it very hard to argue. Perhaps she had been living with her head in the clouds all this time. Perhaps she had so longed to be accepted, both by the Path and the wider Ferdan community, that she had blocked out the sideward glances as she'd walked through the market with the Littles, missing the muttering and the sneers. There was no missing them now. Everywhere she looked, she saw old friends of hers huddled together, heads close, glancing nervously in her direction as she searched for the investigator. Even Grandfer Aurin, the Umbaran who had so often saved her a spot in the market next to their stall, had looked like they wanted to run and hide when she hurried up, relieved to see what she'd hoped would be a friendly face. At least Aurin had some information for her. It turned out that the investigator—a Zeltron woman by the name of Ric Farazi—had quizzed the old droid-monger about the Path, targeting them because of their friendship with Marda and, in the process, completely freaking them out. The first thing Aurin had told the Zeltron was that they didn't want any trouble—a recurring theme, it seemed—and that Marda's regular spot in the market had already been taken, even though there was no one there that day.

Marda tried to change the conversation, to ask Aurin how they were, but the Umbaran only busied themself with a micro-gyro unit, muttering something about needing to get on. They did, however, reveal that they had heard Farazi had left town earlier that day, walking toward the Path's compound, of all places.

Well, wasn't that just great? Marda could have saved herself a lot of heartache by just heading back on the shuttle.

"Don't let it get to you," Kevmo offered as she started the long trudge back to the settlement. "They're not important."

"I thought the Jedi thought *everyone* was important," she countered, the voice that had once excited her starting to grate.

"Yeah, because the Jedi get *every*thing right, don't they?" he responded. "That's why you're alive—"

"And you're dead," she finished for him, wishing it weren't true, that she could see him again—not how he appeared to her now but how he had been when he had held her close and she'd felt so warm. So wanted.

Her mind wandered to Bokana as she neared the compound, a common occurrence over the past few days. At least he always seemed pleased to see her, a little too eager, if anything—although she had started to feel the same way.

She almost hoped she'd see him in the camp as she walked through the gates, but it was not to be. The shuttles were delivering the survivors of Jedha into the center of the compound, but there was no sign of the Ovissian. There was someone new, however, her magenta skin standing out even though the woman's jacket was a similar color to the Path's robes. A deliberate ploy to melt into the crowd, maybe, but Marda's temperature rose as she saw who the Zeltron was questioning.

"Tromak," she called out as she rushed over to the young Gran she had spent so much time looking after before all this had begun.

"Marda," he replied, running to her, arms outstretched and all three eyes wide with alarm. Marda scooped him up, feeling at once how much he was trembling. Did the Zeltron have no shame, haranguing a child? And why was no one else stepping in to check he was all right?

"Because they don't care, not like you," Kevmo told her. "Perhaps you should have stuck with what you know."

"I'm so sorry," the woman said, having the decency to look embarrassed. "I never meant to cause him any distress. I'm Ric. Ric Farazi."

Marda ignored the introduction, stroking the back of Tromak's head. "What are you even doing here?"

"I hoped to meet your leader, your 'Mother,'" Farazi said, flashing what she obviously hoped was a disarming smile. On the surface the Zeltron seemed harmless enough, her face round and her body stout, but the emphasis she had placed on Elecia's title had been dismissive. Marda wished she could tell her to hop on the next transport off Dalna and not return, but that wasn't their way. The Path was open to everyone, even if their motives weren't exactly pure.

"Why?" Kevmo asked beside her, so close that she could feel his stale breath on her neck. "Why welcome someone so obviously out to get you?"

I welcomed you, she thought back.

"And look where that got you."

"The Mother is resting," Marda heard herself say. "Her ordeal on Jedha was . . . somewhat trying."

"For a lot of people," Farazi said, and Marda felt her face flush at the obvious implication. "But I have no desire to put her under any more pressure. I just have some questions about your group. This little guy was pointing me in the right direction, that's all."

The Zeltron attempted to poke playfully at Tromak, but Marda snatched him away.

"I would be happy to answer any of your questions."

"And you are?"

"I am Marda Ro, the Guide of the Path."

Farazi was nodding, taking note of everything Marda said.

"The Guide? Is that a title, like the Mother . . . or the Herald?"

She was fishing, but Marda wasn't going to take the bait.

"It is who I am," she replied. "Can I ask why you are so interested in the Path? Are you looking to join?"

Farazi chuckled, clearly finding that funny. "Not exactly."

"The sheriff said you're an investigator."

"That's what I told her, yes. . . ."

"And the truth is?"

Farazi took a deep breath, raising her hands.

"Okay, I'll level with you. I'm a reporter. A journalist. When I heard about your . . . organization on Jedha, I thought that's a story that would interest my readers . . . so here I am."

She gave that grin again, one that was looking more desperate with every attempt.

"You followed us from Jedha?"

"No, not at all." Farazi looked around at all the activity

in the camp, Path members unloading what few possessions they had from the shuttles. "All of this is just luck. I had no idea you were heading back when I set out. I'd just heard, through my research, that this was where you came from. From Dalna. I thought it would be interesting to see where your movement started. A little background, if you like."

"For your readers . . ."

"Exactly."

"Who are?"

Farazi's smile faltered, embarrassment creeping in. "Well, that's the thing . . . I, um, haven't actually sold any stories yet. I've tried, but I just need that big scoop, you know. That big story."

"And you think that's what this is? What *we* are?"

"I'm hoping so. I mean, it has all the right ingredients." Farazi swept a hand in front of herself as if visualizing a headline. " 'Who are the Path of the Open Hand, that mysterious band of believers who arrived out of nowhere and attempted to save the Holy City?' "

Marda didn't respond, still unsure what to make of the woman.

"Through the Mother's generous offer, I mean," Farazi added quickly. "All those zukkels!" She clasped her hands together. "I was hoping we could help each other?"

Marda shifted Tromak's weight onto her other hip, the Gran getting increasingly heavy as he clung to her. "In what way?"

"I'll tell your story," the Zeltron said. "Your real story, not all the lies and rumors that are circulating."

"So you can make a name for yourself. As a journalist."

"Sure, that's how this works. It's an exchange. A transaction. Your story for my platform."

"I thought you were all about gifts freely given," Kevmo commented.

Marda ignored him. He was right, but there was also an opportunity there.

"You can stay with us," Marda said, her mind made up. "In one of the guest huts. It's probably not the kind of accommodations you're used to. . . ."

"Marda," Farazi said, almost jumping up and down. "I'm a down-on-her-luck reporter who hasn't got two credits to rub together. Between you and me, I didn't know how I was going to pay Lady Jara anyway. I'd *love* to stay here. Thank you so much."

And so it was decided, and Marda felt a stab of pride as she lowered Tromak back to the ground. The Mother had told her to deal with the stranger, and Marda had found a solution that could only make things better, a way to spread their message further than ever before.

Elecia would be so pleased.

FIFTEEN

"You did *what*?"

Marda wasn't prepared for the intensity of the Mother's fury. Even the Elders, gathered in Elecia's listening chamber beneath the surface of the compound, flinched at the sharpness of her response. The Leveler, meanwhile, only glared hungrily.

"I thought . . ." Marda began, her voice smaller than she meant it to be. "I *think* this is a good thing."

"And how *exactly* did you come to that conclusion?" the Mother asked, venom dripping from her words.

"Everyone is talking about us," Marda said, forcing back

tears, unsure if she wanted to weep from frustration or disappointment. "Your offer to the Convocation . . ."

"My more-than-generous offer . . ."

"Your generous offer," Marda conceded, "hasn't been as effective as we hoped."

"It was your idea," the Mother claimed—not true, but Marda was willing to let that pass.

"And it certainly helped, but you didn't see how the people looked at me, Mother. Even friends, like Grandfer Aurin. They've heard rumors . . . lies. . . ."

"And so, to counter this poisonous tittle-tattle, you invited a journalist into our midst."

"Yes!" Marda exclaimed. "I did as you asked."

"I asked you to deal with them in my absence."

"You asked me to be the Guide. To listen to the Force."

The Mother uttered a sharp, cruel laugh. "And now she thinks she's a prophet."

"I think I'm the person you made me. *You* made me Guide. *You* put your trust in me."

"And where did that get us?" the Mother spat like a spoiled child. "Yes, I listened to you. You wanted to go to Jedha and I took us to Jedha."

"Because she wanted the Rod of Daybreak," Kevmo pointed out. "You should remind her of that."

"You wanted to return to Dalna, and we returned."

"That's not how it was," Marda tried to argue.

"We returned to recover, to rebuild," Elecia continued,

talking over her. "To meditate on what has happened, and now? Now you bring a *viper* into the very heart of our community."

"Ric can tell our story," Marda pleaded.

"'Ric' will tell the story she wants to tell," the Mother yelled back. "Why are you so naive, Marda? Why?"

Marda looked to the Elders for support, for one of them to speak out on her behalf, but no one did, their eyes searching the floor instead of searching for the truth. Only Bokana, standing behind Elecia alongside Jukkyuk, looked at her with anything resembling kindness, his dark eyes full of empathy.

"Please. You might as well throw yourself at him," Kevmo sneered in her ear.

The tears were coming. Marda jammed her nails into her palms, anything to stop herself from breaking down in front of them all.

"It's not naivety," she insisted, trying to keep her voice steady. "I know what I'm doing. I will deal with Ric personally."

"And what will that do?" Elecia asked.

"It will ensure she only publishes the truth."

The Mother rolled her eyes.

"This will work! You just have to give me another chance."

"No, Marda. No, I don't." The Mother sank into her high-backed chair, deflating like a balloon.

"What do you mean?" Marda asked, her mouth dry.

Elecia looked up at the Elders, dismissing them with a wave of her bandaged hand. "Leave us. All of you."

They did as she commanded, filing out of the chamber

without a word, followed by Jukkyuk and Bokana, who took up positions on the other side of the door. At least Bokana flashed her a supportive look as he left, trying to tell her with his eyes that everything would be all right.

Marda wasn't so sure as the door clicked shut.

"Mother, I—"

Elecia silenced her with a raised hand before pushing herself painfully from her chair. Marda tried to help her, but the hand went up again.

"I can manage."

The Leveler growled.

The Mother limped over to a small computer terminal in the corner of the room and brought up a file on the screen. "Shea intercepted this transmission not long after you showed the Farazi woman to her accommodation."

She pressed a button, and a voice issued from the device's tinny speakers.

"I'm in, and I have their trust. At least, the trust of the child they've put in a position of authority. An Evereni, no less, although I've never seen a shark with so little bite. It's sad, really."

Then the tears came, running silently down Marda's cheeks. "That's—"

"Your reporter," the Mother said, pausing the recording. "The transmission was highly encrypted, but Shea had no problem breaking their code."

"Of course she didn't," Kevmo said, but Marda was in no mood for his spite.

"She said she wanted to help."

The Mother laughed sadly, leaning heavily on the terminal. "She said what you wanted to hear. That's her job, Marda, and you fell for it."

"I will ask her to leave."

"And she will tell the galaxy that we threw her out," the Mother said, turning back to Marda. "I can just see the headlines, if she is who she says she is."

Marda frowned. "What do you mean?"

"One minute she's an investigator, the next she's a reporter."

"She said she was trying to get to you."

"Exactly." The Mother placed a hand against her chest. "And what if she's not a reporter. What if she's a bounty hunter, or an assassin?"

Marda shook her head. "I don't think she is. . . ."

The Mother stepped forward, her back hunched. "But you don't know, and that's the problem, Marda. You never even stopped to ask." Elecia clenched her hand into a fist. "It's my fault, not yours."

"What?"

"I expected too much of you."

"No."

"You weren't ready, weren't prepared for the responsibility

I gave you. The others said you were too young, too inexperienced, but I didn't listen. I couldn't admit I'd made a mistake."

"Who?" Marda asked, her head spinning. "Who said I wasn't ready?"

"The Elders. The Herald. Even Yana."

"That's not true," Marda said.

The Mother looked hurt. "You're calling me a liar."

"No. I mean, what they said. About me. I know I've made mistakes, but I can learn from them. I can put it right, all of it."

Elecia hobbled over to her and put her hand to Marda's cheek. Her fingers were so cold.

"I know you think you can, but you can't. It's too late."

"No." Marda was openly sobbing, like one of the Littles. "Please don't say that."

"I'm sorry, Marda, but it's for the best."

There was a rap on the door. The Mother's hand fell away, and Marda grabbed it. The Leveler jumped to its feet.

"Don't answer it," Marda pleaded with her, ignoring the animal. "Please. We can sort this out. *I* can sort it out."

"You're hurting me," the Mother said, pulling at Marda's grip.

She let go. "I'm sorry."

There was another knock on the door.

"Come," Elecia said, turning away from Marda.

"She's right, you know," Kevmo whispered. "It *is* too late. For you. For her."

The door opened, and Sunshine Dobbs entered with two beings Marda had never seen before. One was a powerfully built human with a face full of tattoos, and the other was a Trandoshan female with piercing bionic eyes.

"Elecia," Sunshine said, the prospector's voice as oily as ever as he stepped forward, totally ignoring Marda. "I have the ships you wanted. Pilots, too. The best in the business."

"Ships?" Marda turned to the Mother. "Why do we need ships? We have the *Gaze*."

Elecia smiled at her benignly. "You should go, Marda. Take some time. Rest for a while."

"You're being dismissed," Kevmo said. "Just like the Elders. Surplus to requirements."

"But—" Marda began, only to be cut off.

"I've made my decision." The Mother's voice was colder than ever before.

There was no point arguing. Her cheeks burning, Marda marched from the listening chamber, not wanting to cry in front of Sunshine and the others.

SIXTEEN

The three ships sat on the makeshift landing pads the Path had constructed since their return to Dalna. Sunshine's broken-down vessel, the *Scupper,* rested on the largest elevation between two newcomers: the boxy *Moon of Sarkhai* and the *Bonecrusher,* a sleek cruiser owned by Galamal, the tall saurian Marda had initially mistaken for Trandoshan but who turned out to be a Barabel, a species Marda had never encountered before. She sat watching from the porch of what had once been Elder Jichora's hut, not believing her eyes as Jichora stood on the other side of the temporary landing bay deep in conversation with Ric Farazi.

Marda couldn't understand it. After everything Elecia had said, the journalist was still there. What was the Mother playing at?

"Why don't you ask her," Kevmo said, standing where no one could see him. "Oh, you can't, can you? She's cast you out."

The Padawan was a lot crueler now that he was dead. That was probably why Marda ignored him most of the time, that and the fact that looking at him made her want to cry. She'd cried too many tears the past few days. Instead she sat and glared at Farazi, all the time turning Kevmo's scarred lightsaber over and over in her hands. It had been sent with the rest of her meager belongings from the *Gaze*, and once again, she'd considered throwing it away, especially as the Padawan continued to needle at her. Then why was she still holding on to it? Why had it found its way back to her belt? Because she'd lost so much in such a short space of time? Because she needed something to hold on to, a memory of life before all this torment?

"Or maybe you want to use it?" Kevmo said. "Just in case the Mother decides you're the next sacrifice. In case they throw you to the ice gators."

But that was stupid. The Mother would never do that to her, however far she'd fallen from favor, and Marda would never ignite the beam again; of that she was sure.

"Marda, Marda, come play with us."

The sound of children's voices snapped her back to the compound. She looked around to see some of the Littles running toward her, their robes dusty and disheveled. Jerid led the way, fighting for breath as Utalir and Tromak followed close behind.

"We're going to play hide-and-go-seek in the lompop fields," Jerid announced as they reached her. "Elder Waiden says the rains are coming, and we want to make the most of the suns."

"Really?" Marda said. "The rains aren't due for another month."

The brown-skinned boy shrugged. "That's what he said."

"Will you come with us?" Utalir asked, the Mikkian's golden head-tresses almost as messy as her robes. "Please?"

It was tempting. Playing with the younglings was exactly what Marda needed. Unlike the others . . . unlike the Mother . . . the Littles still needed her, still wanted her around. The rest of the Path were keeping their distance, the news of her dismissal already spreading. First the town had shunned her, and then the Path. Perhaps she should have stayed with Yana on Jedha. Marda had the sneaking suspicion that if her cousin were still alive, she would've finally taken the opportunity to fly off into the stars, far away from a cause she never really believed in.

"If only you felt the same, huh?" Kevmo muttered. "If only you could run away."

"Marda?" Tromak said, pulling at Marda's robe. "Marda, did you hear us?"

Marda ignored the Gran, asking a question of her own. "Have you heard anything about what they're doing on those ships?" Across the way, equipment was being loaded onto the three vessels: crates, netting, and what looked suspiciously like blaster rifles.

When they didn't answer, Marda finally turned back to the Littles. "Well? Have you?"

"I-I don't know," Utalir stammered, her bottom lip quivering. "That's grown-up stuff."

"Do you want to play or not?" Tromak asked.

"Not," Marda said, a little too forcefully.

"There's no need to shout," Jerid said, pulling the others with him. "Come on. Let's go."

Marda's shoulders slumped as the three kids ran off. "I'm sorry," she called after them, but they didn't look back. "I didn't mean to snap."

A drop of rain hit her cheek as they disappeared from sight. She looked up to see clouds coming in. Old Waiden had been right, and Marda had been beastly to the people she loved the most.

"Well," she said out loud, "aren't you going to say anything? I screwed up again, right?"

But the ghost of her former love was gone, and Marda was more alone than ever.

Marda rubbed eyes sore from too many sleepless nights. Farazi and Jichora were gone, no doubt taking shelter from the coming rain, and the activity around the ships had slowed, the supplies loaded. All three captains—Dobbs, the human, and the lizard woman—were examining their crafts, checking fuel lines and gauges. Marda knew very little about spaceflight, but it was clear they were preparing for takeoff, so where were their crews?

As if waiting for their cue, three groups approached the vessels, each made up of Path members, some of whom Marda knew and some who were relative strangers recruited on Jedha. All, however, had swapped their robes for flight suits and combat fatigues. There was Wole, a Rodian mercenary who had come to the Path not long before they'd left for the Pilgrim Moon. Then there was a human female called Nanda and an Ithorian called Tragor, who had recently joined their number along with his son, a serious little boy with the most intense eyes. But the boy was nowhere to be seen. Tragor was lugging a heavy-looking pack on his back, accompanied by . . .

Marda stood up, surprised by the final two figures in the group. It was Jukkyuk and Bokana, both wearing fatigues, both with weapons slung across their backs. If the Mother was sending her own guards, this mission—whatever it was—was more important than she'd guessed.

Now she *had* to know what was going on.

"Bokana!" she shouting, slipping the lightsaber beneath

her robes and sprinting toward the ships. "Bokana, wait up!"

The Ovissian turned and sighed as he saw who it was.

"You're going with them?" she asked breathlessly as Jukkyuk lumbered on, rumbling something in Shyriiwook she couldn't understand.

"Yeah," the Ovissian said, hefting his heavy blaster. "We'll be back before you know it."

He went to continue toward the ships, but she stopped him, grabbing his arm.

"Bokana, please. Where are you going?"

He stopped again, looking uncomfortable. "We're not supposed to say. We're . . . fetching something, that's all."

She wasn't about to let him get away with that. "Fetching something? Fetching what? For the Mother? Is that why she's letting you go?"

Bokana looked around as if worried they were being watched. "Marda. Please. It's . . ."

"What?" she demanded. "Secret? Are you Children now? Is that what this is?"

"It's complicated," he said, turning his back toward the ships and, most noticeably, Sunshine, who glanced up at them from the *Scupper*'s hatch. "Sensitive."

"I am the Guide of the Open Hand," she insisted, even though she knew the words didn't mean anything anymore. Instead, she tried something else that she hoped was still true. "I'm your friend."

Bokana glanced back at the ships, hesitated for a moment,

and then, gently taking Marda's arm, guided her toward the huts.

"It's that Dobbs guy," he told her when he was sure they couldn't be overheard. "He's been working on something for the Mother."

"Working on what?"

Bokana's brow creased. "You know that creature, the one that is with her all the time."

"The Leveler."

"Dobbs says that he knows where they come from. That there are plenty more."

"And?"

He shrugged. "That's where we're going. To gather their eggs." He swallowed, obviously not enamored at the thought. "As many as we can carry."

"But why?"

"The Mother had another of her seizures. Like on the ship."

"Is she okay?"

"She said it was another message from the Force, a warning that the Jedi are coming for us."

"Because of Kevmo and Zallah?"

"I don't know. Because of them, because of Jedha. She says we need protection, something that will stop them if they come here. That's why she sent Dobbs away after her first vision on the *Gaze*. She knew something was coming. He's been planning this ever since."

"For her?"

Bokana nodded. "Hiring the other ships, planning the route. He says it's going to be difficult, like flying through hell itself. The eggs are on a world he's calling Planet X. Apparently, it has no name of its own but is surrounded by something called the Veil."

"And what's the Veil?"

"That's the million-credit question," Bokana admitted. "Dobbs said that navigating through the Veil is almost impossible and most pilots don't make it back."

"Is that why there are three ships? Just in case you don't all make it back?"

"Yeah, thanks for that. . . ."

She put a hand on his arm in apology, but her mind was racing. It made sense, although she hated the thought of anyone coming to hurt the Path. But as the Mother had said, Dalna had tunnels that could be defended.

And it wasn't just about defending the Path; it was about defending the Force. Everything that had happened on Dalna and Jedha could be traced back to one moment: when she first met Kevmo and he misused the Force to try to impress her, lifting a flower in the air.

He'd thought it a harmless trick, but the consequences were dire. The caves had flooded soon after his stunt with the flower, and Kevmo once again used the Force, that time to save the Path. A noble act, yes, but one that had only caused more imbalance. What if his actions in the cave, and her acceptance of them, had caused the bloodshed on Jedha? What if *that* was why fighting had broken out in the Holy City? And what of the Jedi who used the Force to quell the uprising, Silandra Sho and the others? What devastation would that cause? What horrors were to come? None, if the Mother had her way, gathering enough Levelers to stem the tide, to stop the Jedi in their tracks.

It could work.

But you won't be a part of it, a voice said deep inside her, not Kevmo this time but herself, realizing what she had to do if the Mother was ever going to look to her again to be the Path's guide.

"When do you leave?" she asked.

"About five minutes ago. I have to go."

"Yes," Marda agreed. "We do."

"We?"

Marda didn't wait for him to try to change her mind. She was already striding toward the ships, Bokana chasing after her.

"Marda. Wait. What are you doing?"

His problem was that he knew *exactly* what she was doing but couldn't stop her, and neither could Kevmo, whom she suspected she'd never hear from again, if he'd even been there at all.

The past was done and she was taking hold of the future.

Sunshine Dobbs was standing at the bottom of the

Scupper's ramp as she marched forward, Bokana still hurrying to catch up.

"You're late," he called to the Ovissian, ignoring Marda.

"Sorry about that," she said, stepping on the ramp. "My fault."

"Whoa there, little lady," Sunshine said, raising his datapad to block her path. "Where do you think you're going?"

"There's been a change of plan. I'm coming with you."

"Says who?"

"I am the Guide of the Open Hand. The Force wills it, as does the Mother."

"Well, that's just a lie, and we both know it." His expression hardened. "Take your foot off my ship. Now."

"I'll do no such thing, but if you *really* want to delay launch, then we can go back to the listening chamber together. You can hear for yourself. I mean, she'll be disappointed with you. Angry even . . ."

She let the words hang, hoping that her gamble would pay off. Everyone close to Elecia had seen the Mother's effect on Sunshine Dobbs. The man was smitten with her. Marda just hoped the thought of her disappointment would be enough to support her blatant fabrication.

"She speaks the truth, Dobbs," Bokana said, surprising them both. "The Mother had another vision from the Force. It said that Marda's presence was vital to our mission, that we won't make it off Planet X without her."

Sunshine snorted. "I've never heard such rubbish. If you think I'm falling for any of this, you're as stupid as you look."

Marda was about to retort when Bokana stepped forward, his broad chest to Sunshine's face. "The choice is simple. You accept the change of plan, or the gig's off."

Sunshine held his ground, glaring up at the Ovissian. "Is that so?"

"No mission. No payment, not for you or your friends on the other ships."

There was movement at the top of the ramp as DZ-23, Sunshine's maintenance droid, trundled out of the gloom of the ship. Marda looked up at the squat unit as it bleeped, blooped, and whistled down at its less-than-desirable owner.

"Sounds like someone else is impatient to take off," she said.

"That storm *is* coming in fast," Bokana agreed.

Sunshine looked up at the darkening clouds and frowned, holding up the datapad to shield himself from the heavy raindrops that were already starting to fall.

"Oh, very well," he finally said, turning his back on the pair of them to stomp up the ramp. "Just stay out of my way. This isn't going to be a pleasure cruise. You puke, you clean it up. Understand?"

Marda understood and also questioned if *anyone* had cleaned the ship for decades as the *Scupper* lurched its way through Dalna's atmosphere. But it wasn't the turbulence that threatened to make her throw up, or the fact that it smelled like a bantha had curled up and died in the main hold. It was the enormity of what she had done. How much she had lied. Would the gamble pay off? Would the Mother see this for what it was, proof that she still walked Elecia's path, that she had been right to make Marda the Guide?

She just had to convince the rest of the crew. Tragor and Nanda had both boarded the *Moon of Sarkhai*, but Jukkyuk shot both her and Bokana suspicious glances as they walked on board, as did Shea Ganandra, who had barely said a word to Marda since their encounter on the *Gaze*. At least Marda knew Shea, unlike Calar, a Setaran who was checking that the supplies were safely secured. The dome-headed being was another newcomer, a convert from an order known as the Sacred Circle. As far as Marda could tell, Calar never spoke, mainly because his species possessed nothing resembling a mouth. Instead, the pale-skinned neophyte breathed by means of long delicate gills that ran from the bottom of his neck to a set of jutting cheekbones that perfectly framed a pair of deep-set but inquisitive eyes. Marda fought a shudder when they turned toward her quizzically as she entered the hold.

The party was completed by Ort, a crimson-skinned Reesarian with long plaited hair and almost simian features. Ort hadn't been the same since her bond partner passed away a few seasons before, and Marda was surprised she'd volunteered for the mission, changing out of her usual robes and into the heavy-duty fatigues everyone but Marda wore.

"Take these," Ort said, handing over a pair of neatly folded coveralls. "They're old, but they should fit."

"Thank you," Marda said, touched by the kindness.

"Don't mention it," Ort said, heading over to help Calar. "You might need a belt."

"See?" Bokana said, flashing Marda an encouraging smile. "You're fitting right in."

"Because of you," she said, looking deep into his eyes. "That's the second time you've covered for me."

He threw her a cheeky smile. "I guess I just like having you around. Besides, maybe you coming with us *is* the will of the Force."

"We'll find out soon enough," she said, swaying slightly as the *Scupper*'s artificial gravity kicked in. They'd left orbit.

"You better get changed," Bokana told her, and she nodded, surprising him—and herself—by standing on tiptoe to plant a kiss on his green cheek. Then she was gone, searching for somewhere to change into the strange clothes before she could see him blush. The *Scupper* rattled and rolled as Sunshine prepared to make the jump into hyperspace. Marda found a closet that was empty except for a few tools and a lot of shipweaver webs. It would do.

The new clothes felt odd after wearing robes for so long, but the pants just about fit and the jacket was pretty roomy. Turned out Ort was roughly the same size as her.

"What do you think?" she asked out loud, trying to see herself in the dull reflection of the metal wall. She didn't expect an answer. Maybe Kevmo really was gone. Probably for the best. She opened the closet and headed off to find Bokana instead. This was good. This was all good.

Now all they had to do was come back alive.

PART TWO
THE BATTLE FOR THE PATH

SEVENTEEN

"Are you coming?"

Oliviah Zeveron stood on the ramp of the Hoopaloo's craft, looking back at Matty, who was standing with Tey Sirrek, the Sephi having negotiated a remarkably good price for their voyage to Dalna.

"I'll be right there," Matty shouted up to the older woman, wrapping her robes around herself in the cold Jedha air. "I just want to say goodbye."

Oliviah sighed, stopping short of rolling her eyes, but only just. "Don't be long," she called back, turning to disappear into the ship's hold. "Captain Strat is eager to leave."

"Sounds to me he's not the only one." Tey chuckled, watching her go. "Not the warmest coal in the brazier, is she?"

"Hmm?" Matty asked, distracted.

The purple-skinned thief nodded toward the ramp. "Your friend, Jedi Grumblepants."

That made Matty laugh. "She's hardly a friend. An acquaintance maybe. An associate at best."

"I thought you've known her for years?"

"I have, but that doesn't mean we're close. Far from it. Oliviah has always kept herself to herself. When she arrived . . ." Matty stopped herself, a flush blossoming along her already red cheeks.

"Oh, don't stop now," Tey said, wiggling his ears. "Not when it's just getting interesting."

Matty smiled, shaking her head-tails. "When she first arrived, I may have developed the *tiniest* of crushes on her."

"Matthea Cathley!" Tey exclaimed, putting a hand on his chest in mock outrage. "How wonderfully non-Jedi of you."

"Jedi have crushes," she insisted. "At least I did. But it soon passed. She just seemed so aloof. Unknowable."

"Colder than a wampa's back passage," Tey added.

"She's not that bad," Matty said, punching him in the arm.

"Ow!"

"You deserved that."

"I deserved that," Tey agreed, rubbing where her fist had

made contact and watching her as she looked around the spaceport. "You'll be okay, you know?" he finally told her.

"What? Oh, I know, I know," she said, trying to cover how she was feeling, not that it worked. "I'm just . . ."

"Scared?"

"Jedi don't get scared."

"Nerf crap!"

"Tey!" she exclaimed.

"Oh, don't try to tell me you're offended. You've lived on Jedha for most of your life. You know far more colorful language than that. I've heard you use it. And I know when you're lying. Your head-tails twitch."

"They do not!"

"There they go again!"

She snorted and then sighed as Tey waited for her to explain what was going on in her head.

"If you really want to know," she began, crossing her arms to stop them flapping around as she spoke, "it's been a while since I've left Jedha. The last time I was here, at the spaceport—"

"You were meeting Vildar off the cruiser from Abregado-rae."

"How did you know?"

"He told me."

She screwed up her face, fearing the worst. "And did he also tell you I talked too much?"

"He might have mentioned it, at least once or seven hundred times, but most importantly, he told me how impressed he was."

That took Matty by surprise. "He was?"

"He said you were the most confident Padawan he'd ever met and that he couldn't get over how well you fitted in all this . . . all this . . ." Tey waved a long index finger around to take in the bustle of the busy port.

"Chaos?"

The grin returned. "Yes. Chaos. Vildar may be your master now, but he's learned a lot from you, Matty. We both have."

"But that's just it. I know lots about Jedha. Probably too much, but up there . . ." Matty looked up at the darkening sky, the stars starting to peek through the desert moon's atmosphere. "Up there's a different matter. Especially with Oliviah. Especially without—"

She wanted to say Master Leebon's name, but the words wouldn't come. Then Tey's arms were around her, pulling her close. She fell into the hug, burying her face in his green scarf so he couldn't see her tears.

"You're going to be fine, kiddo. Better than fine, you're going to be brilliant. *We'll* be the ones lost without you."

She sniffed, not believing him for a minute but appreciating the kindness.

"And we *all* get scared from time to time . . ." Tey continued. "Guardians, daring-but-handsome thieves, even overtalkative Padawans. The question is how we deal with it. Do we run and hide, or do we face our fear and damn the consequences?"

"Which do you think I'll do?" she asked, still not looking up.

"If you get scared?"

"Yeah."

"I think you'll find out for yourself when it happens, and you'll be surprised how well you cope. Not because you're a Jedi, not because of the robes or the lightsaber or even the Force, but because of who you are inside, where it matters."

Matty could have stayed there forever, holding her friend, but she knew that Oliviah would return any minute, demanding they leave. She gave Tey one last squeeze, let go, and stepped back, wiping her nose on the back of her hand.

"How do I look?" she asked, adjusting her robes.

"Like someone ready for adventure," Tey said, beaming at her. "Like a Jedi."

"That bad, huh?"

"Hey," Tey said, shrugging. "What can I say? You people are growing on me. Now go catch your flight before Jedi Grumblepants bursts a blood vessel."

EIGHTEEN

Yana dozed on the last stretch of what had been a torturous journey back to Dalna. Getting off Jedha had been easy enough, thanks to Kradon, who had arranged passage in the hold of a cargo hauler heading for Ord Mantell. They had jumped off at Port Mackie, although getting another craft to take them to Dalna had been more difficult, especially as the entire sector was apparently in the middle of a communications crisis. In the end, they'd found Okut Dand, a silver-whiskered Tarsunt who was transporting a consignment of bergruutfa to the Marat system, the enormous but docile creatures huddled into cramped pens on the Tarsunt's ship. The last member of Dand's crew had recently quit, claiming that they'd rather work in a spice mine than spend another day shoveling bergruutfa dung or mopping up the copious amounts of drool that flowed from the animals' tusked mouths. It had been the Herald's idea to volunteer, Werth surprising Yana by throwing himself into his new role as ship hand and quietly forming a bond with the massive creatures. The stink from the animals was unbelievable, although Yana thought it was still preferable to traveling with Sunshine Dobbs. Then there was the colony of small scuttling lizards that had also taken up residence on the ship, nesting in the vessel's many nooks and crannies, including—most annoyingly—the mattresses in the crew quarters, no doubt another reason Dand's people had abandoned their captain long before. Yana offered to trap and dispose of the pests, but their temporary employer had merely shaken his snout-nosed head. Why dispose of a constant source of food? Yana could think of a dozen reasons, most notably the fact that the reptiles spooked the bergruutfa, the skittish pachyderms trumpeting loudly every time one of the damned things scampered through the hold. Then there was the diet of fried, baked, or poached scuttler, broken up every now and then by a pot of stewed scuttler entrails.

She'd never been happier than when Werth stopped by her quarters to say they were coming up on Dalna.

"Have you persuaded the captain to land, or do we have to jump?"

The Herald smiled. "We're landing on the pretense of

needing fuel. I may have also mentioned that there could be a market for 'gruutfa dung in Ferdan."

"Clever."

She pulled on her jacket, ensuring she still had the Rod of Daybreak. "I suppose we better check on the big lumps one more time."

But the Herald didn't move from the doorway, hovering awkwardly on the threshold.

"Is everything okay?" Yana asked, not knowing how to deal with the situation, a dilemma that only deepened when he replied.

"I realize that I never said thank you."

"Oh. That's fine. Really."

"No, it's not," he said, the door closing as he stepped in, a severe look on his face. So they were doing this now, after all the days of awkward silence mucking out the poodoo machines. "You could've left me at the Convocation's mercy, and yet you came back."

"You would've done the same for me," she offered unconvincingly.

"No, I wouldn't."

"No," she had to agree, "you wouldn't."

The excruciating hush returned, and Yana went for the door, but he stayed where he was, blocking her exit.

"*She* would've come for you," he said. "Kor. She would've broken through every door in that temple to get to you."

Yana tried a smile. "She was stubborn like that. Got it from her father."

"She loved you."

Her smile faltered, but there was only one answer she could give. "Yes. And I loved her."

"I realize that she was the reason you helped me escape," he continued, the man who had murdered Oranalli just a few days before with no remorse whatsoever now struggling to look her in the eye. "Out of loyalty to her, not the Path and definitely not for me. I just need to know, are you committed to what we're doing?"

"I'm here, aren't I?" she said, wishing at this precise moment she could be anywhere but.

"And I'm glad," he told her. "Glad it's you, I mean. Someone I can trust. Someone Kor trusted."

Yana breathed, unwilling to have her emotions played with anymore. "What's this about, Werth?"

The Herald stepped closer to her, his voice more urgent.

"We need to keep my return to Dalna secret."

"Secret?" This was unexpected. Yana hadn't been quite sure what she expected the Herald to do when they made planetfall, but it wasn't this.

"You said it yourself, the Mother has turned against me, used me as a scapegoat. Who knows what lies she's told the rest of the Path. I need you to go to the compound with the Rod of Daybreak. Tell her that you stole it, leaving me where I was to . . ." He paused, searching for the right expression.

"Take the heat?" Yana suggested.

He smiled, amused by the vernacular she had picked up on her travels. "Precisely."

"Won't she be suspicious?" she asked.

"She'll welcome you back with open arms. Yana, the returning hero, who did everything in her power to complete her mission."

"And what about you?"

"Do you remember the barn on the edge of Ferdan that used to be part of old Haq's farm?"

"The guy who was as friendly as a Hutt's armpit?"

"It's been abandoned ever since he died."

That much was true. Haq the horrid had no relatives, and the place had fallen to ruin long before a heart attack finished him off.

"I'll bed down there, wait for your reports."

"My reports?" So she was his soldier now.

"There's one more thing," he said, suddenly less assured. "Something I'd ask Kor to do if she was here."

And there he went again, pulling at her heartstrings.

"I need you to check on my wife."

"On Opari."

He wiped his lips. "I dread to think what they've told her, if she's even still alive."

"You don't think . . ." Yana started, not really knowing

where she was heading with the sentence before trying another. "She was doing so well before we left."

"She was sick, and heartbroken over Kor," Werth said matter-of-factly. "She'd eat, drink, and sleep, but it was like watching a droid." He tapped his fist against his chest. "Nothing was left of her spirit, of the woman I married. The woman I love."

Yana had to admit she was surprised. This was the first time he'd mentioned Opari since they'd escaped the temple. Kor had been devastated when her mother was struck down by the wasting disease that almost killed her. Opari would have died if it wasn't for the medicine that the Mother had provided.

"What if they've let her suffer, Yana?" Werth asked. "What if they've stopped giving her the medicine or left her out in the cold?"

"They wouldn't," Yana told him, almost believing it. "The Elders love Opari. They love you."

"They used to, which is why the Mother came to our aid. Back then, I thought she did it for Opari, but I was blind. The only reason the Mother does anything is for herself. She wanted to keep me on her side, to stop Kor leaving like you wanted her to." There was no point arguing with that. "The Mother knew that as long as we were there, as long as I vouched for her, the Path would do anything she wanted, and now I'm a traitor and Opari is alone."

Yana knew she was being manipulated and that the

Herald was hoping her love for Kor would keep her on his side. He wasn't that different from the Mother, but she had come this far already, and there was no point turning back. Like it or not, she owed it to Kor to make sure Opari was all right.

"Fine," she said, waving the proverbial white flag. "I'll go to the camp and I'll check on Opari."

"And you'll tell me what the Mother is doing?"

"Yes."

He smiled, pleased to have gotten his way.

"You won't regret it, Yana."

Somehow, Yana wasn't so sure.

NINETEEN

"Hold on."

"What do you *think* I'm doing?"

The journey to the nameless planet had been unremarkable enough, even in Marda's limited experience. The only thing unusual had been the number of short sharp jumps Sunshine Dobbs had made, throwing the *Scupper* in and out of hyperspace with no discernible plan or pattern. The ship groaned, the deck beneath their feet shuddering while Sunshine and Deezee barked at each other, the maintenance droid moonlighting as a nav unit. At first, the crew had crowded into the *Scupper*'s filthy cockpit, braving the discarded food wrappers and general detritus that spread out from Sunshine's pilot chair, although Ort had turned the fetid air blue with a surprising array of curse words unbefitting a member of the Path. Marda could forgive the Reesarian as they all tried to remain on their feet.

The other ships seemed to be in the same state, the Barabel captain of the *Bonecrusher* hissing repeatedly at Dobbs over the comm, while the gruff captain of the *Moon of Sarkhai* told the prospector that they were going to need a new thruster rig.

It was only when Jukkyuk lost his footing and took out DZ-23's scomp link on a particularly sharp turn that Dobbs ordered everyone out, yelling that he needed to concentrate.

Everyone had retreated to the holds that doubled as common areas. Shea and Ort tried to kill time by playing Dantooine double-hand on an upturned crate, while Jukkyuk surprised everyone by pulling out a romance tablet from his pack before settling down to read. Marda was a mass of nerves, made all the worse by Calar, who sat on the other side of the hold, peering at her with pupilless gray eyes. Marda turned away but could still feel the Setaran's gaze on her. Why had she thought forcing her way on board the *Scupper* was a good idea?

Because you thought you could prove yourself, said a voice inside her head that didn't belong to her. Nor did it belong to Kevmo. It belonged to someone new, someone who knew what she was thinking, someone with no mouth and the creepiest eyes.

"Marda?" Bokana walked into the hold at the exact moment Marda jumped up, her skin crawling as the Setaran continued to peer at her, his ridged head cocked to one side. "Marda, what's wrong?"

She barged past Bokana, not stopping as he continued to call her name. She thought about returning to the cockpit, thinking that even Sunshine would be better company than Calar, but realized she had taken the wrong corridor, ending up in a cupboard that seemed to double as a galley, if the multiple packets of self-freezing ronk burgers were anything to go by.

Some Guide. She couldn't even find her way around a ship the size of a matchbox.

"Stupid," she told herself, banging her hands down on the filthy counter. "Stupid, stupid, stupid."

"Well," came a voice behind her, "if you're going to hit something . . ."

She whirled around to see Bokana standing in the doorway, a smile on his face and a pair of fighting staffs in his hands.

"They're not shyrran, but if you want to let off some steam . . ."

"Don't sneak up on me like that," she said, her heart racing.

Bokana swayed slightly as the *Scupper* listed, the accelerator compensators struggling to handle another unexpected turn. "Sorry. I was just worried. The way you ran off. The way Calar was looking at you . . ."

She shuddered, her skin crawling all over again. "He was in my head, Bok."

The Ovissian smiled.

"It's not funny!"

"No," he said quickly. "It's not that. You called me Bok." He shrugged a shoulder and moved in closer, leaning the sticks against the wall. "I liked it, that's all."

"Do we know anything about him?" she said, the galley suddenly seeming even smaller than before.

"Like how he eats? Beats me."

"Like why he's on this mission."

"That I *do* know," Bokana said, his body closer than ever. "Shea says that he's an excellent tracker. All Setarans are, apparently. A gift from the Force."

"You don't mean a gift that he uses?" she said, trying to ignore the fact that she was more upset over Bokana talking to Shea than she was over Calar misusing the Force.

"We don't have to talk about him," Bokana said, his voice husky.

"I don't think there's room enough in here. . . ."

"Hmm?"

She glanced past his arm. "To spar."

"There are other ways to relax."

"Bokana!" She slapped his chest but didn't remove her hand.

"I know everything's been screwy," he said, peering into her eyes. "And I know I'm not him."

A lump jumped to Marda's throat. "Him?"

Bokana chewed his lip nervously. "The Jedi."

"You know about Kevmo?"

"People talk, Marda. But it doesn't matter. Not to me." He reached out and brushed a strand of hair over her ear. "I meant what I said to Dobbs. Not about the vision—that was an out-and-out lie—but I truly believe we need you on this mission. *I* need you."

He went to pull his hand away, but Marda reached up, holding it in place against her cheek, enjoying the warmth of his touch. She looked deep into his eyes, seeing the truth of his words in his gaze. He *did* need her. More than that, Bokana *wanted* her, and in that moment, she wanted him right back.

The kiss had been long and gentle, different in so many ways from the brief moments she'd shared with Kevmo, but somehow all the more satisfying for it. With Kevmo, there had been the thrill of the unknown, the sense that worlds were colliding, two competing paths becoming one. With Bokana, everything just felt right—being in his arms, holding him tight. For the first time in weeks, Marda felt at peace, like she belonged. Not even the flight to Jedha, with the Path hanging off her every word, had felt like this. Then she was grieving, and now she felt whole.

Perhaps this was all the will of the Force. All the trials of the past few months, meeting Kevmo only to lose him, journeying to Jedha only for Jedha to burn, even being elevated to the Mother's side only to be cast down again. Everything had led to this moment. Without all that pain, she would never have met Bokana, never forced herself onto this ship, never taken her destiny into her own hands. The old Marda had dreamed of reaching out into the stars, and now there she was, on the greatest adventure of her life, and for once she wasn't alone.

Bokana smiled, and she smiled, too, pulling his head toward her, their lips searching for each other as a Wookiee's roar echoed through the ship.

They jolted apart, startled by the sudden noise.

"What's happening?" Marda asked, wishing she understood Shyriiwook.

"Sunshine wants us in the cockpit," Bokana said, clearly not wanting to leave. But duty called, no matter how much Marda wanted to stay there with him.

"Sunshine needs to make up his mind," she told him, planting one last kiss on his lips before leading Bokana out of the galley by his hand.

No. It wouldn't be their last kiss. She'd make sure of that.

They were still holding hands as they reached the cockpit, not that anyone noticed. They were all gaping at the sight in front of them: a kaleidoscope of colors twisting in the space beyond.

"Is that it?" she asked, squeezing Bokana's hand all the tighter.

Sunshine swung around to face them. "That is the Veil," he intoned, his eyes flicking down to their interlaced fingers for a second—not that Marda cared.

"There's a *planet* under all that?" Galamal hissed from the bridge of the *Bonecrusher*, her incredulity evident despite the poor connection.

"Under? No," Sunshine responded, his chair squeaking as he returned to stare at the anomaly. "Through! The most beautiful planet you've ever seen."

"Is it liquid?" Ort asked, nervously twirling one of her crimson braids around a long finger.

"Liquid in space?" Shea questioned, not taking her eyes off the shifting mass. "That's impossible." She turned to Sunshine. "That *is* impossible, right?"

"We thought so, Spence and me," he replied.

"Spence?" Bokana asked.

"The prospector I was working with when we discovered the Leveler's egg."

"And where is he now, this prospector of yours?" the *Moon of Sarkhai*'s captain asked over the comm.

"We parted ways a long time ago, although his ship is still down there, for all I know."

"He left it behind?"

"He didn't have much choice," Sunshine snorted, lost in

his memory for a moment. "The *Silverstreak* took a beating punching through the Veil."

"And you want us to go through there . . ." Shea scoffed. "To the place where your friend lost his ship."

"The *beautiful* place," Ort reminded her, with sarcasm as thick as her tresses.

Sunshine sighed and leaned forward on the controls, peering into the Veil. "It is beautiful, but it's also dangerous, for more reasons than you can possibly imagine. But yes, that's where we're heading, because that's where the Mother wants us to go."

"For her eggs," Galamal muttered on the comm.

"For her eggs," Sunshine confirmed.

"So, what's the plan?" Marda asked, hoping she sounded more confident than she felt.

"Our plan," Sunshine replied, flicking a series of switches above his head, "is to punch our way through that crap before the crap punches its way through our hulls. Shea's right, the Veil is a liquid, but unlike anything you've ever seen. It's alive and it's angry."

"How can a liquid be angry?" Marda said.

"Why don't you ask it when we make our way through, if you can be heard above all the screaming and the dying?"

"You're really not selling this, Dobbs," Galamal said over the speakers.

"He's just trying to scare us," Shea muttered.

"Got it in one, sweetheart," Sunshine said, swinging around to face the redhead. "Because scared, we might just make it through. Make no mistake, the minute our ships hit that stuff, that stuff will try to hit us. Are we ready?"

"We better live long enough to get paid," Galamal grumbled, and Sunshine laughed, flicking one last control.

"That's the spirit, Gal. What doesn't kill us only makes us richer."

TWENTY

To say that the tone of the Path's presence on Dalna had changed would be an understatement. Yana had noticed it the minute Dand's ship had touched down at the spaceport. Ferdan felt different, more on edge. The locals' heads were either down as they hurried through town or huddled together in little groups. In days gone by, Yana would have put it down to the rain that was falling steadily. This in itself was surprising. The rainy season wasn't due for another couple of months, but that alone surely didn't account for the sense of unease that permeated every street and alleyway.

Then there was the Path itself. Blue-and-gray robes were everywhere, Path members meditating in the middle of the market square or standing on street corners, handing out leaflets. Yana watched as an Anx passed an Ithorian boy she didn't recognize, the youngling thrusting the literature into the Anx's yellow hands. The reptilian didn't even give the leaflet a second glance, screwing it up and throwing it away as soon as they had walked on.

Yana scooped up the crumpled ball and straightened it out, marveling that the leaflet existed. Who used paper? Who even *made* paper? Yana knew some of the Elders had the skill, a throwback to a bygone age, but to produce the literature meant building equipment to process the pulp, not to mention a rudimentary printing press. Why go to that effort? And why now?

Yana scanned the creased sheet in her hand, becoming more concerned with every word she read.

The Force is precious. The Force is life.

There are those who would use it for their own ends, endangering our families and our homes. Endangering our entire planet. They come from the stars with a message of hope, but they are hypocrites who think only of what the Force can do for them, how they can twist its incredible power to fulfill their own desires. But their unnatural practices cause imbalance, putting us all in danger.

Join us to combat this evil. Join your neighbors, the Path of the Open Hand. Together we can strive for freedom, justice, and purity in the face of such irresponsibility. Together we can free the Force from their tyranny.

The tract ended with an invitation to a public meeting in the Path's newly purchased meeting house in Ferdan, another difference and one that made Yana swear beneath her breath. The address given was on old Haq's land, the very place the Herald was planning to hide. Should she warn him? Well, he'd soon find out, especially if Path members were putting as much effort into restoring the barn as they had into producing their propaganda. It was the language that concerned Yana the most, the talk of evil and tyranny. It was clear whom the writer meant. They might as well have mentioned space wizards with laser swords. And then there was the change to the central tenet of their belief; the freedom was still there, but justice and purity? That was the very definition of fighting talk.

Yana shoved the paper into a pocket and turned her collar up against the rain as she headed for the city limits. Even there, she found evidence of a change in the group. Dinube, a Harch Elder Yana had always thought of as a moderate voice in the community, was standing on an upturned koyo-fruit box, berating passersby for ignoring the plight of the Force. There was no mention of gifts freely given. This was condemnation. This was judgment.

There was no avoiding the arachnoid's gaze as Yana hurried by. Dinube's fuzzy gray face lit up in recognition, and she called out to Yana: "Sister Yana, Sister Yana, you have returned to us."

Sister? Another change. The Path had never spoken in

such terms. There was the Mother, sure, the Children, too, but the way Dinube said that made her shiver beneath her wet clothes.

"I need to get back to the camp," Yana said, hands thrust in pockets, fingers wrapped around that troubling paper. "It's good to see you."

A lie, yes, but one she hoped would appease the spider-like being, a hope that was dashed as Dinube called after her, waving all six of her arms in rapture: "The Force has delivered you from our enemies, Yana. Praise the one true prophet. Praise the oracle of the Force."

Not long before, Yana had thought the Path had no enemies. Now it looked like they were doing their best to make as many as possible. Of course, there was also a chance that she might be labeled an enemy herself, but there was no going back now.

"There could be," Kor whispered to her as Yana squelched through the mud. "There is."

Yana carried on anyway, not looking back.

The rain was lashing down as she reached the compound. A defensive wall surrounded the camp, rivertree trunks stripped of their bark and lashed together to form a perimeter. At least there didn't seem to be guards posted at the thick gates, which were thrown open, allowing her to slosh into the place she'd once called home. Inside the new defenses, the settlement was essentially how it had always been, except for one startling difference. The place was deserted. No one was hurrying between the shacks to get out of the rain, no smoke curling from chimneys. There weren't even any children playing in the open, which Yana had to admit wasn't all that surprising considering the deluge, but neither were they sheltering on the porches, fussing over dolls or lacing flowers together the way Marda had taught them.

The thought of her cousin only quickened Yana's steps. She needed to find Marda and see that she was all right. Yes, she'd made a promise to Werth and would absolutely check on Opari, but her own family came first.

If no one was in the compound, there was only one place they could be: down in the caverns, sheltering from the elements. Yana made her way to the entrance but was forced to stop short when the door refused to open. An entry coder had been wired into the frame, another line of defense that hadn't been there before. With no idea of the code, Yana was forced to press a call button and wait for an answer, rainwater running down her neck. Eventually, a mechanical voice responded, a droid she couldn't place.

"State your name and your business."

"It's Yana. Yana Ro. I have returned from Jedha, with an artifact for the Mother."

"Yana Ro," the droid repeated soullessly over the comm, pausing as it checked her name against whatever list it had been provided.

"Well?"

"Yana Ro. Yana Ro of the Children of the Open Hand."

"Yes," she snapped, wishing she could snap the sentry's metal neck in the process. "Open up, will you? It's freezing out here."

There was a click and a buzz, and the door slid open.

"Welcome home, Yana Ro," the droid said. "The Force shall be Free."

There was no sign of the officious little chiphead as the doors slid open, the droid no doubt stashed away in a control room, not that it mattered. Yana had no time to deal with droids. She just needed to find out what the hell was going on.

A voice rang out ahead, from the direction of the large assembly cavern the Path often used as a meeting place, or to gather in the dead of winter for the solstice celebrations. But there was nothing celebratory about the tone or the language, although the speaker herself was all too recognizable, even from a distance. Yana's sharp nails ached at the thought of seeing the Mother again, her contempt for the woman mixed with apprehension about the reception she might receive.

In the end, it turned out that no one even noticed her creep into the large domed cavern. The place was packed, a sea of gray and blue, but all eyes were on the Mother, who sat on what looked disturbingly like a throne on a newly raised platform at the far end of the cave. Yana couldn't help being taken aback by Elecia's appearance. The woman looked as if she had aged twenty years. She hunched forward, gloved hands curled around the chair's grand arms like talons, her once vibrant eyes sunken into a gaunt, skull-like face. But there was nothing small about her voice. That rang out strident and true, the cavern's natural acoustics amplifying her words as well as any sound system.

"We have done well, my brothers and sisters," she continued, the Leveler curled at her feet. "We have worked our fingers to the bone at the urging of the Force, for its glory, for its protection. The prophecy I received on the way from Jedha has yet to be fulfilled, but that doesn't mean we should become complacent. You only have to look to the skies to see the effect the meddling of our enemies is having on our world. This should be a season of light and renewal, and yet our crops are drowning in the fields. I weep when I think of what is happening to this and other worlds, the crisis we now face. The more the Jedi and their kin abuse the Force, the more they strip it of its power and the wider the devastation spreads. Even today, I received news from beyond Dalna. The entire galaxy is in tumult. There is disease and famine on every planet and every moon, children born with terrible deformities while the elderly die in their thousands, hungry and sick. The Republic . . ." Here Elecia paused as if even saying the word left a bad taste in her mouth. "The Republic tells us all will be well, that we have nothing to fear, and why? Because they are the puppets of the Jedi and their kin."

Shouts of agreement rang out around the chamber, the crowd working itself into a frenzy as the Mother continued.

"None of this is being reported on holonet channels because the media, like the Republic, cannot be trusted. My sources know the truth, as does the Force, a truth that is being silenced in every corner of the galaxy. This is why we must remain vigilant, why we must spread the word to our neighbors in Ferdan and beyond. Only together can we stand firm, united in the Force, united in our pursuit of freedom, justice, and purity. Even now, as our brothers and sisters brave the elements to spread the word, help is on the way, help to defend ourselves against those who would silence our message, who would silence the truth. Brother Dobbs and his team are traveling deep into the farthest reaches of the galaxy to secure the weapons we need for the battle that is to come. Meanwhile, our benefactors . . ."

A Path member cried out as the Mother faltered, a strange clucking noise coming from the back of her throat. The cries continued as the Mother's back arched and her entire body went rigid. Even from a distance, Yana could see her eyes rolling up into their sockets before she toppled from her seat, the Leveler already on its feet, maw nuzzling Elecia's contorted face.

The crowd surged forward as the Elders jumped onto the platform, Jichora raising her teal-colored hands to call for calm.

"Stay back. There is no cause for alarm. What you are witnessing is a miracle from beyond the Veil. The Mother is communing with the ebb and flow of the galaxy, with the Force itself. We are blessed, my brothers and sisters, truly blessed."

Yeah, Yana thought bitterly, *and the Evereni are welcomed with open arms everywhere they go!*

She'd waited long enough, distracted by the pantomime playing out on the platform. Diving into the crowd, she pushed toward the front, ignoring the clamor and confusion. Members of the Path were clambering over each other to see the miracle in action, while even more rocked back and forth on their heels, raising brikal-stained palms high as they babbled in a language Yana neither recognized nor believed existed. Something had snapped in these people, something that could have come only from the Mother.

Yana pushed and jostled, not caring whom she shoved to get to the front.

"Please!" she shouted as she jostled her way toward the platform. "Let me through. I need to get through!"

But the crush of people was too intense, the hysterical Path members squashed together tighter than the bergruutfa on Dand's ship.

"Jichora!" Yana cried out when the sheer number of bodies stopped her progress. "I need to speak with you. Jichora!"

The Twi'lek looked down into the crowd, her hazel eyes going wide. "Yana? Sister Yana, is that you?"

Now that she was nearer, Yana could see how haggard Jichora looked, almost as wretched as the Mother, who convulsed at the Leveler's feet. Exhausted or not, the Elder indicated for Yana to be brought forward, a sea of hands suddenly propelling her up to the platform.

"It *is* you," Jichora said, tears brimming in her tired eyes. She grabbed Yana and pulled her into a hug that was impossible to escape. When she could finally extract herself, Yana had to shout to be heard, the noise in the cavern reaching fever pitch. She had two questions that she needed answered, though not necessarily in the order they were delivered: "What the hell is happening, Jichora? And where is my cousin?"

TWENTY-ONE

The Veil was everything Sunshine said it would be and worse.

The *Scupper* barreled forward, Sunshine yelling to brace a split second before the cruiser's stubby nose hit the edge of the Veil. It was like hitting an asteroid. Sparks rained down as the yacht's acceleration compensators immediately overloaded, and Marda was thrown forward in her seat, the belt she had hastily buckled seconds before threatening to cut her in two.

"Are you all right?" Bokana called to her, his voice almost lost in the din that filled the cockpit—a cacophony of straining bulkheads, exploding circuits, and crackling flames. She couldn't reply, knowing that if she opened her mouth, she would be sick. The theory was put to the test seconds later as a sudden jolt had her screaming out in pain. She didn't get sick; at least she didn't think she did, as her senses were immediately overloaded.

The unnatural colors of the Veil, swirling outside the *Scupper*'s rapidly warping plasteel viewscreen, bled into the cockpit, confounding years of experience by making everything she saw strange and new but also utterly terrifying. The interior of the ship was awash with a color that was impossible to describe. Not red, purple, green, or blue, but somehow all at once. Outside, the Veil screamed, and Marda felt its cry deep within her bones.

"You need to move forward," Sunshine shouted against the noise, and for a moment, Marda wanted to cry back that she couldn't, that she feared she'd be dashed against bulkheads that seemed to be breathing like living things. Then she realized that the prospector was talking to the other captains, Galamal telling him that he was insane.

"You need someone to watch your approach," he shouted back into his headset. "Your sensors will be scrambled and you'll never see them coming."

"What?" Marda called out. "What won't they see?"

Sunshine didn't have to answer. She could see it for herself. Outside, balls of viscous liquid were swarming toward them like a shoal of piranha eels, ionized energy crackling over their wildly undulating sides.

They're going to eat us. They're going to consume the ship whole.

"Don't let those things touch you," Dobbs cried, trying to steady their course. "They touch you and you're dead."

"What will happen?" the captain of the *Moon of Sarkhai* asked, but he never got an answer because the *Scupper* suddenly shook as if it had been caught in the jaws of a gigantic hound and was being thrashed back and forth. Marda dug her nails into the frayed arms of her chair to steady herself, but Bokana wasn't so lucky, his head smacking against the nearest terminal with such ferocity that the tip of his horn snapped clean off. The Ovissian yelled, and then his head slumped forward as if it was too heavy for his neck.

"Bokana!" Marda cried out, but he didn't respond, his head flopping around lifelessly as the cockpit almost flipped over.

Frantically, Marda fought with her buckle, but the belt wouldn't release, which no doubt saved her life as the *Scupper* suddenly tilted forward, a crash sounding from deep in the ship.

"The supplies have come loose," Sunshine shouted at Jukkyuk. "They'll be smashed to pieces if we don't secure them." The Wookiee didn't hesitate, hauling himself out of his seat to stagger from the bucking cockpit.

"I'll come with you," Ort yelled, and Jukkyuk grabbed the Reesarian as she released herself from her harness.

How could they be so brave when the galaxy was turning itself upside down? Marda couldn't even get out of her seat, while Jukkyuk and Ort were risking their lives for the sake of the mission.

"The Force will be free," Marda muttered under her breath to calm herself. "Say it with me, Bok. The Force will be free."

Bokana didn't answer. Why didn't he answer? He *needed* to answer.

Ahead of them—or maybe it was above; there was no way to tell anymore—the strange globules massed on the other two ships in their convoy, both the *Moon* and the *Bonecrusher* pushing ahead as Sunshine had commanded. As promised, the prospector called out a warning, but there was no response.

"They're coming for you, *Moon*," he repeated, trying to boost the signal. "Can you hear me? Hal? Hal, open fire."

Marda didn't recognize the name but realized it must have been the imposing captain of the *Moon of Sarkhai* as the cruiser unleashed its laser cannons. The bolts screamed into the Veil, immediately finding their targets. Three of the murderous blobs burst on impact, and Marda thought she heard Hal cheer over the comm, although the cheers turned to screams as every blob suddenly changed course, leaving both the *Bonecrusher* and the *Scupper* alone to slam into the *Moon of Sarkhai*. The cruiser disappeared beneath the onslaught, its hull buckling and then vaporizing in a sudden burst of flame.

They were gone, quick as that. Marda had only just learned Hal's name, and he was dead, along with his crew.

The face of Tragor's son back on Dalna flashed in front of Marda's eyes. The Ithorian was an orphan now, just like her.

"Go, *Bonecrusher*!" Sunshine screamed into his headset. "Give it everything you've got. Straight ahead, now!"

They were slammed back into their seats as Sunshine fired his engines, the *Bonecrusher* shooting ahead. Outside, the impossible colors blurred together as the undulating balls of death locked on to their trajectory, rushing in as a scream ripped through the cockpit. Was it Bokana? No, he was still unconscious, and it didn't sound like Shea. Who, then? Marda prayed that it wasn't Sunshine. The last thing they needed was the prospector losing his mind as he navigated through the maelstrom. That was when it struck her. The scream wasn't coming from outside. It was in her head, but didn't belong there. It wasn't her, wasn't her voice, or even Kevmo's. Instead, it was the same voice she'd heard as Calar had peered at her so intently in the hold. He was doing it again, screaming impossibly at her, the cry becoming words and the words becoming shouts:

Need to go back.

Need to go back.

Need to go back.

If Sunshine could hear the voice, he wasn't listening. The ship plowed forward, plunging deeper into the Veil. If Marda had been able to think straight, she might have wondered how they could still be traveling at full speed through the anomaly. Surely, they should've reached the planet by now?

Time lost all meaning as they traveled improbable distances but never reached their destination. And still the words jabbered on in her head.

We shouldn't be here. This is wrong. We need to go back. Go back. Go back!

"We can't, Calar," Sunshine shouted from the pilot's seat. "Don't you get that?"

That meant Marda wasn't alone in hearing the voice, although the fact that the Setaran could broadcast his thoughts with such ferocity was too much to bear.

The Force will be free, Marda thought in an attempt to drown out Calar's voice, but he was still there as the *Scupper* gained on the *Bonecrusher*, almost coming alongside the other vessel.

Need to go back. We must *go back.*

The two ships were nose to nose now, racing to avoid the deadly liquid.

Why won't you listen? You'll kill us all. Kill us. Kill us. You'll kill us all.

Ahead something appeared in the distance, a gap in the madness. That was it: the planet. It had to be. They were going to make it.

It's not too late. Not too late. Have to go back. Have to turn around.

Something slammed into the ship, a crack spiderwebbing across the viewport. At his station, Deezee's dome exploded, peppering everyone with shards of shrapnel that stung like waspworms.

"Deezee!" Sunshine wailed as he struggled to maintain their course. Another globule slapped against the viewport, blocking the sight of the planet as Calar continued to rant.

What did I tell you? We should have gone back. We will go back. Go back. Make you go back.

Out of the corner of her eye, Marda saw Calar slap open his belt and propel himself out of his chair.

The Force will be chained. The Force will die. The Force will be consumed. All will be consumed.

"Don't," Marda managed to say, realizing that Sunshine had said the exact same word at the same time. The prospector spoke again, Marda doubling his words as if she had already learned his speech: "You're doing this, Calar. Attracting them to us."

It wasn't just her. Shea was screaming the words, Bokana slurring them under his breath, everyone but Calar speaking in unison. "You need to sit back down, before you get us all killed."

All killed, came the response in their heads. *Yes, all must die. Die and die and die so the galaxy will live.*

All the time, Calar struggled forward, reaching for Sunshine, every step an effort, his thoughts louder still.

I didn't know it before, but I know it now. They will come for us. The Nameless Horror. The Shrii Ka Rai. They will come for us all. The storm shall rise and the stars fall, all because you cross the Veil. Because of you. The Force will die. The Force no more.

Behind the controls, Sunshine pulled his blaster and pointed it at the Setaran.

"This is your last warning, Calar," they all cried alongside him. "Get back in your seat. Stop this."

But the Setaran didn't listen. He kept coming as the Veil closed in on them, ready to smother them forever.

The Force will be chained. The Force will be chained. The Force will be—

Sunshine fired and Calar fell back. Ahead of them, the gap in the Veil yawned open as Sunshine threw his blaster to the side and gunned the engines one more time.

All of a sudden, they were through. No more Veil. No more lightning. No more screams.

Planet X was below, but the danger was far from over. The Veil had gone, but so had Sunshine's control over the ship.

"What's happening?" Marda screamed at him, pleased to realize that they'd stopped speaking as one, although the relief was short-lived.

"The engines have failed," Sunshine called back, desperately pulling up on the yoke as the planet's surface rushed toward them. "We're going to crash!"

TWENTY-TWO

"Yana, you made it home. Thank the Force."

Home. Yana had to stop herself from laughing. Dalna had never been her home, not like it was for Marda or even Kor.

"Then why are you here?" Kor whispered to her. "Do what you wanted to do. What you *always* wanted to do. Run away."

There was no condemnation in Kor's voice, only a yearning for Yana to be free, a yearning Yana shared more than ever if she was honest with herself, but one that was impossible until she knew what had happened to Marda.

"Let me look at you."

They had been ushered from the assembly cave to the

Mother's private listening chamber the moment Elecia had stopped thrashing on the floor, her seizure finally coming to an end. Elecia looked thoroughly washed out, that damned monster of hers pacing at the back of the chamber as the Mother swapped her throne on the platform for a sofa strewn with cushions. They were alone, the Elders having been dismissed, although Yana suspected they were hovering outside the chamber's large doors.

"Where's Marda?" she asked, ignoring the skeletal hand that reached out to her.

"I wish I knew," the Mother said, giving up and calling the Leveler to her instead. "No one has seen her for days."

That didn't sound good. Nothing about this was good.

"I thought she was your Guide."

"So did I," Elecia admitted, "but it seems I was wrong. The choices she was making . . . the things she said. It appears that while the Force is infallible, I am anything but. Perhaps you know where she could be hiding, a favorite place from your childhood, maybe?"

There was the torinda tree, although that had always been more Yana's place than Marda's. The lompop fields, perhaps? But Yana wasn't about to help Elecia. She'd look for Marda herself, once she was away from there.

"What about the others? Have they run off, too?"

The Mother's brow furrowed. "The others?"

Yana looked up where Elecia's honor guards used to stand. "Qwerb and Jukkyuk."

"Qwerb never made it off Jedha."

"I'm sorry to hear that."

"He was faithful to the last," the Mother told her, "while Jukkyuk is offworld at present, on a mission of vital importance for the entire Path."

"With Sunshine Dobbs," Yana deducted, spitting out the name as if it were poison.

Surprise creased the Mother's features. "How did you know?"

"Your little sermon to the faithful out there."

Elecia's tired smile returned. "Ah, yes. The Force rather took me back there."

"I noticed. It was . . . spectacular."

Spectacular and terrifying.

"You mentioned a weapon," Yana prompted.

Again, the Mother's hand found the Leveler's head, the monster almost purring as it nuzzled her palm. Stars, it had gotten so big, much larger than when she'd seen it last on Jedha.

"Sunshine is looking for more eggs like the one he gave me before we left for Jedha," the prophet said.

Yana's mouth went dry. "And more eggs would mean . . ."

"More protection," the Mother added quickly, her smile widening, and Yana couldn't help recoiling at the sight of the woman's teeth.

"You're bleeding," she said, her hand going to her own mouth.

The Mother sat up, quickly running her tongue over her teeth.

"Should I call the Elders?"

"No," the Mother said sharply, pressing her hands against her teeth to check the blood. "I will rest soon enough, but first I must know . . ." Her eyes came up, bloodshot but still piercing, almost to the point of mania. "Did you find it? The Rod of Daybreak?"

Yana was surprised it had taken so long for the question to come. She nodded, swinging the rod from her back, the artifact wrapped in a protective cloth they had purchased in Enlightenment for an exorbitant price.

"Give it to me," the Mother demanded, jumping to her feet. "Give it to me now."

Like Yana had any choice! Elecia snatched it from her, the Leveler jumping back like a startled tooka cat. The Mother tore at the covering, the creature whimpering and then falling strangely silent, its head dropping between its paws as the cloth fell to the floor.

"Yes," the Mother cried in triumph, clutching the relic in both hands for a moment before pulling the Rod of Seasons from where it hung at her belt, the small skulls around its shaft glinting in the candlelight. As her robes shifted, Yana caught a glimpse of something else hanging alongside the artifact, a metal tube. So the Mother was still carrying Zallah Macri's lightsaber as Marda carried Kevmo's.

"She'd use it on you," Kor warned her silently. "She'd run

you through without a second thought, killing you as she killed me."

Yana could believe it, but for a moment, she wondered why the Mother needed protection when her pet monster never left her side, especially now the vile creature was almost prostrating itself as the Mother brought the two rods together. They connected with a sharp click, a bright purple glow erupting the length of the now combined staffs, the same color as the large gem sheltered beneath the Rod of Seasons' blade.

The Leveler threw back its giant head and howled. Yana couldn't tell if it was a cry of pain or triumph, but for a moment she thought the Mother was going to join the creature in its frenzied song, her head also tipped back and her eyes closed in ecstasy as the color flooded back to her face.

"Oh, thank you, Yana," she exalted, throwing her arms wide as if she still had an adoring congregation before her. "Thank you from the bottom of my heart."

But when she opened her eyes again, she didn't look at Yana at all but at the Leveler, cowering before her.

"It was all worth it," she breathed, walking slowly toward the creature, who backed away as if scared of the woman. "All worth it indeed."

She thrust the combined rods out toward the Leveler and shouted: "Stop!"

The Leveler froze.

A sadistic smile spread across her face, revealing teeth now cleaned of blood.

"Roll over."

Yana thought she was joking, but the beast obeyed her, rolling onto its back like a trained hound.

The Mother laughed.

"Do you see, Yana, how important this is? The Rod of Seasons alone helped control the animal, but with both rods, we can dominate it completely." She raised her voice again, issuing another command at the visibly shaking creature. "Run up to my cottage on the surface. Go."

The Leveler rushed for the doors, knocking them open with such force that the Elders who had been listening outside cried out in alarm as it thundered past. They watched it go, looking back at the Mother like younglings caught with their hands in the candy jar.

"Go to the Path," Elecia commanded the Elders, with the same authority she'd used on the Leveler. "Tell them I have recovered, that the future is secure."

Jichora and the others scurried away as, somewhere above them, the Leveler bayed once more in the distance.

"You going to leave it up there?" Yana asked.

"For a while," the Mother said, examining the staff. "Until my strength has returned."

"Will it control the others?" Yana said, nodding at the relic.

"Others?"

"The monsters that Sunshine will bring back from his travels."

"We shall have to see," the Mother said playfully before her expression darkened. "But before then, there's something I need to know. . . ." Her gaze fixed on Yana, the whites of her eyes as clear as her teeth. "The Herald. Is he—"

"Dead," Yana said, the lie Werth had supplied tripping from her tongue with surprising ease.

"How?"

"Killed while attempting escape."

"Jedi?"

"Guardian of the Whills."

The Mother nodded, suddenly solemn.

"I suppose you heard—"

"Your broadcast? What you said about him?"

"I had to," Elecia said. "I never wanted to abandon him, but I had to think of the Path. Do you think he understood why?"

"I'm sure he did," Yana told her, safe in the knowledge that the Herald understood everything there was to know about the Mother of the Open Hand.

"I just find it curious that none of my contacts told me," Elecia said, and Yana's heart jumped to her throat. The Mother still had informants on Jedha. "In fact, they've been strangely quiet. Usually, I can't shut Oranalli up."

She knew. She knew it was all a lie. Yana thought about

running for the door, but her escape path was blocked as the Leveler bounded unexpectedly back into the chamber.

"You didn't call it back," Yana said, looking from the creature back to the Mother.

"Oh, I did," Elecia told her. "You just didn't hear me."

The creature stalked toward Yana, its head low. Yana's hand went for Oranalli's blaster, expecting the monster to pounce, but it changed direction at the last moment, heading for the Mother instead.

"Fascinating, isn't it?" Elecia said as the animal curled around her legs. "All I have to do is think and the Leveler obeys. If only everyone were as easy to control."

"Mother," Yana began, her mind racing. "I—"

"I expect I will hear the sad news about the Herald soon," Elecia said, cutting her off. "The communication blackout is playing havoc with interplanetary communications."

"Yes," Yana said, trying not to sound relieved. "I'm sure that's it."

"But I'm glad you made it back to us," the Mother continued, walking toward her, the Leveler staying where it lay. "A battle *is* coming to Dalna, and there is much to do. We need fighters, Yana. Fighters like you. Even if Sunshine's mission is a success—and I'm sure it will be—there is no guarantee the eggs will hatch in time. I need you to train the Path."

"Train them for what?"

"To defend the camp. To defend this entire planet if needs be. The imbalance will be put right, but only after a great deal of suffering. The Force has shown me that. We must be ready." She looked at Yana expectantly. "Will you help?"

"Tell her no," Kor whispered to her from beyond. "Find Marda, find my mother, and get as far as you can from this place."

But what about Werth? Yana thought, hoping that she hadn't spoken out loud.

"Father can look after himself. This is his fight, not yours."

Yana considered Kor's words, recognized the truth in them, and then asked the Mother what needed to be done.

TWENTY-THREE

Marda's first thought was for Bokana. Sunshine had managed to pull the nose of the craft up, but even then, the impact had been intense, the ship plowing through dirt and rocks and Force knew what else. As soon as they had come to their final, juddering stop, Marda slapped her buckle and pushed herself from her chair, ignoring the stiffness already freezing her joints.

"Bok?"

She knelt in front of the Ovissian and raised a hand to his head, fearing to turn it but desperate to see how bad the injury was. Bokana groaned and moved, as if he could hear her thoughts, shifting his head so she could see the horn that had slammed into the terminal. The tip was missing, much like the tusk he'd lost on Jedha, but the break looked clean. She just had to hope that there was no hidden damage, that the impact to the horn hadn't fractured his skull or caused internal bleeding.

"Marda?" he slurred, his eyes fluttering open.

"I'm here," she said, leaning in on instinct to kiss him happily on the lips.

"Do we all get one of those?" came Shea's lethargic drawl from the other side of the cockpit.

Marda pulled away, flushing with embarrassment as Shea fumbled with her belt on the other side of the cockpit.

"Are you okay?" Marda asked Bokana, trying to ignore the other woman.

"Ask me when I'm not seeing three of you."

"Three? That sounds bad."

He smiled, pained but genuine, a spark of life finally returning to his eyes. "Not from where I'm sitting." His hand came up to touch her face. "The more of you, the better."

"I think I'm going to throw up," Shea said.

Bokana told her to go, and Marda picked her way across the cockpit, navigating around debris and trying to ignore the body that was slumped against the rear bulkhead.

"Let me help," she said, reaching for Shea's buckle.

"I can do it," Shea said, slapping her hand away and finally getting the belt apart.

"Do you still think you're going to be sick?" Marda asked.

The redhead looked her straight in the eye. "Not now that you two have stopped making out. Talk about a time and a place."

Marda's cheeks flushed, not out of embarrassment but anger. "I was worried about him!"

"We're all worried about someone," Shea said, grabbing the back of her chair as she pushed herself up. "If anything's happened to Geth . . ."

"Geth?" Marda asked.

"Never mind," Shea snapped, shoving Marda aside to lurch toward the front stations. "I just want to know if we can get back off this rock when the job's done. Dobbs?" She shook Sunshine's shoulder. The prospector was sprawled over the controls, his head resting awkwardly against the yoke. "Dobbs, you still with us?"

"Is he—" Marda began, rushing to his side.

"He's alive," Sunshine groaned, "but his head is ringing like a Ferrixian chime, so back the hell off." The prospector shoved himself up and rubbed the bruise that had already blossomed across his greasy forehead, wincing sharply. "Okay, someone remind me not to do that again."

"Fly into a planet?" Shea asked.

He rubbed his neck. "Touch any part of me that hurts, which is pretty much everything."

Sunshine sank back in a chair that seemed more rickety than ever and looked at the dirt piled high against the viewport. "But we're down and in one piece, more or less. I didn't think we'd make it for a moment there. But you know what they say: any landing you can walk away from is a bloody miracle, right, Deezee?"

A shadow fell over the prospector's face as he remembered, turning to view the burned-out shell of a droid that sat beside him. "Oh, Deezee."

For a moment, Marda actually felt sorry for the man. For all his faults—and Sunshine Dobbs had many—he'd just lost an old friend.

Unfortunately, as a group, they'd lost a lot more. As if thinking the same thing—a disturbing concept considering what they'd experienced—the three of them turned toward Calar's body.

"You all heard him, right?" Shea asked. "When we were up there?"

"In our heads," Marda confirmed, the memory sickening her.

"And we talked back," Bokana said from his seat. "Together."

"You remember that?" Marda asked. "I thought you were out of it."

"And I thought it was a dream," he admitted.

"More like a nightmare," Shea said, shuddering.

"It was the Veil," Sunshine said flatly. "Think of it as a defense mechanism. Your boy over there was Force-sensitive. That's why the Mother sent him."

Marda couldn't believe it. "No, she can't have. No member of the Path is permitted to use the Force."

"Not consciously," Sunshine said. "From what I gather, Calar had taken a pledge to stay out of people's minds. But sometimes a person can't help themself. Take it from someone whose daddy didn't think twice about cracking open a crate of gutrot every evening. He'd taken a pledge, too." Sunshine pointed a stubby finger at the body. "Calar was a tracker, although there was nothing natural about his talent."

"It was the Force," Marda said.

"And that's what those blobs homed in on, what they used to try and bring us down. If I hadn't shot the poor bastard . . ." Sunshine rubbed a grimy hand over his mouth, the bristles of his beard rasping against his rough palm. "Well, now we're down a valuable resource. . . ."

"Resource?" That wasn't right, and Marda knew it. Whatever he was, Calar deserved better than to die on a ship like this at the hands of a man like Sunshine Dobbs. But her outrage had to wait because Ort appeared at the door, eyes alive with wonder and awe.

"You have to see this. It's *incredible*."

It was the smell that hit Marda first as they approached the exit. She'd always loved flowers and hadn't realized how much she'd missed weaving them into her hair until the air rushed through the dusty old ship, so pure and clean.

Jukkyuk was already outside as Ort led them from the ship.

The *Scupper*—which surely would never fly again—had plowed a deep furrow as it skidded to a halt, its nose buried deep beneath the soil. But on either side of the ship was a meadow of such beauty that Marda found it hard to breathe.

"What did I tell you?" Ort said, clapping her hands like a child, her leathery face appearing instantly younger.

"It's stunning," Bokana breathed, pulling Marda in close, while Shea delivered her own verdict in typically more colorful language. Everything Marda had felt in the cockpit, the anger and disgust, was washed away, along with her doubts and fears. Tears streamed down her face, not the tears of shame or sorrow she'd wept so often in recent days but those of pure, unfettered happiness.

They stepped from the ramp onto a rainbow of colors. The grass was the greenest any of them had ever seen, the yellow and orange daisies in the meadow shining like stars. Even the purple trees in the distance seemed sharper than anything she'd experienced on Dalna, more vibrant. Marda sank to her knees, running a hand through the grass, the petals of the flowers like silk beneath her fingers. Never before had she felt so much life, so much vitality. Even the Veil shifted above them in the sky, brighter than any sun. It looked beautiful from below, although the *Moon of Sarkhai*'s crew would no doubt disagree. She felt a pang of sorrow as she realized they would never know the joy of this place. Her only hope was that the *Bonecrusher* had made it down, that Galamal and her crew were nearby, experiencing all this for themselves.

"Marda," Bokana called out from behind. "Look at this!"

He was crouched in the furrow the *Scupper* had plowed, running his hand across the churned dirt.

Tiny shoots were already growing, pushing up through the soil.

"This can't be right, can it?" he asked. "Nature doesn't work like this. Not this fast."

It wasn't just the grass. Marda reached up and brushed his face. The cuts on Bokana's cheeks had already closed, the bruise beneath his horn almost gone. Maybe he hadn't been as severely injured as she'd first thought. He looked so alive, so handsome.

Marda kissed him, holding him tight, his arms pulling her closer. She didn't care what Shea and the others thought, if they were staring as Bokana kissed her in the shadow of the downed ship. What did it matter? All Marda cared about was feeling Bokana's lips against hers. She wanted it to always be like this, the two of them together. She had never wanted anyone this keenly before, never lo—

Marda pulled away sharply before she could complete the thought, pressing her hand to her mouth. Bokana laughed, brushing her hair over her shoulder. "What is it?"

She stood up, turning away, needing to catch her breath. Her head was spinning, giddy with the color and the smells and the kiss . . . and what she'd just felt.

"Marda?"

She turned to him, searching his face to try to make sense of it all. She had meant every thought that had raced through her mind as she pressed her body to his, their embrace all that mattered. She *had* needed Bokana, and, yes, yes, she had realized she loved him.

But that was impossible. They barely knew each other. And what about Kevmo? In the first flush of their kiss in the galley, Marda had questioned whether everything that had happened over the past few months—including the feelings she'd experienced for the young Jedi when he first arrived on Dalna—had led to this point, but love? Was love possible? Could it happen so fast?

"What's wrong?" Bok asked, and as soon as he took her hand in his, Marda knew she was worrying about nothing. She *had* cared for Kevmo, but this, this was strong. Unexpected, yes, but real and true. Maybe that was why she couldn't hear Kevmo anymore, why she hadn't heard him from the moment she and Bokana had kissed. Perhaps it was time to let go of the past. Perhaps it was time to be happy.

She pulled Bokana close, holding him tight.

"Nothing," she said, meaning it with all her heart. "Nothing is wrong at all."

A voice interrupted, Sunshine Dobbs still standing on the *Scupper*'s ramp. "How are we all doing? Feeling good?"

Marda didn't try to pull herself from Bokana's embrace, grinning from ear to ear. "Good? I'm feeling great!"

"Pleased to hear it," Sunshine replied, although the prospector's face didn't show it. He looked around the rest of the group. "And I'm guessing the same goes for all of you. It's this planet. It gets inside you, makes you feel alive like never before. I mean, look at it." He threw his arms out wide like a showman. "What's not to love? You can *feel* the energy in the air."

"You can feel the Force," Ort replied, and Marda knew at once that the Reesarian was right. She'd often wondered what it was like to feel the Force the way the Mother did, the way Kevmo had, not in the abstract way Marda knew it was there, but like something she could reach out and touch.

"Right," Sunshine agreed, "the Force. And this is just the beginning. The things you'll see . . ." He shook his head, barking out a laugh. "The things you'll experience, they'll blow your mind. You'll never want to leave."

Leave? Standing with her arm around Bokana's strong waist, Marda couldn't think of a single reason why *any* of them would want to leave somewhere like this. Why would they? It was a paradise.

"The thing is," Sunshine continued sternly, "you're going to have to. All of us. Our job is to gather more of those eggs for the Mother and transport them back to Dalna as soon as possible. You remember that, don't you? Because it's all too easy to forget when you're here. All too easy to forget who you are."

Marda let her arm fall away. The prospector was right,

though it pained her to admit it. They were there to protect the Path. She had to keep that at the forefront of her mind. On the ship, Sunshine had mentioned his father, who, by the sound of it, had liked a drink, maybe a little too much. Marda had sampled plenty of gnostra berry wine growing up, but never too much, not like Yana, who she'd seen rolling around with Kor after a bottle or two. Marda had never wanted to lose control. Is that what was happening? Too much wine lowered your inhibitions, intensified whatever you were feeling. Did this planet do the same to you? Was she drunk on the Force?

She looked up at Bokana and felt the same swell of love as before, but couldn't be sure that it wasn't the planet amplifying feelings that might come in time into something more immediate. She needed to remember who she was now, not who she might be in the future. She was the Guide. She had to be strong.

"So, what's the plan?" she asked, walking back toward the ship with as much authority as she could muster.

Sunshine still hadn't stepped down from the ramp. "We need to make contact with Galamal. I have no idea if the *Bonecrusher* made it down in one piece, but I hope to hell it did, because one thing's for certain, my old girl is never going to see the stars again." He looked up at the yacht he'd called home for the best part of his life and tipped his hat. "Sorry about that, darlin'."

"And what if they didn't?" Shea asked, her smile finally

dropping away as if she'd also remembered something important to her.

"Hmm?" Sunshine asked.

"What if the *Bonecrusher* didn't make it?"

Sunshine didn't answer at first, taking a breath and finally stepping off the ramp. They were all forced to watch him for a second as he closed his eyes and breathed in deeply, his lips quivering slightly. When he opened his eyes again, they were wet, but he tried to remain businesslike, only a slight tremor in his voice betraying how he felt to be back on Planet X's soil. "You're an engineer, aren't you?" he said to Shea. "You worked on the Mother's ship."

"On the *Gaze,* yes, but please don't tell me you want to fix that old crate." She pointed at the *Scupper,* a literal blot on the landscape. "I don't care how much you love your 'old girl,' it ain't happening."

"Not the *Scupper.* The *Silverstreak.*"

"Your partner's ship?" Marda asked. "But you said—"

"It's still out there," Sunshine said quickly, "and will be in better condition than the *Scupper,* even after all this time."

"I'm not a miracle worker," Shea told him.

"No, but Elecia said you were good, which is why you're here. There was always a chance we'd come in hard. You were my insurance policy."

"So it's lucky you blasted Calar and not me."

"*Who* blasted Calar?" Ort asked, suddenly realizing the Setaran wasn't there. "Calar's dead?"

"I'll explain on the way," Sunshine said, pulling a holo-projector from his belt.

"Is that to contact Galamal and the others?" Bokana asked.

"No, this is for contacting Gal," Sunshine said, pulling a comlink from his belt and tossing it to the Ovissian. "This is to help us find the *Streak*." Sunshine flicked a switch, and a three-dimensional map of the area appeared above the projector. The prospector looked from the map to the forest in the distance, the strange wood more like fungi than trees. "Yup, thought so. This way."

He marched off, the map buzzing slightly, and Shea, Ort, and Jukkyuk started after him.

"Are we going with?" Bokana asked, moving to Marda's side.

"Of course," she said, rubbing his arm. "It's all just a little overwhelming, you know?"

He smiled back and ran a finger along her jawline before lifting her face toward his. "Then it's good that we're experiencing it together."

They kissed, and Marda watched him set off after the others, already trying to activate Sunshine's comlink.

It was good, all of it. More than good. Being there, in that place with Bokana, was all she'd ever wanted.

And that was what scared her the most.

TWENTY-FOUR

The forest was even more incredible up close. The trees on Dalna had been tall, but these were gigantic, with trunks so broad that even Jukkyuk couldn't reach around them. Even stranger, Marda should have been in shadow as she followed the others, Sunshine leading the way. The canopy above their heads was vast, each leaf the size of a reek, but somehow light still managed to find its way through. It took Marda a while to work out that it wasn't light from above that was sneaking through but the leaves themselves that glowed, illuminating the forest floor. In fact, the deeper they pushed into the forest, the more *everything* glowed: from the bell-like flowers that sprung up from the ground to the trees, their smooth, almost spongy bark shining gently as the crew passed by. Marda stopped, pressing her palm against one of the trees, feeling the bark give slightly beneath her fingers. Her first impression of the forest had been right. The trunk's surface felt more like a mushroom than wood, more like flesh. At any other time, it would have sent a shiver up her spine, yet she found it somehow comforting that the trees here were warm whereas on Dalna they were cold. Then there was the slight pulse beneath her palm, as if the tree had a heartbeat. She let her eyes close and imagined she could feel the entire planet beneath her fingers—every plant, every creature, every stream that rushed through the forest, and every breath that stirred. She felt so small, but safe. The planet was so much bigger than any of them, larger than their struggles and concerns, and beneath it all was warmth and safety and—

The Force will be chained. The Force will die. The Force will be consumed. All will be consumed.

Calar's face rushed out at her from thick, suffocating darkness, a gaping wound in his head, his eyes burning with fear.

"Marda?"

She was back in the forest, her hand in front of her where she had snatched it back from the tree.

"Marda, are you all right?"

Bokana was beside her. She hadn't heard him return from

where he'd been standing on a fallen tree, trying to get a signal on the comlink.

She hadn't heard anything but Calar's voice, but now that Bok was beside her everything was better. It was like waking from a bad dream, the world suddenly put right.

"I'm fine," she said, squeezing his arm, ignoring the fact that she was still shaking.

"There it is," Sunshine called out from the front. "The *Silverstreak.* We've found it."

The others were already running, leaping over gigantic roots, Jukkyuk making huge bounds and looking at home among the giant trees.

"Come on," Bokana said, holding out his hand, but Marda slapped him playfully, setting off in a run.

"You'll have to catch me first."

He laughed, taking off after her. "Just try to stop me." And they were running and cheering and waving their arms to scatter the gently glowing bugs that swarmed through the sweet air in front of them.

The Force will die.

The Force will die.

The Force will—

The *Silverstreak* had obviously been an impressive ship, at least from what they could see. When they'd first come to Dalna, Yana and Marda had found the ruins of an ancient hermit's hut far beyond Ferdan's city limits. Nature had reclaimed the structure, moss carpeting the walls as tall weeds burst up through cracks in the floor. Something similar had happened to the old prospecting ship. The sleek mirrored hull was almost completely covered with flowers, as if the ground had tried to swallow the spacecraft whole, determined to transform the wreckage into a small hill.

"It's a good thing this planet makes me feel like I can take on the galaxy," Shea said, hands on her hips, "otherwise I'd be crying right about now."

"There's no way that is going to be able to fly," Ort said, although Jukkyuk muttered something in Shyriiwook that sounded a tad more confident. As they watched, the Wookiee dug into the turf, popping out claws that easily lifted the soil to reveal the ceramic-plated hull beneath.

"The damage really isn't that bad," Sunshine said, scratching his beard.

"Bad enough that you abandoned it in some wood," Shea pointed out.

"Yeah, but how did it end up here?" Bokana asked, looking around the clearing where the *Silverstreak* had come to rest. "The *Scupper* carved up the countryside, but here . . ." He pointed at the trees that ringed the glade, each as mature as the next. "These look like they've been here for centuries. What happened? Did the ship drop like a stone, landing in the middle of a clearing by pure luck?"

"No," Sunshine admitted. "Spence and Dass were lucky to

walk out alive, but they definitely brought down a few trees on their descent."

"Then where are they?" Ort asked. "The fallen trees? Where's the damage caused by the crash?"

"Repaired," Marda said. "Like the flowers sprouting in the wake of the *Scupper*." She wondered how much of the churned dirt behind Sunshine's ship would still be there if they went back now, or whether it had all been reclaimed by the meadow.

"You mean those trees are *new*?" Ort asked, jabbing a gnarled finger at them. "That they grew back in . . ." She turned to Sunshine. "How long was it since you were here?"

"A year," he replied. "A year and a half at the most."

Bokana laughed. "Those trees are not a year or so old."

"Yes, they are," Marda said. "The planet put everything right." She turned to Ort and Shea. "Do you remember when the Mother first came to Dalna? How she planted a garden?"

"A garden that bloomed overnight?" Ort said.

"That was impossible," Marda reminded her, "but it still happened, because the Force was with her."

"Still," Shea argued, crossing her arms. "A few lompop flowers are one thing. Those trees are another."

"What about us?" Marda asked, turning to Ort. "Were you injured when the *Scupper* came down?"

The Reesarian shrugged. "Maybe a little. Jukkyuk caught me when I fell."

"That was it? You weren't hurt?"

"I jarred my back, that's all."

"And how's it now?" Marda said, turning to Bokana. "And how's your head?"

"Just dandy." He grinned, making her smile back. But it was true. The bruising was gone. Even his missing tusk looked like it was trying to grow back, jagged keratin peeking out of the scar on his chin.

"The planet repairs itself," she said, turning in a circle to take in the entire group. "It's the Force. It's so strong here. So *alive*."

"Then it's a shame it can't bring back the dead."

Marda should've been surprised by the voice, and yet somehow she knew it was coming. They all did by the way they turned as one as Galamal and the rest of the *Bonecrusher*'s crew stepped from between the trees.

"Geth!" Shea shouted in delight, running to a tall, pale-skinned human Marda knew from Dalna. She hadn't known they were in a relationship, a fact confirmed as Shea and Geth held each other tight. Shea's comments in the *Scupper* after the crash suddenly made more sense. The rest of the party was made up of a human woman called Shalish, a lanky Rodian called Wole, and a quiet Duros whose name Marda didn't know. Galamal, meanwhile, made straight for Sunshine, blaster rifle held tight in her scaly hands.

"I should kill you where you stand," she hissed. "And don't give me that nonsense about watching our backs."

"This is about Hal, isn't it?" Sunshine said, having the good sense to retreat a couple of steps.

"We've known each other for years," the saurian snarled, "and yet you set him up without a second thought, letting him fire on those things knowing full well what would happen."

"I told him it was dangerous. Told him that not everyone would make it back alive."

"Because of you!"

"Because of this *planet*," Sunshine shouted back. "Because of the Veil. Think what you want of me, but I'd much rather Hal was here."

"Especially with a working ship," Geth added.

Galamal growled at the back of her throat, her quarrel with Sunshine temporarily derailed. "That looks like it's been here a long time."

"Not as long as you'd think," Bokana told her, "but hopefully, Shea can get it off the ground."

"Otherwise, you're going to have to take a lot more of us home in the *Bonecrusher*."

"What's wrong with your junk heap?" Galamal asked Sunshine.

"Even more junk than usual," the prospector admitted. "We lost more than the *Moon of Sarkhai*. The *Scupper*'s gone, Deezee too."

"And Calar," Ort reminded him.

"Your tracker?" Galamal asked.

"The person I hoped would help us find the eggs,"

Sunshine said. "But luckily, we have you and your wonderful senses, Gal, unless you're about to kill me where I stand?"

"What are you thinking?" Marda asked, butting in before the saurian could remember that actions spoke louder than words.

Sunshine slipped the map projector into one of his many pockets, retrieving what appeared to be a fragment of precious stone.

"Is that . . . ?" Marda said, recognizing it straight away.

"Part of the Leveler's shell. I was hoping that Calar could use it to work his magic."

"So, what now?" Galamal asked.

Sunshine held the fragment out to the Barabel. "That's up to you."

"Me?"

"I thought you could smell it or something, catch its scent."

"What do you think I am? A Corellian hound?"

"I *thought* you were a hunter."

Galamal gave another of her troubling growls. "I *am*, but not like that. I follow trails, not my nose."

"Then I suggest you don't kill me just yet," Sunshine said, tossing the shell aside and patting his pockets.

"Second on the right," Bokana said, pointing at his jacket.

Sunshine smiled as he retrieved the projector, Marda wondering how Bok had known that was what he was looking for.

The map reactivated, and Sunshine pointed out a route. "We found the egg here, me and Spence."

"That doesn't look like the forest," Marda said, peering closer at the flickering terrain.

"It's not," Sunshine replied, zooming in to reveal a gorge beyond the trees. "I suppose you'd call it a canyon or a ravine. The topography changes dramatically at this point, as does the wildlife."

"We haven't seen much wildlife yet," Shalish said, the first time Marda had heard the woman speak.

"You will," Sunshine promised. "And if you thought this place is incredible—"

"How far to the canyon?" Galamal asked, shutting him down.

"Less than an hour."

The Barabel held out a scaled hand. "Then we'll see you back here in two. I'll take the map."

Sunshine killed the hologram and slipped the projector back into his pocket. "Oh, no you won't. This is still *my* expedition."

"And *I'm* the hunter."

"We'll all go," Marda said, realizing that someone had to break the deadlock. "How many hands do you think you need to fix the ship, Shea?"

The engineer rubbed her neck. "Depends how bad it is inside. Geth, for sure. He worked with me on the *Gaze* and *usually* knows what he's doing."

"Is that right," the bearded human said, feigning insult.

Shea smirked at him before continuing: "We could do with some Wookiee muscle, and Wole knows his way around an engine. Shalish, too, for that matter."

The Rodian jabbered something Marda didn't understand, but he didn't seem too worried about not traipsing for hours through an alien landscape.

"Fine, so that leaves me, Bok, Ort, Sunshine, and Galamal."

"Don't forget Tareen," Shea said, pointing out the Duros who had remained at the back of the group. "He doesn't say much, but he keeps his head in a crisis."

"It's certainly big enough," Geth joked, prompting the blue-skinned alien to bare a mouthful of crooked yellow teeth in a mock grimace.

"And Tareen, as well," Marda concluded. "We're going to need as many hands as possible to gather the eggs."

"And who are you to make the call of who goes and who stays?" Galamal said, baring some teeth of her own.

"Haven't you heard?" Sunshine smirked. "That's the Guide."

TWENTY-FIVE

It had been a long time since Matty had set foot on a new world. She had come to Jedha as a young Padawan, and Master Leebon hadn't ventured far from the Pilgrim Moon. Matty tried her best to hide her excitement as the Hoopaloo's cruiser dropped into Dalna's atmosphere, already imagining the hatch opening and the air of a different world filling her lungs—not that it seemed to work.

Oliviah Zeveron smiled across the passenger compartment, which was empty save for the two Jedi. "Looking forward to stretching your legs?"

"Yes," Matty said, forcing herself to contain the flutterbugs that were rioting in her stomach. "It's been a long journey."

Oliviah leaned forward, her robes shifting to tumble over her shoulders. "I was the same, when I was a Padawan. Every world was a new adventure. Every moon. My master said she thought she was going to have to strap me in a harness to stop me leaping through the doors of our cruiser every time we touched down."

"Did you travel a lot?"

Oliviah nodded, rubbing her hands together as she remembered. "All the time. Master Fitan was a great admirer of the teachings of Fin-So-Rowan and believed a Jedi's place was traveling the cosmos, teaching not just our ways but the doctrines of the Luminous themselves. We were always hopping from one world to another, never stopping long but hopefully making an impression with those we encountered." She laughed, her eyes losing their focus as she recalled a long-forgotten memory. "Fitan even designed a puppet show to entertain the local younglings."

"A puppet show!"

"Made all the puppets herself, as well as a booth with a small stage for us to perform side by side, barely large enough to swing a norg. 'The Legend of the Noble Bonbrak.' It had to be seen to be believed. Probably a little melodramatic, if I'm honest, but the children loved it, and most of the adults, too, especially when our hapless hero found himself at the mercy of Darth Voord, a terrifying Sith who just loved boiling oceans with his devastating heat ray."

"Your puppet show . . . had a *Sith Lord*?" Matty said, wondering if Oliviah was teasing her.

The Jedi spread her hands. "What can I say? Kids love a baddie."

"Probably because they haven't met many yet."

The brown-skinned woman laughed. "True. Either way, there are worse ways to spend your apprenticeship than zipping from one place to the next, a different sky every week, different soil beneath your feet. And the food. Oh, the food, Matty. Old Fit used to make a beeline for the first food stall she saw the moment we set down, ordering the strangest, most exotic thing on the menu."

"She sounds wonderful."

"She was, and don't let anyone tell you otherwise. Shortest Ugnaught you've ever seen, but the owner of the galaxy's biggest heart. Played the omnipipes with gusto if zero talent, danced as if the galaxy *was* watching, and told jokes that would make a Taratoff blush. Of course, after a while I tried to hide my excitement whenever we visited somewhere new, to prove how mature I was." Oliviah pulled herself up in her seat, brushing down her robes and adopting an overtly dignified demeanor. "Do you know what Fitan did the *very* first time I tried to hold it together, on the day we were supposed to be greeted by a delegation from the Alnarian Collective?"

Matty shook her head-tails.

"She let out a fart. The most beautiful, perfectly timed

trumpet that had ever been heard. And if that wasn't enough, she used the Force to ruffle her robes as if they'd been caught in the backdraft. The Collective's first impression of the brave and noble Jedi was a fifteen-year-old Padawan and her master giggling like younglings."

Matty laughed, wishing she could've seen it for herself, although Oliviah's smile soon dimmed, her whole bearing changing as a strange sadness took hold. "I should've followed in Fitan's footsteps when I had a chance, should've taken on the 'Noble Bonbrak' after I was knighted, but instead I ended up on Jedha, an aide to Master Leebon."

"That wasn't too bad, was it?" Matty asked, taken aback by the sudden change of mood.

Oliviah smiled again, but the light didn't quite reach her eyes this time. "I liked Master Leebon. I liked her a lot, but Jedha wasn't for me. All the talk and the debate, it . . ." She looked away for a moment, eyes focused on a point just beyond the hull. "It just seemed so dusty, you know? So lifeless."

"I think Jedha has seen enough life over the last few weeks."

"You're right," Oliviah conceded, standing up so her immaculate robes fell back into place. "Enough for several lifetimes. What do you think? About time I embraced my inner Padawan?"

"You want me to break wind?" Matty offered, immediately blushing. Luckily, Oliviah took the comment in the way it was intended.

"That wouldn't be my first choice, no, but we could stop at the first food stall we see. What do you say?"

Yet no local delicacies were waiting for them on Dalna, or any welcoming parties, for that matter. Instead, there was a muddy field and rain sheeting down, forcing the two Jedi to raise their hoods.

"So," Matty said, slipping her hands into her sleeves as she felt the eyes of every local on them. "Here we are. What next?"

"How did Tey put it? We start sticking our noses where they don't belong."

"According to the glares we seem to be attracting, that's pretty much anywhere around here."

Behind them, the Hoopaloo's taxi ship took off, its other passengers disembarked and getting as wet as the Jedi.

For a moment, Matty forgot all about her earlier excitement and wished she'd jumped straight back on board the craft before it left, but Oliviah was already marching—or should that be squelching?—past the drinking establishment and heading toward town.

Matty hurried after her, trying not to slip and thinking it would have been nice if her partner—the woman who had dragged her halfway across the galaxy—at least checked to see if she was following. They'd been getting along better in the latter stages of the flight, Oliviah starting to thaw from the early days of their journey, which were made up of a great deal of brooding with a little introspection on the side to break the monotony. Matty never thought she'd miss Vildar and Tey's squabbling, yet here she was, Oliviah's shutters back down, all stories of puppet shows and omnipipes forgotten. She still didn't even know *why* they were there, beyond Vildar's suspicion that Oliviah wasn't telling them everything. From where Matty was standing—or rather trying her damnedest not to fall on her backside—Oliviah had gone back to not saying anything at all.

At least someone was talking as they reached the edge of the mire. Or rather, shouting. Shouting very loudly.

"I thought you weren't using the landing strips," a large Gormak yelled at a much smaller human. The Gormak was wearing bright yellow oilskins that were jollier than his demeanor, while the human's blue robes, drenched though they were, instantly marked them as a member of the Path of the Open Hand, the now-familiar face paint having washed off in the downpour.

The pair were standing in front of a cargo ship, the hauler's Gamorrean deckhands unloading large crates onto carts pulled by lyuna, stubborn but hardworking animals that were used all across the frontier.

"You said your ships were heading straight to that compound of yours, that we wouldn't see your sort around Ferdan anymore," the Gormak continued, water running down the ornate frills that swept up from his noseless red face.

"Is there a problem?" Oliviah asked, approaching the reptilian. The Gormak looked them up and down with orange eyes, his mandibles twisting into an even more pronounced sneer.

"And what are you two supposed to be?"

"We're supposed to be what we are," Oliviah replied pleasantly. "Jedi travelers."

"Jedi!" the Gormak exclaimed, his frills flaring. "Well, it's about time. You come to teach these brikal heads a lesson, have you?"

"The only lessons we seek to impart are those of peace and harmony," Oliviah said, turning to the Path member, who was squinting through the rain.

"There is no problem," he informed her, "except the presence of defilers such as yourself on Dalna."

"Defilers?" Matty repeated, the word smarting more than it should have.

The Gormak crossed his thick arms, chuckling at the Path member. "Looks to me like your days are numbered now that these ladies are here. I can't wait to see them kick you back to whatever hole you crawled from."

"I come from here," the Path member responded, taking a step forward that could only end in trouble. "I was born on Dalna—unlike you, I might add. I belong here."

"Is that right?" The Gormak also stepped forward, towering over the smaller man. "Is that why you're buying up every spare shack in Ferdan, or are you just trying to force us from our homes? Is that it, brikal head? You gonna start a riot like you did on Jedha?"

That surprised Matty. She had no idea the news of Jedha had spread so far, especially with communication lines so fractured in the sector.

"*We're* from Jedha," she said, trying to diffuse the situation and immediately making it worse. "There's no evidence the Path was behind what happened, only a few agitators acting of their own volition."

"Matthea . . ." Oliviah warned under her breath, but the damage was already done.

"Ha! Did you hear that?" the Gormak said, jabbing a clawed finger at the bedraggled Path member. "Agitators. What did I tell ya? Better start packing your bags."

The last thing Matty expected was for the Path member to produce a weapon, yet that was exactly what he did. One second all he had in his hands was a dripping-wet datapad, and the next he'd retrieved a snub-nosed blaster from his robes.

Matty's hand dropped to her holster, but Oliviah moved first, putting herself between the two locals before Matty could draw her saber.

"That is enough," Oliviah said firmly, a hand raised to the blaster's muzzle as if she were prepared to catch the weapon's bolt if it was fired. "No one is starting a riot, and no one is packing their bags." She turned to the Path member, whose aim was as steady as a droid with a bad motivator. "What is your name?"

"I told ya," the Gormak sneered. "He's a brikal head."

Oliviah silenced the reptilian with a raised finger, her gaze never wavering from the man holding the gun, the same man who now shook his head.

"No," he said, his voice trembling almost as much as his blaster. "You're not going to play with my mind. The Force is not your plaything, defiling wretch. The Force will be free."

"No tricks, I promise. Only an honest question. My name is Oliviah Zeveron and you've met Padawan Cathley. We only want to help."

The blaster didn't drop, but a little of his defiance did.

"Xander," the Path member said, his eyes still brimming with fear. "Xander Cran."

Behind Oliviah, the Gormak scoffed, only to have the Jedi fix him with a stare. "And you are?"

"What's it to you?"

"I want to understand what's going on here, what it means to you. Often, the first step in understanding someone is knowing who they are."

The Gormak rolled his eyes, the muscles of his arms bunching as they crossed against his broad chest. "Athul Taran."

"Thank you, Athul. Now, as we all know each other, we can dispense with names such as 'defiler' and 'brikal head.' We can speak to each other as people. People who have no need to point weapons at each other."

Reluctantly, Cran lowered his blaster. "I just want to go about my business," he said, still glaring at the Gormak.

"Buying up the town, you mean. First Haq's place and then Gurso's kitchen. Why's that, *Xander*? Just so you can spread your 'message'?"

The emphasis Taran put on the last word made it obvious what he thought of the Path's mission.

"This planet is in danger," Cran said. "*Our* planet, Athul."

"In danger from what?" Matty cut in, feeling a sudden burst of frustration from Oliviah. What? Wasn't she even allowed to ask questions?

"From the likes of you," Cran spat back. "Look what's already happening," he added, glancing up at the storm clouds.

"You mean the rain?"

"The Force is out of balance. It has been ever since that boy and his master came to Dalna. Ever since we were opposed on Jedha for speaking the truth."

"The rains *have* come early," Taran agreed, unfolding his arms as he suddenly found himself in the strange position of finding common ground with his enemy. Matty was glad the two men weren't shouting at each other but still wanted to back up some. "What do you mean, 'that boy and his master'?"

"Hmm?"

"What boy? What master, for that matter?"

"The Jedi apprentice Marda was messing around with," Cran told her. "And the Soikan, too."

"Soikan?" Oliviah cut in. "Do you know their name?"

"Why would I?" Cran replied. "All I know is they tried to steal from us."

"And you're *sure* they were Jedi," Matty pressed, struggling to believe a word of this. "Stealing isn't really what we do."

"They weren't thieves," Taran scoffed, hooking his thumbs in his belt. "They *helped* Cran's lot, when their caves flooded. At least, that's how I heard it."

"The Jedi helped," Cran acknowledged. "But only so they could inveigle their way into our community."

"Ha!" Taran barked. "Listen to him! Inveigle indeed."

"*That's* why we can't trust them, Athul," Cran insisted. "Why we can never trust them."

"And where are these Jedi now?" Oliviah asked, but the Path member shrugged, finally slipping his weapon back beneath his sopping robes.

"Don't know. They left when they couldn't get what they wanted."

"Which was?" Matty pushed.

"I don't know," Cran admitted, sounding as frustrated as Matty felt. "Something from the Mother. Relics or some such."

Matty and Oliviah exchanged looks. At least that made some kind of sense. The Herald had been caught looting treasures. The Path had form, as Tey Sirrek would say. Was that what these mysterious Jedi had been doing on Dalna, trying to return artifacts to their rightful owners?

Taran, meanwhile, had other concerns. "This is all very well and good," he grumbled, stabbing a scaly finger at the cargo ship behind Cran. "But it doesn't answer what all *that* is."

It was a good point. More of the containers had been offloaded onto the three carts, all of which were full.

"Supplies," Cran answered as if it were the most obvious thing in the world. "Dried rations, rice and seeds sent by our benefactors."

"That's a *lot* of rations," Matty said, counting at least eight crates.

"Exactly," Taran said, enjoying the victory, small though it was. "And it's the third shipment in the same amount of days."

"We have a lot of mouths to feed," Cran insisted. "Especially since the Republic has decided to use us as a scapegoat for their mishandling of Jedha. Our brothers and sisters face persecution wherever they've tried to settle, and many are being forced to return to Dalna."

"More of the brikal heads," Taran exclaimed, rolling his orange eyes. "Just what we need."

"The rains have decimated our crops," Cran insisted. "The Mother was concerned that what little we stored for the winter wouldn't go around."

"Then why don't you just stock up from Gurso's kitchen?" Taran sneered, notching up another win. "That's obviously why you bought it. To look after your own."

"Yes," Cran admitted. "We did. We bought the kitchen to look after everyone. The Path *and* the people of Ferdan. We're all going to be affected if the rains continue, Athul. All of us."

That at least stopped the Gormak in his tracks, although he wasn't about to give much ground. "We don't need your charity."

"Not yet, maybe. But you will. We'll all need each other if the imbalance isn't corrected."

"It sounds like a kind gesture to me," Matty said before Taran could find something else in Cran's words to complain about. "Something to be encouraged."

Taran harrumphed. "You'll forgive me for not trusting someone who hides a blaster beneath their robes. We only have his word that there are supplies in those. How do we know it's not more weapons?"

"He could show you," Matty said. "Isn't that right, Xander? You could let Athul see inside one of your crates?"

Suddenly, the Path member didn't look so sure. "I don't know. If the rain got into the supplies . . ."

"Just a peek. That shouldn't hurt, should it?"

"Very well," Cran finally conceded, stomping over to the cart, his fellow Path members looking somewhat surprised to see a Gormak and two Jedi accompanying him.

"We need to open up one of the crates," he grumbled, checking the manifest. "That one maybe, on the middle cart."

"No point moving those," Oliviah said, pointing instead

to the latest crate that was being lugged off the cargo ship by the Gamorreans. "That one will do. Much easier for everyone."

Xander Cran looked like he was about to argue before backing down. "Very well. Open it up, would you?"

The Gamorreans shrugged and, grunting to each other, did as they were told, removing the lid with practiced ease.

"What are they?" Taran asked, peering at the tiny yellow seeds inside.

"Starbeam legumes," Cran said, reading from his datapad. "Direct from Hetzal. Would you like to check to the bottom?"

Oliviah ran her fingers through the dried seeds. "No need. I'm sure these will make an excellent stew."

"Enough to feed everyone," Cran agreed. "If they don't get too wet."

The lid was replaced and the crate loaded onto the last of the carts, its lyuna snorting in the rain.

"Well, if everyone's mind has been put to rest . . ." Cran prompted, signing for the consignment so the ship could leave.

If anything, Taran looked disappointed that his suspicions *hadn't* been confirmed. "I still don't like it, but I suppose you people need to feed yourselves."

"And others," Matty pointed out.

"Pah! I won't be eating that muck," the Gormak announced before sloping off, a sore loser to the very end.

Oliviah, however, was more gracious, smiling at the Path member. "I'm sorry you had to go through that, but I appreciate your cooperation."

"I didn't do it for you," Cran huffed as the others threw a waterproof sheet over the first cart. "Now, if you'll excuse me, I need to get these back to our compound."

"Of course," Oliviah said, indicating that Matty should help her cover the cart at the rear. "We should be getting into town ourselves."

"I'm sorry if you thought I spoke out of turn," Matty said as they pulled the rubberized sheet into place. "I was only trying to help."

Oliviah didn't reply but pointed underneath the cover before it could be secured. "In here."

Matty looked at her as if she'd gone mad. "What?"

"Just get in."

Too shocked to argue, Matty clambered under the sheet, and Oliviah scrambled after, one of the Gamorreans noticing what they were doing.

"We continued into town," she told him before he could raise the alarm. "You saw us leave."

The cargo hand grunted and buttoned down the covering, sealing them underneath.

Soon the cart was bouncing along a track, the rain hammering down on the canvas.

"You have nothing to apologize for," Oliviah said, finally acknowledging Matty's comment. "You were following your instincts. We both were."

"And what are we doing now?" Matty whispered, banging her head-tails as the cart rolled over a rock.

Oliviah smiled. "I couldn't see our Xander Cran inviting us back for a look around, could you?"

"So we're sneaking in?"

"I *did* say I wanted to embrace my inner Padawan."

"Yes, because this is *precisely* what we do, all the time."

Oliviah grinned cheekily. "Thought so."

Matty wasn't about to complain, though. She was itching to poke around the Path's camp herself, especially after the revelation that Jedi had already been there, including a Padawan who had "messed around" with one of the Path's own.

That wasn't what disturbed Matty. She had messed around herself enough over the years, and sometimes hadn't even been caught. The troubling thing was the emotion she felt from Xander Cran when he told them about the Soikan and their apprentice. It wasn't anger but something else, just as potent and twice as worrying.

Guilt.

TWENTY-SIX

The walk across Planet X should have been arduous, but Marda couldn't remember when she'd felt so happy. They covered kilometers, but their legs didn't seem to tire, even when taking turns pulling the repulsor sled they'd recovered from the *Silverstreak* over the uneven terrain of tree roots and rainbow-colored fungus mounds. Marda had even been able to shake the gloom of Calar's doom-laden warning. There was no way the Force could die. This place was proof of that. Everyone could feel it, even Galamal, who strode on at the front of the group with Sunshine, laughing heartily at the prospector's jokes (most of which were distinctly unsavory) and pointing out fruits and berries they should try on the way to the canyon (all of which were delicious). Ort had at first worried about picking produce on an unknown shore, noting that they had no idea what was poisonous, but Sunshine had assured her that Galamal was not only the greatest tracker he'd ever known but a galaxy-class forager, too. Sure, as Galamal admitted, the Barabel would rather snack on small rodents and lizards, but she'd studied plants, berries, and herbs on a thousand expeditions and long before had worked out that there were universal constants that could be employed to determine which produce would give you the energy you needed or have you rolling around with severe cramps . . . or worse.

Not that Bokana seemed concerned. The big lump was like a Little at a feast, forever reaching up for the bounty of succulent delights that weighed down the branches or cracking nuts between his teeth. At first, he would check with Galamal before sampling a fresh treat but soon seemed to know instinctively what was good and what should be avoided, impressing the Barabel with his intuition.

"I guess I'm a quick study," Bok said, the bright orange juice of a particularly plump peach running down his tusk.

"But a messy eater," Marda said, laughing as she wiped away the pulp to plant a kiss on lips that tasted sweeter than usual. "You should slow down. You'll give yourself a tummy ache."

"Aww, are you worried about me?" he joked, poking her playfully in the ribs. "Don't want me to get sick?"

"I'm only worried that there won't be anything left. At this rate, you're going to strip the planet bare."

"Then you better stop me," Bok said, pulling her in for another kiss.

That fruit really did taste great.

They only broke off when Bokana stumbled back against a tree trunk, the slap of his skin against the spongy wood sending a swarm of flutterbugs the color of the morning sun flapping up into the canopy. Marda leaned back in Bok's arms and watched them go, vowing never to forget the wonder she felt. How would she ever leave this paradise behind?

"Why should we?" Bokana said, shocking her away from the beauty of the insects' iridescent wings.

"Why should we what?" she asked, looking in his eyes, which seemed more alive than ever.

"Why should we leave? We could help the others find the eggs and then stay."

Marda's smile faltered. "Stay? Stay here?"

Bok was babbling like an excited child. "We could build a house, maybe scavenge material from the *Scupper* or use timber from the wood. There's plenty to eat, and it's not like we'd be a strain on the environment, not with how quickly everything regenerates. What do you think?"

What did she think? Marda pulled away and felt a tug on her heart as disappointment flashed across Bokana's eager face.

"Marda?"

"How did you know?"

"Hmm?"

"How did you know that's what I was thinking? About not wanting to leave?"

Bokana's lopsided grin returned and he looked at her as if she'd temporarily lost the plot. "You must have said it?"

She shook her head. "I didn't."

He went to pull her close again, but she stepped back. "Then I guess I must have read your mind," he joked. "What does it matter? It would work, wouldn't it? You and me, here in this place. Perhaps that's *why* we were brought here. Perhaps it's the will of the Force."

Marda was suddenly very aware that they were alone. "We've lost the others," she said, looking around for the group.

"They can't have gone far."

"We should catch up with them."

She started to move, but Bokana caught her arm. He looked deep into her eyes, deep enough to see her soul. "It could work. I'm serious."

She forced a smile, wiping more pulp from his chin. "You're drunk on fermented fruit! Come on, let's go."

Chuckling, he let her grab his hand and pull him after the others. Within seconds, he seemed to have forgotten about his sudden proposition and instead chatted happily about everything they saw or heard, from glowing bees to the call of strange birds overhead. Marda let him whitter on, enjoying the sound of his voice while also trying to ignore the disquiet she suddenly felt. She didn't know what had unsettled her most, the fact that Bokana had known what she was thinking or that the idea of setting up home on a strange planet with a man she'd only just met seemed like the most natural thing in the universe.

The doubts gnawed at Marda all the way back to the group, who barely seemed to have noticed they had left her and Bok behind, although Ort did raise a knowing eyebrow at them that had Marda slipping her fingers from Bokana's hand. Whatever emotions were washing over Marda, they had a job to do, and she and Bok had to stop treating the mission like a lovers' stroll.

In fact, the entire party's mood seemed to shift as the forest gave way to more rugged landscape, the ravine Sunshine had described suddenly yawning in front of them.

"You found the egg down there?" Marda asked, stepping to the front of the group, Bokana staying close.

Sunshine held up the holomap, matching the terrain to the projection. "There are caves near the bottom of the canyon. The egg was in the mouth of one of them, lying out in the sun. We saw it glistening as we made our way down."

"How?" Ort asked. "Don't tell me we have to climb?"

"There's a path," Sunshine confirmed, pointing toward a narrow pass on the right side of the ravine. "It's a little treacherous at times, but nothing we can't handle."

"Even with this?" Tareen asked, indicating the repulsor sled the Duros had been pushing for the last stage of their trek.

"It'll be fine, as long as we take it slowly."

Galamal gazed up at the sky, her slitted Barabel eyes narrowing. "We might not want to wait around for long."

Marda looked up. A pair of large reptiles circled above them, leathery wings stretched wide. "You think they're hostile?"

"Nothing has been so far," Bokana pointed out.

"Sunshine said the fauna changed around these parts."

"And they did," the prospector confirmed, "but don't worry about those babies. We saw them last time, but they stayed where they were, didn't bother us at all. It's the creatures in the caves that you have to watch out for."

"And where do we think we'll find more of your eggs?" Marda asked, already fearing the worst.

Sunshine's mournful expression said it all.

"Great," Ort groaned.

"We're doing this for the Mother," Marda said, feeling the need to take control before the mood soured even more. She could understand how they were all feeling. Back in the trees, the excitement had been palpable, but exposed to the impossible skies with their whirling reptiles, an unmistakable sense of dread had started to take hold, a feeling that they should turn back without delay. Not even Bokana would want to set up hearth and home out there. But they couldn't go back empty-handed. "The sooner we find the eggs, the sooner we can get back to the others."

Marda knew she was talking to the group like she used to cajole the Littles when they didn't want to venture into Ferdan to give out flowers, but the tactic worked. As she strode in the direction Sunshine had pointed, the group followed without complaint, although there was little of the boisterous chatter that had accompanied them through the woodland. Now everyone was quiet, on high alert as they started their descent, glancing up at the circling reptiles to make sure they were staying where they were. She wouldn't blame the creatures if they were tempted from the skies, especially with such a group of tasty morsels just crying out to be plucked from the path.

However, Sunshine's assurances were justified, as they made their way without incident. Bokana broke from her side to help Tareen guide the repulsor sled down the path. Galamal joined her at the front, while Sunshine walked behind, one hand constantly brushing the ravine wall to keep his balance.

The temperature had notably cooled when they finally reached the bottom, Marda's sweat suddenly cold against her skin. Bokana was back beside her in an instant, asking if she was all right, but she nodded eagerly, not wanting him to cause a fuss. Above them, the walls of the chasm rose like giants on either side, a sharp wind whistling along the valley to throw up dust that immediately found its way into her mouth, coating her tongue. This time she didn't refuse Bok as he offered a canteen of water he'd replenished from a crystal-clear brook in the forest. She drank deeply before offering the bottle to Ort, who took it gladly.

"Well?" Galamal prompted Sunshine before glancing back up at the reptiles that looked more like rock-vultures with every passing minute.

"The egg was over here," Sunshine responded, waddling toward a crop of boulders on the ravine floor.

"I thought you said it was near a cave?" Marda asked, following him.

"Near a cave next to these boulders," he replied, annoyance creeping into his voice. He'd switched off the map but still clutched the holoprojector in his fist, ready to use it as a bludgeon if required.

They reached the spot and found it devoid of any eggs, the chance of finding another lying on the ground just waiting for them too much to hope for.

"And you think they'll be in the caves?" Galamal asked.

Sunshine shrugged, pulling down his goggles to protect his eyes from the dust. "That's what Spence theorized."

"But you never looked?"

"We're looking now, aren't we?"

"But where to start?" Ort said, shielding her eyes as she took in the myriad cave entrances lining both sides of the gorge. "There's so many."

"Any ideas?" Sunshine asked Galamal.

"How am *I* supposed to know?" the Barabel replied, kicking the dirt at her feet. "There are no tracks, no sign that anything living has been down here for years." The reptilian looked over at Marda. "Maybe it's time your *Guide* proved her worth?"

Marda touched her chest. "*Me*?"

Galamal shrugged. "Doesn't the Force guide your way?"

"Not like that. I don't speak to the Force. I can't."

"Then what are we supposed to do?" Tareen asked, leaning on the sled and running a hand over his domed head. "Start at one end and work our way through the caves until we get lucky?"

"We could split up," Ort suggested, but that was shot down by Galamal.

"Only if you have a death wish. We've no idea what is in those caverns."

Again, Marda felt all eyes fall on her. She squirmed, feeling out of her depth. Why wasn't Sunshine jumping in? He was the only one who had been there before.

But it was Bokana who spoke up, scratching his lost tusk. "Do you still have that fragment of shell?"

"From the egg?" Sunshine's hand went to the front pocket of his jacket. "Sure."

Bok held out his hand. "May I?"

Sunshine pulled out the glistening chunk. "All right. Although I'm not sure what good it will do."

Bokana didn't answer but just took the fragment and

held it up to the light, his face taking on a purple tint as the light streamed through the gem.

"Bok?" Marda asked, moving in closer, her stomach tightening, although she didn't know why. There was something about his expression, something she couldn't place.

"I just wondered . . ." he said, peering down the valley. "Just had a feeling . . ."

He turned and leaped up onto the nearest boulder before she could quiz him more, then scrambled onto an even larger rock, all while carefully holding the piece of shell in his hand.

"What you doing up there, greenie?" Sunshine shouted up as Bokana turned on the spot, his eyes scanning the cave mounts. "Making yourself an easy target for those terror-birds?"

"They're not going to attack," Bok called back, although Marda didn't know how he could be so sure. "They won't come down here. Not while the Under-Dweller is on the prowl."

"Now that doesn't sound good," Galamal hissed, eyeing the caves with suspicion. "What's an Under-Dweller?"

"Beats me," Sunshine replied, although Marda had a sneaking suspicion that he was being economical with the truth.

"Just what wildlife *did* you encounter down here?" she asked the prospector.

"There," Bokana called out before Sunshine could answer. "That one."

He had stopped turning to leap down from the boulder

like a mountain cub. Bok dashed off the moment he landed on the ground, his booted feet kicking up dust.

"Which one?" Marda shouted after him as he quickened his steps, breaking into a run toward one of the smaller caves, the opening in the rock barely larger than Bok himself.

"Do you have glow rods?" he called back, ignoring her question as he reached the cave mouth.

Sunshine fished around in his pack, pulling out a light and holding it out to the Ovissian without question. Galamal was more cautious, placing a scaled hand on Dobbs's arm before Bokana could take the tool.

"Mind telling us where we're going?" the Barabel hissed.

Bok took the glow rod anyway. "Following a hunch."

"A hunch?" Marda asked, more concerned than ever. "What are you talking about?"

Bokana looked frustrated to be asked and hurt that she didn't automatically trust him. "You must have felt it, too? Ever since we arrived, I've just been so sure of everything. Where we were heading, the fruit on the trees."

"We've been following Sunshine's map," she pointed out.

"Yeah, but it's more than that. When we got left behind, in the forest, I knew that the others weren't far ahead. I felt it here." He tapped his chest, over his heart. "As strongly as I knew that we belong here, Marda. That we can make this our home."

"Make it your what now?" Ort asked, Marda squirming beneath the Reesarian's gaze.

“I don’t know how I know,” Bokana continued, oblivious to Ort’s scrutiny, “but the eggs *are* in there.”

“In this cave?” Marda asked, and Bok nodded.

“More than we’ll ever need. This is where the Force has brought us.”

And there it was, the words that Marda had dreaded. Suddenly, she knew where she had seen the look on Bokana’s face.

Kevmo had looked the same every time he manipulated the Force.

TWENTY-SEVEN

Matty and Oliviah had lapsed into silence for the rest of the uncomfortable journey to the Path's compound. The relentless thrash of the rain against the sheeting above their heads would have drowned out conversation anyway, but there was no point tempting fate, not that Matty felt like talking. Oliviah had apologized for her reaction to Matty's trying to help with the disagreement between Xander Cran and the Gormak, but she couldn't put it out of her mind. Maybe her experience with Master Vildar and Tey had spoiled her. Not the constant danger of imminent death—that she could live without—but the way both men treated her as an equal. True, Vildar hadn't immediately warmed to her—or vice versa, if she was frank—but in a relatively short period, he had come to trust her judgment, enough that now she, in turn, could trust him to be her Jedi Master. With Oliviah, it felt like she was back at square one, a Padawan who should be seen but only heard when deemed appropriate by more experienced Jedi. And for all Oliviah had started to open up about Master Fitan, the Jedi *still* wasn't sharing what was on her mind, or even why they were there. There was something off about the Path, although Matty couldn't fault the plan to open a soup kitchen, but with Oliviah keeping things so close to her chest, Matty didn't feel she could say how she felt. They weren't partners, nor would they ever be unless Oliviah started to talk. Perhaps she never would, which meant the only way Matty could really get to the heart of what had brought them to Dalna was to force the issue, broaching the subject before events overtook them.

The only question was how. As Master Leebon had pointed out on countless occasions, Matty had no problem speaking her mind, but there was something about Oliviah that had always been intimidating. Why was Matty so afraid? What did she think would happen if she challenged the Jedi Knight? A lightsaber duel? Well, that was ludicrous. The silent treatment, then? If so, how was that different from what she was enduring already?

Her thoughts were interrupted as the cart suddenly came to a halt, their driver bringing his snorting lyuna to a stop.

TWENTY-SEVEN

Oliviah pulled a corner of the waterproof covering aside and peeked out, checking before indicating silently for Matty to follow her. Zeveron slipped from the cart, landing on the wet ground like a cat. Matty, on the other hand, landed with the grace and elegance of a happabore, mud decorating her legs and robes as she splashed into the center of a puddle so large that it could have been a pond. She froze, appalled that she was more worried about Oliviah rolling her eyes than the possibility of alerting the cultists to their presence. Luckily, Oliviah merely beckoned for Matty to follow, pulling her robes tight around her so they didn't flap in the wind.

The carts had stopped in front of a weathered barn, the convoy halting so Cran could open its large doors. The creak of the hinges covered the sounds of Oliviah and Matty's sloppy footsteps as they ducked down the side of the structure, finding an open shelter filled with machinery and spare parts. They crouched behind a plow well past its prime and surveyed what they could see of the settlement, a collection of modest dwellings huddled against the rain, most of which appeared abandoned. The pathways between the huts were empty, although the lack of people probably had much to do with the weather. That said, Matty couldn't see a single light shining from any of the squat buildings. The windows were as dark as the clouds above, and the only sound was the rain and the lyuna's hooves as they were led inside.

"Over here," Matty whispered, spotting a crack in the

thick planks that made up the barn's walls. They made their way through the collection of farm equipment that time had forgotten and peered inside to see Cran and the others removing the lyuna's heavy harnesses before leading the creatures to troughs heaped with straw. She would have expected nothing less from a group that preached the sanctity of all beings connected to the Force, especially after a trying journey through the rain. Likewise, the time the three men spent rubbing the grazing animals dry was hardly surprising. However, Matty's eyebrows shot up as, husbandry done, Cran and his compatriots returned to the carts and, with the press of a button, disappeared into the floor, carts and all. A hydraulic lift in a tumbledown barn? What else was the Path hiding under the ground? Minutes later, the lift returned empty, the carts having been pulled clear by unseen hands. There was no way that Cran and the others could have shifted the burden themselves. Maybe they had droids down there, or more lyuna working in . . . what? An underground lair? That was ridiculous, surely. But there was nothing ridiculous about the skill required to build such a device. Oliviah and Matty stole into the barn at the first opportunity, finding a smaller entrance toward the back of the building. Unless you knew it was there, you'd never be able to locate the hidden lift. The join was flawless, Matty barely able to feel the edge as she ran her fingers across the ferrocrete floor.

The rest of the camp was just as innocuous. The buildings were as empty as Matty had suspected, with no sign that anyone lived in them at all. The two Jedi peered through windows and creaked open doors only to find basic furniture, although all the tables were empty and the beds free of covers. Unless the Path practiced the most frugal of lifestyles, Matty doubted anyone had inhabited any of these places for a long time. A thin layer of dust covered everything, which begged another question: Why *was* the Path buying up property in Ferdan when they had so many empty huts on their own land?

At least, the *majority* were empty. As they crept from building to building searching for signs of life, Matty spotted smoke curling from a chimney on the other side of the camp. They hurried across the ghost town, finding a cluster of buildings with dim lights flickering inside. Matty stepped onto the porch of the nearest structure and peered through the window, although there was nothing to see, plain curtains drawn on the other side of the dusty panes. Oliviah meanwhile headed to the next hut and tested the door, which opened easily. She nodded to Matty, who ducked under the covered porch and followed the older Jedi inside.

The interior of the hut couldn't have been more different from the other dwellings. Yes, the rustic furniture was the same, but there was a cloth on the small table in the front room, accompanied by a bunch of brightly colored flowers arranged in a simple wooden vase. A fire burned brightly in the hearth, and a candle flickered on a cabinet beside a freshly made bed in the next room.

Matty fought the urge to call out, to see if anyone was home. There was no need. They could both feel the presence of the living soul somewhere in the building, and there was no way to know how they would respond to two Jedi suddenly invading their strange abode. Not until, that is, they heard the unmistakable sound of retching coming from the back of the house. Matty moved before Oliviah could stop her, fully aware that they should still be cautious. Whoever was back there, on the other side of a door on the other side of the bedroom, was obviously in discomfort.

"Hello?" she called out, walking toward the door. "Are you all right? Do you need any assistance?"

"One minute," came the choked reply from the other side of the door. "I'll be right out."

Matty paused, Oliviah shooting her a chastising look as she joined her, waiting somewhat awkwardly in the strange room. Matty shrugged, fed up with feeling inadequate in the woman's presence. They were Jedi, weren't they? Wasn't it their mission to help those in distress?

Luckily, she didn't have to endure Oliviah's glare for long before there was the sound of water being sloshed down a pan and a Zeltron emerged from the bathroom, dabbing their lips with a flannel. Matty had only met a few Zeltrons in her time, but never one who looked so unwell. The woman's magenta complexion was waxy, and the whites of her bloodshot eyes were an unhealthy shade of yellow.

"Jedi?" she said, her throat thick. "You're the last people I expected to see here." She swayed slightly, pressing the cloth to a mouth that was breaking out with sores.

"Do you need to sit down?" Matty asked, moving to catch the woman, whose color had faded even more.

"Actually, yes," the Zeltron agreed, letting Matty help her to the edge of the bed, the squeak of the springs beneath the eiderdown confirming that at least one bed in the camp came with a mattress. "I seem to have picked up a bit of a bug. You'd think I would've learned by now."

"Learned what?" Oliviah asked, still keeping her distance while Matty crouched in front of the ill woman.

"To stock up on supplements before I jump on a space-hopper," the Zeltron replied, smiling wanly. "I've always been the same, getting sick the moment I leave the Core. My mother always said I was a bad traveler, that I spent the first few days of any vacation in bed. It's the only thing she and Suzi ever agreed on."

"Suzi?" Matty asked.

"My wife. She and mom never saw eye to eye, unless they were ganging up on me about my health." The Zeltron smiled, running her tongue over her teeth before dabbing her mouth again. "Sorry. I'm rambling. Spending half the morning with your face down the evac tube will do that to you. I really should stay at home."

"Then what brings you to Dalna?" Oliviah asked, her

eyes taking in the woman's clothes, a simple vest top, dyed dark with sweat, and a pair of loose-fitting pants tucked into heavy boots. "You don't belong to the Path."

"Nor am I looking to sign up." The Zeltron chuckled. "The name's Ric Farazi. I'm a journalist investigating the Open Hand. Or I was before . . ."

She nodded in the direction of the bathroom, both Jedi immediately getting her meaning.

"They've been looking after me. It's more embarrassing than anything, being hit with this. I would say it's something I ate at the boarding house in Ferdan, but I'm always the first to catch a bug."

"Not that you're in danger of spreading to others," Matty said. "There's no one else here."

Farazi pointed to the ground. "They're in the caves. Beneath the surface. All this up here, that's where they *used* to live, from what I can gather, but they've got more than a little paranoid recently. Not sure I helped, snooping around. They offered to set me up with a cave of my own when I started getting sick, but I didn't like the thought of being underground when I'm like this."

"We should get you back to town," Matty told her, fighting the urge to press her hand against Farazi's forehead to take her temperature. "Get you to a doctor."

Farazi nodded and licked her lips. "If you'd told me that yesterday, I would have argued with you, said I could sleep it off, but the way I'm feeling this morning . . ." She belched, the cloth immediately going back to her mouth. "Not even an audience with the Mother could persuade me otherwise."

"The Mother?" Oliviah finally moved, stepping forward and crouching beside Matty. "You've met her?"

"Not yet, but I was told that she would find me some time today, if her duties allowed."

"What duties?" Oliviah asked, more animated than Matty had seen so far on their journey.

Farazi didn't answer right away, asking instead for space so she could struggle to her feet. Both Jedi leaped up, Matty reaching to help, but the Zeltron waved her off, using the bed to lever herself up. "That's better," she said, not sounding it. "It comes in waves, you know?"

"But you haven't found out anything new about the Mother?" Oliviah asked, continuing to push.

"Anything more than the general tittle-tattle that has been filling the comm lines?" Farazi shook her head. "Not really. The Path members said she came to them out of the blue, claiming to have visions from the Force. Once accepted by the community, she rose to the top like cream, or scum in a sewer, depending on your point of view. The thing is, before I arrived, I heard rumors of a black market operation working out of Dalna. Antiquities, looted treasures, even weapons."

"And you think the Mother is involved?"

Ric dabbed the sores at the corner of her mouth, wincing slightly. "It's a hunch, nothing more. I certainly saw no sign of criminal activity in Ferdan, even when I started scratching beneath the surface. The place seems clean, the people even more so, but here's the thing. I had a contact at Port Haileap that told me messages from Dalna ceased a week or so before the trouble on Jedha, the exact time that the Path shipped off. Coincidence? I don't think so."

"But it could have been the Herald," Matty pointed out. "The Mother said he was responsible for the riot in Jedha City."

"Well, she would, wouldn't she? With all eyes on him . . ."

"She's free to carry out her operation here."

"Or on her ship. Have you seen the size of that thing? No wonder the Path can pay for repairs on Jedha. Don't be fooled by the cabins. There's money here, I can feel it, and I'd bet my admittedly laughable reputation that it didn't all come from generous patrons."

"Does the Path know the truth of what she's doing?" Oliviah asked, and there was something in the Jedi's eyes that disturbed Matty. Oliviah's interest in the Mother seemed to be increasing all the time.

"I don't know," Farazi replied. "The majority of them seem genuine enough. Borderline fanatics, yes, but they think a supernova shines out of the Mother's backside."

"So she could just be using them as a front?" Matty asked.

"Why don't you ask them yourself?" Farazi said, nodding toward the front of the house. "Maybe you'll have more luck than me."

Matty and Oliviah turned to see a group of younglings huddled together in the doorway, concern written all over their small faces. A Gran stood in the middle of the trio, holding a tray containing a covered bowl, accompanied by a human girl whose poor face bore puckered scars, and an Ithorian clasping a jug of water in his long fingers.

"Ric?" the Gran said, his voice full of questions. "Are those—"

"We are Jedi," Oliviah said quickly, raising her hand so the children could see they weren't a threat. "We don't mean you any harm."

"You shouldn't be here," the girl said, looking like she wanted to bolt. The last thing they needed was a bunch of kids raising the alarm that Jedi were skulking around the camp.

"What are your names?" Matty said, staying behind Oliviah but flashing what she hoped was her very best smile. "I'm Matty, and this is Oliviah."

"We're friends of Ric's," Oliviah added. "We hadn't heard from her for a while and wanted to check she was all right."

The ease with which lies came to the older Knight was worrying—and Matty had spent time with Tey Sirrek! Luckily, Farazi seemed willing to go with it.

"This is Tromak," the journalist said, pointing at the Gran before turning her attention to the human and Ithorian. "And that's Naddie and Boolan. They've been bringing me food. What is it today, kids?"

"Moss-goat soup," Tromak said, still seeming unsure.

"Sounds lovely," Farazi said, not sounding convinced. "Why don't you put it down on the table."

The Gran didn't move. "Your friend is very sick."

"The Mother said that she picked up something in Ferdan," Naddie added. "It's the imbalance of the Force."

Matty frowned. "The imbalance?"

But Oliviah was back on what seemed her favorite subject. "You know the Mother?"

The children nodded.

"Do you know where she comes from?"

"Comes from?" Naddie replied. "She doesn't come from anywhere. She's part of the Path, like us."

"Why do you want to know about the Mother?" Boolan asked, his vocalizer translating his native Ithorian.

"We're just interested, that's all," Matty cut in before Oliviah could continue her interrogation. "We're interested in everything about you."

"You're the enemy," the human girl said. "You abuse the Force."

"No," Matty said, concerned by the venom in her voice. "That's not true."

"You're the reason for the rains," Boolan agreed. "And Ric's illness."

"They're really not," Farazi told him, her voice wavering. "I've told you. It's just . . . just a . . ."

The reporter never completed her sentence. Matty moved

before Farazi's knees buckled, not needing a prompt from the Force to guess that the woman's condition was about to take a turn for the worse. She caught the Zeltron before she collapsed in a heap, her head lolling forward.

"We need to get her to a doctor."

"Agreed," Oliviah said, turning back to the children. "Do you have a medic?"

But the younglings were looking at them in horror. "The imbalance," the Ithorian croaked. "The Jedi are *killing* her."

"Killing her?" Matty couldn't believe how quickly *that* had escalated. "No. She's ill. She needs help."

And Farazi wasn't the only one as the younglings fled into the rain, soup slopping over the porch as the Gran threw the tray aside.

Soon the camp was teeming with life as the children screamed in unison: "The Jedi are here! The Jedi are here! They've killed Ric!"

TWENTY-EIGHT

The tunnel was not what any of them had expected. The complete opposite, in fact. The valley outside had been as barren as the forest had been lush, and no one could have been blamed for expecting that the cave Bokana had led them into would be the same. The Path of the Open Hand was accustomed to life underground, the caverns beneath their compound on Dalna the same as countless cave systems the galaxy over. This subterranean world couldn't have been more different. Yes, there were the expected stalagmites and stalactites, but the walls Bok's glow rod picked out weren't the smooth rock of home but passageways covered in what looked strangely like kelp, more usually found swaying at the bottoms of lakes and oceans than lining underground tunnels. Away from the water, you'd expect the vegetation to lie flat, draped over the rocks, and yet it stood, defying gravity with no perceptible stalk or spine. Even more miraculous, the passageway wasn't as dark as they'd expected. Bokana's lamp helped, as did the other rods Sunshine dished out, but their way was lit dimly by tiny glowing bugs that flitted around them like midges, never biting or even brushing against them. The beating of their minute wings was less a buzz and more a tinkling, like the wind chimes Marda had over her bed back on Dalna, a rare present from Yana from one of her missions.

Once again, little about this planet made sense, not that Marda gave much thought to these latest curiosities. Her mind was consumed with the realization that Bokana was somehow using the Force to guide them deeper underground. He was striding ahead, the fragment of shell held out in front of him as if it were a dowsing rod, muttering repeatedly under his breath that they were on "the right path."

The right path! The only path they should be treading was the Path of the Open Hand, the philosophy she had dedicated her life to, forswearing any misuse of the Force for the sake of the galaxy. And yet the Mother had sent Calar on the mission, expecting the Setaran to make use of his . . . what? His *talent*? His *profanity*? And what good had it done them? Calar had nearly gotten them all killed. If anything, the tragedy that had played out in the *Scupper*'s cockpit had only proved the Path was right, while also adding the slight concern that the Mother would so willingly abandon such truth to get what she wanted.

"Are you *sure* you know where you're going?" Ort asked, articulating the question the rest of the group had been thinking. "I mean, I'm seeing a lot of weird crud but no eggs."

"Just through here," Bokana said, squeezing through a gap barely larger than his body in the wall ahead.

"But how do you know?" Galamal asked, although Marda knew the answer and it sickened her. Bokana was just like Calar, just like Kevmo. He was an abuser of the Force who even now was bending its energy to his will. But that wasn't his worst betrayal, not by a long shot.

Sunshine went to follow the Ovissian, but Marda pushed ahead, squeezing through the gap to have it out with the person she'd thought she knew. Instead, she found him looking at her, face split in a stupid smile.

"See, what did I tell you?"

Behind her, Sunshine puffed his way through the aperture in the rock and clapped his hands in glee.

"I knew it," he wheezed, slapping Bokana on the back. "What did I say? The boy knows what he's doing."

"I must have missed that," Galamal said, appearing through the gap, although a similar smile spread over her reptilian features.

Bokana had been as good as his word. The cavern had several different entrances, all notably wider than the narrow gap they'd used, but that wasn't what Sunshine and his team were gaping at. The walls of the chamber were pitted with natural alcoves sunk deep into the kelp-covered rock, and each contained at least two of the large eggs Sunshine had presented to the Mother. Marda tried to count them, but there were too many, each sparkling in the light of the glow bugs. She reached out to touch the biggest of the three gems nearest to her. It was cool against her skin, but she pulled her hand away sharply as it moved. Was that a creature inside, waiting to hatch, an animal just like the Leveler? Was every egg incubating such a beast? If so, and if each had only a fraction of the Leveler's power, the Path would be safe from the Jedi for a very long time. Nothing would be able to harm them again.

But at what cost?

Marda's gaze drifted down. There was something ahead of her, a shadow in the carpet of thick kelp. She picked her way forward, holding her glow rod at arm's length as the rest of the group made plans for how to gather the eggs.

"We'll never get the sled through that gap," Tareen said. Ort agreed and wondered if they could find their way to one of the other openings, all of which looked big enough to handle the floating platform.

"We haven't time for that," Sunshine said, insisting that they simply pass the eggs one by one through the cleft in the wall.

"What's the hurry?" Galamal asked. "It's not like you've got a working ship to get back to."

"What about the *Bonecrusher*?" Sunshine asked.

"I told you, there's not enough room for everyone."

"And if Shea and the others can't get the *Silverstreak* space-worthy?" Ort cut in.

"Galamal won't leave us behind," Sunshine insisted, not sounding convinced. "But whatever state the *Streak* is in when we get back, I'd rather not hang around. Those are a lot of eggs."

"Which is a good thing, right?"

"Yes, until you remember that something had to lay them."

A chill ran through Ort's voice. "Something like the Leveler."

Marda didn't have to turn around to imagine Sunshine nodding. "And the Leveler is little more than a baby itself, relatively speaking."

It wasn't a pleasant thought. The Leveler was disturbing enough, but there was no telling how large a fully grown adult might be. As she crept forward, Marda's imagination went into overdrive, picturing a gigantic version of the creature filling the cavern, its mandibles writhing beneath a pair of staring eyes. She shivered, the glow rod tumbling from her grip as she stumbled at the edge of a yawning chasm stretched out in front of her. She slipped, crying out, but a strong hand grabbed her arm before she could follow the rod into the abyss.

"What do you think you're doing?" Bokana asked breathlessly as she clung to him. "There's no telling how deep that thing goes."

"Really?" she said, remembering herself and pushing away from his arms. "I thought you knew everything these days."

"What?"

She wanted to punch him, to pound against the same chest she'd found so comforting not two hours before.

"You lied to me!"

"When?"

"From the moment we met!"

"I have no idea what you're talking about."

Marda held out a palm. "Give it to me."

"What?"

"The fragment of shell. I assume you still have it?"

"Yes," he said, fishing it from his pocket. "But I don't see what—"

She snatched the fragment from him and squeezed it between her hands.

"Careful! It's sharp!"

It was too late. The edges had already sliced into her palms, but she didn't care. All she wanted to do was feel something from the fragment, for it to prove that the power Bokana had suddenly manifested had come from the gem, not him, but there was nothing but pain from the cuts and a sinking feeling in the pit of her stomach.

She flung it aside, the fragment spinning into the pit after her glow rod.

"Hey! Why did you do that?"

"What does it matter? It did its job, didn't it? Or rather, *you* did."

She turned, looking down into the blackness of the hole that had almost claimed her.

"What *is* this, Marda?" Bok said, lowering his voice and moving closer with a tenderness that made her want to throw *him* after the shell. "What's going on? Is it the planet? The mission?"

"No, it's you," she said, pushing him away, her eyes as hard as his were kind. "Have you any idea how much I wanted it to be the shell? How much I hoped it was the reason you found this place?" She didn't give him time to answer before she turned back toward him, blood dripping through her clenched fingers. "But I felt nothing except this." She held up her hand so he could see the gashes. "It didn't speak to me or tell me anything, other than I should never have trusted you." Keeping her voice down was taking all her control, even as she felt the blood running down her arm in rivulets. She wanted to shout, to bawl in his face, but didn't want the others to hear, not yet. "When were you going to tell me?"

"Tell you what?"

"What's really going on! About you and the Force."

Bokana sighed, shaking his horned head. "I honestly don't know."

"You're just like the others. Like Kevmo and Calar. You abuse the Force without a thought for what damage you are causing."

"It's not like that," he said, reaching for her.

"Isn't it?" she said, slapping his hand away, her blood splattering across his arm. "Then tell me what it *is* like, Bokana. Tell me how long you've been hiding your 'talent.' Since Dalna? Since Jedha?"

"I haven't been hiding anything. Not really."

"Not really?"

"I mean, there have been times when I've known things would happen before they did, found things that others thought were lost."

"Like knowing which fruit to eat in the forest," Marda challenged him, struggling to keep her fury in check, "and which to leave alone? No wonder you could lead us into the caves. No wonder you knew what was here."

"I always thought it was just coincidences, that's all," he insisted, but Marda wasn't listening. A terrible thought had occurred to her, making her blood flow cold.

"None of it was true, was it?"

Bokana's face creased in confusion. "What?"

"Us. The way we were on the ship. In the forest. The way we felt about each other."

"Marda," he said, reaching for her. "Please . . ."

She batted his hand away again, not wanting to listen. She felt sick, her head spinning. "You *made* me feel those things. I knew it wasn't right. I knew it was too soon. I knew it that first time we nearly kissed on the *Gaze*, and, Force save me, I knew it on the *Scupper*, too. I tried to fight it, but I couldn't. How do I know it wasn't you, all this time, playing with my mind?"

Hurt flashed across Bokana's features. "I couldn't. I wouldn't. I promise you, this is all new to me, the way things suddenly make sense, but one thing that has *never* changed is the way I feel about you. I felt it the moment I saw you on Jedha. And yes, when we returned to the *Gaze*. I thought you felt the same."

She turned away, unable to even look at him. "Leave me alone."

"Marda, I can't do that."

"I said, leave me alone!"

Everyone looked up when she shouted. Of course they did. She might as well have used a loudspeaker the way her voice echoed around the chamber.

"Is everything all right?" Sunshine asked, one of the gems in his pudgy hands.

"You better help them," Marda said quietly.

"No, we need to talk about this," Bok insisted, but she had nothing else to say.

"Well, if you won't, I will," she said, raising her voice to address the others as she marched purposefully toward Sunshine. "How many have we got so far?"

The prospector took a few steps to meet her, keeping

his voice down, his eyes flicking from Marda's stony face to Bokana, standing where she'd left him.

"You *sure* you're okay? Do we have a problem?"

She shook her head. "No problem. There's a sinkhole or something back there, so we'll have to be careful collecting eggs from the other side of the cavern." She stopped, looking Sunshine dead in the eye, almost challenging him to press the point. He didn't, although his gaze dropped to her hand, and she wondered if he could see the blood dripping down her fingers. She pulled her hands behind her back, just in case.

"That shouldn't be an issue," he said warily, looking back up at her face. "There's more than enough on this side. More than the sled can carry anyway, although we have some bags we could fill. We should be able to get two or three in each. Four if we're lucky."

"How many eggs did the Mother ask for?" Marda asked.

"You tell me. You're the Guide, after all."

Was she? Did she even deserve that title? What had Ric Farazi called her? A shark with little bite. Perhaps the Mother had been right, after all. Perhaps she wasn't ready.

But if the Mother had known about Calar . . . had she known about Bokana, as well? Known he could abuse the Force? Doubts whirled around Marda's mind. About herself. About Elecia. Everything had seemed so easy before, and now . . . now . . .

She felt tears coming but remembered her promise not to cry in front of Sunshine Dobbs. She needed to get away from there, away from Bokana. If he wanted to set up home on the planet, he could do it on his own.

Marda stepped around Sunshine, grabbing one of the gems and yanking it from its nest, the egg coming loose with a sucking noise. She joined the others passing the eggs through to Tareen and Ort, not looking up as Bokana started to gather eggs, as well. He tried to talk to her as they moved back and forth, but she snubbed his hushed advances, worried that she'd start screaming at him and never stop. They had a job to do and that was the end of it. Everything else could wait.

Soon the crates on the sled were full, but the job still wasn't done. Sunshine produced a number of empty sacks. Marda sought out a clutch of eggs she could pry loose, one as far away from Bokana as possible. Even then, she could feel his eyes on her as he cast hurt looks. What business did he have being hurt? She was the one who'd been wronged, not him. But a few furtive glances were the least of their worries.

At first, Marda didn't pay much attention to the sounds of scrabbling. She put it down to Galamal, who had taken to climbing up the empty shelves to retrieve the eggs that nestled on the higher levels, her claws scraping against the rocks. Yet the noises continued after the Barabel stopped climbing.

"What *is* that?" Galamal asked, her head cocked to one side.

"I thought it was just me who could hear it," Sunshine added.

"It's coming from the pit," Bokana said, and as much as Marda hated to admit it, the Ovissian was right. The scrabbling was getting louder by the minute and was now accompanied by a strange clicking noise.

Klakka-klakka.

Klakka-klakka.

Marda had been carefully placing the eggs in her pack but shoved the last one roughly in through its neck. "Is it something climbing up?"

"Maybe we've gathered enough eggs," Sunshine said, swinging his pack onto his back. "We should go."

"You think?" Galamal snorted.

"Do you think it's the mother?" Marda asked, closing her pack with a sharp pull of the string. She tested its weight. Individually, the eggs were relatively light, but with three inside the sack, it was heavy. She would never have managed four.

Sunshine was already cramming his ample girth through the cleft in the rock. "Don't know and not sure I want to find out."

The noises got louder still. Closer still.

Scrabble. Scrabble.

Klakka-klakka.

Sunshine disappeared, and Marda made for the gap, Galamal waving her through. The Barabel's pack was on her back, her rifle aimed squarely at the pit.

"Here," Marda said, passing her bulky sack through to Ort. "Take this."

"Got it," the Reesarian said, but the bag caught on the rock as Ort tried to pull it through.

"Hang on," Marda said, trying to see how the pack had gotten snagged, but Ort didn't wait, the eggs grinding together in the sack as she heaved.

"Careful!"

"I *am* being careful," she told Marda, but the bag still wouldn't budge.

"What's the holdup?" Galamal said, and at first Marda assumed she was talking to them, until the questions continued. "Bokana, what are you doing, man? Get back from there."

The Ovissian was standing perilously close to the sinkhole, his back toward them, arms hanging loose at his sides.

"The Under-Dwellers," he murmured, not turning around. "They're coming for us. They want out."

Whether she was furious at him or not, Marda didn't like the dreamlike, almost drugged slur to his words. "Bokana," she said. "We need to go."

"And they need to survive. To spread. A blight upon our lands. Upon our lives."

"Bokana." Now it was Galamal who issued the warning, her gun moving subtly from the pit and toward the back of Bok's head.

"No, Galamal, don't," Marda shouted, leaving Ort to cope with the bag so she could place a hand on the captain's scaly arm. Galamal shrugged it off, her aim not wavering.

"Not now, princess. Your boyfriend is *really* starting to worry me!"

"He's *not* my boyfriend."

"I don't care what he is. He needs to step back from the hole."

The scrabbling was becoming more frantic, that strange chittering underlining Bokana's words.

"They're coming."

Klakka-klakka.

"We're doing what they've wanted."

Klakka-klakka.

"They're going to kill us all!"

Sunshine was right. They needed to go, but whatever she felt about Bokana, she wasn't about to leave him there or let Galamal shoot him in the head.

"Bokana, that's enough," she said, hurrying toward him. "We need to move, now!"

She tried to spin him around, but he wouldn't shift.

"The blight. The blight will come."

Scrabble, scrabble, scrabble. Klakka-klakka-klakka.

"Bokana!"

"The blight will spread and *nothing* will be able to contain it."

Finally, she managed to pull him around, gasping as she saw the expression of pure fear on his face—fear and madness.

"The Force will be chained, Marda. The Force no more. Death to the Force."

Marda stumbled back. Those were Calar's words spilling from lips that had tasted so sweet but were now slack and drooling.

Marda clasped her hands to her ears as a shriek burst from the pit, a clawed hand following a second later.

TWENTY-NINE

Yana had no intention of training the Path for battle, not how the Mother intended. Yana had said what she said for two reasons: to get as far away from the listening chamber as possible and to be given free rein to investigate the comings and goings in the caves with Elecia's blessing.

The results were worrying.

The caves were bustling with Path members building barricades near the various entrances and stockpiling weapons—actual weapons, from blasters to stun batons—that had either been smuggled into the compound in recent days or—and this was where it got *really* alarming—had been part of a hidden arsenal that seemed to have existed for quite some time.

Then there were the plans to expand the already sprawling caves. Yana had discovered Elder Dinube rather gingerly checking through a cache of detonite-based charges, another new delivery. When quizzed, the Harch told Yana it was all part of a scheme to open up a previously unexplored network to the north of the system, giving the Path even more space if they needed to survive underground for longer periods. She'd pressed Dinube for details, but the usually genial arachnoid had only snapped at her that it was the will of the Force, immediately shutting down the conversation.

"The will of the Force?" Kor had echoed as Yana walked away. "Sounds like paranoia to me."

As paranoid as listening to a voice that Yana knew wasn't really there? Maybe, but there was no escaping the fact that the tension in the caves was mounting, which made it all the more worrying that Marda seemed to have vanished completely. The only person who had any recollection of seeing her was Utalir, one of Marda's former Littles. With tears in her eyes, she had told Yana that Marda yelled at them before Sunshine Dobbs's convoy set off for Planet X. That was another concern. Marda would never have shouted at her precious Littles in the past. Utalir hadn't seen Marda since and, when pressed, revealed that the altercation had happened at the makeshift landing bay set up in the middle of the camp. According to Utalir, Marda had been watching the ships before they took off on their mission. Yana didn't need Kor to point out the suspicion growing inside her. If Marda had fallen out of favor with the Mother, she would have done anything to rebuild that trust, even jump on a ship on a fool's errand to gather monster eggs.

Yana stopped in the middle of a damp corridor and drew a breath. She was catastrophizing, filling in the gaps of what she actually knew with the worst possible scenarios. The only problem was that it all made sense. The Path was preparing for war, and Marda—poor zealous Marda—just wouldn't have done the right thing and run for the hills. She would have only gotten herself in deeper. She always did.

"Sounds like a family trait to me."

Yana closed her eyes and ran a hand across the wall's dark-pink rock to ground herself.

"Not now, Kor."

"You're the same, the two of you. You both have the opportunity to escape, yet you won't cut the cord. This place will kill you."

"Like it killed you?"

There was no response. Figment of her imagination or not, Kor never liked to lose an argument, a trait that seemed to have continued beyond the grave. Maybe she'd been more like her father than she wanted to admit, a father who was currently waiting for Yana's report back in Ferdan. Yana opened her eyes and turned, ready to head to the surface, already rehearsing her excuses if she was challenged along the way about why she was leaving. Then she stopped, chilled, thinking for a moment that she could hear Kor crying.

Why couldn't her subconscious leave her alone?

But the sound wasn't a dream, and it certainly wasn't a ghost. It was coming from farther down the corridor, through a door that was slightly ajar—ragged sobs that made Yana's heart ache, although she couldn't understand why.

She realized as soon as she gingerly pushed the door open, poking her head into the room. There was a reason she had thought it was Kor, something that had nothing to do with the afterlife, even if such a place existed. The chamber on the other side of the door was small and stark, a mattress resting in an alcove carved into the rock itself. The air was thick with a strange musty smell like something had gone bad, but there was no food in the room, either on the floor or next to the basin of scum-covered water set into the opposite wall. There was a wooden table beside the bed, but that contained only a solitary glass of cold tea and a small holoprojector. No, the smell was coming from the body lying on the mattress, face turned to the wall and shoulders hunching as they cried.

As *she* cried.

Yana hoped that she was right about Kor, that her girlfriend's spirit's continued presence was only the result of her grief-stricken mind. No one needed to see this, not even the dead.

"Opari?"

When she'd last seen Kor's mother, Opari Plouth had been doing better, the terrible wasting disease that had ravaged her body halted, if not cured, by a course of medication supplied by one of the Mother's generous benefactors. Now the Nautolan was little more than a skeleton, her head-tendrils curled beneath her head like a pillow.

Yana put a hand on Opari's shoulder, wincing as she felt bones beneath the woman's almost translucent skin.

"Opari, it's Yana."

"Yana?"

When Yana heard Kor's voice, it was close to her, still strong, even in death. Opari's voice was like a whisper on a dying breeze.

The Nautolan tried to turn over, the movement causing her to cough violently.

"Here," Yana said, grabbing the beaker of tea. "Drink this."

Opari lashed out with a fragile arm, knocking the glass from Yana's hand. It smashed, splattering its contents over the unswept floor.

"I don't want to drink. I want her. I want my baby."

For a moment, Opari's watery eyes met Yana's, and her expression became urgent. "Is she with you?" she asked, grabbing Yana's arms with emaciated webbed fingers. "Have you brought her back?"

"Kor's gone, Opari," Yana told her, immediately regretting her tactless if painfully truthful answer.

"She's gone," the woman wailed. "They've all gone. Kor. Werth. Left me alone. Never coming back."

"No." Yana couldn't bring back Kor, no matter how much she wanted to, but she could do something about Opari's errant husband.

"The Herald is on Dalna, Opari. Do you understand me? I can bring him to you."

But Opari wasn't listening. She had curled into a ball, lost to her tears. "They left me. Left me alone. Left me to die."

For a moment, Yana considered gathering the sick woman into her arms and carrying her out of the caves. Maybe she could take her to Ferdan in a lyuna cart or carry her the whole way on foot. It wasn't as if there was much of her. Yet, while she could make excuses for her own sudden departure, there was no way she could smuggle Opari back to town without people asking questions. Not that anyone was looking after the sick woman, Yana thought angrily. Was it a punishment for the Herald's alleged crimes or simple neglect, Opari having merely outlived her usefulness? Certainly, with both Werth and Kor gone, there was no need to secure the expensive drugs Opari needed to stay well. Either way, Werth had been right to worry. The conditions in the chamber were disgusting. He would lose his mind if he saw his wife like this, and as for Kor . . .

"I won't be long, I promise," Yana told Opari gently, and after adjusting the woman's sweat-drenched robes, she hurried back into the corridor.

THIRTY

The creature's roar finally broke whatever spell had held Bokana in its power. The Ovissian looked up at the monster that had reared from the pit, the color draining from his face as Galamal opened fire.

"Run!" the Barabel commanded, her bolts bouncing harmlessly from the abomination's boney carapace. A muscled knot of a body towered over Bokana on four spiderlike legs. Smaller arms hung from its midriff, taloned fingers flexing as its long segmented tail thrashed like a flail. Worst of all was its head, with a cluster of bulbous black eyes that were set above yawning jaws that bristled with sharp teeth.

Marda grabbed Bokana's hand as the monster bellowed, its anger directed at Galamal, whose shots were having little effect other than infuriating their target. The creature sprang forward, leaping over Bokana and Marda as they raced toward the gap in the wall. According to Sunshine, Galamal had been a gifted hunter and a ruthless captain, but she was no match for the horror that dropped on her, snapping her spine beneath one of its feet. Marda heard Galamal's terrified cry cut short, followed by a splintering of bone and the slurp of a long tongue plunged into a once beating, now still heart.

"Get that out of the way," Marda shouted, pushing against the pack that Ort was still trying to haul through the gap. Who cared if the gems cracked? Better a few alien eggs than her skull. The bag finally cleared the narrow space as Bokana emptied his blaster into the creature that had already finished its meal.

Marda swung her fighting staff from her back and propelled it through the gap, narrowly missing Ort, who thrust a leathery hand through the cleft to grab Marda's wrist. Marda could have managed but accepted the help gratefully, ignoring the sting from the rock that scraped her cheek as she was yanked from the chamber. Sunshine and Tareen were already running back to the surface, pushing the heavily loaded sled, and for once Marda couldn't blame them for saving their own skin first.

"Go!" she yelled at Ort, the Reesarian needing little in

the way of encouragement. Ort scooped up Marda's sack and took to her heels, the glow bugs parting as she raced after the others.

Marda snatched up her staff, yelling through the gap as Bokana continued firing. "Bok! Get out of there!"

He backed toward the exit, carrying not just his own bag but the sack Galamal had packed before her messy demise. He'd never make it lugging that much weight, broad shoulders or not.

"Just leave them," Marda shouted, but he didn't listen.

He had reached the gap, still firing at the spider-thing, aiming not for its body but its hideous face, not that the blasts seemed to be inflicting any damage at all.

"Take this," he yelled, shoving the first pack through, the second following as Marda pulled it clear. Then it was Bokana's turn, walking sideways through the gap so his horns cleared the rock, his other hand firing blindly. He slipped through as though oiled, remarkable for someone so large, but screamed in agony as he turned to run, something long and sharp bursting through his right shoulder. It took Marda a moment to realize what it was, barbs locking the monster's tongue in place before the creature pulled Bokana back, pinning him against the wall. "Get away," he wheezed as the blaster tumbled from his suddenly useless arm, but Marda shook her head. She reached for the vibroknife on Bokana's belt and pulled it free of its sheath. Trying to avoid the barbs, she grabbed the squirming tip of the tongue and, activating the knife, sliced through the thick muscle. The Under-Dweller howled in pain on the other side of the wall, Bokana joining in as the tongue retracted. There was no way to know what damage the barbs had caused on their return journey, but Bokana didn't squander the chance she'd given him. He lumbered forward, grabbing one of the egg packs, refusing to listen as Marda told him to leave it where it was. She grabbed the other, and they ran as the creature threw itself repeatedly against the wall, the cleft widening. They hadn't gotten far before the wall gave way, rocks streaming after them as the monster burst through, its massive body filling the cramped passage as it roared in victory. Any hope Marda had that the tunnel would be too small for the creature evaporated as the Under-Dweller surged after them, all four of its legs skittering against the walls as its muscular arms grabbed for them. Bokana stumbled, nearly falling but shooting out a hand to steady himself.

"Don't stop!" she barked at him.

"I'm not about to!"

And all the time the Under-Dweller bayed in anger and . . . frustration?

Marda glanced back and gasped, not quite believing her eyes. The kelp-like vegetation, so soft and tactile, was sticking to the creature's claws and attaching itself to the Under-Dweller's arched back. The creature struggled and thrashed as the glow bugs swarmed around its monstrous head, blinding eyes accustomed to the dark and flying deep into its maw, causing the creature to hack and choke. It was as if the organisms were fighting the Under-Dweller, or at least giving the pair of them the chance they needed to escape. Like the rest of the planet, that made no sense, but Marda didn't care as long as they got away.

The Under-Dweller was still screaming as they bolted out into the blazing light of the valley. Up to then, Marda had been operating on pure adrenaline, pushing her body beyond its usual limits to escape the creature, but the sudden glare of the surface almost stopped her in her tracks. She kept going, her survival instinct kicking in, but as her vision cleared, she saw that Bokana hadn't been so lucky. His legs must have buckled the second they were outside, the pack flying from his shoulder as he'd crashed to the ground. Marda tried to pull him up, but he was dead weight.

"Just leave me," he wheezed, but Marda couldn't do that, not even after everything she'd said to him. The others had almost crossed the gulley, but Sunshine was running back toward them. For a moment, Marda thought he was about to help her with Bok, but instead the prospector grabbed the bag the Ovissian had thrown clear.

"What are you doing?" Marda shouted at him as he pulled her own pack from her shoulder.

"Easing your load," he said, sweat running from beneath his ridiculous hat. "I'll take the eggs. You help the big guy."

She had no time to argue or even consider if she believed the obvious lie. Sunshine was already halfway across to Ort and Tareen, who were attempting to shove the sled back up the slope, its weighed-down repulsors dangerously near the edge of the path.

In front of Marda was freedom and behind was the horror in the tunnels, clawing its way ever closer in the darkness. She could run, leaving Bokana to his fate, but then what kind of person would she be? The Force would be free only if people like her stayed on the path she had chosen, the path that offered gifts freely given, including the gift of life.

"Take this," she said, banging down the end of her fighting staff in front of Bokana. "Use it as a crutch and put your injured arm around me."

He did neither; he only gasped for breath, his face dangerously pale.

"I didn't lie," he wheezed, not looking up. "I didn't lie to you. I would never lie to you."

"I don't care," she screamed at him, which was a lie in itself. "You could tell me you're a Jedi and it wouldn't matter because any minute now a monster is going to burst out of that tunnel and tear us both to pieces unless you move that pathetic excuse of a body right this minute."

The rebuke worked. As the roars got louder, Bokana grabbed hold of the staff, grunting as he pulled himself up. Marda slipped under his other arm, gripping his waist and trying not to think of the blood still pouring down his chest or the rattle in his breath. Together they hobbled to the bottom of the path, the others already halfway to the surface.

Bokana coped better with the slope than Marda had expected, and they were almost at the top when the Under-Dweller burst from the cave entrance, its back and legs smothered in the vegetation that had somehow saved their lives. The creature wailed as the light hit its eyes but charged on regardless, leaping up when it reached the bottom of the slope. The path was too small for such a large beast, but that didn't stop it, its claws scrabbling at the rock face as it closed the distance between them.

"We're not going to make it."

"Yes, we will," Bokana told her, his voice stronger than it had any right to be, considering the condition he was in. "We're not on our own."

"What do you mean?"

"In the caves. Something else. A protector."

"Protecting what?"

"We *will* get off this planet," he said, ignoring the question. "I promise you."

Behind them, the Under-Dweller slipped, falling back, the rock face crumbling beneath its claws. They'd reached the top by the time it had resumed its chase, the forest in front of them, along with the sight of Sunshine Dobbs disappearing into the trees with the two packs bobbing on his back. Marda and Bokana followed, legs burning and chests tight, convinced that the Under-Dweller was about to pounce at any moment. The last thing they wanted to do was look back, as if somehow seeing the monster would root them to the spot, and yet Marda glimpsed something out of the corner of her eye as they cleared the slope, a flash of blue streaking across the floor of a ravine. Another monster or the protector Bokana had mentioned? It didn't matter anymore. All that mattered was getting away.

THIRTY-ONE

Yana questioned the decision to leave Opari behind all the way to the surface, memories of past times spent with Kor's mother flashing through her mind: the meals, the festivals, most of which Yana had tried her best to avoid but now wished she'd made more effort to attend.

Up top, the rain had stopped, although the swollen clouds promised the break was only a temporary reprieve. There were more Path members in the camp now, a small crowd gathering around one particular hut, a dwelling usually reserved for visitors. There were shouts, raised voices, and an argument well underway.

Yana called out as one of the Littles ran past, the Ithorian she had seen earlier.

"Hey, what's going on?"

The Ithorian didn't stop, his little legs splashing through puddles as he raced for the caves. "Jedi," was all his translator shouted back, repeating the word a second time as if it explained everything.

That was the last thing they needed, especially with paranoia in the camp at an all-time high, but sure enough, the group was crowding around a tall, brown-skinned Jedi who was doing her best to calm the situation.

"What's going on?" Yana asked, pushing her way to the front of the mob.

"The Littles found them sneaking about," a Quarren Path member replied, her tentacles writhing.

"We were attempting to make contact with your leader," the Jedi claimed.

"Liar," the Quarren shouted. "All Jedi are liars. You abuse the Force."

"Look," someone else said, and a younger Jedi, a Twi'lek with a Padawan's braid made of delicate twine curled around one of her head-tails, pushed her way past the older Knight. "What matters is that we have a sick woman in here."

"Matthea . . ." the other Jedi scolded, but the Twi'lek stood her ground.

"I'm sorry, Oliviah, but it needs to be said." She turned

to the Quarren, addressing her directly. "Your guest is sick, really sick, and we need to get her back to Ferdan."

"If she's sick, we can deal with her. We have medics."

"Who haven't done a very good job so far, have they?"

"Padawan Cathley," the older Knight—Oliviah—cut in. "I'm not sure insulting these good people is the way to achieve our goals. I'm sure if we explain what . . ."

The Jedi Knight suddenly swayed, throwing up a hand to grab Matthea's shoulder to support herself.

"Oliviah, what is—" the Padawan started before her eyes rolled back in their sockets.

The crowd immediately stepped back, the Quarren slamming into Yana.

"What's happening to them? Are they casting a spell?"

"Jedi don't cast spells."

"They're wizards!"

"They're *ill*," Yana said, pushing to address the two Jedi directly, both of whom looked as if they were about to collapse in a heap. "Hey. Hey, are you all right?"

The Twi'lek—Matthea—grabbed Yana's hand, squeezing it tight. Too tight! "Something's wrong. Something's very wrong."

"With you?"

"With the world. Everything's spinning. I can't stop it."

"Let's get you sat down," Yana said, trying to guide the girl toward the wooden bench beside the open door.

"No," the older Jedi shouted, throwing up a shaking hand. "Leave her alone."

Yana was pushed back, not by the Jedi, but by an unseen force.

By *the* Force.

"There!" the Quarren screamed. "What did I tell you?"

"It's okay," Yana said, throwing up her hands to try to stop the mob from turning ugly.

"No, it's not . . ." Oliviah snarled, sweat beading on her brow. "What have you done to us?"

"We've done nothing," Yana promised as the Padawan found the bench for herself, falling onto it and holding the arm as if she were caught in the middle of a groundquake. "You're ill. Perhaps you caught something from whoever is in there."

"Then maybe we should put them *all* in quarantine," came a familiar voice from the back. The Path parted to reveal the Mother and the Leveler padding beside her. Suddenly, everything became clear. The Jedi weren't sick; they were being affected by that damned monster, which looked ready to pounce, only the influence of the combined rods in the Mother's hand holding it back.

Oliviah turned to face the Mother, the movement finally overbalancing her so she dropped down to a knee. Elecia smirked as if she'd been waiting for this day all her life, a Jedi kneeling at her feet.

"You . . ." Oliviah wheezed, squinting as if it was difficult to focus. "You're here."

"Of course I'm here," the Mother replied, smiling sweetly. "This is my home. You are the ones who don't belong, but the Force demands we care for anyone who is brought to our door, even those who misuse its gifts." She turned to the others. "Take them down into the caves, the journalist, too. We will nurse them back to health if that is what the Force demands of us."

"No," Yana said, putting herself between the Jedi and the Mother. "If they are ill, then taking them into the caverns will be a mistake. We have no idea what disease they might be harboring."

The Mother reached down and stroked the Leveler's head, the beast almost vibrating with hunger. "Oh, Yana, we know exactly what's wrong with them."

"But how can we be sure?" she replied, dropping her voice so only Elecia could hear. "Ignoring the fact that we have a *journalist* in the camp, if she's as sick as the Jedi say, there might still be a threat to the Path."

The Mother's expression hardened. "There is no threat, trust me."

"But how do you know?" Yana was almost nose to nose with the woman, a danger to be sure but one worth taking. "And what if more Jedi come looking for them?"

"We will be ready."

"Before Sunshine returns from his little jaunt? Sending them away will buy us time, Mother, time we desperately need if the defenses your people have been building are anything to go by."

"'*Your* people,' Yana?" Elecia purred. "Don't you mean *our* people?"

She ignored the challenge. There wasn't time for that. "The Jedi are a complication, one we could do without. Let me take them to Doc Nindle in town."

Elecia's eyebrows shot up. "You?"

"Just in case you're right. Just in case they're not sick and need . . . handling. . . ." Yana's implication was clear.

"You'd see to it yourself."

Yana nodded, anything to get away. "Far from the camp . . . where they can't be linked to us."

"You'd have to be careful."

"I'm *always* careful."

The Mother looked at her for a long time and then at the crowd, who had all retreated to a safe distance to avoid contracting whatever plague was making two Jedi whimper and shake.

"Fine. Do it. Take them, and then come straight back. Do you understand me? We have much to do."

You better believe it, Yana thought as she called for the Quarren to fetch a cart.

THIRTY-TWO

At first, Marda had thought they'd gotten lucky. She'd spent the first few minutes in the forest expecting the Under-Dweller to come crashing after them, splintering the trees as easily as it had rocks, but the farther they ran, the more obvious it became that they weren't being followed.

Had the creature fallen from the slope? Was it lying broken at the bottom of the ravine? Marda honestly didn't care, which was probably the intoxicating effect of the forest. The energy of the place had immediately revived their weary limbs, so much that Bokana no longer leaned heavily on her. He still used her staff, slamming it into the ground, but was actually running instead of hobbling, and his wound, while severe, was no longer bleeding or slowing him down. Was the forest regenerating him, just as it had already healed the cuts on her palms? Maybe he'd be whole by the time they made it back to the ship, as long as that creature didn't catch up with them. He certainly seemed as agile as before, leaping over roots and scrambling up slopes. Tareen and Ort were way ahead of them, the eggs clacking together in their crates.

In a while, they came across a fork in the path, Tareen instinctively swerving to the right.

"Where are you going?" Ort asked, making a grab for the sled. "The *Silverstreak* is straight ahead, thataway!"

"No," the Duros insisted, swerving farther so Ort's hand missed. "You go back to that wreck, but I'm heading for the *Bonecrusher*."

"Galamal is dead," Marda said, catching up with them.

"So?" Tareen shrugged. "*I'm* a pilot. I can get us out of here."

"And back through the Veil?" Ort asked.

"The return journey shouldn't be so bad," Sunshine said, panting heavily. "It makes sense. You head for the *Bonecrusher*—"

"Taking the repulsor sled?" Ort interrupted.

"Taking the repulsor sled," Sunshine confirmed, "while we see how Shea and the others are doing with the *Streak*."

"Sounds like a plan," Tareen agreed, starting to move off, but Sunshine slapped a thick hand down on the sled. "Just promise me you won't fire a thruster until you hear that our ride is space-worthy."

Tareen's crooked teeth showed in a wicked smile. "You worried I'll leave you behind?"

"I would if the situation was reversed," Sunshine admitted, "but I'm a grizzled old spacer and you're a member of a spiritual community."

"I thought you were, too . . ." Tareen commented.

"Hmm," Sunshine muttered, neither confirming nor denying, before removing the bags he had thrown on top of the crates as they'd escaped the ravine. "Just go, before I change my mind."

"Should I go with him?" Ort asked as Tareen disappeared into the trees.

"That's not a bad idea," Bokana said, only slightly out of breath. "He may be a pilot, but taking off will be tricky on his own."

"Agreed," Sunshine said. "And maybe you can make sure he doesn't leave us behind."

"I'll do my best," Ort said, running in the direction the Duros was headed.

"And then there were three," Bokana said.

"Three people and four bags," Sunshine said, holding the bags he'd recovered from the sled out to them. Bokana took the first and swung it onto his back, narrowly missing the wound on his shoulder.

"No," Marda said, taking the other. "I'll have them both."

"I'll be fine," he said, already sprinting away. "I feel great!"

She felt pretty good herself as they continued in silence, Sunshine bringing up the rear. That suited Marda just fine. She was still cross with Bok—so, so cross—but the thought of leaving him behind in the ravine had been too terrible to comprehend. She'd already lost Kevmo. There was no way she would lose someone else, even if they had a complicated relationship with the Force—a relationship that suddenly had him crashing to a stop.

"It's found us," he said, leaning on the staff.

"What has?

"What do you think?"

Noise exploded behind them, cracking wood and trampling feet. It had to be the Under-Dweller. So it had survived, after all.

"Run," she said.

Sunshine looked over his shoulder as they pelted straight ahead, and screamed out: "It's in the trees!"

What an understatement that turned out to be. The Under-Dweller wasn't just in the trees; it leaped from trunk to trunk, branches snapping beneath its weight to crash to the forest floor. They stumbled and fell as it gained on them, tripping on roots and swearing as their packs hit the ground. It would be a miracle if *any* of the eggs survived, let alone them!

Sunshine raced on, the fastest of them all, living proof that appearances could be deceiving. Marda followed close behind, carrying just one bag to Sunshine's two, but Bokana soon began to lag, his body eventually moving faster than his legs, causing him to crash onto his face.

Marda dropped her bag and raced back to help, but it was obvious the Ovissian wasn't getting up.

"I'm not leaving you," she said, the monster screaming in the trees.

"You're going to have to. I can't keep up, and you're not going to die on my account."

In the end, the choice was taken out of Marda's hands as the Under-Dweller dropped on top of them.

THIRTY-THREE

Matty had felt something like it once before, back on Jedha when the fighting first broke out. The Herald had just made his disastrous appearance in front of the Convocation only to be dismissed out of hand. Matty had followed Vildar and Oliviah out of the building as the spurned Path member had addressed the crowd in the Square of the Supplicants, stoking the embers of discontent that smoldered beneath the surface of the Holy City. At any other time, the Jedi would have been able to calm the crowd, but suddenly it felt like reality had turned inside out. Her vision had blurred, the people around her, both friends and strangers alike, transformed into hideous versions of themselves, monsters that looked ready to tear her apart. And it wasn't just the Jedi who had felt it. The other members of the Convocation had reacted in fear and surprise, lashing out at the baying crowd and only escalating the violence.

It had felt as though the Force itself had forsaken them, leaving them lost and alone.

This was no different. In fact, it felt much worse.

It had happened so quickly. Ric's condition was worsening as Oliviah argued with the Path members on the doorstep, and Matty had decided enough was enough. Whatever her traveling companion thought of her, she wasn't about to let the journalist suffer while Oliviah Zeveron tiptoed around the Path members. If there was one thing she'd learned from Vildar and Tey, it was that action was about one billion times better than prevaricating. Of course, Oliviah hadn't been happy when Matty butted in, telling the Path members precisely what she thought about them, but in all honesty, Matty had stopped caring what the other Jedi thought. She just wanted to get Ric the help she needed, a desire that was knocked sideways as the wave of nausea hit her like a blockade runner. Suddenly, she couldn't focus on anything. She knew the others were there, and she could even hear the sound of their voices but couldn't work out what they were saying, their words mashing together. All she wanted to do was curl into a ball and hide from everything, all the colors and the sounds. Most important, she wanted to hide from herself. It was like she was falling into a great pit, down and down and—

Down.

Matty opened her eyes. She could see, though not clearly. Everything was still blurred together, but nothing was spinning. It took her a moment to work out where she was, lying on a blanket that seemed to be swaying gently. A cart. She was back on a lyuna cart, the animal snorting and farting as the wheels jolted over the uneven ground. Ric Farazi was laid out beside her, groaning with every bump in the road, while Oliviah was crammed in the corner of the cart, her legs pulled up to her chest, head pressed against her knees.

Matty glanced back at the driver, seeing only the hooded robes of a Path member, Ferdan's city limits in the distance.

Trying not to make a sound, Matty crawled over to Oliviah, her head pounding. She didn't dare say the Jedi's name, nor could she seem to reach out in the Force to get Olivia's attention, her focus still shredded by whatever had happened in the camp. She stretched out a hand, ready to brush Oliviah's arm, when the Jedi started, her head snapping up to reveal wide, scared eyes.

Get away.

The instruction was a feeling rather than words, accompanied by a shove from the Force that sent Matty flying back to crash into the driver's seat.

"What in Storm's name?" the driver exclaimed, twisting around as the lyuna brayed, shocked by the sudden commotion. Matty felt like braying herself but instead snatched the lightsaber from her belt and hit the activator.

"Stop the cart."

"Okay, okay," the driver said, pulling on the reins. "There. Stopped."

"Where are you taking us?" Matty asked, holding her hilt with both hands to keep the blade from shaking, a goal she *almost* achieved.

"To town," came the reply. "To the local doctor. You became ill. I had to get you out of there."

Matty felt a surprisingly calm presence behind her. It was Oliviah, who had drawn herself to her feet but stopped short of lighting her own saber.

"Why?" Oliviah asked plainly.

The woman—a member of a species Matty had never seen before, with gray skin and pointed teeth—didn't lower her hands. "Because it was the right thing to do."

"She's lying," Matty said out loud, silently cursing that she'd lost the power of internal dialogue, before remembering that she'd never had it anyway.

"Do you know what happened to us?" Oliviah asked.

"I think so, but I don't know what's wrong with her." The woman nodded to Ric, who had stopped moaning, which, considering her pallor, wasn't a good sign. "We need to get her to Doc Nindle. He'll know what to do." She looked around, as if checking to see if they were being watched. "It isn't safe here. If you're spotted waving that thing around."

Beside Matty, Oliviah pulled her robes about her. "Lower the saber."

"But—"

"But nothing. Our friend . . ." Oliviah waited for the gray-skinned woman to reveal her name.

"Yana."

"Our friend Yana is correct. Your lightsaber is only going to attract attention, so . . ."

Clenching her jaw in frustration, Matty deactivated her blade. The woman in the driver's seat relaxed, her shoulders slumping. "Thank you."

"How long till we arrive?"

"At Doc Nindle's place? Ten minutes or so. It really isn't far."

Oliviah checked on Ric, feeling for her pulse. "Then you better hurry."

Yana, if that truly was her name, returned to the reins and, with a sharp command to the lyuna, started the cart back on its way.

Matty dropped down beside Oliviah, who was still examining Ric. "How do we know we can trust her?"

"The Evereni?" Oliviah replied, keeping her voice low. "We don't, especially as I can't get a read on her. Can you?"

Matty shook her head. "Back there, at the camp, did you—"

"Something happened." Oliviah sat back, leaning against the edge of the cart. "Something I can't explain. It was as if . . ."

"You suddenly couldn't see anything?"

Oliviah turned to meet her eyes, Matty sitting beside her, shoulder to shoulder.

"It happened to you, too?" she asked.

Matty swallowed. "I thought I was going to die."

Oliviah looked away again, her expression haunted. "There was a woman there, the Mother, I think, and she had a . . . well, I don't know what it was. There was something at her feet, something I couldn't focus on, but I saw her face, even as everything turned upside down, and if I'm right . . ."

"What?" There she went again, keeping secrets, shutting Matty out. "What aren't you telling me?"

Oliviah glanced up and shook her head, mouthing *Not here* before retreating into her thoughts.

If not here, then where? thought Matty. And *when*, for that matter?

Yana had thought it was game over when the Twi'lek lit her lightsaber. Even in Matthea's weakened condition, there was no way Yana could have reached her blaster before the Jedi took her down. And yet the galaxy had smiled on her for once in her life, and she'd made it to the doctor's surgery without losing either a limb or her life.

Doc Nindle appeared as soon as the lyuna pulled up, the Mon Calamari fussing over Farazi as the Jedi helped carry the woman from the cart.

"What happened?" Nindle asked, but Yana shook her head.

"I wasn't there. You need to ask them, not me."

And ask, Nindle did, barraging the Jedi with questions as he bustled them inside.

"Are you coming?" Matthea asked, glancing over her shoulder as they disappeared inside the building.

"Of course," Yana replied, making a show of tying the lyuna to a post. She had no intention of following them in. She had delivered them where they needed to be, and she had other business to attend to; not least of which was the tall figure standing in the shadows of a warehouse across the narrow street.

The Mon Calamari medic had barely started to examine Ric Farazi before he sighed, shaking his bulbous head.

"Doctor?" Matty asked.

"It's what I thought," Nindle replied. "Or rather feared. This is the second case I've seen today."

"Second case of what?"

"Severe stomach cramps, sickness, and discoloration of the skin. This is by far the worse of the two cases, but the similarities are all there."

"Who else is ill?" Matty asked, Oliviah seeming strangely disconnected from the conversation.

"A young boy, son of an old friend of mine." The Mon Cal

gave a sharp laugh. "Well, just about everyone is a friend in a town as small as this. But Yvanna and Garda . . . well, they've had a bad year. Yvanna suffers from krinjaffi syndrome, you see, and can barely work. The family was just about getting by before her husband was killed in a farming accident. I tried to save him, but the injuries were too severe. Ever since then, Yvanna has barely managed to rub two credits together. She's a proud woman. I had to talk her into visiting the Path's soup kitchen myself, but at least it meant the boy would eat."

"Not the Mother?" Oliviah asked, finally engaging.

Nindle shook his head. "Turns out she couldn't. Has an allergy to the legumes the Path use in their cooking. Diagnosed it myself, you know. But she was happy that Garda had a warm meal inside himself nonetheless. The Path were happy, too, from what I understand. Their first customer, so to speak."

"But then the boy got sick?"

"Sadly, yes. A terrible business, although not as severe as this poor woman, thank the stars. It can't be a coincidence."

"How so?"

"I'll show you," the Mon Cal said, leaning over Ric to gently pull back the Zeltron's eyelids. "There. Do you see?"

It was hard not to. The whites of Ric's eyes were now wholly yellow.

"Could they have been in contact with each other, before she went to the camp?"

The Mon Calamari stroked his barbels. "It's a possibility.

Your friend was asking a lot of questions around town, mostly about the Path and the Mother."

"Do you know her?" Oliviah cut in.

"Not personally, no. The Path keeps themselves to themselves, at least until recently. I always assumed they had their own medic."

"But Ric could have met the boy when she was asking questions," Matty suggested, wanting to keep focused on the matter at hand. "At the soup kitchen, possibly."

"It's a distinct possibility and would explain their condition. Maybe it's a virus the Zeltron brought from offworld or something Garda picked up in town, but there's something about those eyes that worries me. They're as yellow as mine."

"Which means?"

"It could mean all kinds of things, but combined with the trouble breathing, the gastric issues, and the sores in the corners of their mouths . . ." The Mon Calamari looked up at them, his face grim. "If I'm right—and I hope I'm not—I fear they might have been poisoned."

THIRTY-FOUR

The ground shook. It wasn't the Under-Dweller dropping on them, but the heavy tread of a very different beast.

"The protector," Bokana breathed as the second creature came into sight, pushing through the trees as it charged straight at them, as majestic as the Under-Dweller was horrifying. It ran on all fours like a lion, powerful legs that ended in hooves churning the forest floor as it thundered forward. Its face was proud and noble, with long whiskers flowing back like a mane. Marda wasn't sure if it was covered in fur, but its entire body glowed with a deep blue luminescence, from the top of its massive head to the end of its long branched tail. Marda knew she should run, dragging Bokana with her, but she couldn't move, transfixed by the strange vision that would surely trample them within seconds if the Under-Dweller didn't sink its teeth into them first.

Time slowed, the Under-Dweller roared, and the newcomer leaped.

The sound their bodies made when they met in midair was like thunder. Marda threw up an arm—as if something so puny could stop them from being crushed—and the beast passed over them, knocking the Under-Dweller forward. It screamed in frustration and surprise, hitting the ground hard, the two creatures rolling in a deadly embrace. Somehow the Under-Dweller came out on top, but its victory didn't last long. The newcomer swiped up at the monster, what Marda had thought were hooves unfurling into long, powerful toes. It had been running on its knuckles and now revealed long claws that slashed at the Under-Dweller's jaw. The pit creature was thrown to the side, its opponent pouncing on top of it before it could right itself. They exchanged blows, snapping at each other with powerful jaws, the horrific violence of the moment finally breaking Marda out of her spell. They couldn't wait to see who would claim the victory. Their unlikely champion had given them a second chance they couldn't squander.

"Run!" she shouted at Bokana, echoing the word he had said to her earlier. She grabbed her bag and dragged him with her, the warring creatures blocking their way. She pulled

Bokana to the side as the Under-Dweller was thrown at a tree, the trunk splintering as if it were driftwood. They slid down a slight incline, ducking as the newcomer's tail whipped dangerously close to their heads, followed by the animal's body as the Under-Dweller regained the upper hand, sending both creatures tumbling toward them.

Marda and Bokana jumped forward, Bokana crying out in pain as they narrowly avoided being crushed by the rolling bodies. She yanked on his arm, knowing that she was probably hurting him but desperate to get away. He stayed on his feet, barreling into the trees with her as the fight carried on behind them. Marda glanced back to see the protector closing its jaws around the Under-Dweller's neck and thrashing its head back and forth. There was a crack, but Marda couldn't tell if it was the monster's neck or another felled tree. All she knew was that they'd escaped for now.

Marda's chest felt like it was going to explode by the time they caught up with Sunshine Dobbs.

"What the hell was that?" he asked, but neither she nor Bokana had the breath to answer, not if they wanted to keep running.

Her legs finally gave way as they burst out of the trees to find the *Silverstreak* exactly where they'd left it and in much better condition. Shea raised her welding mask, a frown plastered across her oil-streaked face as she looked down from the top of the ship. Marda landed in a heap near the *Streak*'s newly exposed hull.

"What happened to you?" the engineer asked.

"Didn't you hear the monsters?" Marda wheezed, leaning on arms that refused to stop shaking.

"Monsters?" Shea lifted the welding torch she'd been using. "I couldn't hear anything over this baby. What monsters?"

"We'll explain when we get on board," Sunshine told her, hauling Marda back to her feet before making for the ramp. "We need to go."

Shea slid down the hull and landed beside them. "Go? You mean like *go*, go? Take off."

"That's the general idea," the prospector replied, disappearing inside.

"What's the hurry?" Shea asked as she joined Marda and Bokana, who limped up the ramp, every step an effort. "And what happened to you?" she added as she took in Bok's injuries. "Are the others still coming?"

"One at a time," Marda gasped as they made it inside, relieved to be slipping the heavy pack from her shoulder.

"Actually, it can all wait until we're in orbit," Sunshine said, looking around the ship. "If we *make* it into orbit. I thought you were going to fix this thing."

"We *are* fixing it," Shea insisted, although Marda wasn't convinced. Cables hung from the ceiling, while most of the wall panels had been removed to expose a snake's pit of wires and conductors underneath. Jukkyuk appeared, carrying a toolbox, and barked a question when he saw Marda's party had returned.

"No, they're not back," Shea said, glancing at the forest with a slight frown. "Not yet, at least."

"Who's not back?" Sunshine asked, standing in front of her so she had no choice but to answer his question.

Shea sighed and threw her torch onto a crate that was doubling as a workbench. "Geth and the others. They went to the *Bonecrusher* to fetch parts."

"And do you need those parts to fly?" Sunshine pressed.

"What?"

"It's a simple enough question, Shea: can we take off?"

"Are you kidding?" Marda cut in as Bokana leaned against the wall, breathing heavily. "Look at this place. It's still a disaster."

Jukkyuk threw back his shaggy head and brayed something that finally put a smile on Sunshine's grubby face.

"Are you saying what I think you're saying, my fine furry friend?" This time the prospector punched the air when the Wookiee responded with a nod.

"Finally, some good news," the prospector declared, straightening his cap.

"Why?" Marda asked. "What did he say?"

"He said that, yes, the *Silverstreak is* a disaster," Shea translated, "but it's a disaster that can take us home."

"You did it," Bokana said, finally able to speak. "You fixed the ship."

"I think so," Shea responded, scratching her cheek. "I mean, I've always been good, but here, working on this thing, everything just snapped into place, you know. It was as if all the circuits . . . all the power systems . . . were suddenly mapped out in front of me. I could just see how to fix them."

"Sounds too good to be true," Marda said, ice clawing at her gut.

"Sounds like the Force," Bokana said, grinning.

"No, it can't be," Marda snapped, turning on the Ovissian. "Shea isn't like that. She isn't like you!"

"Isn't like him, how?" Shea asked, bewildered by the exchange.

"It's been a long day," Sunshine interrupted, as if that explained everything. "And everyone's just a little bit frazzled, but whatever's happening, we need to prep for takeoff."

"What about Ort and Tareen?" Shea asked as Sunshine made for the cockpit.

"They're heading to the *Bonecrusher*," he called over his shoulder, "and will be leaving, too, if they've got any sense."

"But we haven't even run any tests!"

"The tests can wait," Bokana said, his voice suddenly grave.

Shea threw her hands into the air. "Not you, as well. Anyone would think you want us to fly apart."

"There's no time. It's coming."

"What is?"

"Listen."

Marda could hear it now, a pounding beneath their feet, shaking the deck plates, shaking the entire ship.

"It's coming," Bokana muttered, staring at the trees. "It's angry."

"One of those things?" Marda asked. "Which one, Bokana?"

"It knows we're leaving. . . ."

"Which one?"

"Wants them back."

The footfalls were getting nearer by the second.

"That's it," Sunshine said, disappearing from the hold. "Decision made. Get everything battened down."

"What about Geth and the others?" Shea called after him, but the prospector was already gone. "What about the *Bonecrusher*?"

The engineer swore under her breath and turned toward the hatch. "You all need to help," she shouted as she sprinted down the ramp. "We'll take off okay, but half the ship's access panels are still open. We won't survive five seconds in the Veil unless we lock them."

There was no time to argue, let alone think, which Marda took as a blessing. The four of them—Marda, Bok, Shea, and Jukkyuk—raced around the *Silverstreak* slamming panels shut and disconnecting cables. Marda had no idea what she was doing and so blindly obeyed Shea's hurried instructions, the footfalls outside now accompanied by deep, resonant grunts.

"Well, that's a good sign," Shea said as the *Silverstreak*'s engine rumbled to life.

"What is?" Marda asked.

The engineer smirked. "That it didn't blow up."

Bokana laughed, but Marda didn't find any of this funny, not the fact that a creature was charging toward them through the forest or that Shea seemed to be exhibiting heightened abilities that, like Bokana, could only have come from the Force. Even if Bok was telling the truth, even if his powers had been somehow awakened by this strange planet after a lifetime of lying dormant, why now? Was it a gift freely given by the Force or more evidence that the universe was out of kilter?

Vents opened beneath the *Silverstreak*, steam billowing as Sunshine prepared to depart.

"That'll have to do," Shea called out, ushering them toward the ramp. "Everyone on board before Beardy leaves without us."

Marda had no intention of being left behind, especially with a monster racing toward them. She was the last one on the ramp, Shea and Jukkyuk already on board. She had started after Bokana when the creature in the woods bellowed, vibrating the ramp beneath her feet.

That wasn't the Under-Dweller.

Behind her, the beast Bok had described as a protector

burst from the trees but now looked neither noble nor proud. It looked furious, its lips drawn back and its flanks bleeding from deep cuts. The Under-Dweller hadn't gone quietly, and neither would they.

The *Silverstreak*'s thrusters fired, and the ship lurched into the air, Marda losing her footing and crashing down.

"The ramp's not closed," Shea yelled, but there was no way Sunshine would be able to hear her. Marda slid down the ramp, grazing her palms on the metal grating until her fingers found purchase.

"Forget the ramp," she shouted, her legs dangling over the edge. "What about me?"

Bokana was already clambering down to help as the animal leaped, a giant paw slamming down beside Marda's head. She scrambled up as the other paw clawed at the ramp, skinning her knees as the creature was taken with them, the *Silverstreak*'s labored engines whining. Marda yelped as the creature snapped at her heels, its shoulders bunched as it fought gravity to haul itself after her.

It was no good. She couldn't hold on. Marda's fingers slipped, and she fell back only to jolt to a halt as a hairy hand grabbed her wrist. She looked up to see Jukkyuk stretched over the top of the ramp, his long arms able to reach farther than Bokana ever could. The Wookiee pulled, and all of a sudden Marda was safely in the hold. Jukkyuk propelled her toward the protective meshing that lined the walls, grabbing hold of the netting himself. Marda looped an aching arm through a gap, anchoring herself in place as the crate Shea had been using as a workbench slid down the steep incline of the deck to tumble out of the hatch. It slipped down the ramp, bouncing off the creature and knocking one of its huge paws loose. The beast hung by one arm, thrashing wildly, before its claws found the grating again.

"Can you raise the ramp?" Marda yelled to Shea, who was crammed against the bulkhead on the other side of the hatch, Bokana clambering up beside her.

"What do you think I'm trying to do?" the engineer responded, slamming her hand against the button that should seal the ship. "Whatever that thing is, it's too heavy. The mechanism can't take it."

Outside, the sky was darkening, another ship rocketing after them. It was the *Bonecrusher*, Galamal's ship finally making its own escape from the planet. Marda had a wild thought that they could shoot the creature from the ramp, but the reality was that the blast would probably take the *Silverstreak* with it.

But that was nothing compared with the terror that awaited if the beast clawed its way in before they hit the Veil. It was only a matter of time, the creature halfway up the ramp, crawling paw over paw. It reached up, its claws wrapping around the edge of the hatch as Marda joined the others in pulling themselves toward the front of the ship. They'd never make it in time—she knew that—but they had to try, even if it meant barricading themselves in the cockpit with Sunshine as the creature tore up the ship.

That was when she realized they weren't all trying to escape. She turned, hanging from the netting, to see Bokana looking straight at her from the other side of the hold.

All at once, she knew what he was going to do before he did it, and she called out to stop him, not that it did any good.

He didn't reply, not with his voice at least. He just smiled, eyes brimming, and words appeared in her mind. It wasn't like listening to Kevmo, or even Calar. There was no bitterness or fear, no condemnation or anger. Instead, there was love and sorrow, compassion, and sincerity.

I didn't lie to you.

Bokana let go of the strap he'd been holding and fell toward the ramp. Marda screamed his name as he shot out of the hatch, flying straight into the creature's head. The animal tried to throw him clear, but Bokana held on, wrapping a muscular arm around its neck as he slid onto the beast's back. He pulled, yanking back with all his might, and the creature's claws squealed against metal as it lost its grip on the hatch.

Bokana held tight as the beast bellowed, scrabbling against the ramp, but it was too late. They were both snatched away, there one minute, gone the next, their bodies locked together as they tumbled back to the planet's surface far below.

Across the hold, Shea hit the button one last time, and the ramp rose unsteadily to seal the hatch. Marda wailed, letting go of the restraints and slipping toward the closed ramp as the acceleration compensators finally kicked in. She slid to a halt, tears streaming down her face, her heart breaking as the *Silverstreak* punched its way through the Veil.

THIRTY-FIVE

No sooner had Doc Nindle delivered his verdict than Ric Farazi started to convulse on the Mon Calamari's examination table.

"What's happening?" Matty asked, feeling helpless as the doctor rushed to a drawer, pulling out a tray filled with stim packs.

"She's going into shock," Nindle replied, returning to the table with a fully loaded injector in hand. "Help hold her down, will you? This should stabilize her."

Both Oliviah and Matty did as they were asked so the doctor could administer the drug, which seemed to have no effect at all.

"That's not good," Nindle said, returning to his box of shots. "Maybe if I try cordabenzalyne?"

On the table, Ric stopped thrashing beneath Matty's hand, her head slumping to the side.

"Doctor?"

"She's gone into arrest," the doctor said, abandoning his drugs to begin basic resuscitation. "There's a defib kit back there. Fetch it for me."

"Where?" Oliviah asked, moving right away.

"In the cupboard," Nindle replied between chest compressions. "Next to the desk. A blue box, can't miss it."

"Can you save her?" Matty asked as Oliviah rifled through the shelves behind them.

"That. Is what. I'm trying. To do," Nindle insisted, his sentence punctuated by his efforts to keep the Zeltron's heart pumping. "But it won't be any good if we can't work out what she's ingested."

"Don't you have antitoxins?"

"I gave her an antitoxin," he snapped back. "This isn't exactly a top-of-the-line medcenter, young lady. We do what we can."

"Here," Oliviah said, returning with the blue case.

"Open it up," the doctor instructed, not looking up from his patient. "It should be already charged."

Matty didn't wait to see Oliviah struggle with the clasp and instead made for the door.

"Where are you going?" the older Jedi called after her.

"To find out what they gave her."

"Who?" Oliviah asked as Matty disappeared outside without answering. It was obvious, wasn't it? Ric Farazi had been staying with the Path, eating their food and drinking their water, while Garda, the boy Nindle had so affectionately described, had been taken ill after eating at the Path's soup kitchen. It couldn't be a coincidence. The galaxy didn't work like that.

If only Matty had ducked back outside when Yana failed to follow them inside. Yes, she'd been distracted by her concern for the Zeltron, but she wasn't about to let herself—or the Evereni—off the hook that easily.

At least she couldn't have gotten far. The lyuna and cart were still there, although there was always the possibility that she'd planned to abandon them all along. But why take them to a doctor in the first place? Why not finish them off in the cart?

Fortunately, while the sky was still thick with clouds, the rain had held off, meaning that the Evereni's footprints hadn't been washed away. They led across the muddy road, where they disappeared around the side of a warehouse. A helping hand from the Force or just luck. Matty frankly didn't care as long as she caught up with the woman. True, there was still the mystery of what had happened to her and Oliviah in the camp, but one mystery at a time, right? Besides, a Jedi always thought of others before themself. A woman's life hung in the balance.

Matty followed the trail, slipping down the narrow alleyway beside the building. There were hushed voices ahead, coming from a yard at the back of the warehouse. Her heart jumped as she recognized them both, but surely that couldn't be right. The first was the woman's, but the other was a deep baritone she had first heard on the steps to the Convocation building on Jedha.

Matty slowed as she reached the corner of the building, peering into the yard to see Yana talking to a tall man in a dark cloak, the hood almost but not quite disguising the tendrils that had been slashed years before, leaving stumps Matty had last seen in a cell beneath the Temple of the Whills.

Her suspicions were correct. The Herald of the Open Hand was free and back on Dalna.

Werth had listened to Yana's report with barely a comment until she got to the part concerning his wife.

"They are keeping her *where*?"

"In a room within the caves."

"Not our quarters?"

Yana shook her head, and the Herald bared his teeth. "First that woman took my daughter and now she humiliates my wife?"

"The entire place feels like it's about to go up. The Mother has everyone wound tighter than a power coil. Something bad is coming, but I don't know what. She even has Sunshine off goodness-knows-where, hunting for more Levelers."

"And your cousin?"

"There's no sign of her. I have a horrible suspicion she's gone with Sunshine, but there's no way of knowing for sure."

Werth started to pace, his cloak billowing. "We must save the Path. We must save Opari."

"But how? Everyone thinks you're responsible for Jedha. That you betrayed the Path. Elecia even has them believing that the damned weather is somehow linked to everything that happened."

"The Force thrown dangerously out of balance," he growled, coming to a stop with his back still to her. "She is the only one who has disturbed the balance, and it ends today." He turned, pulling his hood down and approaching her again. "Is there anyone who hasn't yet fallen for her lies?"

"Not that I could see," Yana admitted, "but if you go to the Elders, tell them what *really* happened on Jedha . . ."

"I'll tell them more than that," the Herald promised. "It's time we told them the truth, Yana. About Kor. About how she died."

Finally, Yana thought, wishing she'd done it herself the moment she realized that the Mother had set them up. How much aggravation could have been avoided? How much violence?

That was when the comlink chimed.

"Matty? Matty, are you there?"

Matty swore, fumbling with her comlink to switch it off, but the damage had already been done.

In the yard, Yana spun around, her hand going to her blaster, but the weapon was gone. It had been taken by the Herald, who was already raising it toward the Jedi.

Matty's lightsaber jumped to her hand, and she lit the beam before the first shot was even fired. Yana was already running for cover, heading for an exit on the other side of the warehouse. The Herald backed up toward her, the blaster he'd lifted barking over and over as he continued to squeeze the trigger.

Matty was still suffering from the aftereffects of whatever had happened to her in the camp, but she was recovered well enough to bat the bolts back at the fleeing Nautolan, a blast almost slamming into his head. Instead, it smacked into the wall, sending out a plume of chipped brickwork as he ducked after Yana.

Matty could have chased after them, but where was the fun in that when there was a roof to be had? She ran and jumped, the Force propelling her to the top of the building. She crossed the roof, then launched herself off the edge to land in front of Yana and the murderer. The Herald's weapon fired again, but Matty spun on her heel, sending the bolt screaming back at them. It hit Yana in the shoulder, more by chance than design, twisting her around. The Herald was already turning, but Matty pulled her free hand back, calling on the Force. It was as if the Nautolan had been caught on a fishing line. He flew toward Yana, the blaster tumbling from his hand to skitter across the ground as he landed at her feet.

"Stay where you are," Matty commanded as he lunged for the gun, only to freeze when he realized the tip of a lightsaber was pointing toward his head.

"I think she means it," Yana called from where she was crouched on the ground, clutching her shoulder.

"I really do!" Matty confirmed, actually still reeling from how well that had gone. If only Vildar and Tey could have seen her—Oliviah, too, for that matter. Maybe then the Jedi Knight would have finally taken her seriously.

"May we at least get up?" the Herald asked, and Matty nodded, keeping her lightsaber trained on him.

"Slowly. And leave the weapon where it is."

"*My* weapon," Yana snarled at the Nautolan as they pushed themselves up, the tip of Matty's blade rising with them. "A gift definitely *not* freely given."

Matty wasn't about to take any chances. She reached out with her empty hand, using the Force to pluck the blaster from the ground. It slapped into her palm barrel first, but she couldn't have everything. She probably shouldn't have enjoyed the look of disgust on the Herald's scarred face, either, but it had been quite a day.

"What now?" Yana asked as the Herald merely glowered.

"Now you come with me," Matty said, trying to flip the blaster around in her hand and almost fumbling it.

"Having trouble?" the Nautolan sneered.

"Not at all," Matty lied, finally getting the grip in her palm and her finger around the trigger. The feel of a blaster in her hand was wrong, but she went with it all the same, hoping she wouldn't have to discharge it.

"You should be on Jedha," Matty said to the Herald, but it was Yana who replied.

"He was framed."

Matty couldn't suppress a bitter laugh. "I don't think so. He's a thief and a murderer."

"In your eyes."

"In *everybody's* eyes. You're going straight back to Jedha to answer for your crimes."

"And then you will never get to the root of the problem," Yana cut in. "Yes, we stole treasures, and yes, people died, but send the Herald back to his cell and the real villain escapes, just as she planned."

"The real villain?"

"The Mother," the Herald growled, his distaste clear. "She has betrayed us all, taking something pure and defiling it to serve her own ends."

"And that is why you're here?" Matty asked. "To take back your cult?"

"It is not a cult!" the Herald snapped.

"And you are not innocent. You didn't have to steal. You didn't have to kill."

"The Force will be free."

"Tell that to the woman who's dying on Doc Nindle's table."

"Look," Yana said, daring to step forward despite the glowing lightsaber. "We come from different sides, but I'm willing to bet anything we're here for the same reason. That's why you're on Dalna, isn't it? You're investigating the Path. You're investigating the Mother." The gray-skinned woman didn't wait for Matty to answer. "We can work together, no matter what we believe. None of us want any more blood on our hands."

"Well?" Matty asked, turning to the Herald, who'd remained suspiciously quiet.

The Nautolan pursed his lips, looking like he'd rather kiss a mynock than team up with a Jedi. "I am willing to consider a temporary alliance, but this doesn't mean that I condone your methods."

"Likewise," Matty said, lowering her lightsaber as a sign of good faith. "You'll come back to the surgery?"

"We will," Yana promised. "Although I'm not sure what good it will do."

"It could save a life."

"Only if you extinguish that," the Herald said, pointing at her blade.

"He has a point," Yana said, shrugging. "I'm not sure a

Jedi being seen leading prisoners through town is a good idea."

"Agreed," the Herald sneered. "You wouldn't want to start a riot."

Tey Sirrek would have punched the Herald in the nose, watching with satisfaction as blood washed that sneer away. Vildar Mac might even have done the same, but neither of her friends was there, so Matty merely took the jibe on the chin and stepped back, her blue blade sliding into its hilt.

In many ways, this was a victory. An alliance had been forged, after all.

The only question was how long it would last.

THIRTY-SIX

I didn't lie.

I didn't lie to you.

I would never lie to you.

The words echoed around Marda's head as the *Silverstreak* was buffeted by the Veil. She could hear Shea and Sunshine shouting in the cockpit, trying to stop the hastily repaired ship from being torn apart all over again.

A ship repaired by a woman who suddenly seemed able to use the Force to fix power lines and injector matrices.

A woman who had never exhibited any sign of Force sensitivity before they had arrived on the nameless planet with its monsters and its eggs and its death.

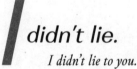

Bokana's death.

Bokana whom she'd trusted, whom she'd given herself to, but whom she hadn't known.

I didn't lie to you.

"Are you sure about that?"

No. It wasn't an answer to the question but a reaction to the voice that had returned from the ether, taking up residence where it didn't belong.

"Leave me alone."

"I can't do that," Kevmo said. "Not anymore. Look what happens when I do, Marda."

He was standing in front of her, clearer than ever in the light of the hold. His skin was gray and flaking, but his eyes burned with disgust. Beautiful Kevmo. Dead Kevmo.

Kevmo, who knew her better than she knew herself.

"No," she shouted, this time out loud, as she leaped from the deck where she had been rocking back and forth. "You're not real. This is the Veil. Making me see things."

"Like it made you hear things, Marda?" Kevmo chuckled. "In your head?" He stepped toward her, forcing her back against the bulkhead, his breath like rotting meat. "Calar tried to warn you, but you didn't listen. The Force will be chained, Marda. The Force will be consumed. You will all be consumed."

Marda shook her head, sidestepping the ghost that couldn't be there, not wanting to listen, not wanting to hear his voice ever again. She should've guessed that wouldn't stop him. He came with her, matching her step for step, his feet silent, his colorless hair stirred by a breeze that shouldn't be there.

"He tricked you, Marda," he wheezed in her ear. "Hid his abilities from you. . . . You said it yourself."

"I was wrong. He told me. It was the planet."

Kevmo cackled, the sound like shards of glass scraping together. "It was the planet. It was the planet. Can you even hear yourself?"

Marda started to run. Why was this corridor so long? Where was the cockpit? Why weren't there any doors?

"You were just as bad as him. You know that, don't you? You wanted to stay, wanted to enjoy how the planet made you feel. What about the Path, Marda? What about the Force? Don't you want it to be free? Do you want it to burn?"

Marda burst into the cockpit, not expecting the flight seats to be so near a door that seconds earlier she could barely see. Kevmo was gone, but Shea was very much there, in the navigator seat that Marda barreled into, unable to stop.

"Watch it," the engineer snapped. "I'm trying to hold us together."

"It's worse than before," Sunshine yelled, wrestling frantically with the controls in the seat beside her. "The Veil really doesn't want us to leave this time."

As if to prove his point, something struck the ship from outside, the deck beneath Marda's feet suddenly becoming a wall. She tumbled back, slamming into the rear stations.

"Strap yourself in, for Void's sake," Sunshine shouted back at her, clicking unresponsive buttons above his head. "The last thing we need is for you to smash your brains out on a bulkhead."

"There might not *be* any bulkheads if we don't get moving," Shea told him, checking a fault locator panel to her right that was lighting up like a bough of Life Day orbs.

"That's not encouraging," came a voice tinged with static. It took a moment for Marda to realize that it had to be Geth, speaking from the *Bonecrusher.*

"It wasn't supposed to be," Shea told him, punching the fault locators to see if it made a difference. "I'm assuming you're in just as bad shape as us?"

"Probably worse."

"It isn't a competition," Sunshine told them both, glancing up at the viewport, where the *Bonecrusher* could be seen doing its best to avoid the same swarming masses that had destroyed the *Moon of Sarkhai.*

"Just show us the way out," Geth responded. "Our systems are crashing one by one."

"I wish I knew how," Sunshine shouted back.

"You found it once before," Marda reminded him.

"Yes, but this is different. We should be through the Veil by now."

"It's getting bigger?"

Sunshine nodded as the *Bonecrusher* narrowly avoided being vaporized. "Like it's expanding from the planet."

"It can do that?" Shea asked in disbelief.

Sunshine swung them to port, Marda realizing she was sitting down only when she clutched the arms of the chair.

"Apparently so."

"What if we made a hyperspace jump?" Geth suddenly asked over the comm.

"From inside the Veil?" Sunshine scoffed. "It will never work."

"Wole thinks he can do it!"

"Then Wole is an idiot."

"At least let him share his course," Shea urged. Sunshine told her that it wouldn't do any good, but the engineer was already studying the details Geth had transmitted from the *Bonecrusher.*

"What do you think?" Geth asked when she was done.

"I think Sunshine's right."

The prospector sniffed. "Told you so."

"Unless . . ."

Sunshine looked at her as if she'd gone mad. "What are you talking about?"

Shea didn't answer but instead started punching data into the navicomputer.

"Shea!"

"I'm concentrating, shush."

"You know what she's *really* doing, don't you?" Kevmo whispered to Marda, appearing beside her as they watched Shea work. "She's tapping into the Force. Just like she did when she needed to fix the ship. She's killing the Force so that you will live. Is that what the Path would want, Marda? Is that what the Mother wants?"

"Try this," Shea said, unaware she was being mocked by a being that shouldn't exist. "I'm transmitting a path now."

There was a beep as the data was broadcast, followed by the sound of a Rodian complaining on the other side of the comm.

"Well?"

"Wole says the coordinates are nonsense," Geth told Shea.

"Not if we realign the hyperdrive."

"What does that even mean? Marda asked.

"It means she's breaking the galaxy," Kevmo told her as Shea transmitted another batch of data.

"I'm following a hunch," the engineer told the other ship. "But if you want to do the same, you're going to have to adapt your jump thrusters." She flicked another switch, cursing as the fault locator took its revenge and went wild. "That's all we need. Jukkyuk, are you still hanging in there, buddy?"

The reply from the Wookiee over the internal speakers didn't sound encouraging. "Well, there's not much I can do about that right now. I need you to get to the field stabilizers."

Jukkyuk replied again, using what Marda guessed were several Shyriiwook swear words.

"I don't care if the door to the power core is stuck. I'm rewriting the known laws of hyperspace up here. Unstick it, pronto."

"He won't be able to," Kevmo whispered to Marda. "You're all going to die here while she plunders the cosmic Force. Everyone is going to die."

"I'll help him," Marda said, pushing herself up. Anything to escape Kevmo's voice. It didn't work. The Padawan was with her every step of the way as she pounded down the corridor to the ship's meager engineering section. "Did you see how Shea looked at you? She knows you can't help, but is glad you're gone. This keeps happening to you, doesn't it? The Mother didn't want you. Nor did Bokana, not really. Weak, Forceless Marda."

She found Jukkyuk in a corridor, trying to claw open the door that gave access to the hyperdrive. He rumbled something at Marda as she staggered toward him, barely able to keep on her feet.

"Let me help," Marda said as Shea continued to harangue the Wookiee from the cockpit.

"Yeah, that should do it," the engineer sneered. "Finally, a bit of muscle."

Marda ignored her just as she'd ignored Kevmo, tucking herself in front of the Wookiee, trying to get purchase on the edge of the door, but it was hopelessly jammed, buckled in its own frame.

"Shea's right, you know," Kevmo said. "If the Wookiee can't open the door, what hope do you have? You're going to die, just like the Force is going to die. There's nothing you can do."

But he was wrong. There was something she could do that Jukkyuk couldn't, something she had that he didn't.

"Step back," she told the Wookiee, who complained but did as he was asked.

"We need those adjustments," Shea demanded.

"Working on it," Marda said, fishing Kevmo's lightsaber, the weapon she'd vowed to never use again, out from her robes.

The dead Padawan snorted. "What are you going to do with that?"

"I'm going to win," Marda yelled, trying to ignite the blade. The last time she'd pressed the toggle, the burst of energy had scorched her hands. This time, there wasn't even that. Kevmo laughed as she pressed the button over and over, not caring if it burned the skin from her palms. She needed it to work. Why wouldn't it work?

"Why can't you do anything right?" Kevmo hissed.

With a roar of frustration, Marda slammed the hilt into the bulkhead once, twice, three times. Why was she being punished like this? Why did the Force hate her?

But the Force didn't hate her. The Force was a blessing.

She pressed the toggle again, not expecting to get a result, and the weapon burst to life. The yellow blade was no longer smooth as it had been in Kevmo's hand. It was jagged, the plasma crackling, but it would do the job.

"Stand back," she commanded Jukkyuk, thrusting the saber into the door. Her teeth grinding together, she carved a ragged arch in the buckled door, all the time imagining the face of the Kyuzo she'd killed on Jedha. But now she felt neither regret nor disgust, only power. For a moment, she fancied she was carving the blade through Kevmo himself, not the boy she had loved but the bitter phantom conjured in his absence, the shade that existed only to taunt and belittle her. There was no taunting now. Now he screamed and begged as she kept the blade moving. She was through with being ridiculed, through with feeling helpless. She was the Guide. The Guide of the Open Hand.

Molten metal splashed onto the deck as she completed the imperfect arch. Jukkyuk punched his way through the gateway, the redundant metal thudding to the floor. The Wookiee wasted no time, ripping a panel from the ship's main stabilizer conduit and going to work as Shea badgered him from the cockpit. Was he done yet? What was taking so long?

Their voices continued, Geth telling Shea that they were ready, Shea questioning whether they'd made the right adjustments.

"There's only one way to find out," Geth replied over the comm. "We'll see you on Dalna. I love you."

Jukkyuk slammed the stabilizer cover shut, roaring at Shea that he was finished. Shea told them to get clear of the core and yelled at Sunshine to punch it. Jukkyuk and Marda were already running from the drive room as the two ships propelled themselves into hyperspace.

Suddenly, the deck wasn't under their feet and Marda was tumbling forward, Jukkyuk's arms closing around her.

Somewhere far away, there was a scream and an explosion and everything went dark, but Marda didn't care. There was a voice missing in all the confusion and noise, a voice she never wanted to hear again.

Kevmo was gone.

THIRTY-SEVEN

Yana didn't know what had disappointed her most, that the Herald had managed to lift her blaster from its holster or that she hadn't stopped him. The longer this all went on, the more she wanted it to be over. The trouble was that she had no idea what she would do with her life now that Kor was gone.

"Anything you want," Kor said as the Twi'lek led them back to the doctor's surgery. Well, wouldn't that be lovely? No more orders. No more compromises. Perhaps she could even leave now that she had done the impossible, forcing a parlay between the Jedi and the Herald. The thought almost made her laugh out loud. Perhaps that was what the future held for her, the galaxy's most unlikely diplomat.

However, her newfound mediation skills were tested the moment they stepped inside Nindle's room and Yana saw the sheet the Mon Calamari was pulling over Ric Farazi's still body.

"Oh, no," Matty said behind her. Oliviah turned toward the door, her face hardening as she saw who had entered the room.

"You!" she exclaimed, taking a worryingly aggressive step toward the Herald. "The Guardians let you go?"

"Not exactly," Werth replied, never one for making an awkward situation easier.

"We made a deal," Yana cut in quickly before anyone could go for their lightsaber.

"A deal?"

"Well, not a deal exactly. An understanding."

Oliviah looked toward Matty. "Padawan?"

The apprentice didn't move from behind them, blocking their exit. Like it or not, the girl was good.

"They say the Mother is behind everything. That she masterminded the riots on Jedha."

"She blamed you," Oliviah reminded the Herald.

Werth shrugged. "She had to save her skin somehow."

"Or she was onto us," Yana added.

The Jedi's eyes narrowed. "Onto you, how?"

Yana told them how Elecia had sent the Children out to steal artifacts, only to betray Yana and the others when they'd outlived their usefulness. The Jedi listened, Matty letting down her guard more the longer the story went on, the empathy she obviously felt for their plight getting the better of her. A gap in the armor? That was how the Herald would look at it, but Yana found something comforting in the Padawan's gaze. The same couldn't be said about Oliviah, whose eyes had become guarded but had shown their true colors when they flashed with anger as she realized the Herald had escaped. Yana had heard the Jedi didn't experience anger or fear, but she wasn't sure she believed it, especially now.

"And what does the Mother want with the artifacts?" Oliviah asked, her hands clasped in front of her, maybe to stop her from putting them to use with her lightsaber.

"She told us we were liberating them," Yana said. "Protecting them from those who would do them harm."

"Or misuse their power," the Herald added. "The truth is that we suspect Elecia has been selling them on the black market."

The two Jedi exchanged looks.

"What?" Yana asked. "What is it?"

Oliviah rested a hand on the table, which had become a slab for the Zeltron's corpse. "Ric Farazi told us that she suspected the Mother was at the heart of a smuggling ring here on Dalna, possibly using the Path as a cover."

"Or someone else to blame if everything goes wrong," the

Herald pointed out. "The woman told you this before she died."

"Before she was *poisoned*," Doc Nindle interjected.

"You think the Mother had Farazi killed?"

"Her and others," Oliviah said, crossing her arms. "The doctor believes the Path are attempting to poison the people of Ferdan."

"The entire town?" Yana asked. "That seems extreme. I'm not saying the Mother is innocent, but you're talking about mass murder. I can't believe the Path would go along with it. Not knowingly."

"We've seen it with our own eyes," Nindle told her. "First Garda, and now this woman."

"Garda?"

"A young boy who has been eating at the Path's soup kitchen," Oliviah explained, the Padawan finally abandoning her post to step forward. "The first to get sick."

"Then we must inform the authorities," Matty said.

"I thought you people *were* the authorities," the Herald said.

"We have no jurisdiction here," Oliviah pointed out. "And neither does the Republic."

"But I do," Nindle said, puffing out his chest. "I can go to Sheriff Pickwick, tell her I've discovered evidence of food poisoning, and advise her to shut down the kitchen."

"And what then?" Yana asked.

Oliviah walked around the examining table to join them.

"The last thing we want is a confrontation, not if the Path have been stockpiling weapons, but perhaps we could go to the Mother together."

"Tell her the jig's up?"

"Voice our concerns. Give her a chance to confirm or deny our suspicions."

"And if she doesn't listen?"

Oliviah shrugged. "We have you now. You and the Herald could appeal to the Path as a whole while we deal with the Mother."

"Us?" Matty asked, surprised at the sudden turn of events. "What about the sheriff?"

"We don't want an angry mob arriving at the compound's gates, armed to the teeth."

The Herald snorted. "But lightsabers are fine?"

"I'm *trying* to stop a bloodbath," Oliviah insisted, irritation sneaking into her voice. "We are highly trained in such matters, unlike . . ."

She stopped herself, but it was too late.

"Unlike whom?" the Herald said, bristling at her words. "Us? You have no idea how we've been trained or what resources we have at our disposal."

"Resources?" Matty repeated, looking worried. "What do you mean?"

Things were getting out of hand, and Yana was suddenly painfully aware that her blaster was tucked into the

Padawan's belt. "Look," she said, putting herself between Oliviah and the Herald. "We haven't told you everything."

"Yana . . ." the Herald growled in warning.

"They deserve to know," Yana snapped back.

"Know what?"

Yana turned to Oliviah, whose hand had dropped to her belt, dangerously close to her waiting lightsaber. "What you felt, earlier in the camp, when I found you—"

Her words were lost in the sudden roar of engines high above them, the doctor's instruments jangling in their drawers and the windows shaking.

"What in Sachar's name?" the Herald exclaimed, rushing for the door.

"It's a ship," Yana said, following him out into the street.

"Of *course* it's a ship, but why is it landing here, rather than the port?"

The sight of the cruiser flying low over the roofs did nothing to answer their questions. Yana had never seen one like it, with its elegant sweeping lines and red-and-white livery. And then she saw the insignia painted on its nose, and her heart sank.

"It's coming down in the marketplace," the Herald shouted, already breaking into a run. Yana chased after him, screwing up her eyes as the vessel descended, kicking up a cyclone of dirt and dust.

"I knew they couldn't be trusted," the Herald snarled

as the landing gear lowered, the ship coming to a rest with almost preternatural grace. "They must have planned this from the start."

"We don't know that," Yana said as Matty and Oliviah caught up with them, stopping short when they, too, noticed the markings on the craft.

"Don't we? They're all the same: hypocrites and liars." He whirled on Oliviah with such ferocity that this time the Jedi's hand found her lightsaber, although the weapon remained in its holster, at least for the moment. "What was that about an angry mob, eh? What was that about finding a peaceful solution?"

"I meant every word," she told him. "I promise you."

"And what about them?" he snapped back, pointing at the figures already marching down the ship's boarding ramp. "Do they agree with you, or were you just stalling for time?"

Zeveron tried to answer, but Yana wasn't listening. She was watching the newcomers, with their pristine robes and knowing eyes, a lightsaber hanging from every golden belt.

So much for being a mediator. The Jedi Order had arrived on Dalna in force.

THIRTY-EIGHT

"This has *nothing* to do with us," Oliviah told the furious Nautolan, but the Herald wasn't ready to listen, and in all honesty, Matty couldn't blame him.

"Stay away from the Path," he spat at her, turning on his heel and running into the crowd already gathering in the marketplace. "The Force will be free."

Yana was already moving to follow, but Matty caught her arm.

"Stay," she said. "Talk to them with us. Explain what's happening."

The Evereni glanced at the Jedi streaming from the ship

and pulled her arm free. "How can I? How can I trust any of you?"

"You can trust me," Matty said, but the woman had already disappeared. Matty considered going after her but knew it wouldn't go well. She didn't recognize any of the Jedi who were approaching Oliviah, but she had her suspicions. The insignia on the front of the craft didn't just indicate the Jedi Order; it marked the vessel as belonging to the High Council itself. Maybe that sigil didn't just represent the High Council; maybe it marked the end of her glittering Jedi career before it started.

"Council members," Oliviah said, addressing the newcomers as Matty fell in beside her. "Masters. Welcome to Ferdan."

The Jedi Master at the front of the delegation, a female Caamasi with a pronounced snout and distinctive black and white stripes through her fur, bowed her head in greeting.

"Jedi Oliviah, this *is* a surprise. Why are you on Dalna?"

"I was about to ask you the same thing, Master Ela. Last I heard, you were still in the Core."

"While you were on Jedha."

"I was injured in the recent troubles," Oliviah said, touching her side. "I requested a leave of absence to return to the Temple to convalesce."

"And yet, as you intimated, Dalna is a long way from Coruscant." This was an elderly Duros with a stern expression on his weather-beaten face.

"This is Master Rinn," the Caamasi said before turning to a cone-headed Morseerian wearing a breath mask to survive Dalna's oxygen-rich atmosphere. "And you remember Gluth Andoi."

"Of course. It is good to see you again, Master Gluth."

Matty didn't know what was more intimidating, the mirrored goggles on Gluth's mask or the Duros's penetrating gaze. Oliviah didn't seem fazed at all, continuing her explanation as if she didn't have a care in the worlds.

"After the events on Jedha, I decided to make a slight detour to investigate various leads the Convocation had received."

"That's quite a detour," Gluth wheezed through his mask, a long rubber tube snaking from the mask to a methane tank beneath his Jedi robes.

"I would have contacted Coruscant directly," she continued, "but, as you're probably aware, communications are down across much of the sector. Is that why you are here?" She paused to glance at the six or so Jedi standing behind the Masters. "In such numbers."

"A good question," came another voice as a human woman pushed her way through the crowd of onlookers. "Another might be why you've decided to land your ship in the middle of my town rather than the spaceport?"

"And you are?" Master Ela asked the newcomer, who regarded the Jedi with barely disguised contempt.

"Someone who has had enough of Core dwellers waltzing in as if they own the place."

"I think Master Ela was hoping for a name," Rinn said. The woman was already rankled; why was the Duros antagonizing her?

"Forgive me if I don't give a spacer's cuss what the 'Master' wants. I'm the sheriff of this town and you are not welcome."

"Sheriff . . ." Ela began, waiting for the woman to provide her name.

"Pickwick. Jinx Pickwick."

"Sheriff Pickwick, I apologize for any inconvenience our arrival has caused, but we attempted to land at the spaceport only to be told that no space was available."

"Which sounds to me like a great reason to turn around and hyperjump the hell away."

Ela smiled, a stark contrast to Rinn's handling of the situation. "I'm afraid that is not possible. Perhaps you remember my young associate from his last visit to Dalna?"

She indicated a tan-skinned human standing at the back of the group alongside a green-domed astromech, both lost in the gathering. Matty's eyes narrowed as the man was beckoned forward, looking less than happy about suddenly being plunged into the limelight. The droid rolled at his feet. There was something familiar about the guy, something she couldn't place but thought she knew.

Sheriff Pickwick, it seemed, had also met the Jedi before. "Ah, yes," she said as he joined the Masters. "I'm afraid I can't remember your name, but you were here looking for those Jedi who went missing, weren't you?"

"Missing?" Matty cut in, feeling increasingly left out of the conversation. "As in the Soikan and her Padawan?"

"Yes," the young Jedi with the droid said, glancing nervously at the Masters, "but maybe we should discuss this elsewh—"

"Rell!" Matty declared, louder than she'd intended.

"Padawan?" Oliviah asked.

"That's his name," Matty replied, pointing at the Jedi. "Azlin Rell."

"It is," Azlin said sheepishly. "But I don't think—"

"We've met?" she said. "No, I don't think we have, but I've seen you, on Jedha."

"Matty . . ." Oliviah warned, her voice low.

"In the archives," Matty continued, ignoring her.

"That's right," Azlin said, his face flushing. "I've passed through from time to time, on the bidding of Master—"

"Of Master Xo Lahru," Matty exclaimed, clicking her fingers. "I *knew* I recognized you."

"Yes, thank you, Matthea," Oliviah hissed, the grit of her teeth telling Matty precisely what she thought of the continual interruptions. "But this isn't the time—"

"For introductions?" Matty asked, now in full flow. "I don't know why, seeing everyone else is getting one." She turned to Master Ela, whose furry eyebrows were raised. "I'm Matty, by the way. Padawan Matty Cathley, and I *realize* I'm only a humble apprentice, but I've been through a lot these last few weeks and thought I was doing okay, but apparently

I'm not. And once I *start* talking, I find it *really* hard to stop, especially when I've been biting my tongue for *days*, and when *everyone*, from a temple delegation to the local sheriff, seems to know a lot more than me about the situation I never asked to be a part of but find myself in the middle of. A situation, I might add," she continued, knowing full well that she should shut up, "I was doing my best to handle when my actually-quite-impressive bridge-building was blown out of the water by a Jedi cruiser dropping out of the sky in the middle of our negotiations!"

There was a shocked silence for a moment when she finally stopped, out of breath and with cheeks that burned like burst-thrusters.

"Are you finished, Padawan Matty Cathley?" Master Ela eventually asked.

"Probably," Matty admitted, wondering if she should hand over her lightsaber or wait for it to be taken from her.

"Excellent," the Caamasi said, an amused glint in her yellow eyes. "Then I suggest we all retire to our ship to discuss what has been happening. . . ."

THIRTY-NINE

Another ship had entered Dalna's atmosphere minutes before the Jedi arrived, a ship that had barely made it through hyperspace in one piece.

A ship that had escaped Planet X as part of a pair but arrived on Dalna alone.

Shea hadn't cried until they set down in the Path compound, her grief for Geth finally catching up to her. None of them had known what to say to her, Sunshine more concerned with the dozen or so eggs they'd managed to get off the planet while Jukkyuk pointed out that he wasn't the kind of Wookiee who gave hugs. Marda, meanwhile . . .

Marda just felt cold.

The explosion she'd heard was the *Bonecrusher*, but no one could explain what had happened. There was a sudden crack over the comm, a yell from Geth, and then a blinding flash of light. When Shea had looked again, the *Bonecrusher* was gone, the *Silverstreak*'s limited sensor bank too frazzled to judge whether the other ship had disintegrated or been thrown from hyperspace. Sunshine made a half-hearted attempt to convince Shea that it was the latter and that Geth and the others were still out there somewhere, but she'd shut him down, blaming Wole. She said that the Rodian had obviously botched the adjustments to the stabilizers. Stupid Wole. Stupid, stupid Wole.

It was obvious she blamed herself and the plan born of her abnormal connection to the Force, a plan that had gotten them home but a blasphemy all the same.

Now that they were home, the others left Shea in the navigator seat, big ugly tears rolling down her cheeks and a hand clutching her belly.

The Mother was waiting for them as Marda joined Sunshine and Jukkyuk outside, the precious eggs in packs over their shoulders as they descended the ramp.

If Elecia was surprised to see Marda exiting the vessel, she didn't say anything. That suited Marda fine. Even Sunshine seemed slightly more restrained around the Mother. Usually, he'd be openly drooling, but he merely asked the Elders where they wanted the assets.

Marda didn't speak as Elders Jichora and Waiden led them down to the caverns, nor when the twelve eggs were carefully retrieved from the bags and placed on a series of pedestals on the assembly cavern's platform as if they were works of art. She didn't even flinch when the Leveler, strangely cowed though it was, sniffed at the lightsaber that hadn't left her grip since she opened the way to the hyperdrive.

She had nothing to say. Not to the Elders and definitely not to the Mother, who had attached a second shaft to the Rod of Seasons. The Rod of Daybreak, maybe, finally retrieved from Jedha? Marda found it hard to care, even when the conjoined rods glowed with purple energy as Elecia swept them over the gems—gems that shook and quivered as if whatever was inside was eager to get out.

The gems that had cost them all much.

Marda didn't even respond when the Mother congratulated her personally, saying that she'd made the right choice to follow the leading of the Force and steal away on Sunshine's ship. The Mother was proud of her. The Force would be free.

But Marda was preparing to speak. She was preparing to scream and shout and rant and rave. She was ready for the fire to be lit deep inside her, a secret place where Kevmo grinned horribly and Bokana told her he loved her. That fire would banish the cold and forge her anew, but it wasn't time yet. That would come.

And then everything would change.

FORTY

Jedi Master Ela Sutan listened to everything she was told, first by Oliviah and then by Doc Nindle and the sheriff.

All the time, Matty fumed at the back of the elegant meeting room on board the Jedi cruiser. In many ways, the space reminded her of the council chamber on Coruscant, not that she'd seen it personally, only in holograms. Nine chairs were set in a circle, seven of which were occupied by Masters Sutan, Rinn, and Andoi; Sheriff Pickwick; Doc Nindle; Oliviah; and Azlin Rell.

The remaining Jedi stood around the plain walls as stoic

as Temple Guards, while Rell's astromech waited patiently behind his master as the conversation continued.

Matty had been instructed to stand with the other Jedi, Oliviah telling her to "stay there" the moment they entered the chamber. She found a place next to a towering Anomid wearing an angular vocalizer mask that covered their entire face. The Jedi didn't even nod in greeting as Matty slipped alongside them. She was being punished, and she knew why. Understood it, even. She had let her frustration about being sidelined run away with her and could just imagine the lecture she would receive from Oliviah once the meeting was at an end: *This is Vildar and Tey's influence. You've forgotten how a Padawan should act. You've forgotten the need for respect.*

But respect went two ways, as far as Matty was concerned. Oliviah hadn't shown Matty one iota of respect since they'd touched down on Dalna. Why agree to her coming along in the first place if Oliviah was going to slap her down at any given moment?

"This is all very worrying," Ela Sutan said, stroking the bristles beneath her snout. "If what you say is true, the Path is preparing for a battle."

"Or a siege," Rinn agreed.

"But it still doesn't explain why *you* are here, Council member?" Oliviah said. "Surely it can't be the disappearance of two Jedi, worrying though that is."

"Indeed," Ela conceded, turning to Azlin expectantly.

"Perhaps you would like to tell our friends what you found when you were last here, Jedi Rell."

The young man cleared his throat, looking distinctly uncomfortable as all eyes turned to him. "Two months ago," he began, "I was dispatched to investigate the whereabouts of Jedi Zallah Macri and her Padawan, Kevmo Zink. They were reported to have left Dalna after coming here to search for an artifact called the Rod of Seasons, stolen from the Hynestian royal family. However, their ship was still here, apparently abandoned, and no one had seen them since.

"On my arrival, Sheriff Pickwick informed me that the Path of the Open Hand had also left around the same time, taking a cruiser they'd been building for years."

"The *Gaze Electric*," Sheriff Pickwick cut in, Azlin acknowledging the interruption with a nod.

"I searched the Path's land," he continued, "discovering a vast network of caves beneath the surface."

"The same caves that the Path has now returned to," Ela clarified.

"And fortified, by all accounts," Rinn added grimly.

"There, within the caverns, I found the . . . remains of both Jedi."

"Their bodies?" Matty asked, stepping forward to rest her hands on one of the empty chairs.

"Not exactly," he told her, seeming to have trouble choosing the right words for what he'd seen. "They were . . . husks . . . their skin almost like stone."

"Husks?" Oliviah asked.

"And that wasn't all, was it, Azlin?" Ela prompted.

Azlin shook his head. "There was a . . . presence in the caves, a feeling that stayed with me long after I recovered the remains and left the planet."

Fascinated, Matty pulled the seat back and dropped into it, leaning toward Azlin. "What kind of feeling?"

The Jedi hesitated, as if not wanting to say the word out loud. "It was fear. Pure, unadulterated fear, clinging to Zallah and Kevmo's remains like a bad smell."

"Something similar to the sensation you felt in the camp, perhaps?" Andoi asked, remembering what Oliviah had told them about their experience when facing the Path.

"And on Jedha, too," Oliviah replied, choosing her words carefully. "It was certainly . . . unnerving."

Unnerving? Talk about an understatement. Matty thought "terrifying" was a better description. "Bloodcurdling," even.

"Azlin came to me on Elphrona, where I am marshal of the local outpost," Master Rinn explained, returning to Rell's report. "I've known the lad since he was Padawan to my old friend Arkoff. . . ."

Matty fought the urge to raise her eyebrows at that revelation, struggling to imagine the Duros being friends with *anyone*.

"Quite naturally, I took the news to the Council on Coruscant," Rinn continued, "traveling with Azlin myself."

Ela Sutan clasped her hands together as she took up the story. "We had heard worrying rumors about Dalna for a while, even before Rinn and Azlin arrived at the Temple."

"And you didn't send anyone to *check* the rumors?" Matty spoke up, ignoring the look from Oliviah.

"Yes, we did, as it happens," Gluth Andoi replied, the Morseerian turning his masked face toward her. "Jedi Master Creighton Sun and Jedi Knight Aida Forte were dispatched to investigate."

"Dispatched here?" Sheriff Pickwick asked, frowning at the new information. "To Ferdan? I wasn't aware that any more Jedi were on Dalna."

"Both Creighton and Aida have a talent for . . . blending in," Ela Sutan replied, choosing her words carefully.

"If they made it here at all," Rinn growled, gripping his knees as if trying to stop himself from leaping out of his seat.

"There's nothing to suggest they didn't," Gluth Andoi pointed out.

"Other than the fact that we haven't been able to raise them," Rinn reminded him. "Either on our approach to the planet or back in the Core."

"Communication systems are compromised. . . ."

"*Sun and Forte* might be compromised, for all we know," the Duros argued. "Especially if the sheriff here hasn't heard of them." Rinn turned his attention back to Oliviah. "I assume *you* haven't made contact, Jedi Zeveron?"

"With Sun and . . ." Oliviah paused, searching for the name.

"Forte," Gluth Andoi provided.

Oliviah shook her head. "I only wish we had. We had no idea *any* Jedi had been on Dalna before we heard of Master Zallah's visit."

"And I thought two was enough," Sheriff Pickwick snorted, crossing her arms. "I didn't know when I was well off."

"We haven't taken this lightly, I assure you," Ela told the woman. "Gluth and I meditated on Azlin's report, the Force advising us to visit Dalna personally."

"But what about the bodies?" Matty asked, exasperated that such an important detail seemed to have been glossed over. "The remains Azlin found. You did test them, right? You found out what happened?"

"Padawan . . ." Oliviah warned, but Master Ela waved away the concern.

"It's a fair question," the Caamasi said. "And one I wish I could answer."

"Jedi Macri and Zink's bodies crumbled as we tried to examine them," Andoi Gluth explained, the breath mask muffling his words. "What was left was little more than ash."

"Ash?" Matty had vowed not to speak out of turn again, but there was no way she could let that pass.

"Padawan?" Ela Sutan asked, leaning forward in her chair. "Are you all right? I sense . . ."

"Master Leebon," Matty started to reply, her throat suddenly tight. "My master . . . I mean, my former master, she . . ."

Her voice cracked, and for once in her life Matty found it hard to speak.

"She died," Oliviah said, with more kindness than Matty had experienced for a while. "In the battle of Jedha. We don't know how, but no body was found, her remains turned to dust."

Matty gave her a smile, weak but grateful, and Oliviah smiled back.

"I see," Ela said, reflecting on the fresh information. "Of course, we have heard about the troubles in the Holy City. The news of the battle reached Coruscant as we prepared to leave, our fellow Council members insisting that a contingent of Jedi Knights accompany us on our journey."

"Even though we are more than capable of looking after ourselves," Rinn muttered beneath his breath, shooting a look at the Jedi keeping guard around the walls.

"A precaution," Ela reminded the Duros. "More for Dalna than us, especially with the communication network still experiencing such difficulties."

"Well, speaking on *behalf* of Dalna," Sheriff Pickwick said, her hands clasped on her knees, "while we appreciate the sentiment, we'd rather you, the Path, and every other Force-whisperer would respectfully clear the druk off our planet."

"Sheriff," Doc Nindle said, trying to stop Jinx before she could say something everyone would regret, but she just raised a hand to the Mon Calamari, shutting him down. "I'm sorry, Nin, really I am, but it needs to be said. The Path used to be no trouble at all, a little weird maybe, but ever since you Jedi have been sniffing around, everything's gotten out of hand. They're buying property in town, poisoning our neighbors. . . ."

"Although we don't know if that was intentional," Doc Nindle added quickly, but Matty suspected he already knew that it was.

"Either way, you have them spooked."

"And what would you have us do, Sheriff?" Rinn asked, glaring at the woman. "Leave you at the mercy of these criminals? If this *is* our doing—and I find that hard to believe—then it's our responsibility to put things right."

"And that's why you're here?" Pickwick asked, looking the Duros straight in the eye. "Not to take revenge for your people's death?"

"Jedi never take revenge," Gluth Andoi replied for Rinn. "Although we are naturally curious to find out what happened to them. Surely, as an officer of the law, you can respect that?

"We have no intention of causing your people distress," Ela Sutan said, speaking directly to the sheriff. "All I suggest is that we visit the camp to see for ourselves."

"Sneak in, you mean."

"No," Ela replied, shooting a glance at Oliviah, who didn't

move but Matty could feel was squirming inside. "That might be misconstrued."

The Caamasi stood, her long robes falling to her feet. "If we approach the Path in peace, I am sure we will be able to reach an understanding. The Force is with us, after all."

FORTY-ONE

"The Jedi are coming. They are coming for the Path!"

Yana had tried to stop Werth, but he was done listening. He tore through the camp, heading down into the caves where the Path was gathered in the assembly cavern, water dripping from the stalactites above. The Mother stood before them on the raised platform, the Leveler at her feet and Marda at her side.

"Herald?" the Mother exclaimed as Werth burst into the chamber. "You've returned to us."

"To reclaim what is rightfully mine," he replied, pushing

his way through the crowd. "What is rightfully *ours.* You do not belong here, Elecia. You will destroy us all."

The Mother didn't respond. She didn't have to. Brikal-stained hands seized Werth, holding him in place.

"Didn't you hear me?" he shrieked as the crowd turned against him. "The Jedi have come to Dalna. They will march on us within the hour. This is what she has brought down on us, our false prophet."

"A prophet you vouched for," Elder Jichora called back.

"To my eternal shame. We must rise up against her tyranny to protect the Path. To protect the Force."

The Mother finally spoke, thrusting the combined Rod of Power toward him. "No, if the Jedi are here, it is your doing, Werth Plouth, the result of your actions on Jedha!"

The Herald barked a laugh. "I was doing *your* bidding, Elecia, bringing you the treasures you sought. And how was I rewarded? You abandoned me to our enemy, the same enemy that now stands at our gates."

"Lies, all lies," the Mother declared. "Throw him from the caves. Let the Jedi have him. It's only what the traitor deserves!"

The Herald thrashed and punched but couldn't break free.

"Tell them, Yana," he yelled as he was dragged from the assembly. "Tell them what she did to Kor. Tell them everything."

Why did he have to bring her into this? They could rip

each other apart for all Yana cared, but the damage was done, anger rippling through the crowd.

She's a part of it. Part of his group.

She's working for the traitor.

Get her!

"No," she said as the first hand grabbed her. "This has nothing to do with me. I only want to talk to Marda. You have to let me through."

But the crowd had become a mob, tearing at her clothes, calling for her blood. All the while, the Mother stood imperiously on the raised platform, Rod of Power in hand, proclaiming that the Path was pure and the Force would be free.

An elbow struck Yana in the side of her head, and she went down, feet trampling her, kicking her. All she could hear was noise and recrimination. There was no way she was getting out of there alive.

That was when a lightsaber ignited and someone shouted: "Silence!"

FORTY-TWO

Everyone stopped. The Path members, the Herald, even the Mother. All eyes turned toward the person who'd spoken, a spluttering yellow blade raised above her head.

"What are you doing?" Marda asked them, standing at the front of the platform. "Isn't this what they want? The Jedi? The Force abusers. Force *killers*! After everything we've been through . . . everything the Force has tried to tell us . . . look at us! Look at what we have become! Fighting among ourselves, tearing each other apart."

The cavern was silent except for her voice. Marda had

never felt anything like this, never felt so sure about herself and her purpose. She was faintly aware that the cousin she'd thought dead was nearby. Yana had even screamed her name when Marda had stepped forward bearing Kevmo's lightsaber, but it didn't matter. Neither did the fact that the Mother was glaring at her with a mixture of fury and fascination. Why should Marda care? Elecia had made her the Guide of the Path, and no one was ever going to take that away, not now that she could see the way so clearly.

Marda lowered the weapon but kept the blade burning, the roar of the sparking plasma underlining her words.

"If the Jedi are here, as Werth says"—she stepped down from the platform, the Path parting in front of her—"if they have arrived to bring us to the sword, then this is our moment. They came to us before, and we took them in. We tried to find a way to make them see the truth, but they threw it back in our faces. Only *their* way mattered to them. Only *their* path. And here we see the results. The Path of the Open Hand broken, at each other's throats. And all the time, the sky weeps above us, our crops rot in the fields, and we do nothing. We cower, and we plot, and we prepare for what, exactly? To survive? To continue our way of life? No. That is not good enough. Not anymore. *We* are the liberators of the Force. We protect it with our lives, for the sake of all."

Marda continued walking, the Path surrounding her until she was in the middle of the cavern, pressed in from all sides. She turned, her blade sizzling.

"I've seen what the Jedi's corruption of the Force has done to us firsthand. How it has twisted us, created abominations in our midst." Her eyes met Shea's, standing at the back of the chamber, her arms across her belly. For a moment, she thought she saw a shadow behind the grieving engineer, an Ovissian with a missing tusk, but she was done with phantoms. Marda Ro was ready for the future.

"If we leave the Jedi unchecked, their evil will tear through the galaxy like wildfire. The imbalance is real. I've felt it myself, seen what it can do and where it leads. The Force will die, and everything will die with it. Every planet, every moon, every star in the sky. How can we fight that if we continue to fight each other? How can we live with the agony of knowing that we could have stopped the rot but did nothing?"

Heads were shaking in the crowd, Path members muttering their accord.

"The Jedi have come looking for the Path of the Open Hand, but they are too late. That dream has broken. That dream has failed. *We* failed, but no more. We offered them a gift freely given, but they wouldn't take it. Now we offer another gift, a gift they won't be able to refuse. A gift we will deliver here on Dalna and in the galaxy beyond. On Jedha. On Eiram and E'ronoh. On Coruscant itself. They did not heed our warning, and now they will pay the price—the price not of an open hand but a closed fist."

Her saber held tight, Marda dragged her other hand

across the markings on her face, her fingers smudging the three vertical lines into jagged lightning bolts.

"Who walks the Path with me?" she called out, the cavern ringing with the sound of her defiance. "Who walks the Path of the Closed Fist?"

FORTY-THREE

Yana couldn't breathe. The atmosphere within the cavern had become stifling, claustrophobic. All around her, arms were raised, fists pumping the air as the same words rang out, over and over.

The Force will be free.

The Force will be free.

The noise was deafening, every member of the community she'd once called home shouting their allegiance to the Path of the Closed Fist in unison.

Shouting their allegiance to Marda.

If Yana had been scared for her cousin before, she was

terrified now. Marda was surrounded, that damned saber blazing in one hand, the other raised high in a brikal-stained fist. But it was the expression on Marda's face that most filled Yana with dread. The fervor burning in her eyes, her head held high. Yana wanted to push through the crowd, to grab Marda by the shoulders and shake her until it hurt, anything to snap her back to reality. But maybe this *was* reality for her cousin, a future as jagged as the lightning bolts on her face.

Yana turned, searching the crowd for the Herald. He'd also been released and was gazing around the chanting assembly in disbelief. She called his name—"Werth. Over here. Werth!"—and their eyes met, desperation in hers, a curious look in his. Then she realized what it was: opportunity.

"No," she muttered beneath her breath as the Herald clenched his own fist, thrusting it into the air as he added his voice to the chorus: "The Force will be free. The Force will be free."

Couldn't he see what was about to happen? Couldn't he smell it in the air? The fanaticism. The hatred.

Of course not. All Werth Plouth could see was a power shift, a chance to rejoin the faithful and bend it to his will. He pushed his way through the multitude, most of whom were copying Marda and daubing lightning bolts on their own faces. She couldn't let him do this.

Not caring who she hit, Yana plowed into the crowd,

elbowing and scratching her way toward him. "What are you *doing*?" she demanded when she finally stood in front of him. "This is going to be a bloodbath. You know, don't you? We won't stand a chance."

He looked at her as if she were a rust-weevil destined to be ground underfoot. "No, Yana. We know they are coming. We are prepared. Are you with us?"

"Us"? Was he insane? "There is no us, Werth. I can't be a part of this. It's suicide."

"Then you should run," he concluded, brushing her aside, "like the coward you are."

Yana lost her footing, landing at the feet of the Path, who immediately started to trample her. She kicked out, trying to pull herself up. How dare he speak to her like that. After everything she'd done for him. All that talk about Kor and his wife? Where was his concern for Opari now? Had he forgotten her that easily? Had he ever truly cared?

Yana fought her way back to her feet. The Herald had made it to Marda as Elecia and the Leveler descended from the stage. All three came together in the middle of the crowd, Marda standing with the crackling saber still raised high, Werth and the Mother on either side.

Yana felt sick.

The Herald raised his hands, calling for silence.

"My friends, the Guide has shown us the way. She has reminded us . . . reminded *me* . . . the truth of our situation.

She is right. Even now, the enemies of the Force seek to silence us and we must stand together, no matter what has happened between us. The old Path is gone; the new Path will light the way. We shall fight for the sake of the Force, for the sake of freedom, justice, and purity. For the sake of all."

The Mother joined her former ally, a general rallying her troops. "In their arrogance, the Jedi think they know what they are facing, but they are wrong. Today we are born anew. Today we face our destiny. This is where we draw a line. This is where we take a stand!"

The crowd responded to her call to action, moving as one for the exits. Couldn't they see this for what it was, what the Mother was? Elecia wasn't drawing a line; she was clinging to power, attaching herself to Marda's fanaticism to stop herself from being pushed aside. And yet the faithful were falling for it, laughing, actually laughing, as they swept from the cavern, as if it were all a game. Yana screamed at them, telling them they were going to get slaughtered, but they didn't listen, the young and the old going off to die.

She whirled around to see Marda, Werth, and the Mother watching them all go, as dispassionate as gods. She stalked toward them, ignoring Elecia and the Herald, even ignoring the Leveler that paced up and down the emptying chamber.

"I need to talk to you," she said, wanting to grab Marda's arm but kept at bay by the spluttering lightsaber.

"This isn't the time, Yana," the Mother said. "We have much to do."

"She isn't one of us," the Herald sneered. "She doesn't even believe in the cause. She's been plotting against the one true Path all along, working with our enemies."

Yana laughed out loud, not believing his audacity. "You can go to hell, both of you." She stepped around the blade, grabbing her cousin's free arm. "This has gone on long enough, Marda. We're leaving."

"You can't tell me what to do, Yana. This is where I belong."

"Why? Because of all this? It's all lies, Marda. They don't care about you. They're *using* you. Why can't you see that?"

The pain came first, even before Yana registered the flash of the lightsaber. She staggered back, unable to fully process what had just happened, her fingers wrapped around the charred stump that had used to be her right wrist.

"What have you done?" she gasped, looking up at her cousin in disbelief.

"What I should have done a long time ago," Marda said, watching her writhe in agony on the ground. "I've cut myself free. Free of you. Free of anyone who's ever told me what to do."

Smiling like a viper, the Mother placed a hand on Marda's shoulder. "Come, my Guide. Leave the traitor where she belongs."

"No, Marda," Yana moaned as Marda was led to the platform, where the strange eggs waited on their plinths. Only the Leveler remained, peering at her with soulless eyes.

"What are you waiting for?" she hissed. "Why don't you finish the job?"

But the monster just turned and walked away, leaving Yana in the dirt.

Marda felt no regret as she took the Herald's hand and let him lead her up onto the platform. Yana had done her a favor, helping her sever the last link to her past. She kept the saber burning as she approached the eggs they'd brought back from Planet X. Such a ridiculous name. The kind of name a Little would conjure up. She preferred the planet remain nameless. Names were power, and she never wanted to think of the place again. Never wanted to think of the girl she had been.

The Mother and the Herald were already discussing tactics. She let them babble, actually amused at how easily they had abandoned their principles the moment she'd seized control. Not for herself, never for herself.

She'd done it for the Force.

"They will be here soon," the Herald said, keeping a safe distance from her lightsaber. "Are you sure the defenses will hold?"

The Mother smiled. "The defenses are the least of the Jedi's worries."

"*Shrii Ka Rai*," Marda said, Calar's strange words returning to her as she gazed at the eggs, although now they brought certainty instead of fear. They brought power. "The Nameless will rise. Champions of the Force."

"Nameless? What are you talking about, Marda?" the Herald asked, but she ignored him, holding out her free hand to the Mother.

"The rod, Elecia. Give it to me."

The Mother hesitated, shaking her head. "Not yet, but soon, I promise."

Marda had spent too many years being told no. She stepped closer to the Mother, allowing the saber's blade to make her point.

"No, not soon. Now."

The Mother tried to smile, but it was a fleeting thing, trembling. "Very well," she said, finally relinquishing the rod. "You are the Guide after all. The Guide of the Closed Fist."

Marda didn't thank her. She didn't need to. Everything that was happening was the will of the Force. The Mother and the Herald took a step back, the Leveler slinking from its former mistress to stand beside Marda.

She thrust out her hand, holding the Rod of Power above the gems. Energy crackled, and the eggs started to quake, gently at first, then with more urgency as the creatures inside began to claw their way out.

PART THREE
THE BATTLE OF DALNA

FORTY-FOUR

"We need to talk."

"No, thank you."

"Matty. You're being childish."

"Then why don't you send me back to the ship? I know you don't want me around."

They were nearing the Path's compound, Master Ela leading the small party, which had swollen in number before they left Ferdan, Sheriff Pickwick recruiting a small army of deputies along the way.

"I never said I didn't want you around," Oliviah said with a sigh.

"You didn't have to. Actions speak louder than words,

Jedi Zeveron. You didn't even introduce me when Ela and the others arrived. I don't know why you agreed to bring me along in the first place."

"Because . . ." Oliviah paused, wiping rainwater from her face. "Because I don't know what I'm following here, where the Force is leading me. I'd considered asking Vildar to come along, but couldn't because of his responsibilities to the Convocation—"

Responsibilities you abdicated, Matty thought but kept to herself.

"And Tey . . . well, I still don't know what to make of Tey."

"No one knows what to make of Tey, most of all himself."

"So when Vildar suggested I take you . . ."

"I was all that was left."

"Yes."

The bluntness of the reply stung, Matty didn't mind admitting. To her credit, Oliviah obviously realized how it had sounded, letting out a sigh.

"Look, this is all new for me. Before the Path came to Jedha, I was struggling."

"You were?"

"You don't have to pretend to be surprised."

"I'm not. I always thought you were so together."

"That's what I wanted you to think. What I wanted *everyone* to think. Master Leebon knew differently, not that I ever told her. She was just . . ."

"Just *her.*"

"Precisely. Then, during the riot, I saw something that"—another pause; this was obviously difficult for her—"spoke to me, through the Force, although I had no idea what it meant. What I was supposed to do. All those times I'd meditated in front of the Sentinel, asking the Force to show me the way, and now, when it answered, I had no idea what it meant."

Matty hadn't even known that Oliviah traveled out to the giant statue in the Jedha desert. She thought she was the only one.

"I'm trying to apologize," Oliviah admitted. "I know I've been difficult. Distant, as well. But I will explain when this is all over."

"When you understand the answer."

Oliviah gave a weak smile. "That's the plan."

Matty smiled back but couldn't say anything else before Ela summoned Oliviah to the front as they approached the Path's gates.

"I'm sorry," Oliviah said.

"Go, go," Matty said, trying not to shudder as she saw the compound's walls.

"Everything okay?"

Matty jumped, not having sensed Azlin Rell's approach. "Yeah," she said, flashing the young Knight a tight smile. "Absolutely."

"Liar."

Luckily, he laughed as he said it, making her chuckle.

"Problems with your master?"

"Oh, she's not my master. We're just . . . colleagues."

"Sounds formal."

"I honestly don't know how else to explain it."

There was plenty she *could* explain. How her frustration and anger had suddenly been replaced with confusion. Ever since she'd agreed to come on this mission, Matty had been so out of her comfort zone that she might as well have been in a different system. Oliviah made her feel so uncomfortable, so small, but that was nothing new. She'd even respected Oliviah for her standoffishness back on Jedha, impressed with how little of a kriff the older Jedi gave about . . . well . . . anything. But now, now she'd discovered Oliviah felt just as lost as she did. If a full Jedi Knight felt that way, what hope did a Padawan have?

"Do you want my advice?" Azlin asked.

"Do I have a choice?" she replied, smirking.

Azlin's smile dropped away. "Keep your head down."

Matty laughed. "That's it?"

"It's better in the long run. Less pressure for a start."

"Right." Matty nodded as if he'd just imparted wisdom worthy of Yoda himself. "Got it. Helpful."

At least that made him grin. "Why do I get the feeling that you're just saying that?"

"Because I am," she replied with good humor. The pep talk would never win any awards, but the support was appreciated nonetheless. "Perhaps you could tell me more about your philosophy of life when this is all over."

"Maybe I can." He looked ahead, the smile fading again. "It would be something to look forward to, anyway. I hoped that I'd never have to come back here, that Rinn would take over the investigation the moment he saw the bodies." He shivered, and Matty doubted it had anything to do with the weather. "The thought of going back into those caves . . ."

She gave him a playful nudge with her arm. "Just keep your head down. It'll be all right."

Azlin chuckled quietly. "Got it. Helpful."

Matty couldn't blame the guy for being apprehensive, though. Just entering the camp made her want to run and hide, not that she ever would. She pulled her cloak tight around herself as they walked through the abandoned buildings, repeating the old maxim she'd been taught by the Guardians of the Whills back home: "The Force is with me. I am one with the Force."

Little did Matty know that she was being observed by hidden cameras set up by Shea Ganandra, who was sitting in a control chamber deep underground, surrounded by dozens of screens. The engineer had raised the alarm the minute the Jedi had passed through the gates, and now watched in silence as the party walked confidently through the buildings.

Would they be so confident if they knew that the crates that had arrived on the transport had been emptied of the grains and seeds, revealing their true contents, so expertly hidden in the offworld supplies? The smuggled units were now secreted in the huts near the entrance to the caves, waiting and watching, just like Shea.

The engineer leaned over and flicked a switch. "They're coming. How long do you want me to wait?"

"Can you . . . sense anyone?" Sheriff Pickwick asked, looking at the Jedi expectantly. "You can do that, can't you? Sense people hiding in the shadows?"

"Sometimes," Ela Sutan informed her, narrowing her yellow eyes. "But there's no one here. No one at all."

The Caamasi looked at the other Jedi, and they all shook their heads, Matty included, although she doubted that her senses were at their best, not with the sand-rats that squirmed in her stomach.

"Hello?" Master Ela shouted, making Matty jump. "Is there anyone here? We've come to talk."

The only reply was the thud of the rain on the once-dusty ground that was now in danger of becoming a quagmire.

"My name is Ela Sutan. I am a member of the Jedi High Council. We are looking for members of our number: Jedi Zallah Macri and Padawan Kevmo Zink. We want no trouble, only to locate our friends."

FORTY-FOUR

"No trouble," Shea repeated in the control hub. "Wouldn't that be nice?"

She hadn't wanted any part of this, not since Geth had died, and there was no doubt in her mind that was what had happened when they tried to escape the Veil. A flash of light and the *Bonecrusher* was no more, the only person she'd ever loved gone with it. She put a hand over her stomach, thinking for a moment she was about to be sick. She deserved to be. It had been her calculations that had gotten Geth killed, after everything they had planned for the future.

She'd wanted to leave immediately, but the Mother had stepped in, offering Shea the money that would have gone to Galamal if she'd help transform the caves into a bunker. Then she could do whatever she wanted. The job had been easy enough, even though she'd seemed to have lost the second sense she'd experienced on Planet X. That was probably for the best. She didn't want to think what effect that place had had on the—

Shea swore beneath her breath. No amount of credits would help if the Jedi invaded the caves, and that damned Caamasi had just stepped over the line the Mother had set as the point of no return.

"Well?" Elecia's voice crackled over Shea's comm. "What are you waiting for?"

Shea pressed a button and activated the trap.

The blaster bolts tore out of the huts without warning. One of Pickwick's deputies went down immediately, the rest scattering as the Jedi stepped into the breach, lightsabers flaring.

"I thought you couldn't sense anyone," Pickwick yelled, but Matty didn't answer. She was too busy batting bolts toward their point of origin. Nearby, Rinn did the same, sending a bolt screaming toward a building already on the point of collapse. The wall crumbled in on itself, revealing a trio of asymmetrical eyes blazing red.

Enforcer droids! No wonder they hadn't sensed anything. They had been trying to detect living beings!

"They're coming out!" Ela warned as the droids emerged from the dwelling, servos whirring and crimson eyes glaring from black faceplates. Matty had seen them once before, in the streets of Jedha, and now they were on Dalna. It couldn't be a coincidence.

FORTY-FIVE

"The droids aren't stopping them!" Shea yelled as she ran into the assembly cavern.

"Droids?" the Herald asked the Mother.

"An insurance policy I cooked up with dear Tilson Graf. Just in case we were followed back to Dalna." She turned to Shea, who looked like she wanted to run for the mountains. "Activate the second wave."

The engineer hesitated. "Are you *sure* that's a good idea?"

"Station them at the cave entrance," the Mother replied, ignoring the question and smiling sweetly at the Herald as Shea retreated back to her control station. "What? Did you think I wouldn't protect our people?"

"As long as you remember they *are* ours, Elecia. Not yours."

"We won't need droids," Marda said, watching the cracks on the eggs widen to reveal a membrane beneath the jeweled shells. "The agents of the Force will protect us."

Beside her, the Leveler bayed in agreement or hunger, maybe both.

"Even so . . ." the Mother began, but Marda cut her off.

"This is about the Path, Elecia. It's about the Force."

"Of course it is," the Mother acquiesced as the first membrane broke, a tiny snout poking into the world. The creature inside looked so pale and fragile compared with the Leveler. It squeaked as it pushed its way out, its siblings joining in as they broke free. The Leveler greeted them all with a howl that reverberated around the cavern, and Marda laughed.

They were small now, but they would grow big. They would grow strong. She could almost feel their hunger, the Leveler's desire to feast stronger than ever, but they could not move until she commanded it, the rod giving her absolute control.

"This is it," she exulted, the tiny monsters scrabbling from the eggs that had carried them from the Veil. They leaped onto Marda, swarming over her body as the rod glowed. She'd never felt power like this. Never felt such a sense of purpose.

Behind her, she was dimly aware of the Mother backing away, holding her robes close while the Herald peered at the creatures with revulsion, but Marda thought they were beautiful.

Beautiful and hungry.

The Leveler was on its feet, its powerful leg muscles ready to pounce. It was screaming in her head, longing for release, its cry stronger than Kevmo's voice had ever been, a sound both discordant and glorious. It wanted to be whole. It wanted balance to be restored.

"Go," Marda cried, spinning around to face the empty cavern. "Free the Force. Free us all."

Finally released, the Leveler bounded from the platform, and the babies followed, streaming from Marda, their tiny claws skittering on the cave floor. Soon they would grow. Soon they would have their fill.

"You have done well," the Mother said, relaxing as soon as the last of the Nameless had left the cavern. "You truly are our Guide."

Ahead, there were shouts and the sound of blaster fire, followed by the all-too-familiar swish of lightsabers in the distance.

The Jedi had made it into the caves.

"I must join our brothers and sisters," the Herald said. "I need weapons."

"There are more than enough," the Mother said, indicating the way ahead.

"Are you not coming?"

She smiled. "I am not a fighter, Werth. Not like you."

He grunted before leaping from the platform to follow the sounds of battle. "We shall talk, Elecia," he said before disappearing into the tunnels, "when this is done."

"I look forward to it," the Mother replied, her smile falling away. "And what of you, my dear?" she said, turning to Marda. "What of our Guide?"

"I will go with them," Marda said, jumping down to the cavern floor, lightsaber in one hand, rod in the other. "The creatures need me."

Once upon a time, she would have asked the Mother's permission to take her leave, but no more. She felt giddy with everything that had happened, the Path's reaction to her speech, the hatching of the Nameless. She glanced down to where she'd left Yana, hoping her cousin, a traitor though she was, could see what she'd become.

But Yana was gone.

"Where is she?" Marda said, spinning around. "Where did she go?" Her cousin's hand lay discarded on the floor, but of Yana herself there was no sign.

"Shea will have seen. She has eyes and ears everywhere," the Mother said, snapping her comlink from her belt and opening the channel. "Shea, Yana is missing."

"And?" Shea's voice came back. "We have more pressing concerns right now, Mother."

"She's in league with the Jedi," Marda shouted, rushing over to Elecia to yell into the comlink. "She's working against us."

Shea sighed over the comms, her tone weary. "And I thought you were the only Ro with a taste for space monks, Marda."

"Just find her," the Mother snapped. "Check the screens."

"I'm looking, and there's no sign. No sign at all."

"I need to find her," Marda insisted. "Before she ruins everything."

"Agreed," the Mother said, holding out a hand. "I'll take the rod."

Marda instinctively pulled the staff back toward her.

"You find your cousin," Elecia insisted. "I can guide the Nameless, just this once. Let me help."

The tables truly had turned. Now it was the Mother asking *her* for permission.

"Very well," she said, handing over the rod. "This won't take long."

"Take as long as you need," the Mother purred as Marda rushed from the cavern.

FORTY-SIX

Yana didn't know where she was going. She had lost her bearings, her breathing shallow and quick. She had crawled from the assembly cavern as soon as Marda had turned her back on her, Yana's existence forgotten. The pain had been excruciating, but at least she hadn't left a trail of blood, the wound where her right hand used to be perfectly cauterized by Marda's blade.

Marda's blade.

Marda had cut off her hand.

Her kriffing hand.

Marda could go to hell.

All that mattered was getting out, leaving Marda and

the others to rot. It would only be a matter of time. The caves reverberated with the sounds of battle, far worse than they had been on Jedha. The sounds of plasma blades, blasters, and screams. And there was something else, unnatural howls that could only mean that the Leveler and its kin had been unleashed on the unsuspecting Jedi.

She should've told them, should have warned the Jedi what they were blundering into. That was something she'd live with for the rest of her life, assuming she got out alive. She was lost; there was no escaping that. The tunnels were a maze at the best of times, and this was definitely *not* the best of times. She needed someone, anyone, to show her the way. She needed Kor.

"Where are you?" Yana cried out, her anguish bouncing off the walls. "Where have you gone?"

But Kor didn't reply. It wasn't a punishment for not heeding her warnings, not running when Yana had the chance, because Kor had never been real. The Evereni couldn't see the dead. Once someone was dead, they were gone. The only curse Yana shared with her people was to end up alone, betrayed by those she trusted, outliving everyone she loved.

"Yana?"

She spun around so fast at the voice that she lost her balance, pain jolting up her wounded arm as she landed on her backside.

"Stars' end. What's happened to you?"

Yana laughed bitterly. Sunshine Dobbs was staring at

her, actual concern written over his greasy face. The galaxy really was trying to kick her when she was down. *This* was the person who cared what had happened to her. The lying, scheming scumslug who'd conspired to kill Kor.

The prospector moved to help her up, but she kicked his hands away. "Don't touch me! Don't come near me!"

He backed off, no doubt fearing the teeth she'd bared were about to sink into his flabby neck. "Who did this to you?"

"Does it matter? Which way is out?"

"Out?"

"Don't waste my time, Dobbs. You always have an escape plan, anything to save your worthless . . ."

Her voice trailed off as she saw what Dobbs had been doing. The doors behind him were open, revealing large backpacks filled with gold, silver, and bronzium.

"The artifacts." She laughed. "You're taking the artifacts."

"Not all of them," he insisted. "She has stashes all over this place, but I'm taking what I'm due, Yana. What she owes me."

"She?" Yana gave another laugh as she realized who he was talking about. "The Mother."

"I don't like being used. Not by anyone, and definitely not by her."

"Used? I've seen the way you look at her, Dobbsy. You *love* her."

"She *made* me love her," Dobbs shouted back, spittle flying from his fat lips. "For all I know, she made *everyone* love her."

"What do you mean?"

"I felt it when we went back to the planet. Where I first got the egg. We'd experienced it before, Spence and me, an overwhelming sense of rapture. Of joy. I don't know if it's a defense mechanism to stop you from leaving, or . . . or . . ."

"Or the Force," Yana answered for him.

"Or the Force. I didn't recognize it until I went back, the same pull I feel when I'm near Elecia. The same euphoria."

"Sounds like an excuse to me," Yana said, picking herself up. "What really happened, Dobbs? Did you make a move and she spurned your advances?"

"She *used* me. Used me to do things I never would have done before." He took a step closer, and Yana tried not to be sick as his foul breath assaulted her.

"It's why I did what I did on that last mission, Yana. Why Kor died."

Yana's claws ached to remove the lying tongue that had dared to speak Kor's name, but like it or not, the tongue made sense.

"Let me make it up to you," Sunshine said, wiping his lips with filthy fingers. "I can get out of here." He pointed at her stump. "Even help you with that. We have the treasures, and I know where to sell them."

"*Her* treasures," Yana growled.

"Yours and mine," Sunshine corrected her. "We stole them for her."

That was true enough. "You have your ship?"

"No, but I have the *Silverstreak*, more or less in one piece. I moved it back to Ferdan when I saw Elecia's new defenses. No sense in letting the old girl get blown up."

"And you *do* know the way out."

Sunshine jabbed a finger down the tunnel that lay ahead of them. "They'll never even know we're gone."

Yana nodded, leaning on the wall to support herself. This was probably her only chance. "Sounds good."

"Excellent." The slimeball actually sounded like he meant it, before his brow furrowed beneath his ridiculous hat. "You strong enough to carry a pack?"

She nodded, licking her lips. "Try to stop me."

"This could be the beginning of a beautiful partnership, Yana Ro," Sunshine chortled before turning back to the vault. "Just the beginning."

"Oh, I don't know," Yana said, planting her foot squarely in his back. "Feels like an ending to me."

Sunshine yelped, tripping over his swag as he was propelled forward. Yana heard the crack of his head on the stone floor and the sharp cry of alarm as she reached in with her one good arm to pull the door shut. Sunshine was already pounding on the wood as she reset the lock, sealing him inside. True, some of those relics would've come in handy, but in all honesty he was welcome to the Path's ill-gotten gains. She had a ship and she had a way out. Anything else was a bonus.

Yana turned, her boot scuffing against something on the ground. She laughed, bending over carefully to retrieve the blaster that had fallen from Sunshine's belt.

"You really are the gift that keeps on giving," she told the trapped prospector, testing the weight of the weapon in her left hand. It felt awkward, but it would do. It would do very nicely indeed.

FORTY-SEVEN

Getting into the caves had been easy enough with Azlin guiding them. There were more droids and more resistance, the Path members surprisingly well-armed, but nothing indicated that the battle wouldn't go their way, especially as word reached Sheriff Pickwick that reinforcements were coming. Ships had been arriving in Ferdan all day, other factions with other vibroaxes to grind against the Path for reasons that were becoming blatantly obvious. This community, with its robes and face markings, was not what it seemed. There were even other Jedi heading toward the compound, a comforting thought as some reports had mentioned pirate ships and even a Hutt Dreadcruiser!

The Path was lucky that the Jedi had reached the caves first.

"For life and light!" Ela Sutan shouted as they pushed deeper into the underground system, coming under fire from all angles. There was no way the bolts would make it past their lightsabers, but there was no point in getting complacent. The tunnels were getting narrow, and the non-Jedi among them seemed determined to take as many risks as possible!

"This way," Pickwick shouted to one of her deputies, a swarthy Aqualish with blaster skills almost as sharp as his tusks.

"No, wait," Azlin shouted, but they didn't listen, peeling off from the main party to head down a tunnel that immediately turned out to be a mistake. Before they knew it, both sheriff and Aqualish were holed up behind an impressive stalagmite that rapidly diminished under increased blaster fire.

"What was that you said about keeping our heads down?" Matty joked as she and Azlin raced to their aid, Gluth Andoi at their heels.

Matty felt a stab of annoyance. Was the Morseerian *really* doubting their ability to save a couple of local law enforcers? Three Jedi was overkill, surely.

"Go with the others," she called back to the Jedi Master. "We can handle this."

"I'm sure you can," he responded, joining the fight bearing no fewer than four lightsabers, one for each arm. "But you know what they say. Many hands make light work."

He stepped into the firing line before she could argue, ordering Matty and Azlin to get the locals to safety. It wasn't the worst plan, but that didn't stop Matty from spinning on her heel to backhand a bolt toward the sniper who had targeted them. The stunned Path member tumbled from their hiding place to land in front of an appreciative Gluth.

"Not bad," he grunted through his mask, his blades flashing as if they were alive. "I must try that myself sometime."

Matty felt a sting of pride that she knew wasn't worthy of a Jedi but enjoyed anyway. She'd meditate about it later. If there was a later. Matty wasn't so sure as the world turned upside down.

It began with a cry that Matty didn't recognize. Was it Pickwick? She turned to see Azlin's lightsaber falling from his hand, his face contorted even before the blaster bolt hit him in the side, twirling him around. That was when Matty started screaming herself. Azlin was spinning like a top, his arms—too many arms—blurring while his legs—definitely too many legs—gave way. Behind her, Gluth staggered, a blast slipping past the Jedi Master's defenses to hit his shoulder. He cried out, the arm blown from its socket. Blood sprayed across Matty's face, but it was the wrong color. Everything was the wrong color. The walls, the floor, Azlin's manically spinning body. . . .

It was happening again, that same confusion as before. She couldn't sense the others, couldn't even remember their names. Couldn't remember anything—who she was, what she was, how it had been to feel the Force surround her and draw on its power. The light was gone. leaving nothing but darkness in its wake.

Darkness and the scrabbling of tiny clawed feet.

FORTY-EIGHT

The ferocity of the Nameless took even Marda by surprise.

Water was running everywhere, the sound of battle almost drowned out by the roar of the underground rivers that were building in some of the lesser tunnels. The entire system was in danger of flooding again, rainwater rushing down into the caves. Marda pushed the worry to the back of her head. She couldn't be distracted, not while Yana was on the loose. There was no telling what her cousin might do, especially wandering wounded and alone. What if she went to the Jedi? What if she warned them about the Nameless?

FORTY-EIGHT

Marda broke into a run, wishing that she'd spent more time studying the tunnel layout before all this began.

But all regrets were banished by the sudden appearance of a Jedi in her path. They weren't like Kevmo or Zallah, wearing instead an angular mask beneath a heavy hood. Was that some kind of rebreather, or what Jedi wore into battle? Either way, Marda hated that she couldn't see their face. What were they hiding?

But she could imagine the Jedi's expression when they noticed the weapon in her hand.

"Drop the lightsaber," they commanded, their voice synthetic and devoid of emotion. A vocalizer then, which would have made it impossible to judge their mood if not for the defensive position they adopted. This was bad. Really, really bad. Marda had felt unstoppable back in the cavern, but standing in front of a warrior, the confidence melted away. She had used the saber against three opponents, one of which was a door, while this Jedi had trained their entire life. There was no way she'd win in combat.

The Jedi raised a gloved hand, and Marda felt a pull on her mind as they calmly repeated the command: "Drop the lightsaber."

Of *course* she was going to drop the lightsaber. She wanted to drop the lightsaber. A lightsaber was the last thing she needed.

Her thumb slipped from the activator, and the blade

disappeared, her fingers loosening around the hilt. Then one of the young Nameless dropped from above, landing on the Jedi, who was already screaming.

Marda realized with horror that the Jedi had been in her head, forcing her to act against her will. Her grip tightened around the lightsaber as the Jedi writhed beneath the creature, the monster growing with every second, its maw fastened to the Jedi's mask. Marda watched, fascinated and appalled, as the Jedi's thrashing limbs slowed before stopping altogether, a horrible sucking noise emanating from the Nameless as it continued its feast. The monster was larger still when it bounded from its prey, crooked spines erupting from its backbone as muscles hardened beneath the pallid skin. It turned, hissing through its fronds, before charging away, already back on the hunt.

All thoughts of Yana forgotten, Marda edged toward the body, almost too terrified to breathe. She kicked the Jedi's hilt from their hand and peered down at the mask, now fractured and cracked. A sudden need to see the Jedi's face consumed her, and hooking the toe of her boot beneath the edge of the broken mask, she flicked it away.

There was very little face left. Marda couldn't tell what species the Jedi had belonged to, only that their skin had turned to stone, their features lost as the face collapsed in on itself.

She wanted to look away, her heart racing, but couldn't, her gaze locked on to the face that wasn't a face. This was the

Jedi's fault, not hers. They'd brought this on themselves by coming here, by refusing to take responsibility for their actions, creating the path she now trod, the Path of the Closed Fist.

Marda wiped the back of her hand across her cheek, and it came away wet. It must have been the water that was pouring through the cave roof. That was the only explanation. She needed to continue. Needed to find her cousin.

Yana was nearly out of the caves. It couldn't be much farther. She'd get to Sunshine's ship and put as many light-years between her and this mess as possible.

There was the slight problem that she didn't actually know how to fly a ship, a challenge that would have seemed insurmountable back when she had both hands, but now . . . now she just had to find a way.

Maybe leaving Sunshine hadn't been such a good idea. She could go back and fetch him. That would be the sensible thing to do, if she could find her way back to the vault, but the tunnels were bleeding into each other now. If she turned back, she'd be lost in seconds. More lost. Loster.

Yana laughed, a high-pitched giggle that she didn't recognize. Hysteria was setting in. She needed to make it outside, to see the sky, feel the rain against her hot skin.

Something scrabbled to her left. Yana spun around, her head continuing to spin after the rest of her had stopped. She *really* needed to stop doing that. Her blaster came up, but dropped the moment she saw what—or rather *who*—stood in front of her.

"Hello," she said to the small Ithorian who cowered in the shadows, the same boy she'd seen around Ferdan and at Ric Farazi's hut. She still didn't know his name, but that was nothing compared to the question of why he was running around a death zone, a bulky satchel clutched to his narrow chest.

"What you got there, kid?" she asked, but the Ithorian didn't answer. "Don't want to chat? I can understand that. Not in the mood myself, but hey, we need all the friends we can get today, right? The name's Yana. You might know my cousin, Marda?"

"The Guide," he barked, twin vocoders translating his native tongue into Basic.

"That's right, the Guide. You got a name?"

"Boolan."

"Good to meet you, Boolan. What's in the bag?"

He backed up, holding the satchel closer. "The Force will be free."

"Not going to show me, huh? That's fine. Guess I'll be on my way then?"

But she had no intention of leaving. Something had glinted in the rock behind the kid, not the sun opals that dotted the walls of the caves, but something that looked terribly familiar.

Boolan jumped as Yana suddenly lunged for him,

forgetting that she didn't have a free hand. She tripped, throwing out her stump, which caught the bag and hooked it from the Ithorian's grip. Boolan screamed and took to his heels, running into the darkness. Yana let him go, dropping her blaster so she could look inside the boy's mysterious satchel.

"Where is she? Have you seen her?"

Shea was packing a bag as Marda stumbled into the watch chamber, yanking pads and components from the bank of equipment.

"What I've seen is death," the engineer snapped. "Lots and lots of death. Some I can explain; you know, blasters, glowing swords, that kind of thing, but some of it, some of it I don't even want to think about. Have you seen what those things do? Those creatures of yours?"

"The Nameless," Marda prompted.

"I don't care what you call them. They're monsters, and so are we for bringing them back with us."

Marda didn't have time to be lectured by Shea of all people. Yes, the number of husks had surprised her as she searched for Yana. Yes, there were more than she'd expected. Most of the victims were Jedi, but some were Path members. That could only mean one thing: there had been more Force users hiding in plain sight. More like Calar and Shea. But now they'd been found out. They deserved it. They deserved everything they had coming.

"Yana," Marda repeated through clenched teeth, her grip on the lightsaber tightening. "Have you seen her?"

"Nope," Shea said, swinging the pack onto her back. "You want to look for her, go right ahead. I'm out of here."

She barged past, her shoulder striking Marda as she went, but Marda didn't care. She only needed the cameras.

Her lightsaber still burning, she moved to the controls, cycling through seemingly endless feeds.

"Where are you?" she muttered to herself, trying to ignore the husks lying on the tunnel floors. "Where are you?"

More than once she was about to give up before—there—a grainy image filled the top display. "No," Marda gasped as she watched her cousin lunge at a terrified-looking Ithorian. At a child! "No!"

Sparks flew as Marda bisected the watch station with a single swipe of her saber. This time Yana had gone too far.

Boolan's satchel was full of thermal charges, the same explosives that Elder Dinube had told her were going to open up the south caves. Then why was a youngling—a youngling for Void's sake—planting them as far away from the south caves as you could get?

No wonder the kid had looked so guilty. He'd been busy, that was for sure. The bag was half empty, its contents crammed into nooks and crannies along the length of the tunnel. Yana stumbled to the next device, not thinking as she raised her right hand to ease it out of the rock. The right hand that wasn't there.

Cursing, she lay the satchel on the floor and reached up with her left hand, trying to pull the explosive free. The cunning little hammerhead had wedged it in well and good. The last thing she needed was to drop the device. She'd be dead the moment it hit the floor. Not that it mattered as she heard the spluttering hum of a lightsaber igniting behind her, its yellow light reflecting on the rock ahead.

Sighing deeply, Yana turned and looked her cousin in the face.

"Hello, Marda," she said grimly. "Come to finish the job?"

FORTY-NINE

Somewhere in the back of her mind, Matty knew that Gluth Andoi was dead. She'd seen him bravely lurch forward, even as blaster bolts peppered his body, putting himself between them and whatever it was that charged toward them in the darkness.

She couldn't see what it was, couldn't focus on its body as it sprang at Gluth, knocking the Morseerian back, but she knew that it was feeding on the Jedi Master, Gluth convulsing beneath the creature she would never be able to describe.

Not that it mattered, because one thing was certain, an

inevitability that was as clear as the tears that ran down her face.

She was next.

The thought was almost a comfort. Time had lost all meaning, and sorrow had consumed her world—sorrow that she could no longer feel the Force, that she had let everyone down, that a Master of the High Council had sacrificed himself for nothing. She had failed. She always failed. There was nothing left for her to do but die.

Do it, she screamed at the animal that was savaging Gluth. *Finish me! Finish everything!*

She didn't know if she yelled the words out loud or only in her head, but she received an answer all the same as the world snapped back to reality.

She was lying on her back, water splashing from the stalactites above. The ground beneath her lekku was real; the stench of death was real; the screams were real.

Not Gluth's screams. He was past that. And not her screams, either.

It was Azlin. Azlin was in pain. So much pain.

The realization had her flipping over. She crawled toward Rell, who was curled in a ball, fists bunched above his head.

"Azlin," she croaked, her throat raw. "You're safe. We're both safe."

She tried to pull his hands away, but he turned from her like a frightened youngling. At least his screams had stopped.

"What in Stars' name?"

Pickwick and her deputy were standing over Gluth Andoi's corpse, staring in disbelief. Matty forced herself up and took a few faltering steps toward them. The sight of Gluth's body had her falling back to her knees, a trembling hand clasped over her mouth to stop herself from throwing up.

It didn't work.

The Jedi Master's methane mask had been ripped clean, his wizened face staring up at the ceiling. His mouth gaped open, his skin ash white. Water splashed against his sunken cheek, running down a head that had turned to stone. At first, Matty thought it had come from the ceiling, but then she realized she was crying, her tears throwing up tiny plumes of dust on Gluth's petrified face.

Zallah Macri and Kevmo Zink had become husks, Azlin had said. That was what he'd found the first time he'd come to these caves, and it had happened again, just as it had happened to Master Leebon.

"What *was* that thing?" Pickwick asked.

"What was what?" Matty replied, sniffing as she gathered Gluth's fallen lightsabers, the only thing she could think to do to honor his death.

"That thing that attacked him," Pickwick said. "I've never seen anything like it."

Matty hadn't seen it at all. She stood, clutching Gluth's sabers to her chest, only vaguely aware that she still had to find her own. "What happened to it?"

"Hmm. Oh, I shot it . . . I guess. Knocked it off of him. It ran off into the tunnels before I could fire again."

"You saved my life," Matty said, forcing herself to clip the hilts to her belt, one by one. "You saved my life when I should've been saving yours."

"Hey, we're in this together," Pickwick said, checking on the Path member Matty had dropped from his perch. "Your friend managed to take out the rest of the shooters, even with an arm down. Never seen anything like it."

"He was a Council member," Matty said, as if that explained everything, spotting her own lightsaber a meter or so away.

"He was damned impressive, that's what he was, but we can't stay here, especially with those monsters running around."

Matty raised her hand, and her lightsaber twitched but didn't fly back to her palm. Her focus wasn't quite there yet. Maybe it never would be again.

"You go. Rejoin the others," she told the sheriff, walking to retrieve the hilt, every step an effort. "We'll follow."

"Are you sure?" Pickwick said, glancing at Rell, who was still curled in a ball.

"No, but I need to help Azlin. We'll be fine."

"Okay, but if you need us—"

"We'll call. I promise."

Pickwick nodded and ran the way they'd come, the Aqualish deputy following close behind. Matty waited for them to disappear before letting the tears come in earnest. She sank to the ground, sobbing uncontrollably, rocking back and forth, unable to stop. She knew it was dangerous, that she would be finished if the creature came back or a trigger-happy Path member found her crying like a youngling, but there was nothing she could do but let the tears run their course.

It's okay, she thought she heard someone say, recognizing Master Leebon's voice in her head. *You're going to be okay, Matty. I believe in you.*

Now Matty just had to believe in herself.

She pushed herself up, flapping her hands in front of her face as if that could dry her eyes. She needed to get a grip, to get moving again.

"Azlin," she said, sniffing. "We have to go on. We have to continue."

The other Jedi didn't respond, his face pushed into his knees.

"Azlin."

"I can't," he finally said, his back toward her.

"You're going to have to."

"Leave me."

"That's not happening!" The ferocity of her shout shocked her, as did the wave of the Force she sent flowing over Azlin, rolling him onto his back. He looked up in shock, his face streaked with tears and dirt.

"I'm sorry," she said, meaning it, "but I can't leave you here. I need you to help me. We need each other."

His eyes dropped to see Gluth. "No," he whimpered, lips quivering. "Not again."

"Get up," she commanded, wiping her nose on her sleeve. "On your feet, Jedi. Don't make me drag you."

He obeyed, an automatic response, fresh tears welling in his eyes. "I can't . . . I can't go through that again."

"People are in danger."

"So?"

"So? We must help them."

"And what if we can't?" he yelled in her face, pointing at the husked Morseerian. "What if we end up like that?"

"The Force is with us."

"It wasn't. I couldn't feel it, Matty."

"The Force *is* with us. We are one with the Force. Say it."

He mumbled the words, not imbuing them with any sense of meaning.

"Again. The Force is with us. We are one with the Force."

This time his voice was stronger.

"The Force is with us. We are one with the Force. The Force is with us. We are one with the Force. The Force is with us. We are one with the Force."

"Okay," he said, cutting them off. "Okay, I believe it."

There was part of her that doubted that, but she'd take the win.

"Ready to go back into battle?" she said, trying to sound light and breezy, although she felt neither.

"Do you really want me to answer that?" he replied, recovering his lightsaber.

"No," Matty admitted, turning toward the sound of fighting, "but what choice do we have?"

FIFTY

"What are those?" Marda snarled, looking at the bag.

"What do they look like?" Yana said, keeping her voice level, her good hand itching to grab Sunshine's blaster.

"You're a coward," Marda said, the lightsaber shaking with fury in her grasp. "You were going to kill us all."

"No, but I was running away, so I guess you're not too wrong."

"Liar!"

That was it. Yana couldn't risk Marda coming at her again with that blade. Yana was a fast draw, even missing a hand. At least Marda stopped when the blaster was pointed at her, glaring at Yana over the fizzing saber.

"You won't believe me whatever I say," Yana told her, trying to stop the blaster from shaking. "You've already made up your mind."

"You're a traitor. I hate you."

"Yeah, you made that crystal clear when you chopped off my hand. Thanks for that."

"Walk away from the bag, Yana."

"Why? So you can kill me?"

"Walk away!"

"What are you even doing here, Marda? Shouldn't you be off leading your people? What kind of Guide runs from the fight?"

"I'm not running."

"And you're not in the thick of it, either. Maybe it's not what you thought it would be, the Closed Fist."

"The Force will be free."

"Have you killed any of them yourself? The Jedi?"

"Walk away from the bag."

"Have you put your credits where your mouth is?"

"Walk away from the bag!"

Yana stepped back, letting Marda approach. The Guide kicked the satchel open, wincing as she saw what was inside.

"Careful!" Yana warned.

"You were going to blow up the caves," Marda said, her voice quiet.

"Not me," Yana told her.

"What?"

"It wasn't me."

Something moved in the darkness behind Marda. Yana shifted her aim and fired, Marda flinching as the blast streamed past her head to slam harmlessly into rock. There was a shriek, and the figure that had been watching them ducked, revealing himself, eyes wide with fear.

"Don't move, Boolan," Yana hissed at the Ithorian. "Don't even blink."

"Yana!" Marda snapped, jumping to the wrong conclusion as usual. "It's a child."

"I know it's a child," Yana said, hating herself for what she was doing. "And I'll let him go if he tells the truth. What do you say, Boolan? Why were you planting the explosives?"

"Lower the blaster, Yana," Marda warned.

"Who told you to plant the bombs?" Yana continued anyway.

"Lower the blaster, or I swear—"

"It was the Mother!"

Boolan's shout stopped them both dead. Yana had expected nothing less from the confession, but Marda was rattled.

"What do you mean?"

"She told us where to put them," Boolan told her. "Where they'd do the most damage."

"Us?" Marda's lightsaber dropped slightly.

The Ithorian looked at her as if she should already know. "Tromak, Utalir, and the others. She said it was our duty to the Path. To the Force."

"Their duty," Yana repeated, not trying to disguise the contempt in her voice. "The duty of children. Your children, Marda."

Yana dropped her aim. She'd never intended to fire anyway. "Go," she told Boolan. "Get the others. Tell them to stop."

"But the Path . . ." the Ithorian said. "My father died. The Mother said this was the only way."

"I was there when your father died, little one," Marda said, warmth seeping into her voice for the first time since she'd found Yana. "There was nothing we could do."

"It was the Jedi!"

Marda shook her head sadly. "No. No, it wasn't. Go to the others. Tell them Marda said to run away. This isn't for them. It isn't for any of you. Go now, Boolan."

The Ithorian waited, just for a moment, and then scampered away, muttering into his translator over and over: "The Force will be free. The Force will be free!"

Marda watched him go, her back to Yana. It would be so easy to take her down.

"It was a child. A child, Yana."

"I wasn't going to shoot him."

Marda turned, her face lit by the glow of the blade. "That's not what I meant."

Shaking her head, Yana dropped the blaster onto the bag of charges.

"There, I'm done," she said, looking her cousin in the eyes. "You can finish me if you want. Everyone else is dying. If the Jedi don't get us, the explosives will. You see that, don't you, Marda? You see what the Mother is doing? Rigging the caves to explode. Sending the Littles to do her dirty work. She's not who you think she is."

"None of this is what I thought it would be."

The yellow blade sizzled into its hilt.

"I was so angry," Marda said. "About the mission, about Bokana. But then I saw them. I saw what they actually do."

"The creatures?"

"I did that. I set it all in motion. I told them to feed."

Yana stepped forward, knowing that Marda could reignite the blade at any minute. "It wasn't you. It was her. It's *always* been her, since the very beginning. She used the Path. She used us all, just like she's using the Littles. The question is, are we going to do anything about it, or are we going to tear each other apart?"

FIFTY-ONE

Matty had never felt so tired. Her entire body ached, and her head felt like it had turned to stone.

No. Not stone. Talk about the wrong choice of words, especially after Gluth.

And he hadn't been the last. Matty and Azlin had found three more husks, all belonging to Jedi they didn't recognize, members of the other parties that had arrived on Dalna. Every corpse made Matty's heart sink lower while Azlin retreated into silence. The young Jedi was barely speaking as they continued through the caves, disarming Path members and taking out Enforcer droids wherever they were found. At first, Azlin muttered beneath his breath as they pushed on, repeating the Guardian of the Whills mantra the way she had taught him, but as the bodies piled higher with every passing moment, Matty realized his words had changed. There was no mention of the Force, only that "they" were out there, and they were coming back.

Coming back.

Coming *back*.

This wasn't encouraging and *definitely* wasn't healthy, but even as he lapsed into silence, there was no change in his abilities with his saber or the Force. That had to be a good thing, didn't it?

Besides, Matty had other concerns rattling around her head. Other worries. No one had seen Oliviah since they'd first entered the caves. Matty couldn't help fearing the worst. What if it was already too late? What if they turned a corner and found Oliviah turned to ash? She knew she was letting anxiety get the better of her, but her nerves were still shredded from what she'd seen and experienced. No one could blame her for that, right? Early in her training, Master Leebon had told Matty to be kind to herself, to accept that sometimes you felt bad, even as a Jedi. *Especially* as a Jedi. "The trick is to acknowledge how you are feeling," the elderly Selonian had told her, "and more importantly, understand *why* you are feeling that way. Then, and only then, will you be able to ask the questions that will help you control your emotions, to overcome the burden you bear." It sounded so easy when the galaxy wasn't going mad, but if ever there was a moment to give it a try, it was when she was advancing through strange tunnels threatened by creatures that could suck her life out of her face.

And, hey, if she was looking for a bright side—and Force knew she needed one—things couldn't get much worse, could they?

The answer, it turned out, was no. It shocked Matty, too, as she'd pretty much set herself up for a fall.

They heard a weapon firing ahead, not a blaster but something percussive. Matty led the way, creeping around the corner to see a group of Path members crouched behind a large boulder. There was a Dowutin with a ridiculously small disruptor pistol and a Twi'lek with a blaster rifle, their shots drowned out by the Herald of the Open Hand. Werth Pouth was firing the most barbaric weapon Matty had ever seen. It wasn't an energy weapon but a flechette launcher pumping out streams of razor-sharp durasteel darts.

And this was the man with whom she'd thought they should ally themselves. This was his kind of weapon.

His target was a group of Ferdan locals who had joined the fight. Now they were being forced to hide behind a low shelf of rock that was gradually being whittled away by the darts. But they weren't alone. A Jedi was crouched behind them, waiting for a break to respond. Relief rushed over Matty as she realized it was Oliviah, her back pressed to the rock. She was alive, if not exactly safe.

The older Jedi turned toward them as she sensed Matty and Azlin's presence, and she nodded sagely as if everything was proceeding entirely to plan. Maybe it was. As Leebon always used to say: "The Force has a habit of slotting things into place when you need them the most, my young Padawan. It's all a matter of trust."

If ever they needed trust it was now.

Oliviah tipped her head toward the Herald, and it was Matty's turn to incline her head, understanding passing silently between them.

Oliviah vaulted over the rocks, her emerald lightsaber glowing as she threw herself into the hail of darts. Blocking blaster bolts was one thing, but projectiles were another. A dart slipped past Oliviah's flashing blade, slicing her cheek, but she kept moving, darts sparking in the air as she cut them down. The Herald roared in defiance, focused completely on Oliviah. He never even saw Matty and Azlin. They pushed with the Force, and the boulder the Path members were using for shelter shuddered and then was shoved out of the way, scraping painfully against the floor. The Herald and his cronies stopped firing, suddenly defenseless. It was all Oliviah needed. She joined Matty and Azlin, slamming the three Path members back into a wall with the Force. There was nothing particularly elegant about the move, but it was followed by stun blasts from the Ferdan fighters, who laid out the Dowutin and the Twi'lek within seconds.

The Herald was another matter, already bringing his brutal weapon about to finish the job. Oliviah sprinted forward, spinning around to slice the launcher in two. The Nautolan threw up his hands to protect himself and, when he looked again, had three Jedi standing before him, the tips of their lightsabers meeting above his heart.

"Hello again," Oliviah said, blood trickling from the cut on her cheek.

"Are you talking to him or me?" Matty asked.

"Both," the older Jedi replied. Azlin kept deathly silent.

"Your tricks won't save you," the Herald sneered, looking for all the worlds as if he was about to impale himself on their blades, a martyr for his cause. "You have no power in these caves."

"That boulder would probably disagree with you," Oliviah told him, and Matty felt the crush she'd had all those years ago return with a vengeance. In all honesty, it was good to feel anything that wasn't abject terror.

"What has been happening to us?" Matty demanded of Plouth. "What have you done to our people?"

The Herald smiled horribly. "I haven't done a thing. You have done this to yourself through your dependence on the Force. You are leeches, parasites, but now we will sever you from what you value most. We shall strip you of your power so the galaxy can see—"

The Herald's words died in his throat as his body stiffened. Matty looked down, checking to see that one of them hadn't accidentally impaled the man.

It was worse than that.

So much worse.

"You will answer the question. You will tell us what you have done."

Azlin's voice was like flint as his eyes bored into Plouth.

"Azlin, don't," Matty warned as she realized what the young Knight was doing. The pressure in the Force was intense as he pushed further than any Jedi ever should.

"Tell us," Azlin yelled, spit flying from his lips. "Tell *me*!"

"No!" Matty shouted, bringing up an arm and throwing him back using the Force. Azlin sailed through the air, his lightsaber clattering to the floor seconds before the man himself.

The Herald gasped for air as if he were being strangled, his knees buckling. He slid down the wall, the color draining from his face. "Animals," was all he could wheeze. "You're all animals."

"That wasn't the way," Matty said to Azlin, who was wiping his mouth on the back of his hand. "It's *never* the way."

"Desperate times," he said, refusing to meet her gaze. "But it worked."

"What did you get?" Oliviah asked him, drawing another appalled look from Matty. *Surely* she couldn't condone what Azlin had just attempted.

"They're using something called the Rod of Power. An artifact strong in the Force."

"Is that it?"

"Isn't that enough?" Matty asked, despairing.

"No," Azlin replied. "There was a name."

"The Mother?" Oliviah asked.

Azlin shook his head. "No. The name he was thinking of is Marda. Marda Ro."

FIFTY-TWO

Yana still wasn't convinced Marda wouldn't stab her in the back and knew the feeling was mutual. The trust between the cousins was broken, maybe forever, but they'd reached an uneasy truce, for now at least.

They tried to avoid the battle that raged in most of the tunnels, Marda leading the way through the passageways she'd used when searching for Yana. There was a worrying amount of water running down the walls, especially near the assembly cavern. If the flood defenses breached, as they had when Kevmo and Zallah first came to Dalna, it would be game over, hidden death charges or not.

At first, they couldn't find any of the Littles, Yana suggesting that Boolan may have done what they'd asked, telling the rest of the younglings to stop planting the bombs.

Then they'd found another device, crammed into a crack in the rock, a young scream reaching them a moment later.

Marda raced toward it, her sparking lightsaber reflected in the water that pooled at their feet. One of the Littles was ahead; Utalir had her back pressed against the wall, the Mikkian screaming at the nameless horror that stalked toward her, hackles raised.

"Leave her alone," Marda yelled as the Nameless prepared to spring.

"I don't think it's listening, Marda," Yana said, drawing her blaster. "Not without the rod."

"It *has* to. It must."

But it didn't. With a horrible hiss, the terror threw itself forward, Utalir's scream reaching previously unknown heights. Yana wanted to fire, but the chance of hitting the girl was too great, especially using her left hand.

Marda didn't hesitate. She swung the lightsaber, the tip of the blade scraping a deep gouge in the ground. But the damage to the creature was worse. The saber sliced through the animal's flank, cutting deep as the animal leaped for Utalir. The Mikkian dropped into a ball, the critically injured monster slamming into the wall where she'd been standing. It hit the floor, writhing in agony, its front legs thrashing as Marda raised the lightsaber above her head. She brought it down, pinning the creature to the ground. Its howl echoed through the chambers, bouncing off walls as the blade of the lightsaber flared, almost buckling as sparks flew from the hilt. There was a sharp flash of light and Marda hurled the hilt aside, yelping with pain. It bounced once and rolled, smoke billowing from its casing, the damage caused by the wargaran finally coming home to roost. The lightsaber was dead, never to be ignited again.

Yana ran to the child, holding her close while Marda raged at the lifeless creature she'd brought back from deep space. "You were supposed to protect us. You were supposed to attack the Jedi, not our children."

"Marda," Yana said, trying to calm her as Marda kicked at the remains.

"You were supposed to attack them. Attack *them*."

"They're supposed to attack those sensitive to the Force," Yana reminded her, the Mikkian sobbing into her breast. "Anyone, Marda, no matter who they are. Like Utalir."

Marda whirled on them, rubbing her scorched hand. "Utalir does *not* use the Force."

"How do you know?" Yana asked. "Maybe it's an ability that will develop in time. Or maybe it will remain dormant for the rest of her life. Either way, that monster could smell it on her. *Your* monster, Marda."

Marda stopped, breathing heavily. Yana could see from

her expression that she'd already realized that truth even if she didn't want to admit it. The Nameless didn't discriminate. They didn't care if your robes were Jedi gold or brikal blue. If you had a connection to the Force, you were prey, and Marda had allowed them to run free.

Marda darted forward, dropping to her knees to check the girl.

"I'm sorry," Utalir wailed still clinging to Yana. "It wouldn't leave me alone."

"No," Marda told her, running her hands through the Mikkian's golden tendrils. "I'm sorry. This is my fault. *All* my fault. I didn't know."

"I doubt she knew herself," Yana said. "I'm no expert, but I don't think you have a choice whether you're connected to the Force or not. How many others have your creatures fed on today, Marda? How many like this little girl?"

Marda was weeping, her tears washing away the lightning bolts that covered her face. She pressed her head against Utalir, and Yana put an arm around them, pulling them in. They huddled together until Marda and the little one had exhausted their tears. Yana cried, too, exhausted but wondering if there was hope for the Ro cousins after all.

Eventually, Marda pulled away, her gaze dropping down to the bag Utalir had been carrying, far too bulky for such a small Mikkian. She reached out and retrieved one of the devices, showing it to the child.

"What are you doing with these, Utalir? Who gave them to you?"

"Am I in trouble?"

Marda shook her head. "No, darling. You're not."

Utalir looked at them both, checking to see they weren't lying before answering.

"The Mother. She told us to hide them in a cave. Said she was going to drop the rocks on the Jedi, so they couldn't hurt us anymore."

"Who else did she give them to?" Marda asked.

Utalir sniffed. "Boolan and Tromak, but Tromak wouldn't do it. He was scared."

"Good. The Mother should never have asked you to do that. The bombs wouldn't just hurt the Jedi. They'd hurt us all."

The Mikkian started crying again. "But why would she do that? Why would she hurt us?"

"Because she isn't who we thought she was," Yana said. "She's like you, Utalir. She uses the Force."

"What?" Marda said, shocked.

Yana shrugged. "That's what Sunshine believes. He said that Elecia uses the Force to make people do what she wants. We've all seen her do it, even if we didn't recognize it for what it was."

"The sheriff," Marda said quietly. "When we returned from Jedha."

"Does that make me bad?" Utalir asked, bottom lip trembling. "Because I'm like her?"

"No," Marda said, leaning forward and brushing away the child's tears. "You could never be bad. Never."

"Even if she's connected to the Force?" Yana asked.

"We're all connected," Marda replied, so quiet it was almost a whisper. She kissed the Mikkian's forehead and stood, rubbing her burnt palm as she tried to work out their next move.

"Where was the Mother, Utalir?" she finally asked. "When she gave you the charges?"

"In her listening chamber."

"Is she still there?"

"I don't know. She has a button. Said she was going to press it when we'd finished."

"The detonator," Yana said.

Marda nodded, pacing up and down.

"Utalir, can you help Yana find the bombs you've already hidden?"

"Yes. It's not that many. I wasn't very fast, and the bag was really heavy."

"Good. That's good."

Yana peeled the Mikkian from her, Utalir helping her stand.

"What are you going to do?" she asked her cousin.

"I'm going to the chamber."

"Then you're not going alone. I'm coming with you."

"No, I need you to do something, both of you, if you'll help me one last time."

"I'll help," Utalir agreed, eager to make amends. Yana sighed, pulling Sunshine's blaster from her belt and holding it out toward Marda.

"Fine, but you're not facing her unarmed."

Marda pushed the gun away, showing Yana her nails. "I don't need a blaster. I have everything I need."

FIFTY-THREE

Matty didn't want to admit how good it was to see the Herald back in restraints. It wasn't the most Jedi of responses to seeing a man in binders, his arms behind his back, but it seemed to be a day of not just bending the rules but breaking several at once.

She'd been feeling good about coming to Oliviah's aid. Proud, even. Perhaps that was why things had soured so quickly, the Force slapping Matty down. Azlin forcing himself into someone's mind seemed a bit much, though. Surely there was a better way to deliver a lesson.

The Dowutin and the Twi'lek—who turned out to be one

of the Path's Elders—had been taken away by the Ferdan reinforcements, who had also provided the cuffs. The Herald was guiding them to the last spot he'd seen Marda, this time acting of his own free will rather than being coerced by a Jedi who should have known better.

"How far is it?" Matty asked, realizing she was starting to obsess.

"Why don't you look for yourself?" the Herald replied bitterly. "That's what you people do, isn't it? Root around in people's minds."

"No," she insisted, shooting a glance at Azlin, who had retreated into himself again. A defense mechanism? She hoped so. Someone needed to look after him.

The Herald snorted, not believing a word she said. "It's not far."

His head turned as they passed a smaller chamber carved out of the rock. Matty followed his gaze, seeing a collection of screens, most of which were in pieces.

"What's this?"

"Shea's watch station. Looks like one of you found her."

Matty could see what he meant. The damage to the equipment looked like the work of a lightsaber.

"Give me a minute," she said, dipping into the room.

"We haven't time," Oliviah said, but Matty ignored her.

"I want to see if it can help."

Most of the controls were smashed, but a few screens still

operated, images streaming from cameras above and below the surface.

"What are you looking for?" Oliviah asked, bringing the Herald in with her while Azlin guarded the door, saber still bright.

The Herald answered for her as Matty cycled past a figure creeping stealthily down a corridor.

"That's her. That's Marda."

Matty flicked back to the image, peering in closer. At first glance, the woman looked like Yana, the Evereni who had saved them from the Mother earlier that day. "Are you sure it's her?" she asked.

"I know my people."

"Where's she going?" Oliviah asked. Her voice became harder when the Herald didn't respond. "Where, Plouth?"

The Nautolan grunted before answering. "She's heading to the listening chamber. To the Mother."

A now-familiar gleam shone in Oliviah's eyes. "Take us there."

Jukkyuk was in his customary place at the door of the listening chamber, a heavy blaster in his powerful hands.

"Let me pass," Marda said as she approached, but Jukk shook his shaggy head. "I need to see the Mother. I need to warn her."

The loyal Wookiee wouldn't move. He'd probably been told not to let anyone pass, not even the Guide.

"Look," she said. "The Jedi are coming right now, coming for you. Do you *really* think you stand a chance against them? They'll be through that door before you even see them coming."

He roared back at her, his pride hurt. She was playing a dangerous game but needed to see it through.

Marda bared her teeth, surprising herself as she hissed, showing the side of the Evereni that the galaxy feared. Jukkyuk towered over her, yet even he jumped back, his broad shoulders hitting the door.

"Pathetic," she sneered. "You wouldn't last two minutes."

He bellowed a second time, angrier still as she pressed home the advantage.

"Go on then, prove yourself. Face the Jedi. Show them the strength of the Path. Free the Force!"

Her gamble paid off. Jukkyuk almost flattened her as he charged forward, racing toward an enemy that wasn't there.

Marda grinned, pleased with herself. The Jedi didn't have the monopoly on mind tricks.

Marda pushed open the door, but the Mother wasn't in the main chamber or the adjoining antechamber. She eventually found her in the boudoir, emptying a drawer of precious jewels into a chest that rested on her bed. "What are you doing?"

"Protecting our legacy," the Mother told her, not missing a beat. Marda felt an immediate burden to accept the words as gospel, to believe anything that spilled out of the woman's mouth. Yana was right; the Mother *was* asserting her will on others. She'd fallen for it before, but never again.

"I need the Rod of Power," she said, moving to grab the artifact that lay next to the open chest.

"No," the Mother said, grabbing the rod simultaneously. "It stays with me."

"The Nameless are going wild," Marda said, trying to wrestle the staff from the Mother's grasp. "Attacking our people. I had to stop one from killing a child."

"You stopped it?"

"They *can* die, Elecia, if they need to."

"No," the woman said, shaking her head. "You don't get to call me that, not here. I am the Mother. The Mother of the Open Hand."

"We're not the Open Hand anymore."

Elecia brought the staff back, its tip striking Marda across the face. Stars burst across her vision and she fell, hitting the floor hard.

"Here's a word of advice for you, 'Guide,'" Elecia sneered, looming over her. "Never believe your own legend. That stunt in the cavern was good, I'll give you that. And the Path bought it like the ignorant rabble they are, but it doesn't impress me. You don't impress me."

Marda stayed where she was, glaring up at the woman she'd adored. "You're leaving, aren't you? After detonating the bombs?"

"Bombs? What bombs?"

"Stop lying, Elecia. I know what you're planning. I can see it in your face."

"Is that right?"

"You destroy the caves, sacrificing everyone so you can escape. It gives you everything you want. Proof of the imbalance, a disaster you can pin on the Jedi while you march across the galaxy, building your part, poor heartbroken Elecia."

"You don't know what you're talking about."

Marda's eyes dropped to a device on the Mother's belt, the remote detonator. "Maybe not, but I know a monster when I see one."

Marda sprang at her, long nails bared. The Mother cried out, grabbing Marda's wrists as she tumbled back, taking Marda with her. They rolled, Marda on top one second, the Mother the next, but Marda was stronger. She flipped Elecia onto her back, clawing at her arms, robes, anything to grab the box. It was all she could do not to sink her sharp teeth into the woman's neck. She had never hated someone as much as she hated the Mother right now. All it would take was one bite, and the detonator would be hers.

But Elecia brought her elbow up, catching the side of

Marda's head. She was only stunned for a moment, but it was long enough for the Mother to plant a boot on her chest, kicking her onto her back. Elecia loomed up, grabbing the Rod of Power. The elegant blade at the staff's tip glinted as it dropped toward Marda's chest, and there was nothing she could do to stop it.

FIFTY-FOUR

The point of the blade stopped just as it was about to plunge into the woman's chest.

The Herald had led them straight to the listening chamber, a little too eagerly, if Matty was honest. Maybe he saw this as his chance to rid the Path of the Mother once and for all, the Jedi becoming his execution squad. The way Azlin and Oliviah were acting, she couldn't blame him. Things had only gotten worse as they had entered the maze of tunnels that led to the Mother's private rooms and found themselves in the path of a charging Wookiee. The hairy giant was racing full pelt at them, a blaster rifle already raised and firing.

The bolt screamed toward them, its light glinting on the precious stones that lined the tunnel walls, but Oliviah merely raised her hand, the shard of energy halting in midair. She gave a push, and it shot back, slamming into the Wookiee's chest. He was knocked off his feet, flipping over to crash onto his face. Oliviah checked his pulse, which Matty took as a hint that the Jedi she knew was still in there, although she was soon marching on, more driven than ever. Azlin, meanwhile, stayed at the rear of the group, checking behind him. What was happening to these people? Was it also happening to Matty and she just didn't realize?

They pushed into the room as the Mother swung her strange weapon toward Marda. Matty only just managed to raise her hand in time, calling on the Force to stop the woman from being skewered. Another flick of her fingers sent the rod spinning from the Mother's grip to land as far away from Marda as possible. It clattered to the floor, breaking in two. Matty had no way of knowing whether it had snapped or was meant to come apart, but a flash of eldritch light burst from the two halves as they separated.

The Mother snarled like a caged animal. "Stay back," the woman said, pulling a small detonator from her belt. "The caves are rigged to explode. I'll bury us alive if you take another step."

The Herald just laughed, stepping forward, hands still cuffed but head held high.

"It's over, Elecia. They've won."

"No," the Mother replied, hair as white as bone tumbling from her hood. "I don't give up that easy, Werth. I'm not a coward like you." Her eyes darted to the Jedi. "The girl attacked me. I was defending myself."

"You're lying," Azlin said. "I can sense it."

"Get out of my head!" the Mother screamed, brandishing the detonator. "I meant what I said. We'll all die together."

"She means it," Marda said, pushing herself up on her arms. "She's had the Littles planting bombs."

"The Littles?" the Herald echoed, not believing what he was hearing.

"You didn't know?" Matty asked.

Plouth glared back over his shorn tendrils. "I'm not a monster. I would never hurt my own. Unlike her. Unlike—"

He stopped as he turned back to face the Mother, Matty feeling a sudden wave of disgust.

"What's happened to your arm, Elecia?"

His question was low, dangerous. The Mother glanced at the arm she'd stretched out, the detonator in her hand. The wrappings she usually wore had come loose, slashed by the Evereni's nails.

"You noticed, did you?" Marda asked, grinning in victory. "I wondered when you would."

"It means nothing," the Mother said, covering the exposed flesh with a hand, but it was too late; they had *all* seen.

The flesh beneath the shredded wrappings wasn't flesh at all. It was stone.

"It's been feeding on you," the Herald rumbled, the coin dropping. "That devil of yours."

"What devil?" Azlin asked, clutching his saber tighter than ever. "What're you talking about?"

The Herald ignored him, continuing his cross-examination of the Mother. "But it only feeds on those who touch the Force, those who manipulate its power."

"She's been manipulating us all for a very long time, Werth," Marda told him from the floor.

"No!" the Herald bellowed, taking another angry step forward, stopping only when the Mother flexed her fingers around the detonator. "You lied to us. The Force hasn't been speaking to you. You've been *mining* it, using it for your own ends. You're the source of the imbalance!"

"You don't know what you're talking about," the Mother sneered.

"But *I* do," Oliviah spoke up, stepping forward to join the Herald. "You see, the Force has always run strong in our family."

FIFTY-FIVE

"What?" It was the Twi'lek who asked the question that was on everyone's lips. "Are you saying what I *think* you're saying?"

The older Jedi didn't respond. She just stared at Elecia, who shook her head, their eyes locked. The same eyes.

"I don't remember much of my life before the Jedi," the brown-skinned Knight said, "but I remember a little. Images mainly. Faces. A man and a woman who *I* think were my parents, although I can't be sure. But I was playing with someone when the Seeker knocked on our door. Another girl. My sister."

The Mother shook her head. "No. It's not possible."

"That's what I thought when I saw you on Jedha. The Force spoke to me, unearthing memories I never knew I had: the two of us playing for the Jedi who'd come for me, showing him tricks. I could make our building blocks lift from the floor just by thinking about it, and my sister, my older sister, could get people to do things for her just by being near them."

"Oliviah." The name was like a curse word on the Mother's lips. "After all this time. I never thought I'd see you again. Even went looking for you when I was old enough, but they wouldn't let me near. And you were on Jedha." She laughed bitterly. "What are the chances?"

"The Force works in mysterious ways," the Twi'lek said.

"Your name," Oliviah continued, "is Elecia."

The Mother snorted. "Anyone could've found that out."

"Elecia *Zeveron*."

The Mother fell silent, but the Herald spoke up, glowering at the prophet he had installed as the head of the Path. "The Jedi came for you when you were young. To train you. To teach you how to bind the Force to your will."

"But they didn't take her," Marda said, the truth suddenly so obvious. "They took her sister instead, leaving her behind . . . because she wasn't good enough."

"You don't know what you're talking about," the Mother spat.

"Don't I?" Marda rose to her feet, feeling everyone tense as Elecia swung the detonator around to face her. "I've spent my entire life being told I was second best to the person I loved most. Told by you, mainly."

"Love her?" the Mother sneered. "I didn't love my sister. She was nothing. They got it wrong. They should've taken me, not her."

"And now you're making them pay. You're making *everyone* pay. For their mistake. For not taking you seriously."

The Mother grinned horribly. "Maybe we are like each other after all, Marda Ro of the Closed Fist. You want to punish the galaxy just as much as I do. Maybe even more. Well, let's start here."

The last thing Marda expected was for the Mother to toss the detonator toward her. She went to catch it, but the device was snatched away, changing direction in midair to be caught by Oliviah.

No, Marda screamed inside. This was going to ruin everything.

"First rule of a con," the Mother said, snatching up the rods and slamming them together, "a little misdirection goes a long way. You think you've won, Oliviah, but you have no idea. The Jedi may not have valued my gifts, but I found my own way to use them."

"By tricking everyone you ever met," the Herald growled.

"That's how you win," the Mother said, brandishing the combined Rod of Power.

The effect was instantaneous. Oliviah doubled over, the

same happening to the Twi'lek and human, who staggered as if intoxicated. Their eyes rolled in their sockets, their faces growing pale, and the human male moaned under his breath: "They're coming back. Coming back to take us. To take us away."

"That's right," the Mother gloated. "They *are* coming, but they won't hurt me. They can't hurt me while I'm holding the rod. Isn't that right, my Guide?"

"Yes," someone said, but it wasn't Marda. It was the Herald, staring defiantly at Elecia. "They can't hurt you, but *I* can."

Werth threw himself forward, the binders around his wrists snapping apart as he lunged for the Mother. She tried to evade him, but the man was too fast, his hands going for her throat. They crashed down beside the bed, the Mother catching the open chest as they fell, multi-colored gems cascading down the Herald's back. He didn't even seem to notice as he throttled the life from the woman who had tricked him for so long.

All the time, the Jedi writhed on the floor, lips foaming as the human continued to babble his manic litany: "We'll all be dust. Dust."

"Marda," the Mother wheezed, powerless to stop Werth. "Help me . . . please."

But Marda helped herself to the rod instead, snatching it from Elecia and holding it tight. She felt the power of the Nameless in her hands once more and gloried in their hunger.

The Herald and the Mother could kill each other for all she cared. This was her moment. She could turn the tide of the battle, restoring balance once and for all.

And then she looked down at the agonized Jedi and imagined Kevmo in their place. This was how he must have died, so alone and scared. And it was happening again, right in front of her. She thought how Bokana would look away if he were there, his heart breaking at the sight, how Yana would judge her for standing by while others suffered. It needed to change, and it would; Marda would make sure of that.

Her decision made, she turned to leave as a lightsaber burst through the Herald's spine.

FIFTY-SIX

Matty started fighting the wave of confusion the moment it rolled over her. She didn't think she could win—far from it—but she had to try. It was like before, she thought, trying to remember Leebon's lesson. She had to acknowledge that reality was turning inside out again. That part was easy enough, especially with Azlin's screams coming from all directions at once. Understanding why was impossible, although she thought she remembered the Mother grabbing the strange purple staff. Maybe the Herald *had* been telling the truth all along. Maybe there *was* an artifact. When this had happened before, Matty had thought there'd been a creature feeding on Gluth, but she could have been wrong.

Good. This was good. The process was working. She'd acknowledged the feeling, and while understanding why it was happening was a work in progress, the answer to how Matty could overcome the madness came in a flurry of images from the past. She saw herself training with Master Leebon, the Selonian's sharp teeth glinting as she laughed at Matty's jokes. Then there were Vildar and Tey, Matty standing in between them, stopping them from arguing, and then fighting alongside them, feeling empowered as they trusted her to defend the Enlightenment from attack. She longed to see them both again, to tell them of her adventures on Dalna, the thrill she'd felt as she'd worked with Azlin and Oliviah to capture the Herald.

That was it. That *was* the answer.

"We need each other," she gasped. "We can't beat it on our own." She had no idea if the others could hear her. She could barely see anything, let alone her friends, but she could see something glint in front of her. There were so many of them, winking in the darkness. Realization hit her like a rail-crawler. They were the precious stones she'd seen in the cave walls, the opals!

"Look at them," she shouted at the others. "Look at the stones. Concentrate on them."

The world swam back into focus, only a little. The opals

were there, reflecting the light of the strange staff. The Evereni woman was holding it now, but there was another light, reflected blue in the sunken gems. Was that a lightsaber? Had one of the others ignited their blade? Or was it hers? It was the right color, but it was too far away, rising up like a rocket from a body on the floor.

The body of the Herald.

"No," she cried out, sick of the death and waste, her thumb finding the trigger of her own blade. It blazed on, so bright it hurt her eyes. She wanted to move, needed to move, to save the Nautolan, but it was too late. He was already dead.

The world righted itself, the chaos fading as the Herald's lifeless body slipped to the side. The Mother rose to her feet, the lightsaber that had killed Werth Plouth in her hands. There was no time to ask where she had found it. Oliviah was already moving, her own saber coming up. The Mother grinned, the family resemblance so strong that Matty couldn't believe she hadn't seen it before. She was still struggling to recover from the attack, her feet weighed down to the floor, but at least the floor wasn't moving.

The lightsabers crackled as they met, the Mother swinging wildly, Oliviah blocking the lunge. Oliviah had trained all her life, but the Mother had the advantage, her opponent still groggy. She hacked and slashed, forcing Oliviah back step by step until Matty grabbed one of the hilts she'd recovered from Gluth and, shouting out, threw it forward. Oliviah caught it, the blade snapping on, a smile spreading over her sweat-drenched face.

Suddenly, she was on the offensive, years of training falling into place. There was no way the Mother could defend herself against two blades, giving up ground at first and then the battle as Oliviah hooked one of her blades beneath Elecia's, burning plasma to rip the saber from her hands.

The Mother tumbled back, landing next to the man she had murdered.

"Thank you," Oliviah said.

"For what?" the Mother sneered.

"I wasn't talking to you."

Matty felt a wave of gratitude and realized not only that she could move but that someone was missing.

"Marda," she said, spinning around. "She's gone."

"Taking the rod with her," Oliviah confirmed. "I'll deal with my sister. You go after the girl. Get the staff before it kills again."

Yes, Matty could do that, unlike Rell, who was still curled into a ball on the floor.

"Azlin?"

It was no good. The young Jedi was locked in his fear. She could help him later, but first she had a job to do.

FIFTY-SEVEN

Utalir's eyes went wide as the uncanny howl echoed through the caves.

"What was that?"

"Your cue to leave," Yana told the Mikkian. "Can you find your way to the surface?"

Utalir nodded, curling one of her yellow tendrils around a finger as she looked at Yana's missing hand. "Are you going to be okay?"

Yana tried to give a reassuring smile. Dealing with Littles was still new to her. "I'll be fine, kiddo. You did well. Marda will be proud."

The Mikkian looked past Yana, a smile breaking across her young face. “There she is!”

Yana turned to see her cousin splashing through the water that had pooled at the bottom of the assembly cavern.

“You got them then,” she said, noting the combined rods in Marda’s hand.

Marda nodded, turning her attention to the youngling. She crouched in front of Utalir and smiled. “You need to run now, darling. We’ll be right behind you.”

“Promise?”

“Cross my heart.”

Marda leaned forward, planted a kiss on the Mikkian’s forehead, and told her to leave. Utalir threw her arms around Marda, holding her tight for a second before scampering from the cavern.

Somewhere near, the Nameless howled.

“Will they hurt her?” Yana asked.

“Not while I have the rod.” Marda stood and looked around the cavern. “This is good,” she said, nodding to herself.

“You sure about that?”

Their eyes met. “It has to be.”

The Rod of Power pulsed in Marda’s hand as the Nameless poured into the cave.

Matty didn't want to run. She wanted to hide. Maybe Azlin had been right all along, curling up against a world that hated him. *Keep your head down. Don't let anyone see you.*

She stopped, her legs heavy. She'd honestly thought she could do this as she'd run from the Mother's listening chamber.

Get the girl. Get the rod. Stop the madness.

Simple.

But that same madness was rolling back toward her, stripping everything else away. She tried to focus on the happy memories she'd recalled in the chamber but couldn't see them anymore. Master Leebon's face was gone. Vildar and Tey, too. She could barely remember Oliviah, let alone anyone from before Dalna. The past was gone, the future was empty, and the present was only pain.

The sun opals glinted in the wall, mocking her, and Matty wanted to do more than hide; she wanted to die.

What had she been thinking, pathetic little Jedi with her head full of dreams? She had one job to do, and there she was sniveling in the dark. Get the girl? She didn't even know where Marda was. Matty was lost, so terribly lost, and everyone would die.

She had to run. Yes, that was what she'd do. Back to Oliviah. Back to safety. Away from the hurt and the fear.

No.

That was wrong. The stones were wrong.

"Jedi can be afraid," she told them as they winked at her from the walls. "Jedi can be scared. There's no shame in it. Everyone is scared at one time or another. The difference for a Jedi is that we know fear is fleeting and should never win. A Jedi never runs from their fear. They face it, safe in the knowledge that the Force is with them, and they are one with the Force. The Force is with them, and they are one with the Force. The Force is with them, and they are one with the Force!"

Matty took a step, and the step became a walk, and the walk became a run. Soon she was pelting along the corridor, teeth clenched and lekku streaming behind her. Today, Matty Cathley wasn't just facing her fear; she was running toward it.

The Nameless flocked around Marda, heads bowed and tails lowered.

"How are we going to do this?" Yana said, worried that any minute the reverence the creatures were showing would turn into the ripping and rending of flesh. They all looked so hungry, so desperate, their bodies impossibly large for creatures that had hatched only an hour or so before. But they were still half the size of the Leveler, who stood in the middle of them, saliva running down its fronds.

Marda didn't take her eyes off it as she fumbled for

something on her belt. It slipped from her fingers and clattered to the floor, the Nameless jumping back and hissing at the noise.

"Careful," Yana warned, wondering if she should pull her blaster.

"I *am* being careful," Marda responded, reaching down with her free hand. "Steady now. Steady."

The Leveler's attention was broken by the sound of approaching feet splashing through the water. The Nameless snapped around as one as a blue glow raced toward them in the gloom. They moved, turning away from Marda, starting for the light.

"No, no, no, no," Marda said. "Stay with me. Stay with me."

But they weren't listening, not to her anyway. Their ears twitched as a trembling voice was heard, reciting the same words over and over: "The Force is with them. They are one with the Force. The Force is with them. They are one with the Force. The Force is with them. They are one with the Force."

Matthea Cathley ran into the cavern, took one look at the Nameless, and froze in terror.

The eyes were everywhere, filling the cavern, brighter and more terrible than a thousand suns. *This isn't real,* Matty told herself. *It's just the rod making you see things that aren't there, making you hear things, too, all the snarling and the clutching and the growling, making you feel their hunger and need.*

And she wasn't alone in her head. Azlin was there, too, telling her that they were coming to take her away. *All you'll be is dust, Matty. Dust. Dust.*

She didn't want to believe it; she had come so far, but there were so many of them. Too many.

And she was already dead.

The Leveler moved, and the pack followed. Marda screamed at them to stop, but they didn't listen, the pull of their blood lust too strong.

Yana drew her blaster and fired, hitting the Leveler in the back. It didn't slow. She fired again, hitting one of the smaller creatures instead. That one fell, its siblings clambering over it to get to Matthea.

"Stop," Marda ordered them. "You must obey me. I hold the rod. I am your Guide."

The Leveler reared up as if it were on a leash, held in place. The rest of the pack howled with it, the Jedi within reach, on her knees, muttering manically beneath her breath, "Dust. Dust. Dust."

Marda kicked something toward Yana. She looked down to see it was a detonator, little more than a small red button beneath a protective clip.

"Pick it up," Marda hissed through clenched teeth, her arms shaking as she stretched the rod in front of her. "I don't think I can hold them for long, not when they're like this."

Slipping her blaster back into her holster, Yana retrieved the box, the metal cold in her hand.

"Get the Jedi onto the platform before you do it," Marda said, backing away.

"No," Yana said, realizing what her cousin had planned. "You're not doing this, Marda. It's not what we agreed."

Marda continued toward the middle of the assembly chamber, the creatures' claws digging into the floor to stop themselves from being forced to retreat. "They'll kill her if I don't, and then I'll never be able to control them. Get to the Jedi, Yana. Help her."

There was no point arguing. Yana knew Marda was speaking the truth. She ran around the baying horde, clipping the detonator to her belt before slipping her good hand under the Twi'lek's arm. The Nameless hissed at them as she pulled the Jedi toward the platform, the lightsaber slipping from Matthea's grip. The Nameless tried to follow but couldn't, not until the Leveler broke from the pack. The monster hauled itself forward, every step an effort, the others following as it began to close the gap. Yana and Matthea were on the platform, but the high ground offered no protection, the Leveler leaping up after them.

It almost looked as if it were smiling.

"Marda . . ." Yana called out as her shoulders hit the back wall.

"Listen," Marda shouted from the middle of the cavern. "You will hear my voice and obey. I am the Guide and the Force will be free."

The Leveler threw back its awful head and roared, the cavern's walls vibrating to the sound of its fury. Then it turned and bounded back down to Marda, the rest of its brood following. The animals crowded around her, the Rod of Power held high above her head.

"Now," she called to Yana. "Do it now."

"I love you, Cousin!" Yana shouted, and pressed the button.

FIFTY-EIGHT

The thermal devices exploded as one, opening large cracks that let the floodwater in, cascading into the chamber like a tidal wave.

Marda held on tight to the rod as the water hit her, colder than she ever thought possible. Clamping her mouth shut, she let herself be carried away by the current as the deluge became a river. The force of the water would do the rest, washing them into the depths of the underground network, both her and the nightmare she'd unleashed on Dalna. The Nameless thrashed in the water, unable to swim, the first of their number already dashed against the rocks. She imagined she heard the Leveler bellow nearby but couldn't be sure. She was too busy drowning herself.

"Marda," Yana screamed as her cousin disappeared beneath the rushing water. The platform beneath them creaked, the struts that held it in place threatening to rip away. Yana pulled Matthea toward a slight ledge at the back of the stage, but it soon turned out that being washed away wasn't the problem.

Above them, the roof groaned and gave way, giant boulders splashing into the water. The entire system was falling in on itself, weakened by the explosions and floodwater. She had to go after Marda, to see if her cousin had survived before it was too late. Leaving the Jedi where she was, Yana sprinted across the platform but never made it to the water as a huge rock smashed down from above. Yana jumped to the side and rolled, coming to a halt as another boulder tumbled toward her. She raised her arms, waiting to be crushed, but death never came.

The rock hung above her, suspended impossibly in the air.

"Well?" came a pained voice from behind. "Get the girl. I won't be able to hold this for long."

The Jedi was lying where Yana had left her, a hand stretched out toward the boulder, her fingers shaking.

"Thank you, Matthea," Yana breathed, crawling to the edge of the platform.

"My friends . . . call . . . me Matty," the Jedi told her as Yana dived headfirst into the water.

FIFTY-NINE

Marda dreamed of Kevmo Zink. He wasn't the corpse she'd seen before, but the boy he used to be, sitting in the lompop field without a care in the world, his skin rich and blue, the tattoos beneath his beautiful eyes glinting in the sun.

He smiled at her as she woke up, looking around bleary-eyed.

"You made it then?"

"Did I?"

He shrugged. "You're here, aren't you?"

She laughed. "Are you going to talk in riddles all day?"

The Padawan pursed his lips. "Maybe. It's kinda fun."

Marda ripped a handful of grass from the meadow and threw it playfully at him. He laughed, wiping the tiny green blades from his face before leaning in for a kiss.

"No," she said, putting a hand to his lips. "Not that."

Disappointment registered in his dark eyes. "You want to kiss *him*, don't you?"

She shook her head. "Bokana isn't here."

"But if he was?"

"I don't want to kiss anyone, Kevmo. Not for a while."

He sat back, leaning on his arms. "You did it, you know? You won."

"Did I?"

"Now who's talking in riddles. You saved the Jedi, Marda. You saved everyone."

"I saved the Jedi," she said, testing the words for herself.

Kevmo frowned at her. "That's what you wanted to do, right?"

Marda closed her eyes, feeling the warmth of the suns' rays against her face. "That's what I wanted to do."

"Good." He sounded convinced. "So, what do you want to do now?"

"Hmm?" Marda said, opening her eyes again. He was grinning at her, so eager. So excited.

"What do you want to do, Marda?"

She sighed, realizing this was all too good to be true. "I want to wake up."

She coughed, water spluttering from her lungs onto the rock. There were no lompop flowers. There was no sunshine.

There was no Kevmo.

Marda looked up as the water rushed past her. The cavern's roof was open above her head, the stars shining in the night sky.

"It's stopped raining," she said to no one in particular, watching the moon as the moon watched back.

Gingerly, she pushed herself up, her limbs aching like never before. She was on a ledge, pressed against a rock that had stopped her from being carried away. She was lucky that she hadn't smashed every bone in her body.

There was no sign of the Nameless, but the rod was at her feet, teetering on the edge. Part of it was, anyway. The Rod of Daybreak was gone, snapped off maybe, leaving her with only the Rod of Seasons.

It began to topple into the water, and she lunged forward, catching it before it could disappear over the edge. She sat there momentarily, turning the artifact over in her hands. It didn't glow or call to her. The Nameless were truly gone, weren't they?

She concentrated, holding it tight. There *was* something, a presence above her, in the open air. Slipping the rod into her belt, Marda began the long climb to the surface.

SIXTY

Matty had let the boulder fall as soon as Yana disappeared into the water. She'd allowed herself a moment to recover, more if she was honest. Centering herself wasn't an option just yet. Stopping the rock from crushing Yana had taken everything she had, and now she was stranded next to a roaring river that hadn't been there a few minutes before. The rest of the platform had disintegrated, and she was facing a challenging climb over treacherous rocks.

That was when she realized she no longer had her lightsaber. It must have gone into the water. "That's okay," she told herself, patting the hilts that jangled on her belt. "Gluth left me more than enough. I'm sure he won't mind."

The tears came then, a strange mix of relief and sorrow. Matty let them flow, not caring if she was discovered while sobbing her heart out. Who could blame her after everything that had happened?

Certainly not Master Rinn, who came to her rescue. Not that long before, Matty would have told anyone—*especially* the Duros—that she could rescue herself, thank you very much, but right now, that didn't seem important. There was no shame in admitting she needed someone else. Jedi worked better together, after all.

The battle was over, but the cost had been high, much if not most of the Path's compound having disappeared into a sinkhole when the Ro cousins detonated their charges. Matty still didn't really understand what had happened or why the Evereni had done what they did. Something about monsters nagged at the corner of her mind, but that must have been an illusion caused by the rod.

Yes, that had to be it.

Master Ela listened patiently as Matty told her what she could remember later that day. They were sitting in the Council member's tent in the middle of the emergency camp the surviving Jedi had set up, with Pathfinder teams who had arrived to assist with the cleanup. The Caamasi told her that Master Leebon would've been proud, which made Matty cry a little more, especially when a couple of newcomers appeared through the flap of the hastily erected tent.

Matty threw her arms around Vildar Mac and Tey Sirrek and sobbed all the more. They'd come as soon as they heard what had happened on Dalna, too late to help with the battle but just in time to hold her tight.

Azlin Rell was already in a relief shuttle being prepared for departure when Matty found him. The young Jedi Knight had made it out of the Mother's listening chamber, running wildly up to the surface before the explosives were triggered. He'd met with his former master, but Arkoff hadn't been able to shake him from the terror that had all but consumed his spirit. The young Knight didn't even look up at Matty as she drew next to his cot. He was sitting up against the wall, scribbling manically on sheets of paper with a blunt stylus. Where in the Light had he found paper? The Path's printing press? Not that it mattered. She needed to calm him.

"Azlin? Azlin, what are you doing?"

He looked up at her voice, his eyes wide and bloodshot, although there was no sign that he recognized her. The papers spilled from his lap.

She bent down to gather them, and he grabbed her shoulder, his fingers digging deep into her flesh.

"Ow. Azlin, stop it."

"Do you hear them?" he asked, not letting go. "You do hear them, don't you? The voices. You hear what they're saying?"

She stood up, shaking him off. "I don't know what you mean."

"The Herald heard what they were," he continued, kneeling on his bunk, eyes imploring her to listen. "He heard, but he didn't understand. He didn't know. The *Shrii Ka Rai.*"

"What?"

"That's what she called them. The Guide. The *Shrii Ka Rai.* Look."

He snatched the papers from her hands and turned them over frantically, searching for something in the scribble.

"Azlin, please," she said, keeping her voice calm. "You need to relax. You need to center yourself."

He shook his head, a manic, frenzied gesture. "No, there is no center. No balance. You'll see. You'll see . . . here."

He had found what he was looking for and thrust the paper back at Matty. She took it, unsure what he expected her to do.

"Read," he said, hugging himself and rocking back and forth on the bed. "Read for yourself. Out loud. Read it out loud so they can hear. So we can all hear."

Matty swallowed, peering at the spiderlike scrawl, but did as she was asked:

"'*Shrii ka rai ka rai.*

They're coming to take you away.'"

Azlin was nodding, mouthing the words silently as she read.

"'They'll do what they can—'"

"And they'll do what they must," Azlin interrupted, completing the line.

"'But when they find you . . .'" Matty continued before stopping, unable to decipher the last few words. "I'm sorry, but I can't . . ."

"But when they find you," Azlin shrieked, snatching the paper back and crushing it against his chest, "all you'll be is dust. Dust. All you'll be is dust!"

She didn't know what to say to give him peace. Maybe this was just the way his mind was processing the horror that had overwhelmed him. Maybe this was how he'd find his way back.

"They'll take care of him on Coruscant," Vildar promised as the shuttle took off, heading to the small fleet assembled above Dalna.

"You could go with them if you like," Tey said. "Lend a hand. Make sure the poor guy gets back on his feet."

Vildar cocked an eyebrow, turning to the Sephi. "Oh, you're in charge of my Padawan now, are you?"

Tey grinned, sticking his tongue through perfectly white teeth. "Someone needs to show you how it's done."

"I'm going nowhere," Matty told them, patting her master's arm. "Except back to Jedha, but before we leave, I want to check in on Oliviah, okay?"

"Of course," Vildar said. "We'll be right here."

"Both of us," Tey added.

The Mother was in another tent that the Jedi were using as a holding area, but she wasn't alone. Marda could see Oliviah Zeveron with Elecia as she approached, Oliviah trying to explain to her sister why the Jedi did what they did, leaving some children behind, only taking those they thought they could train.

"That seems particularly cruel," Marda said, stepping inside. "Taking a child from their family?"

Oliviah jumped up, her hand dropping to her saber, eyes fixed on the Rod of Seasons Marda held. "You need to hand that over."

Marda shook her head. "I can't do that. You see, I thought I'd cleared up all the mess, but there's something left, something I can only handle with this."

The gem at the end of the artifact flared purple, and

Oliviah dropped to her knees, her lightsaber guttering out as it hit the groundsheet.

"No," the Jedi gasped, clawing at the floor, her eyes rolling in their sockets as the Leveler stalked into the tent and glared hungrily at the Jedi.

The Mother clapped, swinging her legs from the bed she'd been lying on. "How marvelous. I thought they were all gone."

"They are," Marda told her, "but the Leveler is stronger than the rest. I found it on the edge of the camp."

"And you came to finish the job." The Mother grinned. "I knew I could rely on you."

Oliviah fell onto her side, her eyes wide but unseeing. The Leveler didn't attack. It couldn't as long as Marda held the rod.

"Did you realize that before or after you tried to kill me, Elecia?" she asked, cocking her head.

The Mother stood, raising her hands in surrender. "I made mistakes, but this is good. We can start again, the Mother and the Guide. We can tell the galaxy how the Jedi destroyed everything."

"Just as you planned."

"Just as the Force revealed it to me."

"It's amazing how the Force always tells you what you want to hear."

"I have gifts, Marda. Gifts I should have shared with you

all, but I was ashamed." The Mother dropped her eyes, rubbing the husked portion of her arm. "I need you to help me, to be my Guide. I'll fight the urges within me, I promise. I'll remain pure."

"For freedom, justice, and purity," Marda intoned.

"Exactly," the Mother said, clasping her hands together. "Will you help me, Marda? Will you guide me along the Path?"

"Don't," Oliviah Zeveron wheezed through her terror, looking up at Marda. "Please."

Marda gazed down at the Leveler, so eager to feed.

"I *will* free the Force," she said quietly. "I will free it of your tyranny, of your abuse. I will make it strong again."

"Yes, Marda," the Mother hissed. "Do it. Show the Jedi the true Path. Release her from the agony of her world."

"I wasn't talking to your sister, Elecia," Marda said, finally looking up and meeting her eye. "I was talking to *you.*"

The Mother screamed as the Leveler pounced.

"Vildar! Tey!"

Her friends came running as soon as they heard Matty's shout.

"Saber's grace," the Kiffar said as they pushed their way into the tent. "What *is* this?"

"Go and get help," Matty told them. "She needs help."

"I'll go," Tey said, taking one last glance at the bed before disappearing back outside.

Vildar dropped to where Matty was holding Oliviah tight, the older woman shivering in her arms, staring at the thing on the bed. It was wearing the robes of the Mother, but its skin was like stone, its ash-colored face frozen in a scream.

"Is Oliviah . . . ?"

"She's not hurt," Matty said, rocking the Jedi back and forth, "at least not physically. But we're going to help her, Vildar. We're going to help her get over this together."

Vildar smiled at his Padawan. "Of course we are, Matty. It's what Jedi do best."

SIXTY-ONE

"Yana?"

She hadn't found Marda. She'd swum so far, her arms aching, body wanting to give up, but there was no sign of her cousin, until now.

Yana turned to see Marda standing behind her. She ran to her, pulling her into a hug that Marda returned happily. "You're alive. Thank the Force."

Marda's tears were wet against her cheek. "I didn't think you believed in the Force."

"No, but I need to thank something."

She pulled away, looking her cousin up and down.

"Are you hurt?"

Marda shook her head. "Only sore."

Yana snorted. "You and me both."

Marda glanced at her stump, ashamed. "I'm sorry."

"It wasn't you."

"It was, and I have to take responsibility for that."

Yana shrugged. "I never liked that hand anyway."

Marda didn't smile but glanced at the woman in the hoverchair Yana had been pushing.

"Opari?"

The Nautolan was huddled under a blanket, looking out into space.

"When I couldn't find you, I just wanted to save someone. Anyone," Yana told her. "I'd made a promise anyway."

"To the Herald?"

"No," Yana said sadly, shaking her head. "To someone who can't hear me anymore. Someone who told me she'd be around as long as I needed her. Thought it was time I repaid the favor."

"Is that one of Cincey's chairs?"

Yana thought of her old friend, another of the Children who had sped through the galaxy on the Mother's bidding. It all seemed a lifetime ago now. It *was* a lifetime.

"Found it in the store. Cincey doesn't need it anymore."

"Where will you go?" Marda asked.

Yana shrugged. "I don't know."

"You could come with me?" Marda said. "Both of you. Leave Dalna how we arrived."

"Together?"

Marda took a step forward, willing Yana to agree. "The Mother had a shuttle. I found it after . . ."

Her voice trailed off.

"I hear the Mother died," Yana said, studying her cousin's reaction. "They say she turned to stone. She became her own monument. One final miracle."

"We can go to the *Gaze*," Marda continued, ignoring the comment. "It's in orbit on the far side of the moon. I don't think anyone has found it yet, and if they have, they won't be able to get on board."

"Marda."

"The Leveler is on the shuttle already."

"Marda, we need to kill that thing."

"No," Marda said, shaking her head. She reached behind her back, pulling the Rod of Seasons from the pack slung between her shoulders. "I have this to control it. I don't know where the other half is, but it'll work well enough. We only have the Leveler. It'll have to do what we say."

She moved closer, her voice urgent. "I'm going to start again, Yana. I'm going to find a new path, and I want you to walk it with me. The imbalance must be put right. The Force must be free."

"Marda."

"No, listen, please. There'll always be people out there

trying to use the Force against its will, stripping it of its power. People like her, people who want to trick us, to make us do things we don't want to do. I did so many things, Yana. So many terrible things."

Her eyes were filling with tears. Yana put a hand on her shoulder and looked her deep in the eye.

"I can't go with you, Marda. *We* can't go with you."

"Is it the Jedi? Are you worried about the Jedi? Because the Leveler will protect us. It will help us find balance."

"It's not the Jedi I'm scared of. It's that thing. What it does to you. You need to let the Leveler go. Tell it to drown with the others."

"I can't do that. I won't."

"And that's why the path you tread isn't for me. I'm sorry, truly I am."

A solitary tear ran down Marda's face. She sniffed and nodded. "I understand."

"Do you?"

Marda pulled her in close again, squeezing her tight. "The Force will be free, Yana. I promise. I'll do it, even if it takes me a thousand years."

Yana laughed, pulling out of her grip. "I don't think Evereni live that long."

"I will," Marda joked. "I'm a Ro, after all."

"Yes," Yana smiled. "Yes, you are."

The *Silverstreak* was where Sunshine said it would be. It was in a sorry state, but it looked like it could fly. At least he hadn't lied about that.

Yana had checked on the vault on the way to collect Opari, but Dobbs had gone. The door was open, the bags gone, too. She'd half expected the ship to have vanished, as well, but its ramp was still down, noises coming from inside. For all she knew, that was Dobbs himself, preparing for take-off. That would be difficult. There was no way in the stars that the old prospector would take them with him, not after what she'd done.

But it wasn't Sunshine Dobbs who tramped down the ramp to make the final checks.

"Shea?"

"Yana," the engineer replied. "What are you doing here?"

"I was hoping for a lift. We were, I mean."

Shea looked at Opari. "Is she . . . ?"

"She'll be fine," Yana told her. "I'm going to look after her. She's the only family I have left."

A strange look crossed Shea's face.

"Shea?"

"It's Geth's," the redhead said, rubbing her belly. "He didn't know. I was going to tell him once we got back from Planet X. I've been thinking of names as I've been trying to get this wreck shipshape. Geth if it's a boy, obviously. Mari if it's a girl."

"Mari?"

Shea looked embarrassed. "My mom's name. Mine too, actually, although I never liked it, until now."

"Sounds to me like you're going to need some help," Yana said. "I mean, I can't fly, and I don't think Opari is much of a pilot, but I can help maintain the ship. We can muddle on together, at least for a while. Maybe become haulers."

Shea laughed. "Haulers?"

"Why not. See the galaxy. Maybe visit Alderaan. I think I'd like Alderaan."

Shea shrugged. "Well, it's not like I have anyplace better to go. Do you need a hand with the chair?"

Yana was already starting up the ramp. "No, I can manage, but I will need a hand when we can afford it," she joked, "maybe after our first job."

The hoverchair jolted, the Rod of Daybreak falling from where Yana had stashed it next to Opari.

"Let me get that," Shea said, recovering the short staff before it could roll away. "What is it anyway?"

"Just something I found in the caves when I was looking for Marda." Yana said.

"A memento?"

"Kind of. You know, maybe I could do with some help, after all."

Together, they pushed the chair into the *Silverstreak.*

Marda sat alone on the flight deck of the *Gaze Electric*. The ship really was a marvel, designed to fly almost single-handed. She guessed that was very much on purpose, the Mother's ultimate escape route.

The Leveler was bedded down in a storage unit toward the back of the vessel, near enough to come running if necessary but far enough that Marda couldn't hear it howling. It would stay there until she said otherwise, the Rod of Seasons on her lap. She would have liked to still have the Rod of Daybreak, just in case, but one would do for now, until she could make plans.

She had chosen the destination at random, instructing the navicomputer to chart a course where no one would go looking. It had come up with a system that was as good as any, as long as there were no caves. Marda had seen enough caves.

Part of her wished that Yana had joined her, but maybe it was better this way. Now she could go where she wanted, when she wanted. No one would tell her no ever again. One day she would free the Force—she knew that, believed it wholeheartedly, in fact—but for now, for the first time in her life, she was truly free.

And if anyone tried to tell her otherwise, well, they would reap a whirlwind of their own.

Smiling, Marda set the Rod of Seasons aside and walked to the station where she had laid out the few possessions she had salvaged from Dalna, the greatest of which was the pot of brikal-shell blue. She lifted the lid and peered inside, noting that there wasn't much left. No matter: it would be enough for now. Dipping her fingers into the mixture, she touched the tips to her forehead and pulled down, painting three jagged lines.